SINS
AND
Seduction

SWEET REVENGE

CAT
SCHIELD

DANI
WADE

JOANNE
ROCK

MILLS & BOON

MIX
Paper | Supporting
responsible forestry
FSC® C001695

Published by
Mills & Boon
An imprint of Harlequin Enterprises (Australia) Pty Limited (ABN 47 001 180 918), a subsidiary of HarperCollins Publishers Australia Pty Limited (ABN 36 009 913 517)
Level 19, 201 Elizabeth Street
SYDNEY NSW 2000
AUSTRALIA

® and ™ (apart from those relating to FSC®) are trademarks of Harlequin Enterprises (Australia) Pty Limited or its corporate affiliates. Trademarks indicated with ® are registered in Australia, New Zealand and in other countries. Contact admin_legal@Harlequin.ca for details.

Printed and bound in Australia by McPherson's Printing Group

CONTENTS

Substitute Seduction

Cat Schield

Cat Schield has been reading and writing romance since high school. Although she graduated from college with a BA in business, her idea of a perfect career was writing books for Harlequin. And now, after winning the Romance Writers of America 2010 Golden Heart® Award for Best Contemporary Series Romance, that dream has come true. Cat lives in Minnesota with her daughter, Emily, and their Burmese cat. When she's not writing sexy, romantic stories for Harlequin Desire, she can be found sailing with friends on the Saint Croix River, or in more exotic locales, like the Caribbean and Europe. She loves to hear from readers. Find her at catschield.net and follow her on Twitter, @catschield.

Books by Cat Schield

Las Vegas Nights

At Odds with the Heiress
A Merger by Marriage
A Taste of Temptation
The Black Sheep's Secret Child
Little Secret, Red Hot Scandal
The Heir Affair

Sweet Tea and Scandal

Upstairs Downstairs Baby
Substitute Seduction

Visit her Author Profile page at
millsandboon.com.au,
or catschield.net, for more titles!

Dear Reader,

I'm excited to bring you the second book in my Sweet Tea and Scandal series set in historic Charleston, South Carolina. When I originally conceived a trilogy about three women taking revenge on the men who wronged them, I knew London McCaffrey needed a man who could muss up her perfect exterior and wake the passion slumbering in her.

Enter race-car driver Harrison Crosby, the hot and sexy brother of the man she's supposed to be taking down. I love this couple's chemistry and their opposites-attract story line.

As always, Charleston makes a wonderful backdrop for the romances playing out among the city's elite. The historic homes, fantastic restaurants and local flavor capture the heart of what makes the South so fascinating. So grab a glass of sweet tea, and I hope you enjoy this scandalous romance.

Happy reading,

Cat Schield

Prologue

"We need to get back at all of them. Linc, Tristan and Ryan. They need to be taught a lesson."

When Everly Briggs had decided to attend the Beautiful Women Taking Charge event, she'd researched the attendees and settled on two women she believed she could convince to participate in a devious plot to take down three of Charleston, South Carolina's most influential men.

Each of the three women had shared a tale of being wronged. Linc Thurston had broken his engagement to London McCaffrey. Zoe Crosby had just gone through a brutal divorce. But what Ryan Dailey had done to Everly's sister, Kelly, was by far the worst.

"I don't know about this," London said, chewing on her coral-tinted lip. "If I go after Linc, it will blow up in my face."

"She's right." Zoe nodded. "Anything we try would only end up making things worse for us."

"Not if we go after each other's men," Everly said, pierced by a thrill as her companions started to look hopeful. "Think about it. We're strangers at a cocktail party. Who would ever connect us? I go after Linc. London goes after Tristan and, Zoe, you go after Ryan."

"When you say 'go after,'" Zoe said hesitantly, "what do you have in mind?"

"Everyone has skeletons in their closet. Especially powerful men. We just need to find out where the worst ones are hiding and let them out."

"I'm in," London said. "Linc deserves to feel a little pain and humiliation for ending our engagement the way he did."

Zoe nodded. "Count me in, too."

"Marvelous," Everly said, letting only a small amount of her glee show as she lifted her glass. "Here's to making them pay."

"And pay," London echoed.

"And pay," Zoe finished.

One

The party celebrating the ten-year anniversary of the Dixie Bass-Crosby Foundation was in full swing as Harrison Crosby strolled beneath the Baccarat crystal-and-brass chandelier hanging from the restored antebellum mansion's fifteen-foot foyer ceiling. Snagging a glass of champagne from a circling waitress, Harrison passed from the broad foyer with its white marble floor and grand columns toward the ballroom, where a string quartet played in the corner.

Thirty years ago Harrison's uncle Jack Crosby had purchased the historic Groves Plantation, located thirty-five miles outside the city of Charleston, intending to headquarter Crosby Motorsports on the hundred-acre property. At the time, the 1850s mansion had been in terrible shape and they'd been on the verge of knocking it down when both Virginia Lamb-Crosby and Dixie Bass-Crosby—Harrison's mother and aunt respectively—had raised a ruckus. Instead the Crosby family had dumped a ton of money into the historic renovation to bring it up to code and make it livable. The result was a work of art.

Although Harrison had attended dozens of charity events

supporting his family's foundations over the years, the social whirl bored him. He'd much rather just donate the money and skip all the pomp and circumstance. Despite the Crosby wealth and the old family connections his aunt and mother could claim, Harrison had nothing in common with the Charleston elite and preferred his horsepower beneath the hood of his Ford rather than on the polo field.

Which was why he intended to greet his family, make as little small talk as he could and get the hell out. With only three races left in the season, Harrison needed to stay focused on preparations. And he needed as much mental and physical stamina as possible.

Spying his mother, Harrison made his way toward her. She was in conversation with a younger woman he didn't recognize. As he drew near, Harrison recognized his mistake. His mother's beautiful blonde companion wore no ring on her left hand. Whenever his mother encountered someone suitable, she always schemed to fix him up. She didn't understand that his racing career took up all his time and energy. Or she did get it and hoped that a wife and family might persuade him to give it all up and settle down.

Harrison was on the verge of angling away when Virginia "Ginny" Lamb-Crosby noticed his approach and smiled triumphantly.

"Here's my son," she proclaimed, reaching with her left hand to draw Harrison in. "Sawyer, this is Harrison. Harrison, I'd like you to meet Sawyer Thurston."

"Nice to meet you," Harrison said, frowning as he tried to place her name. "Thurston..."

"Linc Thurston is my brother," Sawyer clarified, obviously accustomed to explaining about her connection to the professional baseball player.

Harrison nodded. "Sure."

Before he could say anything more, his mother reinserted herself into the conversation. "Sawyer is a member of Charles-

ton's Preservation Society and we were just talking about the
historic home holiday tour. She wants to know if I'd be willing to open the Jonathan Booth House this year. What do you
think?"

This was the exact sort of nonsense that he hated getting involved in. No matter what his or anyone else's opinion, Ginny
Lamb-Crosby would do exactly as she liked.

He leaned down to kiss her cheek and murmured, "I think
you should ask Father since it's his house, too."

After a few more polite exchanges Harrison pretended to
see someone he needed to talk to and excused himself. As he
strolled around the ballroom, smiling and greeting those he
knew, his gaze snagged on a beautiful woman in a gown of
liquid sky. Her long honeyed hair hung in rolling waves over
her shoulders with one side pulled back to show off her spar-
kly dangle earring. In a roomful of beautiful women, she stood
out to him because rather than smiling and enjoying herself,
the blonde with big eyes and pale pink lips wore a frown. She
seemed to barely be listening to her chatty companion, a shorter,
plump brunette of classic beauty and pouty lips.

She seemed preoccupied by... Harrison followed her gaze
and realized she was staring at his brother, Tristan. This should
have warned Harrison off. The last thing he wanted to do was to
get tangled up with one of his brother's castoffs. But the woman
inspired more than just his curiosity. He had an immediate and
intense urge to get her alone to see if her lips were as sweet as
they looked, and that hadn't happened in far too long.

Turning his back on the beauty, he headed to where his aunt
was holding court on one side of the room near a large television playing a promotional video about the Dixie Bass-Crosby
Foundation. In addition to helping families with sick children,
the foundation supported K–12 education programs focused on
literacy. Over the last ten years, his aunt had given away nearly
ten million dollars and her family was very proud of her.

Yet even as Harrison exchanged a few words with his aunt,

uncle and their group, his attention returned to the lovely blonde in the blue dress. The more he observed her, the more she appeared different from the ladies who normally appealed to him. Just as beautiful, but not a bubbly party girl. More reserved. Someone his mother would approve of.

The more he watched her, the more he labeled her as uptight. Not in a sexual way, like she wouldn't know an orgasm if it reached out and slapped her, but in a manner that said her whole life was a straitjacket. If not for her preoccupation with Tristan, he might've turned away.

He simply had to find out who she was, so he went in search of his uncle. Bennett Lamb knew where all the bodies were buried and traded in gossip like other men bought and sold stock, real estate or collectibles.

Harrison found the Charleston icon holding court near the bar. In black pants and a cream honeycomb dinner jacket with a gold bow tie and pocket square, Bennett outshone many of the female guests in the fashion department.

"Do you have a second?" Harrison asked, glancing around to make sure his quarry hadn't escaped.

One of Bennett's well-groomed eyebrows went up. "Certainly."

The two men moved off a couple of feet and Harrison indicated the woman who'd interested him. "Do you know who that is?"

Amusement dancing in his eyes, his uncle gazed in the direction Harrison indicated. "Maribelle Gates? She recently became engaged to Beau Shelton. Good family. Managed to hold on to their wealth despite some shockingly bad advice from Roland Barnes."

Harrison silently cursed at the word *engaged*. Why was she so interested in Tristan if she was unavailable? Maybe she was cheating on her fiancé. Wary of letting his uncle think he'd shown an interest in someone who was engaged, he asked, "And the brunette?"

"Maribelle Gates is the brunette." Bennett saw where his nephew was going and shook his head. "Oh, you were interested in the blonde. That's London McCaffrey."

"London." He experimented with the taste of her name and liked it. "Why does her name ring a bell?"

"She was engaged to Linc Thurston for two years."

"I just met his sister." Harrison returned to studying London. Meanwhile his uncle kept talking. "He recently broke off the engagement. No one knows why, but it's rumored he's been sleeping with..." Bennett's lips curved into a wicked grin. "His housekeeper."

An image of the heavyset fifty-year-old woman who maintained his parents' house popped into Harrison's mind and he grimaced. He pondered the willowy blonde and wondered what madness had gripped Linc to let her go.

"He doesn't seem the type to go after his housekeeper."

"You never know about some people."

"So why is everyone convinced that he's sleeping with her?"

"*Convinced* is a strong word," his uncle said. "Let's just say that there's speculation along those lines. Linc hasn't been out with anyone since he and London broke up. There's been not a whisper of another romance on anyone's radar. And, from what I hear, she's a young widow with a toddler."

Harrison shoved aside the gossip and refocused on the object of his interest. The more Bennett speculated about the reason Linc Thurston had for ending the engagement, the less he liked London's interest in his brother. She deserved better. Tristan had always treated women poorly, as his recent behavior during his divorce from his wife of eight years demonstrated. Not only had Tristan cheated on her the entire time they were married, he'd hired a merciless divorce attorney, and Zoe had ended up with almost nothing.

"Now, if you're looking for someone to date, I'd like to suggest..."

Harrison tuned out the rest of his uncle's remarks as he continued to puzzle over London McCaffrey. "Is she seeing anyone at the moment?" Harrison asked, breaking into whatever it was his uncle was going on about.

"Ivy? I don't believe so."

"No," Harrison said, realizing he hadn't been paying attention to whatever pearls of wisdom his uncle had been shelling out. "London McCaffrey."

"Stay away from that one," Bennett warned. "That mother of hers is the worst. She's a former New York socialite who thinks a lot of money—and I do mean a lot—can buy her way into Charleston inner circles. Honestly, the woman is a menace."

"I'm not interested in dating the mother."

"London is just as much a social climber," Bennett said as if Harrison was an utter idiot not to make the connection. "Why else do you think she pursued Linc?"

"Obviously you don't think she was in love with him," Harrison retorted dryly.

He wasn't a stranger to the elitist outlook held by the old guard of Charleston society. His own mother had disappointed her family by marrying a man from North Carolina with nothing but big dreams and ambition. Harrison hadn't understood the complexities of his mother's relationship with her family and, frankly, he'd never really cared. Ever since he could remember, all Harrison had ever wanted to do was to tinker with cars and drive fast.

His father and uncle had started out as mechanics before investing in their first auto parts store. Within five years the two men had parlayed their experience and drive into a nationwide chain. While Harrison's dad, Robert "Bertie" Crosby, was happy to man the helm and expand the business, his brother, Jack, pursued his dream of running race cars.

By the time Harrison was old enough to drive, his uncle had built Crosby Motorsports into a winning team. And like the brothers before them, Tristan had gone into the family business, preferring to keep his hands clean, while Harrison loved every bit of oil and dirt that marked his skin.

"She pursued him," Bennett pronounced, "because her children would be Thurstons."

Harrison considered this. It was possible that she'd judged the guy by his social standing. On the other hand, maybe she'd been in love with Linc. Either way, Harrison wasn't going to know for sure until he had a chance to get to know her.

"Why are you so interested in her?" Bennett asked, interrupting Harrison's train of thought.

"I don't know."

He couldn't explain to his uncle that London's preoccupation with Tristan intrigued and worried him. For the last couple of years Harrison had increasing concerns about his brother's systematically deteriorating marriage to Zoe. Still, he'd ignored the rumors of Tristan's affairs even as Harrison recognized his brother had a dark side and a ruthless streak.

The fact that Zoe had vanished off his radar since she'd first separated from Tristan nagged at Harrison. In the beginning he hadn't wanted to get involved in what had looked to become a nasty divorce. Lately he was wishing he'd been a better brother-in-law.

"Do you know what London does?" Harrison asked, returning his thoughts to the beautiful blonde.

Bennett sighed. "She owns an event planning service."

"Did she plan this event?" An idea began to form in Harrison's mind.

"No. Most of the work was done by Zoe before…" Not even Bennett was comfortable talking about his former niece-in-law.

"I think I'm going to introduce myself to London McCaffrey," Harrison said.

"Just don't be too surprised when she's not interested in you."

"I have a halfway-decent pedigree," Harrison said with a wink.

"Halfway decent isn't going to be enough for her."

"You're so cynical." Harrison softened his statement with a half smile. "And I'm more than enough for her to handle."

His uncle began to laugh. "No doubt you're right. Just don't be surprised when she turns you down flat."

London McCaffrey stood beside her best friend, Maribelle Gates, her attention fixed on the tall, imposing man she'd promised to take down in the next few months. Zoe Crosby's ex-husband was handsome enough, but his chilly gaze and the sardonic twist to his lips made London shiver. From the research London had done on him these last couple of weeks, she knew he'd ruthlessly gone after his wife, leaving her with nothing to show for her eight-year marriage.

In addition to cheating on Zoe through most of their marriage, Tristan Crosby had manufactured evidence that she was the one who'd been unfaithful and violated their prenuptial agreement. Zoe had been forced to spend tens of thousands of dollars disproving this, which had eaten into her divorce settlement. A settlement based on financial information about her husband's wealth that indicated he was heavily mortgaged and deeply in debt.

Zoe's lawyer suspected that Tristan had created offshore shell companies that allowed him to hide money and avoid paying taxes. It wasn't unusual or illegal, but it was a hard paper trail to find.

"Heavens, that man cleans up well," Maribelle remarked, her voice breathy and impressed. "And he's been staring this way practically since he arrived." She nudged London. "Wouldn't it be great if he's interested in you?"

With an exasperated sigh, London turned to her friend and was about to reiterate that the last thing on her mind was romance when she recognized the man in question. Harrison Crosby, Tristan's younger brother.

A racing-circuit fan favorite thanks to his long, lean body and handsome face, Harrison was, to her mind, little more than a glorified frat boy. Zoe had explained that her ex-brother-in-law liked fast cars, pretty women and the sorts of activities that red-blooded American males went for in the South.

"He's not my type," London told her best friend, returning her focus to her target.

"Sweetie, I love you," Maribelle began, settling further into her native South Carolina drawl, "but you have to stop being so picky."

Resentment rose in London but she studiously avoided showing it. Since the first time her mother had slapped her face for making a fuss during her sixth birthday party, London had decided if she was going to survive in the McCaffrey household, she'd better learn to conceal her emotions. It wasn't always easy, but now, at twenty-eight, she was nearly impossible to read.

"I'm not being picky. I'm simply being realistic." And since he wasn't the Crosby brother she was targeting, he wasn't worth her time.

"That's your problem," Maribelle complained. "You're always realistic. Why don't you let loose and have some fun?"

Out of kindness or sympathy for her longtime friend, Maribelle didn't mention London's latest failure to climb the Charleston social ladder. She'd heard more than enough on that score from her mother. When London had begun to date someone from one of Charleston's oldest families, her mother had perceived this as the social win she'd been looking for since the New York socialite had married restaurant CEO Boyd McCaffrey and moved to Connecticut, leaving her beloved New York City behind. And then, when London's father had been accepted for a better position and moved his family to Charleston, Edie Fremont-McCaffrey's situation grew so much worse.

When she'd first arrived, Edie had assumed that her New York connections, wealth and style would guarantee Charleston's finest would throw open their doors for her. Instead she'd discovered that family and ancestral connections mattered more here than something as vulgar as money.

"It's not that I don't want to have fun," London began. "I just don't know that I want to have Harrison Crosby's sort of fun."

Well, didn't that make her sound like the sort of dull prig who'd let the handsome and wealthy Linc Thurston slip through her fingers? London's heart contracted. Although she no longer believed herself in love with Linc, at one point she'd been ready to marry him. But would she have? London wasn't entirely clear where their relationship would be if he hadn't broken things off.

"How do you know what sort of fun Harrison Crosby likes?" Maribelle asked, bringing London back to the present.

She bit her lip, unable to explain why she'd been researching the Crosby family, looking for an in. There were only three people who knew of their rash plan to take revenge on the men who'd wronged them. What London, Everly and Zoe were doing might not necessarily be illegal, but if they were discovered, retribution could be fierce and damaging.

"He's a race-car driver." As if that explained everything.

"And he's gorgeous."

"Is he?"

London considered all the photos she'd seen of him. Curly black hair, unshaved cheeks, wearing jeans and a T-shirt or his blue racing suit with sponsor patches plastered head to toe, he had an engaging smile and an easy confidence that proclaimed he had the world on a string.

"I guess if you like them scruffy and rough," London muttered. Which she didn't.

"He looks pretty suave and elegant to me."

Maribelle's wry tone spiked London's curiosity and she carefully let her gaze drift in his direction. Not wanting the man to think she was at all interested in him, she didn't look directly at him as she took in his appearance.

The Harrison Crosby she'd been picturing looked nothing like the refined gentleman in a perfectly tailored dark gray suit that drew attention to his strong shoulders and narrow hips. Her hormones reacted with shocking intensity to his stylish appearance. He was clean-shaved tonight, appearing elegant enough to have stepped off a New York runway. Where she'd been able to dismiss the "rough around the edges good ol' boy" in racing attire, London saw she'd miscalculated the appeal of a confident male at the top of his game.

"Apparently he cleans up well," London remarked grudgingly, her gaze moving on before she could get caught staring.

"He's coming this way," Maribelle squeaked.

London's pulse revved like an engine as she took in his elegant appearance. "Get a hold of yourself," she murmured in exasperation, unsure if she was speaking to herself or Maribelle.

"Good evening, ladies." His voice had a deep, rich tone like the rumble of a cat's purr. "I'm Harrison Crosby. Dixie Bass-Crosby is my aunt."

"Number twenty-five," Maribelle responded in a surprisingly girlish tone that caused London to gape. "You're having a great second half this year. I'm Maribelle Gates."

A sexy half grin kicked up one corner of his mouth. "You follow racing?" he asked, echoing the question in London's head.

While his sea-glass eyes remained focused on Maribelle, London stared at him in consternation. Her body was reacting to his proximity in confusing ways.

"I do," Maribelle confirmed. "So does my fiancé. We're huge fans."

As her best friend displayed a surprising amount of knowledge about race-car driving, London began to feel like a third wheel. While the two girls had been best friends since their first day of the exclusive private girls' school they'd attended, certain differences had always existed between them.

Both were from wealthy families, but Maribelle's had the sort of social standing that had allowed her access to the inner circles that had eluded London and her family. And while each woman was beautiful, Maribelle had always fought with her weight and this had led to her feeling less secure about her appearance. But the biggest difference was that for all her lack of social standing, London had always been the more popular of the two.

Until now.

"Oh," Maribelle exclaimed, glancing toward her friend as if suddenly realizing they'd excluded London. "How rude of me to monopolize you. This is London McCaffrey."

"Nice to meet you," London said. Yet as miffed as she was at his earlier lack of interest, she wasn't sure she meant it.

"Nice to meet you, as well." Harrison's gaze flicked from one woman to the other. "Now, it seems as if you know all about me. What is it you ladies do?"

"I'm planning a wedding," Maribelle said with a silly little giggle that left London struggling not to roll her eyes.

Harrison's sculpted lips shifted into an indulgent smile. "I imagine that's a full-time job."

London bit the inside of her lip to keep from snorting in derision. "I own an event planning company," she said a trifle too aggressively. Hearing her tone brought a rush of heat to London's cheeks. Was she seriously trying to compete with her engaged friend for a man she wasn't even interested in?

"Are you planning her wedding?"

London shot her friend a glance as she shook her head. "No."

"Not your thing?" he guessed, demonstrating an ability to read the subtle currents beneath her answer.

"She mostly organizes corporate and charity events," Maribelle responded with a sweet smile that stabbed at London's heart.

"Oh, that's too bad," Harrison said, the impact of his full attention making London's palms tingle. "My brother's turning forty next month and I was going to plan a party for him. Only I don't know anything about that sort of thing. I don't suppose you'd like to help me out?"

"I…" Her first impulse was to refuse, but she'd been looking for an opening that would get her into Tristan's orbit. Planning his birthday party would be an excellent step in that direction.

"Don't usually do personal events, but I would be happy to meet with you and talk about it."

She pulled a business card out of her clutch and handed it to him.

He glanced at the card. "'London McCaffrey. Owner of ExcelEvent.' I'll be in touch." Then, with a charming smile, he said, "Nice meeting you both."

London's eyes remained glued to his retreating figure for several seconds. When she returned her focus to Maribelle, her friend was actively smirking.

"What?"

"See? I told you. What you need is a little fun."

"It's a job," London said, emphasizing each word so Maribelle wouldn't misinterpret the encounter. "He's looking for someone to organize his brother's birthday party. That's why I gave him my card."

"Sure." Maribelle's hazel eyes danced. "Whatever you say. But I think what you need is someone to take your mind off what happened between you and Linc, and in my not-so-humble opinion, that—" she pointed at the departing figure "—is the perfect man for the job."

Everything London had read about him stated that he liked to play hard and that his longest relationship to date had lasted just over a year. She'd decided her next romance would be with a man with a serious career. Someone she'd have lots in common with.

"Why do you think that?" London asked, unable to understand her friend's logic. "As far as I can tell, he's just like Linc. An athlete with an endless supply of eager women at his beck and call."

"Maybe he's just looking for the right woman to settle down with," Maribelle countered. She'd been singing a different tune about men and romance since she'd started dating Beau Shelton. "Can't you at least give the guy a chance?"

London sighed. She and Maribelle had had this conversation

any number of times over the last few months as her friend had tried to set her up with one or another of Beau's friends. Maybe if she said yes Maribelle would back off.

"I'm really not ready to date anyone."

"Don't think of it as dating," Maribelle said. "Just think of it as hanging out."

Since London was already thinking in terms of how she could use Harrison to get to Tristan, it was an easy enough promise to make. "If it means you'll stop bugging me," she said, hiding her sudden satisfaction at killing two birds with one stone, "I'll agree to give Harrison Crosby one chance."

Two

Harrison spent more than his usual twenty minutes in the bathroom of his penthouse condo overlooking the Cooper River as he prepared for his meeting with London McCaffrey.

A woman he'd dated for a short time a year ago had given him pointers on grooming particulars that women appreciated. At the time he'd viewed the whole thing with skepticism, but after giving the various lotions, facial scrubs, hair-care products and other miscellaneous items a try, he'd been surprised at the results and happily reaped the benefits of Serena's appreciation.

Still, as much as he'd seen the value in what she'd introduced into his life, his focus during racing season left little room for such inconsequential activities. Today, however, he'd applied all that he'd learned, scrutinizing his hands to ensure they were grease-free and giving his nails more than a cursory clipping, even going so far as to run a file over the edges to smooth away any sharpness. Although he didn't touch the high-tech race cars until he slid behind the wheel, Harrison often unwound from a race weekend by tinkering with the rare classics his uncle bought for his collection.

Today, however, as he surveyed his charcoal jeans, gray crewneck sweater and maroon suede loafers, Harrison decided that someone as stylish as London would appreciate a man who paid attention to his grooming. And in truth, his already elevated confidence was inflated even further when the receptionist at ExcelEvent goggled at him as he strolled into the King Street office.

"You're Harrison Crosby," the slender brunette exclaimed, her brown eyes wide with shock as he advanced on her desk. "And you're here." She gawked at him, her hands gripping the edge of the desk as if to hold herself in place.

Harrison gave her a slow grin. "Would you let London know I've arrived?"

"Oh, sure. Of course." Never taking her eyes off him, she picked up her phone and dialed. "Harrison Crosby is here to see you. Okay, I'll let him know." She returned the handset to the cradle and said, "She'll be out in a second. Would you like some coffee or water or...?" She trailed off and went back to staring at him.

"I'm fine."

"If you want to have a seat." The receptionist gestured to a black-and-white floral couch beneath the ExcelEvent logo painted in white on the gray wall. "She shouldn't be too long."

"Thank you."

Ignoring the couch, Harrison stood in the center of the room, wondering how long she would leave him cooling his heels. While he waited, he took stock of his surroundings, getting a sense of London's taste from the clean color palette of black, white and gray, the hint of drama provided by the silver accessories and the pop of color courtesy of the flower arrangement on the reception desk. On the wall across from him was a large-screen TV with a series of images and videos from various events that London had organized.

In his hand, his phone buzzed. Harrison sighed as he glanced at the message on the screen. Even though he took Mondays and Tuesdays off during the season, rarely an hour went by that his team wasn't contacting him as they prepared the car for that week's upcoming race. Each track possessed a different set of variables that the teams used to calibrate the car. There were different settings for shocks, weight, height, springs, tires, brakes and a dozen other miscellaneous factors.

For the first time in a long time, Harrison debated leaving the text unanswered. He didn't want to split his focus today. His team knew what it was doing. His input could wait until his meeting with London concluded.

A change in the air, like a fragrant spring breeze, pushed against his skin an instant before London McCaffrey spoke his name.

"Mr. Crosby?"

As he looked up from his phone, Harrison noted the uptick in his heartbeat. Today she wore a sleeveless peach dress with a scalloped neckline and hem, and floral pumps. Her long blond hair fell over her shoulders in loose waves. Feminine perfection with an elusive air, she advanced toward him, her hand outstretched.

Her fingers were cool and soft as they wrapped around his hand. "Good to see you again."

"I intend to call you London," he said, leaning just ever so slightly forward to better imprint the faint scent of her floral perfume on his senses. "So you'd better call me Harrison."

"Harrison." Still holding his hand, she gazed up at him through her lashes, not in a manner he considered coy, but as if she was trying to take his measure. A second later she pulled free and gestured toward a hallway behind the reception desk. "Why don't you come back to my office?" She turned away from him and led the way, pausing for a brief exchange with the receptionist.

"Missy, were you able to get hold of Grace?"

"I had to leave a message. Do you want me to put her through when she calls?" Missy glanced at Harrison as she asked the question.

"Yes. It's urgent that I speak with her as soon as possible." London glanced back at Harrison as she entered her office. Like the reception area, this tranquil space was decorated in monochrome furniture and accessories. "I hope you don't mind the interruption, but I'm organizing a fiftieth wedding anniversary for a client's parents in a week and some things have come up I need her to weigh in on. She's currently out of the country and not due back until just before the party."

"I understand." His phone vibrated with another incoming text as if to punctuate his point. "I'm sure you have all sorts of balls in the air."

"Yes." She gestured him toward a round table to their left and closed the door. "I always have several projects going at once."

"Are you a one-woman show?" His gaze tracked her as she strode to her glass-topped desk and picked up a utilitarian pad and basic pen. No fancy notebooks and expensive writing instruments for London McCaffrey.

"No, I have several assistants," she explained as she sat across from him. "Most of them help me out on a part-time basis, but I have two full-time employees plus Missy, my receptionist."

"I didn't realize your company was so large."

She acknowledged the implied compliment with a slight smile. "I've been fortunate to have expanded rapidly since I opened my doors."

"How long have you been in business?" Harrison leaned back in his chair and let his gaze flow over her slender shoulders and down her bare arms.

She sat forward, arms resting on the tabletop, the pen held lightly in her fingers. "Nearly six years. I started right out of college."

"Why an event planning company?"

Her eyes narrowed as if she'd suddenly noticed that he was interviewing her, but her voice remained smooth and unruffled as she answered. "My mother used to be a socialite in New York and has always been big on the charity circuit. I started attending events when I was in my teens and mostly found them tedious because I didn't know anyone. To keep myself occupied, I would spend my time analyzing the food, decor and anything else that went into the party. When I got home, I would write it all down and make notes of what I would do differently."

Harrison found himself nodding in understanding as she described her process. "That sounds a lot like how I got into car racing. My uncle used to let me help him work on the cars and, when I got old enough to drive, gave me the opportunity to get behind the wheel. I could tear apart an entire engine and put it back together by the time I was fourteen."

"I guess we both knew what we wanted to do from an early age."

"Something we have in common." The first of many somethings, he hoped.

As if realizing that they'd veered too far into the personal, she cleared her throat. "So you said you were interested in having someone organize a party for your brother's birthday?"

"Yes." Harrison admired her segue back to the reason for his visit. "He turns forty next month and I thought someone should plan something."

After meeting London the other night, Harrison had called his mother and confirmed that no one was in the process of planning anything for Tristan's fortieth birthday. In the past, events like this had been handled by Tristan's wife, Zoe, but she was out of the picture now.

She tapped her pen on the notepad. "Tell me something about your brother."

Harrison pondered her question for a moment. What did he know about Tristan? They were separated by more than just an eight-year age difference. They had different ideologies when it came to money, women and careers. Nor had they been close as kids. Their age differences meant the brothers had always attended different schools and Tristan's free time had been taken up by sports and friends.

"He runs the family business since our dad semi-retired five years go," Harrison began. "Crosby Automotive is a billion-dollar national chain of auto parts stores and collision centers in twenty states. We also have one of the largest private car dealership groups on the East Coast."

"And you race cars."

Her matter-of-fact tone carried no judgment, but Harrison imagined someone as no-nonsense as London McCaffrey wouldn't view what he did in a good light. No doubt a guy like Tristan, who put on an expensive suit and spent his days behind a desk, was more her cup of tea. On the other hand, she had been engaged to a baseball player, so maybe Harrison was the one guilty of being judgmental.

"I'm one of four drivers that races for Crosby Motorsports."

"Car twenty-five," she said, doodling a two and a five on her legal pad before encircling the numbers with a series of small stars.

He watched her in fascination. "Yep."

"I've never seen a race." She glanced up, caught him watching her and very quickly set the pen down atop the drawing as if embarrassed by her sketch.

"Well, you're in luck," he said. "I'm racing on Sunday in Richmond."

"Oh, I don't think…" Her eyes widened.

"It's my last race of the season." He made his tone as persuasive as possible.

London shook her head. "It's really not my thing."

"Then what is?"

"My thing?" She frowned. "I guess I don't really have one. I work a lot, you see."

"And that leaves no room for fun?"

"From what my friend told me about a racer's schedule, I'd like to know when you slow down for fun."

"You have me there. I'm on the go most of the year."

She nodded as if that put an end to the topic. "So, how many people are you looking to invite to your brother's birthday party?"

"Around a hundred." He'd secured a list from his mother after realizing he'd better not show up to a party planning meeting empty-handed and clueless.

"And do you have a budget?" London had relaxed now that they'd returned to familiar territory and flipped to a clean page so she could jot notes.

"Keep it under ten."

"Thousand?" She sounded a tad surprised, leaving Harrison questioning whether he'd gone too high or too low. "That amount opens up several possible venues. Of course, the timing is a little tight with it being the start of the holiday season. Did you have a particular date in mind?"

"His birthday is December fifth."

"I'll have Missy start calling around for availability." She excused herself and went to speak to her receptionist.

Harrison barely had a chance to look at any of the several texts that had come in while they'd been talking before she returned.

"Are you thinking a formal sit-down dinner with cocktails before and dancing afterward or something more casual?"

"My mother insists on a formal event. But I don't think dancing. Maybe a jazz band, giving people a chance to mingle and chat." Harrison was even more relieved that he'd checked with his mother because he was able to parrot everything she'd suggested.

"You were smart to get her input," London said, picking up on his train of thought. "I guess my last question for now is whether you had any sort of theme in mind."

Theme? Harrison was completely stumped. "I guess I was just thinking it was his fortieth birthday..."

"A color scheme?"

More and more Harrison wished he'd found a different way to connect with London McCaffrey. "What would you suggest?"

Her lips pursed as she pondered the question. "I'll pull together three ideas and run them past you. What are you thinking about for the meal?"

"Wouldn't it depend on the place we choose?"

"Yes, but it might help narrow things down if I thought you wanted seafood versus steak and chicken."

"Ah, can I think about it?"

With a slight shake of her head, she pressed on. "Give me your instant thoughts."

"Seafood."

She jotted that down. "There are several venues that do an exceptional job."

Although he'd never planned an event like this before, Harrison was finding that the process flowed easily with London in charge. She was proving to be both efficient and knowledgeable.

"You're really great at this," he said.

Her lips quirked. "It is what I do for a living."

"I didn't mean to sound surprised. It's just that I've never thrown anyone a birthday party before and you're making everything so easy."

"If you don't mind my asking, how did you come to be in charge of this particular event?"

Harrison doubted London was the sort who liked to play games, so he decided to be straight with her. "I volunteered because I was interested in getting to know you better and a friend warned me that you wouldn't be inclined to give me a shot."

"Get to know me better?" She looked more curious than annoyed or pleased. "So you decided to hire me to plan your brother's birthday party? You should know that I don't date my clients."

Despite her claim, he sensed she wasn't shutting him down entirely. "You said you usually work with corporate clients. Maybe this would be an excellent opportunity to gain some exposure with Crosby Automotive. And I get a chance to work with a woman who intrigues me. A win-win solution all around."

Interest colored her voice as she echoed, "A win-win solution…"

London's pen flowed across the legal pad as she randomly sketched a centerpiece and pondered Harrison's words.

When he'd called to set up this meeting, she'd been elated. Organizing his brother's birthday party would solve the problem of how she could get close enough to Tristan to figure out how to bring him down. The more she learned about Zoe's ex-husband, the more daunting her task. Frustration welled up in London as she considered the impulsive bargain she'd made several months earlier. What had she been thinking to agree to something that could lead to trouble for her in the future if she wasn't careful? But how did she back out now that Everly and Zoe had their plans in motion?

"Would you like to have dinner with me tonight?" Harrison asked.

The abruptness of his invitation combined with the uptick in her body's awareness of him caught her off guard, and London was shocked and dismayed by the delight blooming in her.

"I…"

She'd been so focused on her goal of helping Zoe that she hadn't considered the possibility of an interpersonal relationship between her and Harrison. Now, with his startling confession, the situation had grown complicated.

"Ever since meeting you at the party the other night, I can't stop thinking about you," he declared, his sea-toned eyes darkening as his voice took on a smoky quality. "You don't date your clients, but there's nothing that says you can't. Let me take you to dinner."

You made this devil's bargain. Now see it through.

"Tomorrow would be better," she responded a touch breathlessly.

"I'm heading to Richmond with the crew tomorrow. Tonight is all I have."

She was on the verge of refusing when his smile faded. An intense light entered his eyes and London found it difficult to breathe. The man's charisma was off the charts at the moment and London found herself basking in the glow of his admiration. At the same time she couldn't help but wonder if he was sincere or merely plying her with flattery to get her into bed. Worse, she wasn't sure she cared.

Maribelle's words came back to haunt her. London could use a little fun in her life and rebound sex with Harrison Crosby might be what enabled her to move on from Linc. If only she wasn't planning to use Harrison as part of their revenge plot.

"I don't want to have to wait another week to spend an evening with you," he continued as she grappled with her conscience.

"I'm flattered," she said, stalling for time.

His lips kicked into a dry grin. "No, you're not."

Harrison wasn't the sort of Southern gentleman she was used to. One she could wrap around her finger. He had a straightforward sex appeal that excited her and made her feel all needy and prone to acts of impulsiveness. The urge to grab his sweater and haul him over for a kiss shocked her.

"Really—" Her instincts screamed at her to retreat. Her susceptibility to this man could prove dangerous.

"You think I'm hitting on you because I want to sleep with every woman I meet."

"I wouldn't dream of thinking such a thing," she murmured in her most guileless drawl as she glanced down at her legal pad and noticed she'd been drawing hearts. She quickly flipped to a clean page and set down her pen.

"Don't go all Scarlett O'Hara on me," Harrison replied. "I'm not going to lie and tell you I don't see us ending up in bed, but I fully intend on making it about the journey and not the destination."

Outrage poured through London, but there was a certain amount of amusement and curiosity mixed in, as well. Damn the man. His plain speaking was having the wrong sort of effect on her.

"You seem pretty sure of yourself," she said. "What makes you think I'm interested in you that way?"

"The fact that you're still here discussing it with me instead of kicking me to the curb."

"Do you honestly think you're the first client who has hit on me?"

"I'm sure I'm not." He didn't look at all concerned by her attitude. "But I'm guessing you're going to give me a different answer than all the others."

It pained her that he was right. Nor could she console herself with the falsehood that she would turn him down flat if it wasn't for this pact she'd made with Zoe and Everly.

"I'll have dinner with you tonight," she said. "But I get to pick the place and I'll meet you there."

"And I promise to behave like a proper gentleman."

She snorted. "There's nothing proper or gentlemanly about you, I think." A delicious shiver worked its way down her spine at the thought. "Do you agree to my conditions?"

"If they make you feel safe, then how can I not?"

His use of the word *safe* made her bristle. She hadn't set conditions because of any nervousness she felt around him, but to make him understand that she wasn't one of those women who flatter and swoon all in the hope of achieving that elusive five-carat sparkler for their left hand.

"How about we meet at The Front Porch at eight o'clock."

"That's perfect."

She then steered the conversation back to the original reason for their meeting. "It would be a good idea if we could meet next week and check out a couple of the venues," she told him, already having a pretty good idea of the sort of elegant evening she intended to organize.

"I'll be back in town next Monday and Tuesday."

She picked up her phone and pulled up her calendar. "I'm open Monday afternoon, say two o'clock? The faster we book a location, the sooner we can start working on the details. And I'll pull some ideas together and send them along to you this week."

"Sounds great."

They'd arrived at an obvious end to their meeting and Harrison stood. As London escorted him to the front door, he asked, "Are you sure you wouldn't want to come watch me race in Richmond?"

London's eyes flicked to her receptionist. Missy was paying rapt attention to their exchange without actually staring at them. Heat bloomed beneath London's skin as she realized that word would soon spread about Harrison's invitation.

"I don't know…"

"You could bring your friend. Maribelle, wasn't it?"

"Yes." To her dismay, London's mood had dipped at the thought of sharing his attention. "I mean, yes, my friend is Maribelle. She's a huge fan. Both her and her fiancé, Beau."

"Bring them both along. I'll get you seats in our suite."

London considered how enthusiastic her friend had been after meeting Harrison. It surprised her that someone who had been trained from birth to epitomize a gracious Southern lady had an interest in such a loud and tedious sport. All the drivers did was go around and around in circles at high speeds for three hours. How could that possibly keep anyone interested?

"I'll see if she's busy and let you know." The words were out before London could second-guess herself.

She needed access to Tristan, and Harrison was the perfect way in. From the way her pulse triggered every time he smiled at her, acting interested wouldn't be a problem. She just needed to be careful that she kept her body's impulses in check and her mind focused on the revenge bargain.

Harrison looked a little surprised that she'd changed her mind, but then a grin slowly formed on his face. "Great."

"Wonderful," she murmured, reaching out to shake his hand.

She'd begun the gesture as a professional event planner, but as his long fingers enveloped hers, a jolt of electricity surged up her arm. The raw, compelling reaction left London wobbly. She couldn't let herself be distracted right now. Not when she had a mission and Harrison played an integral part in accomplishing it.

Capitalizing on his interest in her was one thing. Reciprocating the attraction would only lead to trouble.

"See you at eight."

Aware that they were still holding hands, London pulled her fingers free. "Eight," she echoed, glad Harrison had the sense not to gloat as she opened the front door and gestured him onto the sidewalk. "In the meantime, I'll keep you informed as we confirm availability on the potential venues."

After they said goodbye, she wasted no time watching him walk away, but immediately turned to her receptionist. Seeing that Missy was making a poor effort at busywork, London gathered herself to scold her and then realized if she'd been worried about the scene playing out in front of an audience, she should've taken him outside.

"Let me know what you hear from the venues," she said, heading for her office.

With a whoosh of breath, she plunked down on her office chair and ignored the slight shake in her hands as she jiggled the mouse to deactivate her screensaver. However, as she struggled to refocus on what she'd been working on before Harrison had shown up, peeling her thoughts away from the handsome race-car driver proved challenging.

Unsure what to make of his confessed interest in her and invitation to dinner tonight, she contemplated her legal pad and the mixture of notes and doodles. No fewer than ten hearts lined the margins and swooped across the page. What had she been thinking?

London opened a file on her computer for the event and typed in her notes before tearing the page into tiny pieces.

Going forward she needed to take a firmer grip on her subconscious or heaven only knew what might happen.

Once her initial work on the fortieth birthday party was done, London dialed Maribelle to give her a heads-up about all that had transpired and to extend Harrison's invitation to watch him race on Sunday.

"Beau will be thrilled," Maribelle said. "Do you think Harrison can get us into the pit on race day?"

"Maybe. I can find out what that entails." She traced her fingertips over the twenty-five she'd once again doodled on her legal pad. At least there were no hearts this time. "We're having dinner tonight."

Maribelle's squeal forced London to pull the phone away from her ear. "See, I knew he was interested in you. Where are you going? Is he taking you somewhere romantic? Are you going to sleep with him? I would. I bet he's great in bed. He's so sexy with that dark hair and those blue-green eyes. And that body. I read that he's in crazy great shape. What I wouldn't give to get my hands on him."

Maribelle's rapid-fire remarks left no room for London to speak. She really shouldn't sleep with Harrison Crosby, but any argument about what a bad idea it was would fall on deaf ears.

"Need I remind you that you're engaged? You better tone down your fan-girling," London warned. "Beau might not appreciate you heaping praise on another man."

"Don't you worry. My Beau knows while my eyes might wander my heart never will."

It was such a sweet and solemn declaration that London felt a flare of envy. Had she ever embraced that level of dedication to Linc? Not that she'd needed to. Once she'd settled on him as her future mate, she'd never looked at anyone else. And until the very end, she'd thought Linc felt the same. Her trust in him had never wavered despite all the women she knew must be throwing themselves at him while he was out of town during baseball season. She'd never imagined her competition would be someone so unassuming and close to home.

"You're lucky to have each other," London said and meant it.

"You'll find someone," Maribelle returned, her tone low and fierce. "And he will love you and make you feel safe."

Again that word *safe*. And again, London flinched. She was a strong, capable woman who didn't need a man to make her feel safe. Yet even as her thoughts trailed over this mantra, a tiny part of her clenched in hungry longing. What would it be like to be taken care of? Not physically or financially, but emotionally supported. To be part of a devoted team like Maribelle and Beau.

It was something she hadn't known growing up. Her parents had burdened her with huge—if differing—expectations. Her father was an autocratic businessman who'd impressed upon her that absolute success was the only option. London had spent her childhood living in terror that she would be criticized for not achieving high enough marks. She'd undertaken a rigorous class schedule, participated in student government, women's soccer and debate club, and couldn't remember a time during her high school and college years when she wasn't worn out or anxiety ridden.

Nor was her mother any less demanding. If her father expected her to succeed professionally, her mother had her sights set on London's social achievements. To that end, there had been hours of volunteer work and social events her mother dragged her to. Becoming engaged to Linc had been a triumph. But even then it grew obvious that no matter how much London did, it was never enough.

"I just texted Beau," Maribelle said. "He suggests we fly up on Saturday and back on Sunday. So we can see the practice rounds. Will that work for you? Usually you have parties on Saturday night, don't you?"

As easy as it would be to use work as an excuse, she heard the excitement in her friend's voice and sighed in surrender. "All we have is a small anniversary party and Annette is handling that." To London's surprise, she realized she was looking forward to getting out of town. She'd been working like a madwoman since Linc had ended their engagement. Keeping busy was the best way to avoid dwelling on her failed relationship. "And since Beau is flying us up, I'll take care of the hotel rooms."

"We should go shopping for something to wear. In fact, we should go shopping right now."

London imagined her friend grabbing her purse and heading for her car. "What's the hurry?"

"I need to make sure you wear something on your date tonight that doesn't scream *I'm not interested in getting laid.*"

"I'm not," London protested.

"Have you been with anyone since Linc?"

London winced. "You know I haven't."

"You need a rebound relationship. I think Harrison Crosby would be perfect."

That Maribelle had echoed what London herself had been thinking less than an hour earlier didn't surprise her. The two women had been friends so long they sometimes finished each other's sentences.

"Why do you say that?" London asked.

"Because he's the furthest thing from someone you'd ever settle down with, so that makes him a good bet for a casual fling."

London was warming to the idea of a quick, steamy interlude with the sexy race-car driver. Still, she'd never slept with anyone she didn't have feelings for. Yet with what she, Everly and Zoe were up to, maybe the fact that London wasn't going to fall for the guy was a plus.

"You might be right."

Maybe it would be okay to give sexual chemistry and a casual relationship a quick spin. They were both adults. What harm could it do?

Three

Harrison arrived at The Front Porch ten minutes early and parked himself at the bar in easy range of the entrance to wait for London's arrival. Since leaving her office that morning, he'd been half expecting she'd call to cancel. With each hour that passed, he'd grown increasingly confident that she wasn't going to fight their mutual attraction. Yet now, as he counted down the minutes until she walked in, he found his stomach tying itself into anxious knots.

Her effect on him should've sent him running in the opposite direction. Already he suspected that they were at odds on several fundamental issues. For one thing, she wasn't his type and it was pretty clear he wasn't hers. She was elegant and aloof. Completely the opposite of the fun-loving ladies who hung out at the track, enjoyed drinking beer and weren't afraid to get a little dirty.

He imagined she'd be bossy as hell in a relationship. Tonight was a good example. She'd chosen the time and place, taking control, making it clear if he wanted to play, it would be by her rules. Harrison smirked. She could make all the rules she wanted. He'd bend every one.

The restaurant's front door opened, and before Harrison had fully focused on the woman on the threshold, his heart gave a hard jerk. For someone accustomed to facing near collisions at ridiculous speeds and regularly operating at high levels of stress for long periods of time without faltering, Harrison wasn't sure what to make of the jolt London's arrival had given him.

For the space of several irregular breaths as her gaze swept the restaurant in search of him, Harrison had the opportunity to take her in. She'd changed her clothes since their earlier meeting and looked stunning in a navy dress with a broad neckline that bared her delicate shoulders and the hollows above her collarbones. The material hugged her upper body, highlighting the curves of her breasts, before flaring into a full skirt that stopped at her knees. The dark color contrasted with the creamy tones of her pale skin and highlighted her blue eyes. She'd pulled her hair back into a loose knot at the base of her neck and left long strands of gold waves to frame her face. Her only jewelry was a pair of simple pearl earrings.

When she spotted him, her uncertain smile hit Harrison like lightning. His nerves buzzed in the aftermath as he made his way through the crowded bar toward her.

"You look gorgeous," he murmured, cupping his fingers around her bare arm and leaning down to graze a kiss across her cheek.

Her body tensed at his familiarity, but her smile remained in place as he stepped back and looked down at her.

"Thank you," she said, her voice neither breathless nor coy. She took in his jeans, light blue shirt and oatmeal-colored blazer. "You look quite dapper," she said, reaching out to tug at the navy pocket square in his breast pocket.

"I'm glad you approve," he said and meant it. "And I'm glad you were able to join me for dinner tonight."

"You were kind to invite me."

Niceties concluded, Harrison set his hand on her back and guided her toward the hostess. They were led to a table by the front windows overlooking King Street.

"Do you come here a lot?" Harrison asked after they were seated. He scanned the menu, which specialized in farm-to-table fare, and settled on the scallops with smoked yogurt, beets and pistachio.

"Actually, I've never been, but it's one of Maribelle and Beau's favorite places. They had their first date here and...it's where he proposed." Her eyes widened as if she realized what she'd implied. "They're always going on and on about how good the food is. That's why I picked it."

"Can't wait to see if they're right."

"So, you've never been here before?"

Harrison shook his head. "I don't get out much."

"I find that hard to believe."

"It's true. I'm on the road so much of the year that when I do get home, I like to hole up and recharge."

"You do?"

"Most of my time and attention is focused on cars and racing. Analyzing my competition, studying the track, figuring out how I can improve."

"I did a little research on you and learned you're a big deal in racing." Bright spots of color appeared in her cheeks as he raised his eyebrows at her confession. "Lots of appearances and events."

"All to promote Crosby Motorsports. I'm actually an introvert." He could tell she wasn't buying it.

"You can't possibly be. You're a fan favorite with a huge following."

"Don't get me wrong, I do my share of press events and meeting fans, but it isn't what I enjoy. I'd much rather be tinkering with a car or hanging out with a few of my friends."

She made a face. "I figured you would be out in the public, soaking up the accolades, enjoying your stardom."

Her thorny tone made him frown. "You seem to have a very jaded view of me. Why is that?"

"It's not you." She moved her wineglass around in circles on the white tablecloth and seemed engrossed in the light refracted by the liquid. "I guess it's what you do. I've spent a lot of time around sports stars and most of them love being celebrities. The adoring fans. The special attention they get wherever they go. It makes them act…entitled."

Obviously her attitude had been formed during her relationship with Lincoln Thurston. As a professional baseball player, no doubt Thurston had enjoyed his share of the limelight. Harrison needed to convince her he and her ex-fiancé weren't cut from the same cloth.

"Not all of them," Harrison insisted.

"Most of them."

"Was Linc that way?" He'd asked, even knowing that it was risky to probe for details about what might be painful for her.

"I don't want to talk about him." London's brittle tone was a warning to Harrison that he should tread carefully.

Still, he needed to know where her head was at. "Because you're still not over the breakup?"

How could she be? He'd done his own bit of research on her and discovered only a few months had passed since their two-year engagement ended.

"I am over it." The bits of gold floating in London's blue eyes flashed.

"Are you over him?"

She exhaled in exasperation. "We were together for three years."

"So that's a no?"

London's expression hardened into a look that Harrison interpreted as *back off.* That wasn't going to stop him. This woman was worth fighting for.

"I can't imagine what having him break your engagement must have been like for you, but I am happy to listen if you want to dump on the guy." He paused and then grinned. "Or the male gender as a whole."

From her frown, he could see his offer had confused her.

"Why?"

He shrugged. "Because I think too many men suck in the way they treat women."

"And you don't?" Her earlier tension faded into skepticism.

"I'm sure you can find plenty of women who would complain about me."

One corner of her lips twitched. "So what, then, makes you so different from all the other men out there?"

"Maybe nothing. Or maybe it's the case that I don't take advantage of people because I can. I'm not an entitled jerk like my brother can be all too often." Harrison brought up Tristan to see how London reacted. She'd shown far too much interest in him at the party and Harrison wanted to understand why. "Tristan treats women like they're his personal playground."

"But until recently he's been married. Are you insinuating he wasn't faithful?" London's interest intensified when Harrison shook his head. "I've never understood why men bother being in a relationship if they intend to cheat."

Harrison recalled what his uncle Bennett had told him about Linc Thurston's infidelity. London had every right to be skittish when it came to trusting any guy she perceived as having the same sort of fame and fortune as her ex-fiancé.

"It's a social norm."

London looked positively dumbstruck. "Is that what you think?"

"It's true, isn't it?" Harrison countered.

"What about love?"

"Not everyone believes in love. I don't think my brother does. Tristan chose to marry a very beautiful, very young, woman who was passive and pliable. For eight years she satisfied his need for a decorative and docile companion." Harrison recalled how Zoe's spirit dimmed with each wedding anniversary. "Her only failure was in her inability to make my brother happy."

"Why was that her responsibility?" London asked in surprise. "Isn't marriage a partnership where you support each other?"

"Mine will be." Harrison waited a beat to see how she absorbed that before continuing, "I think Zoe's dissatisfaction with her role grew too strong to be contained. One thing about Tristan—he likes having his way and becomes a bear if events run counter to his preferences. I imagine him perceiving Zoe's discontent as nothing he'd done wrong, but a failing on her part."

London absorbed his assessment for several seconds before asking, "How close are you with his ex-wife?"

"I like Zoe. She's quiet and subdued, but once you get to know her you see that she has a warm heart and a wry sense of humor." He could go on extolling her virtues but decided to keep to his original purpose, which was to make sure London understood that Tristan wasn't a good guy. "She deserved better than my brother."

"I hope she appreciated having you as her champion."

"I don't know about that. If I'd been a better friend, I would've steered her away from marrying Tristan."

"You might not have been able to do that. Sometimes we have to make our own mistakes. It's the only way we learn."

"Maybe, but some mistakes carry harsher consequences than others."

London sat back and let her hands slide into her lap. She regarded him steadily with her keen blue eyes. "You aren't what I expected."

"I hope that's a good thing."

"The jury is still out," she said, an enigmatic smile kicking up the corners of her lips. "So, Mr. Introvert, what is it you enjoy besides cars and racing?"

"The usual guy stuff. Outdoor sports. Spending time with

my friends. How about you? What do you do when you're not working?"

She laughed. "Sleep and eat. Sometimes I get a massage or facial. I have a hard time unwinding."

"Sounds like we're both on the go a lot."

"Like a shark. Swim or die."

The phone in her purse chimed. She'd set the clutch on the table beside her plate and now made a face at it. "Sorry." The tone repeated.

"Do you need to get that?"

"No." She heaved a sigh. "I already know what it's about."

"That's impressive," he teased and was rewarded with a grimace.

"About this weekend..."

Something in her tone made him grin. "You've decided to accept my invitation to watch me race in Richmond."

"I spoke with Maribelle," she replied. "Both she and her fiancé are excited about your offer."

Her carefully worded statement left room for interpretation. "What about you?"

"I'm not sure what I'm getting into, so I'm reserving judgment."

"I guess that's something," he murmured, convinced he would win her over.

"We're flying up Saturday morning," she continued, ignoring his dry remark. "And Beau was wondering if you'd be able to get us into the pit. At least I think that's what he wanted to know."

"Absolutely."

She'd been seated facing the restaurant's entrance and suddenly her eyes went wide in surprise. Harrison drew a breath to ask what was wrong when she shifted her attention back to him and smiled brightly.

"You know..." she began, picking up her purse. "Maybe I should double-check the text to make sure nothing is amiss."

She gave a nervous half laugh. "The pitfall of being the boss is that I'm always on call. Excuse me, won't you?"

And before Harrison could say anything, she'd fled the table, leaving him staring over his shoulder after her.

Everly Briggs strode along King Street, paying little attention to the restaurants, stores and bars clustered along the popular thoroughfare. Her entire focus was on the tall man she was following.

Linc Thurston appeared unaware of the stir he caused as he passed. Usually the professional baseball player paused to chat with fans he encountered, but tonight he seemed intent on reaching his destination.

Since Everly, London and Zoe had met at the Beautiful Women Taking Charge event, Everly had been actively pursuing whatever angle she could to take down Linc. From digging into all available gossip, Everly had gotten wind that the reason he'd broken off his engagement to London was that he'd started cheating on her with his housekeeper.

Once she'd determined that they weren't just involved in a fling, but a full-blown, secret relationship, she determined this would be the best way to get revenge on him. At the moment she had plans in the works to expose the woman's lies and sabotage her credibility. Linc would learn what it meant to be betrayed by someone he loved.

Of course, her plans would completely fall apart if she was wrong about the strength of his feelings for Claire Robbins, so Everly was doing a little spying to see if his cheating was a onetime event or if the man was a typical representation of his gender.

She was so caught up in her thoughts that Everly hadn't noticed Linc had stopped walking until she drew within arm's length. Jerking to a halt would be too obvious, so Everly was forced to sail on past. She did take note of what had captured his interest, however, and spotted London occupying a table beside the large window of The Front Porch. She was obviously having dinner with Harrison Crosby and the couple was engaged in some pretty serious flirting.

What the hell was London doing? She was supposed to be taking down Tristan Crosby, not dating his brother.

Everly's irritation spiked as she reached the end of the block. By the time she turned the corner, she'd pulled out her phone. Pausing, she typed a text and sent it. Although the three women had agreed not to communicate to avoid their plotting being discovered, Everly simply had to confront London.

We need to meet—E

She tapped her foot as she waited for a response. Meanwhile she kept her gaze on King Street, expecting Linc to pass by at any second. She'd intended to continue her surveillance and it annoyed her that London's behavior was forcing her to detour. When her phone didn't immediately chime with an answer from London, Everly rapidly typed a second message.

I saw you having dinner tonight. What r u doing?

When London still didn't answer, Everly knew she had no choice but to push the issue.

Linc had passed by while Everly had been typing her second text. Instead of following him, she doubled back to the restaurant. London sat facing the entrance and Everly made sure the woman noticed her enter. The two made brief eye contact before Everly headed toward the back, where the restrooms were located.

She entered the ladies' room and was relieved to find the stalls empty. She approached the sinks and pulled her lipstick out. Fury made her hands shake. While she was here dealing with London, Linc was getting away.

By the time London pushed through the door, Everly was more than ready to let her have it.

"Why are you having dinner with Harrison Crosby?" she snarled, barely restraining the urge to shout in displeasure. "You're supposed to be going after Tristan."

"What are you doing here?" London countered, pitching her voice barely above a whisper. "We agreed the way this works is to not have any contact with each other. We can't be seen together."

"I came to find out why you're going after the wrong brother," Everly said, ignoring London's objections.

London crossed her arms over her chest and glared back. "Did it ever occur to you that Harrison might be the best way for me to get close to Tristan?"

Everly let loose a disparaging noise. How could London possibly think she was buying that? It was obvious what was going on.

"It's more likely that you find him attractive and plan on sleeping with him." Based on the way London refused to meet Everly's gaze, she'd hit it square on the head. "Do you have any idea how badly that could backfire?"

"Look," London said, showing no sign of being convinced that her actions were flawed. "It's none of your business how I handle my end of the bargain. You and I meeting like this could become a problem if anyone sees us together and it's discovered that you were behind whatever happens with Linc."

"Give me some credit," Everly snapped. "No one's ever going to find out I was the one behind what happens to him."

"Regardless. We agreed this only works if we don't have any contact with each other. So leave me alone."

Before Everly could say another word, London flung open the bathroom door and exited.

For several long minutes Everly fumed. This situation with London and Harrison Crosby was a problem. Now she had to keep her eye on her own revenge scenario and make sure London stayed focused on their plan. And if London couldn't do the job, then Everly would show her what happened when you turned your back on your friends.

Four

With her heart pumping hard against her ribs, London smoothed her palms along her dress's full skirt and slowly wound her way back to Harrison. Everly's texts and subsequent appearance in the restaurant had been disturbing. What they were doing was dangerous enough. If they were caught in some sort of conspiracy, it could ruin all their lives.

Nor could she ignore the question front and center in her thoughts. Was Everly following her? The possibility made her skin prickle. How else could the other woman have known that London was having dinner with Harrison? And what sort of insanity had prompted Everly to confront London in public like this where anyone could have seen them? Had Everly contacted Zoe, as well? London was tempted to reach out to the third member of their scheme, but that was exactly what she'd railed at Everly for doing.

Anxiety danced along her nerve endings as she slid into her seat opposite Harrison. London suspected her distress was reflected in her expression because after a quick survey of her face, he frowned.

"Is everything okay?"

"Fine." London forced a reassuring smile. "I just received a bit of bad news about an event I was going to organize." The lie came too easily, sparking concern over the person she was becoming. "The client had been on the fence about what they wanted to do and decided to cancel."

"You seem rattled. It must've been a big client."

"Not huge, but all my clients are equally important and I'm disappointed that this didn't work out." Even though London wasn't lying, the fact that she was deceiving Harrison left a bad taste in her mouth.

"Maybe they'll change their mind." His winning smile gave her heart a different reason to pound. "I'll bet you can be quite persuasive."

His attempt to make her feel better through flattery was turning her insides to mush and soothing away her earlier distress. She caught herself smiling at him in gratitude as pleasure washed over her. The man had a knack for getting under her skin.

"If by 'persuasive' you mean bossy," London said, recognizing that she had a tendency to stab directly into the heart of something rather than nibble away at the edges, "then I agree. I come on a little too strong sometimes."

"You want to get things done," Harrison said, nodding. "I get it. Winning is everything."

It struck London that maybe they had more in common than she'd initially thought. They shared a love of competition and a matching determination to get across the finish line. Maybe his way of doing things meant he slid behind the wheel of a car and drove at reckless and adrenaline-inducing speeds, making impulsive decisions in the moment, while she tended to be more methodical and deliberate in her approach.

"I don't exactly think of it as winning," London responded. "More like a job well done."

"Nothing wrong with that."

London toyed with her earring as she asked, "Do you win a lot?"

"I've had my share of successes over the years. Generally, I finish in the top ten drivers about two-thirds of the time. Except for the first couple years when I was still learning and a couple of seasons when injury kept me off the track."

"Is that good?" she asked, noting his amusement and figuring she'd just displayed total ignorance of what he did.

"It's a decent statistic."

"So winning isn't important?"

"Of course it's important, but with thirty-six races a year, it's impossible to be on top all the time. If I win four to six times in a season, that's good enough to put me in the top three for the year as long as my stats are solid."

As an event planner, London was accustomed to dealing with a lot of numbers. It was how she kept her clients happy while maximizing their budget and remaining profitable. She was interested in trying to understand the way driver standings were determined.

"How many other drivers are there?"

"Almost sixty."

"What was your worst year?"

"The year I started—2004. I finished fifty-eighth."

"How old were you?"

"Nineteen." Harrison's lips twisted in self-deprecating humor. "And I thought I knew everything there was to know."

London considered what she'd been like at nineteen and couldn't relate. She'd been a freshman in college, away from her parents for the first time and struggling to figure out who she was.

"And now?" she prompted.

"Still learning," he said. "Always improving."

"Those seem like good words to live by," she said.

His blend of confidence and humility was endearing. London softened still more toward him even as she marveled at his gamesmanship.

The waitress approached to check on their meal and London watched the man across from her charm the woman with his friendliness. The contrast between the two brothers struck her again. During her brief introduction to Tristan, the way the man had looked her over had made London feel like running home and taking a shower.

"Did you leave any room for dessert?" the waitress asked.

Harrison glanced her way and London shook her head. "But don't let me stop you from ordering something."

"I hate to eat alone." And once the waitress had left with their plates, Harrison finished, "Besides, I'd much rather grab an ice cream cone at Swenson's."

"I haven't been there in years," London said, remembering what a rare treat it had been when her father had taken her there.

"Then it's time to go, don't you think?" He didn't wait for her answer before asking, "What is your favorite flavor? Please don't say vanilla."

"I don't know." She was struck by rising delight at the thought of enjoying such a simple, satisfying treat with Harrison. "Maybe strawberry."

"A few months ago they introduced a strawberry, honey balsamic, with black pepper ice cream. It's really good."

"You know quite a bit about the place." London's mouth watered as she imagined all those delicious flavors harmonizing on her taste buds. "Do you take all your dates there?" She didn't mean the question to sound so flippant and flushed beneath his keen regard.

"You'd be the first."

"That was rude of me. I'm sorry."

"Are you skeptical of all men?" he asked. "Or is it just me?"

She took a second to consider his question before answering. "Not all men and not you. It's just that since Linc and I..." She wished she hadn't brought up her ex-fiancé's name again.

"The breakup has left me feeling exposed and I lash out at un-expected moments. I'm sorry."

"He really hurt you."

"Yes and no." She really didn't want to talk about Linc over a first-date dinner with Harrison, but maybe it would be good to clear the air. "All my life I've achieved whatever I set my mind to. Except for one thing. Social acceptance in certain circles. In Charleston it's impossible to become an insider. You have to be born into it. When Linc and I got engaged, it opened doors I'd spent my life knocking on."

London sighed as she finished her explanation. She wanted Harrison to understand what had driven her. His own family was self-made, parlaying hard work into a booming automotive empire. Would he view her hunger to belong to a group of "insiders" as petty and shallow?

"Growing up, I attended the right schools," she continued, thinking back to the private all-girl high school she'd attended and the friends she'd made there. Friends who'd gone on to attend debutante classes and formal teas and to participate in the father/daughter skeet shoot. "But I was always on the outside looking in."

"And that bothered you a lot."

Despite his neutral tone, her defensiveness flared. "Shouldn't it?"

"Why did you think you needed the validation? In my opinion, you already have it all."

Delight set all her nerve endings alight and suddenly a life-time of exclusion became less hurtful. "That's kind of you to say, but it never seemed enough." Seeing the questions in Harrison's raised eyebrows, London explained further. "My mother is constantly harping on how frustrating it is for her that no matter how much money she donates or how lavish her dinner parties are, she can't ever gain acceptance."

"So maybe it's your mother's issue and not yours."

If only it was that simple.

"She's pretty determined." London could've said more about her mother's unrelenting pressure on her to marry well, but decided further explanations would only put her family's flaws on display.

"It seems like a lot of pressure."

London shrugged. "I'm no stranger to that. After all, heat and extreme pressure turns coal into diamonds," she said, parroting her mother's favorite quote.

"That's not actually a scientific fact," Harrison replied.

"Fine," she grumbled. "But diamonds need heat and pressure to form."

His lips curved in a bone-melting smile. "True."

The exchange highlighted how easily Harrison could blow past her defenses and signaled to London that she might be mistaken about which Crosby brother presented the most danger to her.

Everly's words came back to London. Maybe the other woman's concerns weren't out of line. Did she have what it took to keep up her end of the bargain when already she was thinking of Harrison in terms of getting to know him better rather than someone she could use?

Fifteen minutes later Harrison opened the restaurant's front door, and as soon as they reached the sidewalk, he took her hand and threaded it through his arm. Already a warm glow filled her as a result of the wine she'd consumed and Harrison's stimulating company. Being tucked close against his body increased the heat beneath her skin and she inhaled the cool fresh air, hoping it would clear her head.

"Thinking about ice cream?" he asked, breaking into her thoughts. They'd reached the corner, and instead of continuing on to Swenson's, he pulled her onto the quieter thoroughfare. "Because I'm not."

"No?" she countered, trembling as he backed her up against the building's brick wall and leaned his forearm beside her head.

His gaze searched her features before settling on her lips. "The only dessert I want is a taste of your sweet lips."

If any other man had delivered that line, she would've had a cynical retort, but something about Harrison told her that he meant every word. Her muscles lost strength, making her glad for the wall at her back. She wasn't sure what to do with her hands. His hard body called to her, but letting her palms roam over his chiseled physique—while tempting—was a little too familiar for their first...dinner...date?

"Okay."

"Okay?" he echoed, his soft, firm lips grazing across hers with deliberate intent.

"Yes." She breathed the word and it came out sounding almost like a plea.

"Are you sure it's not too forward of me?"

He seemed determined to tantalize and torment her with what could be. The suggestion of a kiss did exactly what it was supposed to. It frustrated her and provoked curiosity at the same time. She reached up and tunneled her fingers into his hair.

"Kiss me like you want to," she urged, conflicting notes of desperation and command in her tone as he trailed his lips across her cheek.

"If I do that, we might get arrested." His husky laugh puffed against her skin, making her shiver.

Disturbed by the acute longing he aroused, London laid her palm against his chest. His rapid heartbeat caught her attention and bolstered her confidence. The chemistry she felt wasn't one-sided but sparkled between them, ripe with promise and potential.

"I don't know what to do with you," she murmured, trembling as his hand slipped around her waist and into the small of her back, drawing her tight against his hard body.

"Funny," he said. "I know exactly what to do with you." His fingers coasted over the curve of her butt and he punctuated his claim with a quick squeeze before setting her free. "You are temptation in high heels."

The heavy beat of desire pulsing between her thighs made it hard for London to utter her next words. "I think I'd better go home."

"I'll walk you to your car."

To her dismay, his words disappointed her. As they made their way to the parking lot where she'd left her car, she mulled several questions. How had she hoped the evening might end? That he would press her to extend their time together? Suggest that she come home with him?

He'd demonstrated that he was attracted to her...hadn't he? Wasn't that what he'd meant by his temptation-in-high-heels remark? He spoke as if he wanted her, but his actions hadn't crossed any boundaries she'd set for first-date behavior. His kisses hadn't been designed to blow past her defenses and set her afire. She had no doubt that would happen. The brief contact with him had demonstrated her body was dry kindling and his lips the spark that would set her alight.

"Are you okay?" he asked, breaking into her thoughts.

"Fine." Yet she was anything but. What if there was something wrong with her? Something that caused men to lose interest in sex. Could it be that she was the sort of woman who turned men off? Harrison had barely kissed her. Maybe he'd been uninterested in taking things any further.

London's skin prickled as she pondered her relationship with Linc. For months now she'd been plagued by the worry that the reason he'd broken off their engagement was her lack of desirability. Sure, sex between them had been good. Linc was a fantastic lover and she'd never gone unsatisfied. But there hadn't ever been the sort of rip-your-clothes-off passion Maribelle so often talked about having with Beau. In fact, London had grown surly with her best friend several times after Maribelle had shared stories about her and her fiancé.

"Remember I told you I was an introvert?"

"Yes."

"Aside from the negative impression we can give about being shy, aloof or stuck-up, we have a lot of really positive characteristics. One of those being our ability to take in a lot of information and process it."

Unsure what he was getting at, London asked, "What sort of information?"

"When I'm in the middle of a race, it can be tiny nuances about how other cars are moving that telegraph what their drivers are thinking. I'm also pretty good at reading micro-expressions. I can tell by tiny muscle shifts what someone might be feeling."

"You think you know what I'm feeling?" She disliked being like a bug under a microscope.

"I can tell you're not happy."

Rather than agree or disagree, she raised one eyebrow and stared at him.

"You can give me that face all day, but I'm not the one you're upset with."

"What makes you think I'm upset at anyone?"

"Not anyone. Yourself."

That he had read her so easily should've rattled London, but there was no judgment in his manner. "And I suppose you know why?"

"I could guess, but I'd rather wait until you're ready to tell me."

He couldn't have said anything better, and all at once London wanted to cry. She prided herself on her strength and resilience. That Harrison had whipped up her hormones, roused her insecurities and nearly reduced her to tears demonstrated just how dangerous he could be.

"What if I never do?"

To her shock, he wrapped her in a fierce, platonic hug that left her body tingling and her nerves raw.

"Everyone needs someone to talk to, London," he whispered

and then let her go. Before she could untie her tongue, he continued, "I'll call you later this week with the details about Saturday. I'm looking forward to having you and your friends at the race."

London used the distraction of sliding behind the wheel to grab at her flailing control and reined in her wayward emotions. "Is there anything I should know beforehand?"

"We're looking at sunshine and midsixties for race day, so dress accordingly."

"Okay." London had no idea what to wear to a racetrack, but no doubt Maribelle would have plenty of ideas. "I'll see you Saturday."

"See you Saturday." With a wink, Harrison stepped back so she could close the car door.

"Harrison!" Jack Crosby's sharp tone brought his nephew back to the present. "What is going on with you? All week you've been distracted."

His uncle wasn't wrong.

It was early Saturday afternoon. The qualifying races had run that morning, and instead of revisiting his performance on the Richmond track, a certain blonde kept popping up in his thoughts, disrupting his ability to stay on task.

His usual hyper focus on the days leading up to a race had been compromised while he'd wasted energy regretting that he'd pulled back instead of making a definite move on her like she seemed to expect.

Yet her conflict had been plain. She'd made it clear that he wasn't the sort of man she saw herself with, but their undeniable chemistry tempted her. Based on how she'd begged him to kiss her, no doubt he'd gotten beneath her skin. Which was exactly why he'd retreated instead of wearing down her defenses. The woman was too quick to lay down the law. She had definite boundaries and ideas how courtship was supposed to transpire. He needed to set the foundation for new ground rules.

"I guess I've been a little off."

"A little?" His uncle crossed his arms over his chest. "I've never seen you like this."

"I'm sure it's not that bad."

"Since the day you showed up at Crosby Motorsports and declared that you were going to be our top driver one day, you've been the most focused member of the team. And that's saying something considering all the talent we've assembled. But not this week."

Harrison spied a trio headed their way along the alley between the garages and felt his lips curve into a giant grin. He'd recognized Maribelle right off. The lean, well-dressed man matching her brisk pace had to be her fiancé. And the leggy blonde trailing them looked like a fish out of water as her gaze swung this way and that, taking in the loud cars and mechanics that buzzed around the vehicles.

"Excuse me a second," he said to his uncle before stepping forward to meet the visitors.

"Welcome to Richmond," he said as he drew near enough to shake hands. "Hello, Maribelle. And you must be her fiancé, Beau. I'm Harrison Crosby."

"Beau Shelton." The man clasped hands with Harrison. "No need to introduce yourself. We're big fans." Beau tipped his head to indicate Maribelle and she nodded vigorously. "We appreciate this chance to get a glimpse behind the scenes."

"I'm glad you came," Harrison said, forcing himself to be patient when all he wanted was to push past the couple and snatch London into his arms.

Maribelle winked at him. "Thanks for the invite."

Harrison approved of her sassy demeanor, even as he noted once again how her outgoing personality differed from her friend's reserve. Given how close the two women seemed to be, Harrison hoped it boded well for his own chances with London. Obviously she liked—and definitely needed—someone in her life who encouraged her to have fun once in a while.

"Hi," he murmured to London after the couple stepped to one side to allow him access to their friend. He ignored her tentativeness and leaned down to brush his lips over her cheek. "I'm really happy you're here."

London peered at him from beneath her lashes. "You were kind to invite us."

"You look amazing."

She'd chosen dark blue skinny jeans with strategic tears that gave them a trendy appearance, an oversize fuzzy white sweater and a camel-toned moto jacket that matched the suede pumps on her tiny feet. She looked as if she'd worked hard to dress down, but hadn't succeeded in achieving her friend's casual weekend style. His fingers itched to slide into the low knot she'd fastened her hair into and shake the pins loose. She needed someone like him to mess up her perfect appearance.

"I like your suit." Her deliberate scan of his body heated his blood. "It's very colorful."

Fighting the urge to find a quiet corner where he could kiss that sardonic grin off her beautiful lips, Harrison stuck to polite conversation.

"How was the flight down?"

"It was a little more eventful than usual." Her blue eyes shifted past him and settled on her friends. "Beau is teaching Maribelle how to fly and today she did both the takeoff and landing."

"It was fine," Maribelle piped up. "Just a little windier than I was used to during the landing. I did a perfectly acceptable job, didn't I?" This last she directed to her fiancé, who nodded.

His heart was in his eyes as he grinned down at her. "You did great."

Envy twisted in Harrison's chest at the couple's obvious connection. The emotion caught him off guard. Over the last decade he'd watched most of his team and fellow drivers fall in love and get married. Many had even started families. Not once had he wanted to trade places. But since meeting London, he was starting to notice a pronounced dissatisfaction with his personal life.

"That's my car in the third garage stall on the left, if you want to check it out."

"I've never seen a race car up close before," Maribelle said, tugging at Beau's hand to get him going. "I have a hundred questions."

Harrison let London's friends walk ahead of them. The urge to touch her couldn't be denied, so he bumped the back of his hand against hers to see how she'd react. She shot him a questioning glance even as she twisted her wrist so that her palm met his. As his fingers closed around hers, a lazy grin slid over his lips.

"This is...really something." Her choice of words left him with no idea how she felt, but her gaze darted around as if she half expected to be run over any second. "There's a lot of activity."

Up and down the length of the garage, the crews swarmed their cars, making last-minute tweaks before the final practice of the day. Today was a little less chaotic for Harrison than race day and he was delighted to be able to give London and her friends a tour.

"If you think this is hectic, wait until tomorrow. Things really kick into high gear then."

"So, you look like you're dressed to get behind the wheel." She set her fingertip lightly on his chest right over his madly pumping heart. "What's going on today?"

"We had the qualifying race this morning and there are practices this afternoon."

She cocked her head like a curious bird. "You have to qualify before you can race?"

"The qualifier determines what position you start in."

"And where are you starting?"

"Tenth." He should've done better, but his excitement at seeing London again had blown a hole in his concentration. It was unexpected. No woman had thrown him off his game before.

"Is that good?"

Based on the tongue-lashing delivered by his uncle, not so much.

"In a pack of forty," Harrison said with an offhanded shrug. "It's okay."

Nor was it his worst start all year. A month ago his car had failed the inspection before the qualifying race because of a piece of tape on his spoiler and he'd ended up starting in thirty-sixth position.

"So I'll get to see you drive this afternoon?"

"We have a fifty-minute practice happening at three." He took her hand in his and drew her forward. "Come meet my team and check out the car."

After introducing London and her friends to his uncle and giving them a quick tour of the garage, Harrison directed Beau and Maribelle to a spot where they could watch the practice laps. Before letting London get away, he caught her hand and stopped while they were twenty feet from the stall where his car sat.

"You know, I've been thinking about you all week," he confessed, mesmerized by the bright gold shards floating in her blue eyes.

"I've been thinking about you, too." And then, as if she'd given too much away, she finished with, "We have several venues to look at on Monday and I have lots of ideas to run past you for the decor."

He ignored her attempt to turn the conversation to business and leaned close. "I've been regretting that I didn't take you up on your offer."

Her tone was husky as she asked, "What offer was that?"

He pinched a fold of her suede jacket between his fingers and tugged her a half step toward him until their thighs brushed. At the glancing contact, she bit down on her lower lip.

"When you told me to kiss you any way I want."

"That was in the heat of the moment," she said, her voice soft and a trifle breathless. "I don't know what I was thinking."

"I was kinda hoping you weren't thinking at all."

"I guess I wasn't." She gave him a wry smile. "Because if I had been, I probably wouldn't have gone out with you in the first place." Her lighthearted tone took the punch out of her words.

"I'm gonna guess you think too much."

"I'm gonna guess you do, too," she said.

"Most of the time, but not when I'm around you. Then all I do is feel." Harrison cupped her face and sent his thumb skimming across her lower lip. Her eyes widened in surprise. "In fact, my uncle is annoyed with me because it's been hard for me to stay focused."

The temptation to dip his head and kiss her in full view of her friends, his uncle and the racing team nearly overcame him until she gently pulled his hand away and gave it a brief squeeze.

"You're quite the flirt," she said.

"I'm not flirting. I'm speaking one-hundred-percent unvarnished truth." He spread his fingers and entwined them with hers. "Will you have dinner with me tonight?"

"All of us?" she quizzed, glancing after her departing friends.

"Of course. You're my guests." He liked that she looked ever so briefly disappointed. Had she hoped to have dinner alone with him? "I have a press event at six. How about if I pick you up at eight?"

She glanced at the couple ahead of them. "That should be fine."

"Terrific." His gaze drifted to her soft lips. "A kiss for luck?"

"I thought it was just a practice," she retorted, arching one eyebrow. "Why do you need luck?"

"It's always dangerous when you get onto the track," he said, his voice pitched to a persuasive tone as he tugged her to him. "A thousand different things could go wrong."

"Well, I wouldn't want to be responsible for anything like that." Reaching up, she deposited a light kiss on his cheek.

It wasn't exactly what he'd had in mind, but Harrison's temperature skyrocketed in response to the light press of her breasts against his chest. He curved his fingers over the swell of her hip just below the indent of her waist, keeping her near for a heart-stopping second.

Too soon she was stepping back, the color in her cheeks high. Harrison wondered if his face was equally flushed because he appreciated the cool breeze blowing through the alley between the garages.

"Good luck, Harrison," London told him before turning to follow her friends. "Don't let that kiss go to waste."

With a rueful shake of his head, Harrison returned to the garage and wasn't surprised to find several of his pit crew ready to razz him over his obvious infatuation with London.

"She's obviously a great gal," Jack Crosby remarked flatly. "Now, can you please stop mooning over her and focus on the next fifty minutes?"

Harrison smirked at his uncle. "Jack, if you weren't so in love with your wife of forty years, I might think you were jealous."

Five

Anxiety had settled in by the time the clock on the nightstand in her hotel room hit seven fifty. London stared at her reflection, hemming and hawing over the third outfit she'd tried on.

She'd overdressed for today's visit to the racetrack. What might have suited a shopping trip in downtown Charleston had stood out like a sore thumb at Richmond Raceway. Was tonight's navy blue sheath and beige blazer another misstep? She looked ready for a client meeting instead of a date with a sexy race-car driver. Would he show up in jeans and a T-shirt or slacks and a sweater? Should she switch to the black skinny pants and white blouse she'd packed? London was on her way to the closet when a knock sounded on her door.

For a second her heart threatened to explode from her chest until she remembered that she'd agreed to meet Harrison in the lobby. He didn't have her room number, so there was no way he could be the one knocking on her door. She went to answer and spied Beau standing in the hallway. His eyebrows went up when he glimpsed her.

"You're wearing that to dinner?"

London had grown fond of Beau over the last three years, but having him critique her wardrobe choices was too much. She crossed her arms over her chest and glared at him.

"I am." Why did everyone find it necessary to criticize her appearance? "What's wrong with it?" She meant to sound hostile and defensive but the question came out sounding concerned.

"It's a dinner date," Beau pointed out, "not a business meeting."

"It's not a date," she argued, ignoring the fact that she wanted it to be. She just couldn't get attached to Harrison Crosby. Not when she was using him to get to his brother. "We're just four people having dinner."

"About that…" Beau began, his gaze sliding in the direction of the hotel room he was sharing with his fiancée. "Maribelle isn't feeling well, so we're going to stay in tonight and order room service."

London knew immediately that her friend was completely fine and that the engaged couple had conspired to set London up to have dinner alone with Harrison. Panic set in.

"But it's too late for me to cancel," she protested. "He's supposed to be here right now."

"I'm sure it will be just fine if the two of you go by yourselves." He offered her a cheeky grin and winked. "Just wear something else. And have fun. He's a great guy if you'd just give him a chance."

"Great," she grumbled, closing the hotel room door and pondering Beau's parting words.

Harrison was showing every appearance of being a really great guy. Certainly one who deserved better than what she was doing to him. Guilt pinched her as she went to fetch her purse off the dresser. As she passed the closet a flash of teal distracted her. She'd added the clingy fit-and-flare dress to her suitcase at the last second. The color reminded her of Harrison's eyes, a coastal blue-green she could happily drown in.

Growling at the impulses sweeping through her, London roughly stripped out of the blazer, unzipped her sensible blue dress and let it fall to the floor. A minute later she was sliding the soft jersey over her head and tugging it into place. Almost immediately London's perception of the evening before her transformed. As she turned to the dresser and the bag that held her jewelry, the full skirt ballooned and then fell to brush against her thighs, setting off a chain reaction of sensation.

The mirror above the dresser reflected a woman whose eyes glowed with anticipation. She tugged her hair free of its restraining knot and let it fall around her face before fastening on a pair of long crystal earrings that tickled her neck as she moved. A quick glance at the clock revealed she was now running late. London scooped her clothes off the floor and draped them over the bed before sliding her feet into nude pumps and snagging her purse.

It wasn't until she'd closed the hotel room door behind her and raced toward the elevator that she realized she was breathing erratically. Nor could she blame her agitation on the last-minute wardrobe change. She might as well face that she was excited to be having dinner alone with Harrison.

Since her hotel room was on the second floor, London had less than a minute to compose herself before the elevator doors opened. She stepped forward onto the smooth marble floor of the reception area.

At this hour the lobby was busy with people on their way to dinner or in search of a drink at the elegant bar. Suddenly she realized she hadn't specified a particular location in the large open area to meet Harrison. But even before her concerns could take root, he stepped into her line of sight, looking handsome, desirable and a little dangerous dressed all in black. She released a pent-up breath as he drew near.

"Hi," she said weakly.

"You look gorgeous." He leaned down and brushed her cheek with his lips.

Goose bumps broke out on her arms. "Thanks." London couldn't believe he'd reduced her to single-syllable words. "So do you." To her dismay, she felt her cheeks heat. "I mean, you look very nice."

"Thanks." He glanced past her. "Where are Maribelle and Beau?"

"She wasn't feeling well, so they're ordering room service and staying in."

He frowned. "I hope that doesn't mean they'll miss the race tomorrow."

"I think she'll make a miraculous recovery," London mused.

"Oh?" Harrison raised his eyebrows.

London cleared her throat. "She likes to play matchmaker."

"I see."

Did he? When London peered at him from beneath her lashes, she caught him observing her in turn. His look, however, was bold and openly curious.

"She thinks you're a catch."

"I mean no offense when I say that I'm not interested in what she thinks." Harrison took her hand and led her toward the lobby doors. "I want to hear your opinion."

"Do I think you're a catch?" London knew her breathless state had nothing to do with their pace. It was more about the warmth of Harrison's fingers against her skin. "Of course you are."

He glanced at her as she sailed through the open door ahead of him. "You're a little too matter-of-fact when you say that."

"How else should I be?" Despite her earlier reservations, London was having a wonderful time bantering with Harrison. "Are you hoping I'll spill the beans and divulge that I'm infatuated with you?"

"It'd be nice." But his smile indicated he wasn't serious. "Especially given how much you've been on my mind these last few days. It's getting me into trouble with my team."

He'd recaptured her hand once they'd reached the sidewalk.

Was he serious? They'd only met three times and been out once. Surely he was feeding her a line. It was tempting to believe him. The flattery gave her ego a much-needed boost. Heaven knew it had taken a beating since Linc had ended their engagement.

"You've gone quiet," he continued. "Don't you believe me?"

"We barely know each other."

"True, but I felt an immediate attraction to you. And I think you noticed the same pull. Why else would you agree to step out of your comfort zone this weekend and come watch me race?"

"Maribelle would've killed me if I'd turned you down." It was a lame cop-out and both of them knew it. London gathered her breath. He'd generously arranged this weekend for her and her friends. She owed him better. "And I wanted to see what you did. Watching you during the practice laps was really exciting."

His full smile nearly blinded her with its brilliance. "Wait until you see the race tomorrow. It gets a lot more interesting when forty guys put it all on the line."

"I imagine it does." She found herself grinning back. His enthusiasm was infectious. "Where are we going?"

While they'd been talking, he'd directed her along the downtown street. Now, as they crossed another street, he gestured her toward a red canopy that marked the entrance to a restaurant.

"The food here is really good. I thought maybe you'd like to try it."

"Lead the way."

He'd brought her to a tiny French bistro with wood floors, a tin ceiling and white linens on the tables. Cozy booths were tucked against a brick wall while the opposite side of the room was lined with bottles of wine. The subdued lighting lent a warm, romantic vibe to the place and the scents filling the air made London's mouth water.

The hostess settled them into a booth near the back where it was quieter and London turned her attention to the menu.

"It all looks so good," she exclaimed. "I don't know what to choose."

"We could order a couple things and share," Harrison suggested.

It would ease the decision-making process, so London nodded. "Since you've been here before, I'm going to let you do the ordering."

"You trust me?"

She somehow sensed he had more on his mind than just meal selection. "Let's just say I'm feeling a little adventurous at the moment."

"I like the sound of that."

After the waitress brought their drinks and left with their orders, London decided to grab the conversational reins.

"So where are you staying?"

"In an RV at the raceway," he replied. "You're welcome to stop by and check it out later. It's pretty roomy with a nice big bed in the back."

"I suppose it makes sense to be close by," she said, ignoring his invitation. "I looked at the weekend schedule and they keep you really busy. I'm surprised you had time to have dinner with me."

"I snuck out," he said with a mischievous grin. "My uncle thinks I'm going over the data from today's laps before tomorrow's race."

"Really?" She was more than a little shocked until she realized he was kidding. "I'm learning there's a lot more to racing than just getting in a car and going fast."

"Sometimes the tiniest changes can make all the difference."

"So besides making sure you're super-hydrated," she began, referring to the fact that he was only drinking water and wasn't partaking in the bottle of wine he'd ordered for her, "what else goes into preparing for tomorrow's race?" In stark contrast to her earlier skepticism about being interested in a race-car driver, she was finding Harrison's occupation quite interesting.

"I make sure I eat a lot of carbs the night before. I hope you're a fan of chocolate mousse."

"I can always make room for chocolate of any kind."

"Tomorrow morning I'll have a big breakfast followed by a light lunch. In between I'll make sponsor-related appearances before checking in with my crew chief and team to run through last-minute strategy. After that there's a drivers' meeting where the racing association shares information about what's going on that day. If I'm lucky I'll get a few minutes alone at the RV to get my head on straight, but more likely I'll be doing meet and greets. Finally, after lunch, I'll suit up and head to the driver introductions."

"Wow! That's a packed schedule." She was starting to appreciate that his career wasn't just about driving. He was a brand ambassador for his sponsors and the league as well as being a celebrity. "You really don't have any time to yourself."

"Not really. It's all part of the job. And I wouldn't give up any of it."

"You call yourself an introvert, but don't all the public appearances and demands on your time wear you down to nothing?"

"It's not like I don't enjoy meeting my fans." He buttered a piece of bread and popped it into his mouth. "But when I have time off, I make sure I do whatever it takes to reenergize."

"I'm surprised you're out with me, then."

"Are you kidding?" His broad smile dealt her defenses a significant blow. "Being with you is quite exhilarating."

"That's sweet of you to say…"

"I mean it." He gestured at her with another hunk of crusty bread. "And this is where I should probably confess something."

London barely resisted a wince, thinking about her poorly conceived notion to get close to Harrison as a way of getting to his brother. She had yet to figure out what she could do to take Tristan down.

"Like what?" she prompted, hoping it was something terrible so she could feel better about her own questionable morality.

"I used my brother's birthday party as an excuse to see you again."

"Oh." Her pulse skipped. "Does that mean you don't need me as your party planner?" She considered the amount of time she'd spent working on the party and sighed. He wouldn't be the first client to change his mind.

"Not at all. My mother is thrilled that I've taken the project off her hands. My brother can be quite particular when it comes to certain things and it's better if I take the heat for his disappointment."

"You're assuming he'll be disappointed before you've heard any of my plans?" London frowned, but found she wasn't all that insulted. Neither Harrison nor his brother were the toughest clients she'd ever worked for. "That doesn't speak to your faith in my ability to do my job."

Despite the lack of heat or ire in her tone, Harrison's eyes widened. "That's not what I meant at all. I'm sure you will outdo yourself. It's just that Tristan is hard to impress. He's always been that way."

London remembered that Zoe had said something similar about her ex-husband and nodded. "Challenge accepted," she said, digging in where others might throw up their hands and quit.

Harrison nodded. "You thrive under pressure," he said, admiration in his steady gaze. "So do I. It's what makes us good for each other."

Although his words thrilled her, guilt shadowed her delight. Getting revenge on Tristan had prompted her to agree to work on his birthday party and go on that first date with Harrison. She simply had to get her emotions under control.

"You don't think two competitive people will end up ruining things because they're forever chasing the win?" she asked.

"Not if we do it together. I think if we became a team, there's nothing we couldn't accomplish."

Before she started nodding in agreement, London reminded herself of why she'd begun dating him. Getting close to Harrison was a means to an end. And if that made her a terrible person then that was something she'd just have to live with.

Harrison watched his car, number twenty-five, roll into the truck for the return to South Carolina. He was pleased with his second-place finish. With only one race left until the end of the season, he sat in third place for the year and, based on his points, he'd likely hang on to the spot unless he completely screwed up next weekend.

As the car disappeared, a familiar wave of exhaustion swept over him. Once the race was over and the media interviews finished, his body reacted to the long day by shutting down.

"Nice race," his uncle said. The two men were standing side by side while the team rolled Harrison's race car from one set of inspectors to the next. "I was a little worried about you in the beginning."

Today's race had been unusually challenging since at the beginning he'd had to work twice as hard to stay focused on the track and the cars around him while thoughts of London and their dinner last night dominated his mind. Things had gotten better once he'd passed his hundredth lap and settled into the race, needing to win so he could impress London.

"Just wanted to make it interesting," Harrison replied with a sly grin.

"You did that," Jack grumbled. "Let me know when you're ready to head back tonight. I'd like to get out of here by midnight."

"Actually, I've arranged a lift back to Charleston already."

His uncle raised an eyebrow. "Your new girlfriend?"

"She's not my girlfriend...yet." That last word slipped out, revealing something Harrison hadn't yet admitted to himself. He had more than a casual interest in London McCaffrey.

What was going on with him? They'd only been out twice and he was already thinking in terms of a relationship? The only time he was quick to commit was on the track. But when he was with London, their connection felt right and his instincts had never failed him before.

"You sure she's the right woman for you?" his uncle asked, the question a jarring pothole Harrison didn't see coming.

Acid began churning in Harrison's gut. "You have some thoughts on why she isn't?"

While Jack had never commented on any of his drivers' personal lives, he was operating a business where each driver brought in hundreds of thousands to millions of dollars in sponsor revenue each year. That meant he couldn't afford for his team to operate at anything less than 100 percent. And anything that interfered with that would come under fire.

"I asked Dixie about her."

"And?" Harrison challenged.

"She's a social climber." Jack's expression grew hard. "Apparently she and her mother have been trying to access Charleston inner circles without much success."

"What does that have to do with us dating?" Although he already knew the answer, Harrison wanted to hear his uncle say it.

"I'm just concerned she's going to mess with your head if you're not careful."

"Because I'm not her type?" He'd already figured that out.

"Before Linc Thurston, she'd only gone out with executives and professionals," Jack said. "I don't think she'd have dated a pro ball player if he hadn't belonged to one of Charleston's oldest families. And I'm guessing the reason they're no longer engaged is because Linc figured that out before it was too late."

"I don't think she's as shallow as all that," Harrison said, hoping he was right. "And we're in the early stages of dating. Who's to say where things are going for us."

Jack grunted. "Make sure you figure it out one way or another before the season starts up again in February." His uncle frowned. "I don't need you distracted on the track."

"Hopefully it won't take that long."

Jack nodded and the two men parted ways.

Harrison headed back to the trailer, where he grabbed a quick shower. Even on cooler days like this one, the heat inside the car during the race hovered close to a hundred and thirty degrees. Since the sort of AC in a consumer vehicle weighed too much to be installed in a race car, drivers were cooled by a ventilation system that used hoses and a bag they sat on to blow air on their feet and head. With the average race lasting at least three hours, that was a long time to go without any sort of air-conditioning.

After getting dressed, Harrison slung his duffel over his shoulder and headed to the spot where he'd agreed to meet up with London and her friends. He was intrigued by the fact that Beau had his pilot's license and that Maribelle was learning how to fly. Harrison liked the couple, finding them an upbeat counterpunch to London's reserve.

On the heels of his conversation with Jack, Harrison reflected on his own concerns about what he was getting into with London. If all he wanted was sex, he wasn't going about it the right way given the chemistry that sizzled between them. Take last night, for example. He'd accompanied her back to her hotel room and once again she'd put out a vibe that welcomed physical contact. But instead of backing her into the room and doing all the things he'd been fantasizing about, he'd kissed her on the forehead—not trusting himself to claim her lips—and walked away with an ache in his chest and his loins.

Appreciating the cool night air against his skin, Harrison lengthened his stride, eager to see London and hear her opinion of the race. A silver SUV awaited him near the gate that led to the parking lot. The window was down on the driver's side and Harrison recognized Beau's profile. The easygoing fellow was smiling and gesturing as he spoke to the car's occupants.

"Hey," Harrison said as he approached. "Thanks for the lift."

"Are you kidding?" Beau glanced at his fiancée. "It's the least we could do after the weekend we've had. The behind-the-scenes access you gave us was incredible."

Harrison pulled open the rear driver's-side door and spied

London sitting on the far seat. The sight of her made his chest
go tight. *Damn.* The woman was beautiful. Today she wore
black pants and a denim jacket over a cream sweater. Her hair
was bound in a loose braid with long strands framing her pale
cheeks. A welcoming smile curved her full, kissable lips and
he glimpsed no trace of hesitation in her manner.

Heart thumping erratically, he slid in beside her and became
immediately aware of her subtle floral scent. "So what did you
think of your first race?" he asked, slipping his duffel into the
SUV's cargo area. "Was it what you expected?"

"To be honest, I thought I'd be bored. Five hundred laps
seemed like a lot. But it was really fun. It helped to have these
two with me." She indicated the couple in the front seats. "They
explained a lot of the ins and outs of the strategy. And congratulations on your second-place finish."

"The team had a good weekend," he replied, unsure why he
was downplaying his success. Didn't he want to impress this
woman? From everything he'd been told, only the best would
do for her. "If all goes smoothly next weekend, Crosby Motorsports is poised to finish second this year."

"So next weekend is your last race? What do you do during
the off-season?"

"Rest, play and then get ready for next year."

"How much time do you get off to do that?"

"Season starts again in February. I take a break in December
to vacation and celebrate the holidays with my family. But even
during the off-season I train. Both in the gym and with driving
simulations to keep my reflexes sharp." Harrison reached out
and took her hand in his, turning it palm up and running the
tips of his fingers over her skin. He noticed a slight tremble in
her fingers as he caressed her. "I had a really great time last
night," he murmured, pitching his voice so only she could hear.

"It was fun. Thank you for dinner." Her gaze flicked from
the hand he held to the couple in the front and back to him.

"I'm sorry we had to make such an early night of it."

"You had a big day today. I wouldn't have felt right if I kept you up too late." She sent him a sizzling look from beneath her lashes, banishing his earlier weariness.

Was she feeling bold because they weren't alone?

He toyed with her fingers, imagining how they would feel against his naked body. Yet, to his surprise, the rush of lust such thoughts aroused was matched by a strong craving to find out what made her tick. He lifted her palm to his lips and nipped at her skin. Her sharp gasp made him smile. He'd begun to suspect the route past her defenses might involve keeping her off balance by pushing her sensual boundaries. He would have to test that during tomorrow's hunt for the party venue.

"I think a sleepless night with you would've been worth doing badly today," he murmured.

"I'm sure your uncle wouldn't agree."

"He was young once."

"He's running a multimillion-dollar racing team," she countered, her tone tart. "And even if he forgave you, what about your sponsors?"

Harrison let loose an exaggerated sigh. "One of these days you're going to surprise me by not being so practical."

"You think so?" A faint smile curved her lips.

"I know so."

London subsided into reflective silence for several minutes and Harrison gave her room to think. At long last she said, "It's not part of my nature to be rash and spontaneous. My mother drilled into my head that I should think first and act second. She's very concerned with appearances, and growing up, I never had an opportunity to spread my wings, so to speak."

This bit of insight into her past intrigued him. "What would you have done if your choices hadn't been so restricted?"

"Run off and join the circus?" Her weak attempt at humor was obviously an attempt to deflect his probing. After a second she gave a half-hearted shrug and said, "I don't know. Sometimes I resent that my mother was so obsessed with advancing my position in Charleston society."

"Only sometimes?" he challenged.

London's fingers briefly tightened over his. "When I let myself think about it." For a long moment she sat in silence, but soon his patience was rewarded. "It's hard when your mother thinks your worth is defined by who you marry. That's something other people judge you by, not your own parent."

"Why do you care?"

His blunt question apparently surprised her. Despite the shadowy confines of the back seat, he could easily read the sudden tension in her expression.

She reacted as if he'd attacked some core value she lived by. "I want her to be glad I'm her daughter."

Harrison understood why this was important. Tristan had long sought their father's approval, especially since taking over Crosby Automotive. Harrison's brother seemed obsessed with matching the success their father had made of the company, yet profits had been mostly flat in the first few years Tristan had been in charge. Still, that hadn't seemed to affect his personal spending. Something Harrison had heard his uncle criticize more than once.

"You don't think she admires all you've accomplished?" Harrison asked, returning his thoughts to London's situation.

"I think my dad does." Pride glowed in her voice. "My company is very successful and that makes him proud."

"But not your mother?"

"She might've been happy if I'd married Linc and had several boys and one girl."

"Why only one girl?" Harrison suspected he knew the answer before she spoke.

"Obviously my mother's opinion is that women are worth less than men." London's tone was more matter-of-fact than bitter. "Still, she'd like to have a granddaughter who could do what I couldn't. Become a debutante."

Harrison knew his mother had gone through the classes and been presented at nineteen. But in this day and age, did that stuff even matter?

"Why is it so important to her?" he asked.

"My mother grew up in New York City and was never selected for the International Debutante Ball there, despite her family's connections and wealth. She took the rejection hard." London shifted in her seat, turning to face him. "And then she gets to Charleston and finds all the doors are closed to her. No one cared about her money. All that mattered was she was from *off*." London freed her hand briefly so she could form air quotes around the last word.

"You should talk to my mother," Harrison said. "She rejected becoming a debutante and married my dad, who was not only an outsider but poor by her family standards."

"I'm going to guess she'd tell me to follow my heart?"

"That was the advice she gave me when my dad hassled me about choosing racing over working for Crosby Automotive. If I hadn't, I'd be working for the family business and completely miserable."

"You don't see yourself as a businessman?"

"Honestly, not the sort who sits in an office and stares at reports all day. My plan is to take over for my uncle one day and run Crosby Motorsports."

"And in the meantime you're just going to race and have fun."

"Nothing wrong with having fun. I'd like to demonstrate that to you."

"What sort of fun do you think I'd be interested in?" she asked, her manner serious rather than flirtatious.

"Hard to say until I get to know you better." He had several ideas on the subject. "But would you have guessed that you'd enjoy today's race as much as you did?"

"No, not really. Maybe I do need to look outside my limited circle of activities."

"So that's a yes to new experiences?"

"As long as you're willing to balance adventure with somewhat tamer forms of entertainment," she said, "I'm in."

No sweeter words had ever been spoken by a woman.

Six

Shortly after lunch on the Monday following her weekend in Richmond, London sat at her desk, doodling on her notepad, her cell phone on speaker while Maribelle went on and on about how much she and Beau had enjoyed their time at the raceway. London's attention, however, was not on the race but on the man who'd invited her to it.

Almost as if her friend could read her mind, Maribelle said, "He's really into you. I think that's so great."

Maribelle's remark sent a little shiver of pleasure through London. "I don't know what to think."

But she wasn't being completely truthful. London was in fact thinking that she'd intended to use Harrison to get close to his brother, and the more time she spent with the race-car driver, the more troubling her attraction to him became.

Despite their closeness, London hadn't told Maribelle about the crazy plan hatched at the Beautiful Women Taking Charge event. London knew if she looked too deeply at why she'd kept it from her best friend of fifteen years, doubts would surface about her moral choices. Shame flooded her as London realized how far she'd strayed from the person she'd believed herself to be. Yet to stop now when others were depending on her…

"Are you worried what your mother would think of him?" Maribelle asked, breaking into London's thoughts.

Maribelle had been there for London during high school when Edie Fremont-McCaffrey's frustration with Charleston's society rules had made London's life hell. It wasn't her fault that she wasn't allowed to be a debutante, but that hadn't stopped her mother from raining criticisms down on her daughter's head. Blaming her mother gave London an excuse to be conflicted about getting involved with Harrison so that her real concerns never had to surface.

"She wasn't exactly thrilled with the fact that Linc was a professional baseball player, but he was wealthy and had the old Charleston social connections that she wanted for me." London toyed with her earring. "Can you imagine how she'd feel about Harrison? Not only is he a race-car driver, but his father and uncle are from off with no social standing."

"Why do you care?"

It wasn't the first time Maribelle had asked the question. Nor did it spark the familiar surge of resentment that was always just below the surface. About how easy it was for someone who had it all to downplay their advantages. Add to that how supportive Maribelle's family was about everything she did, and bitterness had often colored London's mood. Today, however, London was feeling less defensive than usual.

"Because fighting her is so much work. It's easier to give in." The admission flowed from London's lips, startling her. And apparently surprising Maribelle, as well, because for a long few seconds neither woman spoke.

"Oh, London."

Sudden tears erupted in London's eyes. Shocked by the rush of emotion, she blinked rapidly, determined not to give in. Her mother had hounded her mercilessly all her life and London had always braced against it. For as long as she could remember,

London had maintained a resilient facade while secretly believing that Edie was right and it was all London's fault.

She picked up the phone and took it off speaker. "My mother is a tyrant," she said in a barely audible whisper, almost as if she was afraid to voice what was in her heart. "She has criticized nearly everything I've ever done or said."

"She's a terrible person," Maribelle agreed, always London's champion. "But she's also your mother and you want to please her. It's normal."

But was it? Shouldn't parents want what was best for their children? That being said, Edie would claim that encouraging her daughter to marry well was the most important thing for London's future, but it was pretty clear that her mother didn't take London's happiness into account, as well.

"Maybe I need a new normal," London groused.

"Maybe you do," Maribelle said, her tone deadly serious. "What are you wearing right now?"

The question came out of nowhere and made London laugh. She dabbed at the trace of moisture lingering near the corner of her eye and found her spirits rising.

"Are you trying to get me to engage in phone sex with you?" London teased, pretending to sound outraged. "Because I don't think either of us rolls that way."

"Ha, ha." Maribelle sounded more impatient than amused. "I'm only asking because I heard you making plans to get together with Harrison today to go venue shopping. I hope you're wearing something less...reserved than usual."

London glanced down at the emerald green wrap dress she wore. The style was more fun and relaxed than her typical uniform of conservative suits in understated shades of gray, blue and black.

"I'm wearing the necklace you bought me for Christmas last year." London had not previously worn the statement necklace of stone flowers in hot jewel tones, thinking the look was too bold for her. But today she'd wanted her appearance to make an impact and the necklace had paired perfectly with the dress.

"Is your hair up?"

London's fingers automatically went to the sleek side bun she wore.

"Forget I asked," Maribelle said. "Just take it down and send me a picture."

Feeling slightly ridiculous, London did as she was told, even going so far as to fluff her blond waves into a sexy, disheveled look, and was rewarded by her friend's joyful squeal.

"I think that means you approve."

"This is the London McCaffrey I've been waiting for all my life," Maribelle declared in rapturous tones. "You look fantastic and it's so nice to see you ditching those dull duds you think make you look professional."

"Thanks?" Despite her friend's backhanded compliment, London was feeling optimistic and excited about seeing Harrison again. Would he approve of her new look? Or was he a typical guy who wouldn't notice?

"You really like him, don't you?"

London opened her mouth, preparing to deny the way her heart raced and nerves danced whenever she was with Harrison, but couldn't lie to her friend. "I do like him. More than I expected to. That being said, it might be that we have a lot of chemistry and there's no possible way we're compatible beyond that." She left an unspoken *but* hanging in the air.

It was getting harder and harder to make excuses for why dating Harrison would be a waste of her time. Unfortunately, the real reason was a secret London could never share with her friend and that made what she was doing all the worse.

"Say whatever you want," Maribelle said. "But I see things working out between you two."

"I don't know. We're so different. We have divergent points of view about lifestyle and the things we enjoy. How do we go forward if we have nothing in common?"

"That sounds like your mother talking. How different are you really? You both come from money. You may not run in the same groups, but your families share some social connections. Both of you are committed to your careers and highly competitive. If you're talking about the fact that he races cars for a living, he makes a boatload of money doing it and I think you'd be bored with some stuffy businessman who only wants to talk about how his company is doing. You need someone who gets you riled up."

"You keep saying things like that, but excitement has never been my criterion for finding a man attractive before."

"How's that worked out for you thus far?"

Before London could protest that she was quite happy with her life, her desk phone lit up with a call from Missy, likely indicating that Harrison had arrived.

"I think Harrison's here."

"Call me later to let me know how it went."

Instead of reminding her friend that this was a business meeting, London said, "I'm sure there won't be anything to tell."

"Let me be the judge of that."

London was shaking her head as she disconnected with her friend and answered the call from her receptionist. Sure enough, Harrison was waiting for her in the lobby.

Before she picked up her tablet containing all the information on the four venues she'd be showing Harrison today, London double-checked her makeup and applied a fresh coat of lipstick. She noted her sparkling eyes and the flush over her cheekbones put there in anticipation of seeing Harrison. The man had certainly gotten beneath her skin. Worse, she was glad of it.

Despite the fact that she'd seen him the night before, London's stomach flipped as she walked into the reception area and spied Harrison's tall figure. Although her primping had kept him waiting, he wasn't checking his phone or flirting with her receptionist. Instead he was focused on the hallway leading to her office. Their eyes collided and a shower of sparks raced across London's nerve endings, leaving her breathless and light-headed.

"Hi," she said, her voice sounding not at all professional. Cursing her body's longing to fling itself against his, she cleared her throat and tried again. "Sorry I kept you waiting." Flustered by his slow, sexy smile, she turned to the receptionist. "Missy, I'll be gone for the rest of the afternoon. See you in the morning."

"Sure." Missy brazenly winked at her. "You two have fun now."

London's mouth dropped open and her brain was scrambling to come up with something to reply when Harrison caught her hand and tugged her toward the door. She noticed how the man smelled delicious as he guided her to his Mercedes.

"Where to first?" he asked as he slid behind the wheel.

Although the entire afternoon's plans were already firmly in her mind, she cued up her tablet, needing something to do to avoid looking at him. After naming an address half a mile down on King Street, she began listing the positives and negatives of the space.

"The best part is their menu. They have an excellent chef. Unfortunately, there is no elevator, so the space is only accessible by stairs. I only mention it in case you have any guests who can't make the climb."

"That shouldn't be a problem."

Harrison found an open spot along the curb a half block up from their destination and parked. They then walked back toward the venue. As Harrison held the front door, allowing her to pass, she noticed his slight frown. The first floor of the narrow building was occupied by a wine bar.

"Don't let the size down here fool you," she said, waving at the manager. "Upstairs is fifteen hundred square feet and feels much more open and airy. There's plenty of room for all your guests and even an outdoor patio if the night is mild." She broke off to greet Jim Gleeson and introduced the manager to Harrison. "Jim has helped me with several corporate functions over the last two years," she explained.

The two men shook hands and then Jim led the way upstairs. "We can set up the space however you envision it," the manager said over his shoulder. "And the room is big enough that we can divide it into a cocktail setting with high tables or couches on one end and large round tables on the other for dinner."

"I think that would be nice," London said.

They'd reached the second floor and Harrison wasn't evaluating the space, but rather, his attention was focused on her.

"Since we'd talked about a jazz band," she continued, determined to treat him like a client in this setting, "we could place them near the bar as people first enter."

At the moment the room was set up for a cocktail party with a freestanding bar at each end and high-top tables scattered along the perimeter.

Jim's phone buzzed and he excused himself, leaving the pair alone.

Somehow as soon as it was just the two of them, the massive room became oddly intimate. Or maybe it was the way Harrison was looking at her as if he intended to penetrate her professional mask and get to the woman beneath. London couldn't stop herself from recalling how disappointed she'd been on Saturday night that he hadn't tried to kiss her good-night. Or the way they'd leaned toward each other on the plane ride back, sharing the armrest as he'd shown her the camera footage from inside his race car.

"What I really like here is all the period details," she began, taking refuge in professionalism to avoid Harrison's hot gaze. She walked away from him, gesturing at the exposed brick and white wainscoting. Her heels clicked on the polished pine floor and echoed off the gleaming wood in the original coffered ceiling. "Isn't this fireplace fantastic?"

"I think you're fantastic."

"I'm picturing ten tables of ten. With big glass vases holding candles and filled with glass beads in the center. Since it's December, we could do evergreen centerpieces, but maybe that's too predictable." Aware that she was rambling, London continued. To stop meant she might give in to the longing pulsing through her. "Or we could do glass pillars with layered candies like peppermints and foil-wrapped chocolates in red and green. Unless you think he's too sophisticated and would prefer crystal with white and silver."

While she'd been going on and on, Harrison had been stalking after her, his expression intent, his gaze narrowed. Now, as she approached the door leading out to the rooftop patio, he set his hand on the doorknob before she could reach it, halting her retreat.

"I think you're fantastic," he repeated, compelling her to stop dodging him. "Everything about you interests me."

"I like you a lot," she admitted, surprising both of them with the confession. "What you do is dangerous and exciting. I never imagined..."

Oh, what was she doing? It was on the tip of her tongue to spill everything about the riotous, treacherous emotions driving her actions. To share how disappointed she'd been Saturday night because he hadn't tried anything when he'd brought her back to her hotel room. Confessing her developing feelings for him was the absolute wrong thing to do. So how was she supposed to get out of the verbal corner she'd backed herself into?

Harrison watched a dozen conflicting emotions race across London's features. Most of the time she'd demonstrated a sphinxian ability to keep her thoughts concealed. Her need to keep herself hidden frustrated him. He wanted her to open up and share what made her tick.

"I've also had great success with hurricane holders filled with rice lights and Christmas balls," she stated in a breathless rush, returning to the earlier topic of centerpieces. "Or glass bowls with candles floating above holly sprigs."

"Never imagined what?" Harrison prompted, ignoring her attempt to evade the real subject.

She shook her head. "This really isn't the place for this conversation."

"Where would you like to go?" He hoped she'd suggest her place. Or his. It was past time he got her alone.

"I set aside my afternoon to help you find a venue for your brother's birthday party."

"London," he murmured, cradling her head in his palm, thumb caressing her flushed cheek.

"Yes?"

Her voice was equally soft and it seemed to him a trace of desperation colored her tone as if with each thump of her heart she was losing the fight to maintain control. It echoed how he felt when they were together. Each moment in her company tested his willpower. He knew better than to pressure her like this. As much as he wanted to go in with guns blazing, she needed to be coaxed. Wooed. Enticed. But damn if he didn't want to feel her surrender beneath his touch.

"I don't really care what venue we choose," he said. "The only reason I'm here today is to spend time with you."

He placed just the tips of his fingers on her spine. A tremor went through her an instant before she tipped her head back and gazed up at his face. The hunger glowing in her eyes transfixed him. Inching closer, he dipped his head until he could feel her breath on his skin. He grazed his nose against hers, ending the move with a slight bump that nudged her head into a better angle. Smiling at the sigh that escaped her, he slanted his mouth above hers, not quite making contact. Although he'd already kissed her on the street in downtown Charleston, that location hadn't offered him the privacy to do it right. Plus, it had been too soon to take things as far as he wanted to.

This time it would be different.

She made a soft impatient noise in the seconds before their lips met and his world stopped being ordinary. Then another sound erupted from her throat as fire flashed through him. Wildness sped across his nerve endings, setting his heart to pounding. Endless fantasies of her and him naked and rolling over his mattress in hungry, frenzied passion flashed through his mind.

Harrison didn't give a damn that the manager might return and interrupt them. The only thing on his mind was the woman making his heart pound and his body heat. Longing had gotten hold of him and wouldn't let go.

With one hand coaxing her forward, bringing her torso into contact with chest and abs, he cupped her cheek with the other and deepened the kiss. It nearly killed him to go slow when he wanted so much more. Her lips. Tongue. Teeth. All of her. And when her lips parted and a soft, helpless groan escaped her, he nearly lost his mind.

In the instant her body melted into his, they were both swept up in a way that Harrison found himself powerless to stop. Despite his best intentions, the kiss went nova too fast for him to rein it in. Instead he surrendered the fight, realizing while he desired this woman more with each encounter, she wanted him just as much.

This was how a kiss was supposed to be. A give-and-take of sweetness and lust. Pure longing and dirty intentions. He slid his tongue across hers, claiming her mouth and driving her passion harder. Her fingers clutched his hair and dented his leather jacket. It was all crazy, frantic fun with a poignant dash of inevitability, and he never wanted it to end.

The sound of footsteps on the wooden stairs behind him jolted Harrison back to reality. Cursing inwardly, he broke off the kiss and gulped in air. Without releasing his hold on London, he blinked several times in rapid succession, trying to reorient himself to their surroundings. When had he ever lost control like that? Who was this woman who could make him go crazy by relating details about square footage, color schemes and table layouts?

"How are we doing?" came a bright voice from the far end of the room.

London jerked in response to the interruption and pulled Harrison's hand from her face. She took a half step back, her eyes stunned and wide as they met his. Her chest rose and fell as she put her hand to her mouth, hiding a dismayed *oh*. Harrison surveyed the hot color of her skin and her passion-bruised lips, unable to resist a smile.

Damn, she looked gorgeous with her vulnerability on display. All softness and submission. But even as this thought registered in his mind, he could tell she was rapidly regaining her poise. Her features shifted into the cool reserve with which she confronted the world. Only her eyes betrayed her in the second before her lashes dipped, concealing her confusion.

"It all looks great," he called to the manager. "I think we'll take it."

"Great," the man replied. "I'll get the paperwork started."

"You go do that," Harrison said. "We have a few more things to talk about up here and then we'll be down."

"I have three more properties to show you," London reminded him in a harsh whisper, regaining her voice even as the manager's footsteps retreated down the stairs. "You can't make a decision without seeing all of them."

He skimmed his fingertips over her cheekbone, admiring her delicate bone structure. "Do you really want to spend the rest of the afternoon pretending to look at properties while what we really want to do is get to know each other better?"

"I..." Her eyes narrowed. "If you think one kiss means I'm going to sleep with you, you're wrong."

No doubt she'd intended to make this declaration in tart tones, but her voice had lacked conviction.

"You have a dirty mind," he scolded, giving her an affectionate tap on her perfect nose. "I like that in a woman."

"I don't have anything of the sort."

"Really?" He raised an eyebrow. "I say I want to get to know you better and you assume that means sex."

"Well, sure." She gnawed on her lip and frowned. "I mean…"

"Table that thought," he growled, dropping his head and giving her a firm, brief kiss on the lips. "What I meant by getting to know each other better was more about how you came to Richmond this weekend to watch me race. I thought it might be nice for you to show me a little of your world."

It had occurred to him after being dropped off the night before that London McCaffrey had learned way more about him than he'd discovered about her.

Her gaze remained glued to him as she gestured toward the room. "This is it."

"What? Do you mean work? There has to be more to your life than just this." When she shook her head, Harrison nodded. Obviously they were two of a kind when it came to their careers. "So we'll continue to plan the party. We've chosen a venue. What's next?"

"The menu. Flowers. Invitations. A theme."

A theme? Harrison kept his thoughts hidden with some difficulty as he imagined the challenge in finding something that would appeal to his brother. Maybe his mother would have some ideas.

"So, let's go downstairs, sign the contract, plan the meal and then go buy some flowers."

She regarded him skeptically. "Really? You want to do that?"

"I want to spend time with you and see what you enjoy doing. If that involves flowers and invitations, so be it."

For several heartbeats she remained undecided, but instead of pushing, Harrison stayed silent and let her sort through whatever it was she was grappling with. At last she nodded.

"But first," he said, turning her around until they were both staring through the glass door leading outside. "Let's talk about this patio."

"Okay."

Her expression as she glanced back at him reflected her puzzlement. Keeping her off balance was part of his plan to discover all the little things she kept concealed.

"How do you see us using the space for Tristan's party?" As he spoke, he grabbed her wrists and slid her hands to the wood portion of the door before pushing her palms flat against the narrow panel. "Keep your hands right there. Now, tell me your thoughts."

She shivered as he ran his hands up her arms to her shoulders before moving aside her hair, exposing her neck. "They can string lights and put out couches."

"What else?"

He dusted a kiss just below her hairline, hearing her breath stutter as his lips continued to play over the fragrant flesh of her neck and run along the neckline of her dress. He dipped beneath the fabric with his finger, baring the top of her spine, claiming her shoulder, collarbone and nape with soft kisses.

She pushed back into his body and moaned as her backside came into contact with his erection. The sound inflamed his already fiery desire and he murmured encouragement as he kissed the shell of her ear and nipped at her earlobe.

"What else?" he repeated. "How do you envision the scene?"

"Um," she said, her breath coming faster. "We could have them set up a bar. Oh, that feels good."

This last was in response to his hand sliding over her stomach and splaying as she rocked her hips, rubbing herself against him.

"How many people do you think could fit out there?" he quizzed, dipping his hand beneath the hem of her dress and running his fingertips up her thigh.

"A couple dozen. Oh." Her head fell back against his shoulder as he grazed the inside of her thigh. "What you're doing to me…"

"Yes?" he prompted.

Did she have any idea she'd parted her legs to give him better access? He raked her neck with his teeth, dying to touch her, to find out if she was wet for him.

"Don't stop."

"Besides the lights and couches, how would you decorate?"

He ran his fingers over the cotton panel of her panties, noting the damp fabric.

"Please." She was panting and rocking against his hand, making low, incoherent noises, trying to ask for more.

"How would you decorate?" he repeated, sliding his fingers beneath he elastic of her panties and cupping her for a long second before dipping his finger into her wetness. With a heartfelt groan he stroked her, absorbing her shudders as he discovered just how she liked to be touched.

"Candles." She ejected the word like a curse. "Lots and lots and lots of candles."

She was coming. Hard. Her hips rocked and bucked as her spine arched. The sounds emanating from her stopped being coherent. A storm was rising and it fed his own pleasure. In that moment they were no longer two people but one being, both focused on driving her into a mind-blowing orgasm. And then he felt the first wave of it rush over her. Felt her start to shatter against him.

"Give it to me, baby," he said. "Let me take care of you."

Her nails dug into his thigh. He'd been so focused on her he hadn't even realized she'd gripped him there. But now her touch, so close to his aching erection, caused him to harden to the point of pain.

"Oh, Harrison."

Her words ended in a shudder that seemed endless as she climaxed and he held on, easing his strokes as the last of her pleasure dimmed. Panting and limp, head bowed, she braced herself with one hand on the door frame and sucked great gulps of air into her lungs. The other hand eased its death grip on his thigh and she pushed a lock of hair behind her ear.

"God, I love making you come," he murmured, easing his

hand from between her legs. He placed his palm on her stomach, keeping their bodies together while he dipped his head and kissed her neck.

"Not as much as I love coming," she retorted with a shaky chuckle.

He found his breath wasn't altogether steady as he said, "I've never known anyone like you."

"Really?" Her head swiveled just enough to give him a glimpse of her skeptical expression.

"Really."

Beneath her show of reserve—and he now realized that was all it was, a performance she'd played all her life—lurked a wild woman, unsatisfied with all the restrictions placed on her by society and expectations. He looked forward to coaxing her from hiding.

"You haven't gotten other women off in public?"

"Most of the women I've been with know the score. They're with me because of who I am and are willing to do whatever I'm into." He turned her around and put his hands on her shoulders, waiting until she met his gaze before continuing. "You are with me in spite of who I am. What just happened was all about you. For you. I'm incredibly honored just to be a part of it."

"I can't believe I did that," she murmured, disbelief in her tone. "That wasn't at all like me."

"I think it was. You just don't want to admit it." He paused a beat, noted that she remained unsure and finished, "You were incredible."

"Don't expect that it will happen again."

But they both knew it wasn't the end. He recognized the truth in his gut and saw acknowledgment in her eyes.

"Whatever you want to happen will."

And as she frowned at him, trying to interpret what he meant, Harrison knew that party planning had never been so sexy.

Seven

Chip Corduroy was the sort of Charleston insider London had begun cultivating long before she'd started her event planning business because he knew everyone's dirty secrets and could be counted on to trade information for favors. The slender fifty-year-old had a proud pedigree and expensive taste. Unfortunately, that meant he mostly lived above his means, which was why he loved that London "treated" him to spa days, shopping excursions and dinners out at the best restaurants in exchange for leads and introductions.

"I heard you've been out with Harrison Crosby a few times," Chip said, shooting her a sideways glance.

They were standing in front of the hostess at Felix Cocktails et Cuisine waiting to be seated and London wasn't at all surprised that the sandy-haired man had caught wind of their dates.

"It's business," she responded, keeping her answers short. "I'm planning his brother's birthday party."

"Doesn't really seem your type," Chip persisted, obviously not believing her explanation.

"Because he's a race-car driver?" She heard the defensive note in her voice and inwardly winced.

"Because his family isn't old Charleston."

"There aren't many eligible men who are." London sighed, feeling disingenuous as she fed Chip what he expected her to say. "But from everything I've heard, it seems as if Tristan and I would be better suited." The lie tasted awful on her tongue, but she needed whatever Chip knew about Tristan.

"So you've given up on getting back together with Linc?" From the routine nature of the question, London suspected he already knew the answer. "I mean, you two were the golden couple."

"Maybe on paper."

In truth, the longer they'd been together and the more interest Linc had displayed in settling down and starting a family, the more she'd dragged her feet about setting a wedding date. Frankly, she'd been terrified at the idea that she'd be expected to give up her career and had struggled to imagine herself as a mother. Did she have the patience for children? Or the interest?

And yet none of those same questions or insecurities bombarded her when she imagined herself with Harrison. Not that she saw a future with him. Her mother would disown her if London married a race-car driver. And then there was the revenge plot against Tristan, something she'd have to keep secret from Harrison forever. What chance did a relationship have when the partners weren't truthful with each other?

No doubt the impossibility of a happily-ever-after with Harrison was what kept her anxieties at bay. Convinced they had no future, London was free to daydream about them settling into a house somewhere between downtown Charleston and the Crosby Motorsports complex. With her business growing ever more successful each year and thanks to the hard work of the fantastic staff she'd hired, she was in a position where she could delegate more. They'd have two darling kids. A boy and a girl. Both would have Harrison's sea green eyes and her blond hair. They would grow up to become anything they wanted to be with both parents encouraging their individual interests.

"Have you heard that he's taken up with his housekeeper?" Chip asked, dragging London away from her daydream.

She found herself reluctant to emerge from the satisfying fantasy. "Really?" She forced herself to sound aghast, knowing it would spur her companion to greater gossip even as her actions filled her with distaste.

"He's definitely sleeping with her."

When his mother had encouraged Linc to hire Claire Robbins, London's initial reaction had been to doubt Maribelle's concerns that the pretty military widow was competition and to ignore the fact that Claire and Linc had chemistry. In London's view, Claire was obviously still in love with her deceased husband and utterly focused on her darling toddler.

"Has he come out and said so?" London asked, breaking her promise to not dabble in unsubstantiated rumor about her ex. "Or is that just speculation?"

"They've been going out to dinner and he bought her a pair of earrings." Chip declared this as if it definitively proved his claim. "And the way he looked at her at his mother's party?" Chip fanned himself even as he rolled his eyes emphatically. "There's definitely something going on."

"That's all speculation," she insisted, hoping the gossip wasn't true. Something about Claire was off. She'd been too evasive when discussing her life before Charleston. "Plus, even if he's sleeping with her, it's not going to last."

Chip looked shocked. "Well, of course not."

As the hostess led them to a table, London shoved all thoughts of her ex to the back burner. Linc was Everly's project and London needed to give every appearance of having moved on to avoid any backlash after Everly's revenge plan came to fruition.

As London settled into her seat, she scrambled for a way to shift the conversation to what Chip knew about Tristan Crosby. When no smooth segue came to mind, she decided to be forthright.

"Harrison hired me to plan a surprise birthday party for his brother. What can you tell me about Tristan?"

Chip leveled a speculative look on her before answering. "Dresses well. Loves the finest money can buy. Gives to charities, but not because he cares, more so people will tell him how great he is. Several women have told me he's a sexual predator. Don't let yourself be alone with him or he'll have his hands all over you."

None of this was news, so she pushed for more. "Wasn't he married until recently?"

"Zoe. Nice girl. She had no idea what she was getting into when she married him."

"Girl?" London echoed, picturing the woman she'd met weeks earlier. "I thought she was in her late twenties."

"I'm speaking figuratively. He snapped her up when she was still in college and she always seemed to have a deer-in-the-headlights look about her. She barely spoke when they were out together. Just a decorative bit of arm candy that every guy in the room wanted as their own."

London shuddered as she pondered how it would feel to be valued for her face and figure alone. Although she'd barely met Zoe, their shared experience of personally being wronged by powerful, wealthy men had given her a sense of sisterhood that she hadn't felt with Everly, whose beef with Ryan Dailey had to do with his treatment of her sister.

"You can do better," Chip said, redirecting her attention. "Might I suggest Grady Edwards? Good family. Wealthy. A little obsessed with polo for my taste, but no one is perfect."

"I'll keep him in mind," London replied diplomatically, struggling for a way to return the conversation to Tristan. "Although I heard Landry Beaumont has been seeing him." This was a spurious remark. Rumor had it Landry was chasing Linc. "So what happened between Tristan Crosby and his ex-wife?"

"He dumped her. Something about her having an affair. Later I heard he fabricated the whole thing to get out of paying her anything. The man is ruthless," Chip said, leaning forward and lowering his voice conspiratorially even though no one was close enough to hear their conversation. "Magnolia Spencer told me in confidence that Zoe got next to nothing."

"Because of a prenup?"

"Because there's no money."

"How is that possible? Crosby Automotive does exceptionally well and, from what I hear, Tristan has been remodeling the Theodore Norwood house on Montague for the last five years. A client of mine has done some of the work and said Tristan has put nearly three million into the project."

Chip shrugged as he eyed the menu. The restaurant was known for its creative cocktails and small plates all done with a Parisian flare. "What looks good?"

As much as London wanted to keep the conversation alive, she decided more digging would only make Chip suspicious. Whatever Tristan was doing, his activities weren't spawning the sort of gossip that if it got out might harm him.

London stared at the menu, but her thoughts were far away. Finding an indirect way to take down Tristan seemed impossible.

Zoe had explained that Tristan was incredibly secretive about his finances. So much so that when her divorce lawyer had looked into his assets, it had become pretty obvious that Tristan spent far more than his annual salary from Crosby Automotive and the income he received from his investments.

"I think I'm going to have the tarte flambée," Chip said. "Or maybe the Spanish octopus."

Decisions made, London settled back and listened with half her attention as Chip filled her in on all the latest events. She let her troubling thoughts about Tristan drift to Harrison and the risky path she was following.

What had happened between them at the venue where his brother's party would be held was a perfect example of what a mistake it was to become involved with Harrison. The man held an unexpected and compelling power over her libido. She still couldn't believe she'd had an orgasm like that in a public place where at any moment they could be discovered.

Her cheeks went hot as she recalled how she'd rocked and writhed against him, greedily grabbing at the pleasure he'd offered. She'd never climaxed like that before, and recognized that some of her excitement had come from the danger of being caught with his hand up her skirt.

When London had shared what had happened with Maribelle, her friend had at first been shocked and then wildly encouraging. To say that London had stepped outside her comfort zone was a major understatement. What surprised her almost more than letting Harrison touch her like that was her lack of regret in the aftermath. She'd done something wicked and wanton and failed to hear her mother's voice rain scathing recriminations down upon her head. Maybe she was making progress.

London's phone buzzed. It was Thursday evening and Harrison had flown to Miami for the last race of the season. She was a little shocked the way her heart jumped in anticipation of hearing from him. Still, she left the phone screen down on the table.

Following that incredible encounter on Monday afternoon, Harrison had been a man of his word and accompanied her to choose flowers and pick out stationery.

In the subsequent days, even though he'd been preoccupied with pre-race preparations, he'd sent her several charming messages that made her body sing.

With each text she'd grown more and more impatient to see him again. She caught herself daydreaming about what she would do the next time she got him alone. In all-too-brief moments of clarity, London reminded herself that this behavior ran counter to her real purpose in getting to know him better. She was supposed to be focused on securing whatever information she could to take down his brother. The push and pull of regret and longing was making her question her character and decisions.

Unfortunately, it was too late to back out now.

Her phone buzzed again.

"Do you need to get that?" Chip asked.

Fighting the need to connect with Harrison was too much work and London nodded with relief. "It might be work," she said, hoping that wasn't the case.

It's hot in Miami. Thinking of you in a bikini.

Joy blasted through her, shocking in its power. Giddy with delight, she forgot that she was sitting across from one of Charleston's most fervent gossips.

Missing you.

She stared at the words she'd just sent. Despite the fact that it was true, she couldn't believe she'd opened herself up like that.

You're sure you can't join me?

She bit her lip as temptation raged within her. The corporate event she'd arranged for Saturday night could be turned over to Grace. It would be so easy to jump on a plane and be in the stands cheering him on Sunday afternoon.

Can't. How about dinner Monday? My place.

His response came at her in a flash.

Sure.

She sent a smiley face emoji and returned the phone to the table, aware she was smirking. Only then did she glance at her dinner companion and notice that he wore a bemused expression.

"That wasn't work," Chip said.

"What makes you say that?" she hedged, a flush racing over her skin.

"I've never seen you smile like that before." His eyes narrowed. "Not even when you were first engaged to Linc. You are glowing. Who is he?"

London shook her head. "What makes you think it was a he? It could've been Maribelle."

"It was Harrison Crosby, wasn't it?" Chip countered, displaying absolute confidence in his deductive reasoning. "You're interested in him. He's a catch."

"Is he?" London replied weakly. "I guess I haven't thought of him that way."

Lies, lies, all lies. She'd thought of little else these last few days. London was abruptly appalled at the person she was becoming. Nor did she have a plan to extricate herself from her pledge to take down Tristan even as her feelings for Harrison grew. More and more she was convinced that everything was going to blow up in her face and her actions would end up causing harm rather than helping Zoe.

At a table near the front window of the coffee shop across the street from London's ExcelEvent office, Everly sipped green tea and pondered her ever-deepening concern over London's relationship with Harrison. Stupid idiot. At least she'd picked the inconsequential brother to fall for. Everly would have to kill her if she'd fallen for Tristan.

Her cell buzzed, indicating an incoming call from her assistant. Annoyed with the distraction, she sent the call to voice mail. She refused to make London's mistake and lose focus. A second later her phone buzzed again. It was Nora again.

Blowing out a breath, she unclenched her teeth and answered. "What?"

"Devon Connor is here for your four o'clock meeting," Nora said, unruffled by her employer's sharp tone.

"What four o'clock meeting?"

Everly handled the branding for his numerous golf resorts up and down the coast. In the year since Kelly had been arrested, his account had become the bulk of her business.

"The one I texted and called and emailed you about yesterday and this morning. Where are you?"

Everly silently cursed. "Tell him I've been delayed."

"How long?"

A quick glance at her watch showed it was a quarter past four already. London usually left work by now.

Earlier today Everly had secured a little bit of tech that could help them all out. After deciding London was neither computer savvy enough nor equipped with the right tools to get dirt on Tristan Crosby, Everly had taken matters into her own hands.

The USB drive in her purse had come from a source connected to a friend of her sister's. In college Kelly had run with a group that hacked for fun. Everly hadn't known about it at the time or she'd have warned Kelly away from such recklessness.

The drive contained software that, when plugged into a computer and with a few commands, could bypass passwords and copy everything on the hard drive. The question remained if London was up to the challenge of gaining access to Tristan's computer.

"Reschedule him for tomorrow," Everly said, calculating how much work remained on the presentation for his newest acquisition. "Or if you can push him to next week that would be even better."

"He's not going to be happy."

"Make something up. Tell him I'm dealing with an emergency." Everly spotted London exiting her office. "I have to go."

Hanging up on her assistant, Everly exited the coffee shop and followed London, doing her best to behave like an unremarkable woman window-shopping along King Street.

London walked briskly. Obviously she had some place to be. Rushing off to another date with Harrison, no doubt. The thought made Everly grind her teeth.

Honestly, what did London think she was doing? Did the event planner imagine she and Harrison had any sort of chance? Even if London was merely engaging in a bit of fun with the handsome race-car driver, her priorities were skewed. Irritation flared that Everly needed to remind her of this fact again.

London had almost reached her car. Everly lengthened her stride until she was jogging and her timing was perfect. As London pushed the unlock button on her key fob, Everly drew within several feet of her.

"Where are you running off to in such a hurry?" Everly demanded, speaking with a more accusatory tone than she'd planned, causing London to whip around.

"What are you doing here?" Eyes wide, London glanced from side to side, scanning the area to see if they were being observed.

"Relax. Nobody's going to see us." Everly crossed her arms and regarded the younger woman with disdain. "You've been spending a lot of time with Harrison Crosby. Have you been able to get any information out of him that we can use against his brother?"

Everly suspected she already knew the answer, but asked the question anyway. From the way London's gaze shifted away, it was obvious she wasn't taking their revenge pact seriously.

"Look," London quipped, "it's not as if I can just come out and ask Harrison about Tristan's secrets."

"Of course not." Everly reached into her purse and pulled out a USB drive. "That's why I got you this."

London eyed the slim drive for a long second. "What is that?"

"It's a USB drive with a special program on it. You just need to insert it into a port on Tristan's computer, key in a few commands, and it will get you all the information you need off his hard drive."

"Where did you get it?"

"What does it matter?" Everly snapped, her irritation getting away from her. "All you need to know is that it will work."

"How am I supposed to get access to Tristan's computer?"

London was worthless. She was letting her feelings for Harrison distract her from their mission. Fortunately, Everly had thought everything through and had a plan prepared.

"There's a charity polo event coming up at Tristan's plantation," Everly explained. "Make sure you're invited. It will be the perfect opportunity for you to get the information we need."

"That sounds risky."

Everly wanted to shake the other woman. "Do you think you're the only one who's taking chances here?"

"I don't know." London's gaze hardened. "And isn't that the whole point? That we cut off all contact? With each of us handling the other's problems, no one was supposed to be able to trace anything back to us. A onetime meeting at a random event between strangers. Wasn't that the plan? Yet here you are following me from my company. Giving me some sort of technology that I'm supposed to use. What if I get caught and it gets traced back to you?"

"Don't get caught."

London made a disgusted noise. "Can this be traced back to you?"

"No. The person I got it from is very careful."

"Couldn't that person get into Tristan's files? Isn't that what they do?"

"If I wanted to hire the hacker, you'd be unnecessary. And it would be pointless for me to ruin Linc's life on your behalf." Everly neglected to mention the hacker had already tried and failed to access Tristan's laptop remotely as she shoved the USB drive at London. "Just do your part and it will all work out."

Before London could reply, Everly turned on her heel and walked away.

Leave it to a spoiled princess like London McCaffrey to ruin everything. Of course, she wasn't the only problem. Zoe's progress in taking down Ryan Dailey had stalled, as well. At least Tristan's ex-wife wasn't likely to fall for her target. Crosby had done a number on Zoe during their marriage and subsequent divorce. Chances were Zoe would never trust any man ever again. That worked for Everly. These three men were the worst of the worst and each one of them deserved every terrible thing that would happen to them.

Eight

London spent the days leading up to her dinner with Harrison pondering how she wanted the evening to go. She'd already decided to sleep with him and had prepared her bedroom with freshly washed sheets, flowers and candles for ambience. He probably wouldn't notice any of those touches, but she was an event planner. Arranging the environment to enrich the experience was second nature.

Plus, she didn't want him to catch her off guard a second time. What had happened between them at Upstairs had been amazing, but a little more spontaneous than she was used to. Tonight would be different. She knew what to expect. Could Harrison say the same? Would he realize that she was ready to take things to the next level? After getting her off in a public space, shouldn't he?

By the time he showed up at her door, a bottle of white wine in his hands, she looked poised and pulled together without any sign that she'd spent the weekend cleaning and the last two hours exfoliating head to toe, changing clothes a dozen times, reapplying her makeup twice and generally behaving in a frantic fashion.

"Wow," Harrison said, his sea-glass eyes taking in her appearance.

London had chosen a silky wrap dress in blush pink that flattered her curves and made her feel both sexy and comfortable at the same time. She'd painted her toenails a matching pink and left her shoes in her closet, showing the different side of her personality that came out in her own space.

"Thanks," she murmured. "Come on in."

"Did you know that we're neighbors?" he asked, sliding his arm around her waist and bringing her body up against his. "I live in the building next door." He bumped his nose against her neck right below her ear and breathed deeply. "Damn, you smell good."

"Really?" Her toes curled as she draped her arm over his shoulder and tipped her head to give him more access. "I mean about you living next door."

"Crazy, right?" With a sigh, he set her free and brought up the bottle between them. "You said we were having seafood."

"Scallops with risotto."

"Sounds delicious." He accompanied her to the kitchen, glancing around him as he went. "This is nice. How long have you lived here?"

Her unit faced east, with large floor-to-ceiling windows that overlooked the Cooper River. She'd fallen in love with the condo's hardwood floors and small but high-end kitchen with its white cabinets and marble countertops.

"Three years." She wondered if he'd think the space too neutral. She'd painted the walls a crisp white and paired it with a pale gray sectional, accessorizing with crystal and silver. "How long have you owned your place?"

"Almost five years."

"I'm a little surprised you have a place downtown. You strike me as someone who would prefer a big garage and a lot of out-door space."

"I've thought about selling, but with my schedule it's easier to live somewhere that I don't have to take care of anything." He was standing at the sliding glass door, looking past her wide terrace and the dark river to the brightly lit Ravenel Bridge. Now he swung around and stepped up to the broad kitchen is-land. "Need any help?"

She pushed the wine and a corkscrew in his direction. He filled two glasses and brought her one by the stove.

"You cook, too," he said, sounding pleased. "You're a woman of endless talents."

"I like trying out new recipes. I used to entertain a lot, but it's been a while since..." She stopped abruptly, remembering all the dinner parties she and Linc had hosted here.

"You had anyone to cook for?"

She nodded, wishing she hadn't summoned the specter of her ex-fiancé with her careless words. "Maribelle comes over once a week to update me on her wedding plans, but she's worrying about fitting into her dress and so I tend to serve her healthy salads with boiled chicken."

"You can cook for me whenever you want," Harrison said. "Most days during racing season I'm so busy that I live on pro-tein shakes and takeout. Sometimes the racing wives take pity on me and drop by with a home-cooked meal."

"You poor baby," she teased as her phone began to ring.

London noted the caller and winced. She'd been dodging her mother's calls for a week now. Someone had filled Edie in on the new man in her daughter's life and the four voice mails she'd left London had been peppered with her disappointment and unwelcome opinions.

"Do you need to get that?" Harrison asked.

"No."

His eyebrows rose at her hard tone. "Is something wrong?"

"She likes to put her nose where it doesn't belong."

"And where's that?" Harrison leaned his hip against her kitchen island and kept her pinned with his gaze.

"Everything about my life."

"Has she heard you and I are seeing each other?"

"I really don't want to spoil our evening with a conversation about my mother."

"I'll take that as a yes." He sounded unconcerned, but London didn't want him to get the wrong impression.

"I don't care what she thinks. It's none of her business who I see."

"But I'm not the one she'd choose for you."

"It doesn't matter who she'd choose." A defensive edge shaded her tone. "I'm the one dating you."

"I'll bet she was happy you were marrying Linc Thurston."

For what she had planned later, London needed this dinner to be perfect. That wasn't going to happen if a conversation about her mother's elitist attitude ruined the mood.

"If it's okay with you, I really don't want to talk about my mother or my failed engagement."

"I understand."

Something about his somber response warned her he wasn't satisfied with how the conversation had ended.

"I think the risotto is done," she said. "Do you mind bringing the plates over?"

They moved to the dining table and sat down. Candlelight softened Harrison's strong bone structure and gave his sea-glass eyes a mysterious quality as they talked about his race the day before and she updated him on the jazz group she'd booked for his brother's birthday party.

While they ate, London devoured him with her eyes. He was a daredevil. And a competitor. The sort of man who set his eyes on the finish line and went like hell until he got there. Which was why she'd imagined the evening progressing a different way. She'd figured the sexual tension would build during the meal, leading them to fall upon each other before the dessert course.

Instead, Harrison kept the conversation moving from one topic to another. They discussed their parents and favorite vacations growing up. She discovered he hated any drinks with bubbles and she confessed that she was a French fry junkie. It was fun and easy. Yet as they finished the white-chocolate mousse she'd made, and then worked together to fill her dishwasher, London couldn't stop her rising dismay.

Had she made a mistake when she'd assumed they would end up in bed tonight? Harrison seemed as relaxed as she was jumpy. Each brush of his arm against hers had sent her hormones spiraling higher.

Now, as the dishwasher began to hum, she turned to face him. They stared at each other for a long, silent moment. Hunger and anxiety warred within her as she waited for him to make a move. When the tension reached a bursting point, London lifted her hand to the tie that held her dress closed.

It was time to be bold with him. With a single tug, her dress came undone. Harrison remained silent, watching her as she shrugged the material off her shoulders, letting it fall to the floor.

Standing before him in a silk chemise and matching thong, she gave him a sweet smile. "I thought we might watch a movie," she said, toying with a strand of her hair. "Unless you have something else you'd rather do."

He expelled his breath in a half chuckle, one corner of his mouth kicking up. "We are going to be good together," he declared.

"I know." She twisted a handful of his warm shirt around her knuckles and tugged. "Kiss me."

He obliged, but not in the way she'd hoped. She needed him to claim her mouth and stir her soul. Instead he tormented her by drifting gentle, sweet kisses over her cheeks, eyes, nose and forehead.

"The things I want to do to you," he murmured near her ear.

Relief flooded London even as her breasts ached for his touch. "Like what?"

"Take you into the bedroom." His hand cruised up her side, thumb gliding beneath her breasts, inciting her to arch into his caress with a wordless plea.

If only he'd sweep that thumb over her nipples. Instead he shifted his palm to her back.

"And then?" she prompted, frustration apparent in her voice.

"Strip off your clothes."

Oh...hell...yes. Now they were getting somewhere.

"And...then...?"

"Lay you on the bed and spread your gorgeous legs wide open for me."

"Oh..."

His erotic words made her quake. And she suspected that what this man could do to her with his words wouldn't begin to compare to what would happen when his hands and lips met her skin.

"How does that sound?" he asked.

She nodded, excitement momentarily taking away her voice. "What else?" she asked in barely a whisper.

But he'd heard her and smiled. "I'd kiss you everywhere until you were writhing in pleasure."

"Yes, please."

"I'm going to warn you right now," Harrison said. "I'm going to talk during sex."

"What?" Heart thumping madly, London stared at him in helpless delight. "What sort of things are you likely to say?"

"I'll definitely be discussing how beautiful you are and how much you turn me on."

"Do you expect me to answer?" At this point in their relationship London wasn't sure she was ready to crack open her heart and divulge all her thoughts and feelings.

"No expectations. Just relax and listen."

"Relax?" Was he kidding? Already her muscles were tense and nerves twisted in agonized anticipation of his touch. "I feel as if I'll shatter the second you touch me."

"That's not going to happen," he assured her, easing his lips onto hers.

The contact made her sigh. With the release of her breath came a shift in her emotions. Anxiety diminished, replaced by eagerness and undulating waves of pleasure. Instinctively she knew Harrison wouldn't do something that would break her heart. In fact, he might just heal it. If only she could let him.

Except she couldn't.

A giant lie hung between them, casting a shadow over every beautiful emotion that swelled in her chest. Her subterfuge ate at her more and more each day. She longed to be with Harrison even as she recognized that one day her guilt would destroy everything good between them.

Butterflies whirled in her stomach as he grazed his palm up her arm and brushed the strap of her chemise off her shoulder. She pushed all thoughts of the future away as the silk dipped low on her breast. The slide of the soft material tickled her skin and turned up the volume on her eagerness. A tremor shook her as his mouth skated down her neck and into the hollow of her throat. She wanted him. Wanted this. It was simple and at the same time complicated. But mostly it was inevitable.

His fingertips grazed the lace-edged neckline, sweeping the fabric downward. The material momentarily snagged on her sensitized nipple, drawing a sharp gasp from her lips before it fell away, exposing her warm skin to the cool air.

"Your breasts are perfect," he murmured, sliding his lips over their upper curves.

His words sent desire lancing straight to her core. She sank her fingers into his thick curly hair, her throat aching as she held back a cry of protest when his lips glided away from her aching breasts and returned to her shoulder.

With her free hand she slipped the other strap off her shoulder and bared both breasts. "I need your mouth on me. Please, Harrison."

Instead of doing as she'd asked, he leaned back and regarded her expression. Hunger darkened his eyes, strengthening London's desire and bolstering her confidence.

It wasn't as if she was an innocent. She'd known passion, had given herself over to lust and fast, desperate sex.

But what she felt for Harrison wasn't just physical. She genuinely liked him. Appreciated his wry sense of humor, his ability to read her moods and even his fondness for pushing past her boundaries. Deep in her soul she recognized they'd be good together. Better than good. Fantastic.

She and Linc had been together for three years, and with all the time they'd spent apart, she had rarely pictured them making love and grown so horny that she ached for release. Yet almost from the start Harrison had awakened unstoppable cravings. Cravings that on one occasion, all alone in her bed late at night, had compelled her to take matters into her own hands or go half mad.

"Are you wet for me?" He crooned the words, driving her hunger even higher.

"Yes." She gasped the word as his fingers moved between her thighs and grazed across the narrow panel of her thong, sending pleasure lancing through her. She rocked her pelvis in search of more.

"So you are," he purred, stroking her again. "Can you get even wetter?"

"Keep that up—" Her voice broke as he applied light pressure to the knot of nerves between her thighs. A blissful shudder left her panting. "And see."

He gave a husky little laugh.

"What if I bury my face between your thighs and taste you?"

Her legs had been on the verge of giving out before his offer. Now yearning battered her, making her achy and needy. But mostly it made her impatient.

"Harrison," she blurted out.

Every part of her was shaking. Her knees were threatening to buckle. But instinctively she knew he'd take care of her. She wouldn't crumple to the ground. He'd be there to lift her and carry her into pleasure unlike anything she'd ever known.

"Yes, London?"

His clever fingers slipped beneath the elastic of her panties and stroked her so perfectly she thought she might die from it. She clenched her eyes shut and struggled to draw enough breath into her lungs to tell him what she wanted.

"I don't want our first time to be here," she said, though she was on the verge of not caring that she'd spent hours setting the stage for a perfect evening. "Take me," she gasped with what air his skillful touch hadn't stolen from her, "to the bedroom."

Harrison didn't care where their first time was as long as she was happy.

Without a word, he bent down and lifted her into his arms. She gave up a joyous laugh as she roped her arms around his neck and dropped soft kisses along his jawline while directing him down a hallway.

Her bedroom was like the rest of the condo. Cool and refined with a few decadent touches like a fuzzy throw rug, a vase of pink roses on the dresser to scent the air and a dozen flickering candles casting wavering light over the gray walls.

She'd planned this, he realized. Invited him for dinner with the purpose of sleeping with him. What a woman.

He set her on her feet inside the door and pulled her into his arms for a long, sexy kiss. Electricity jolted through him as she drove her tongue into his mouth and let him taste her desire. Rich and vibrant, the kiss promised fantasies he hadn't yet dreamed up.

Tonight was about finding out more about London. And something told him she was going to surprise him.

"I'm obsessed with your mouth," she said when he broke

off the kiss and set his forehead against hers. Trembling fingers skimmed over his lips. "I can't stop thinking about all the places I want you to kiss me."

He answered her with a smile, letting his eyes speak for him. Gaze locked on his lips, she sighed.

"I've tried to fight this," she continued. "Tried to remain sensible, but just hearing your voice gets me hot."

Harrison smoothed his palms along her spine and across her hips. He didn't want to say or do anything that would stop this confession. She made him feel things he'd never known and it was heaven to hear her echoing his own needs and desires.

"How hot?"

"My skin burns. My nipples ache. I want you to take them in your mouth and suck hard."

His groan was ragged and rough. "Keep going." The command was nearly incoherent as he set his lips against her shoulder.

She looped her arms around his shoulders and tipped her head, baring her long, white neck to his determined seduction. Taking advantage of what she offered, he lowered his lips to her skin and brought both tongue and teeth into play. Her muscles jerked as he nipped and a low moan rumbled up from her chest.

"Oh, Harrison." Her husky voice hitched, betraying how turned on she was, and despite the almost painful ache below his belt, he grinned.

He backed her toward the bed, divesting himself of shirt and shoes as he went. Hooking his fingers into her thong, he pulled the bit of silk and lace off her hips and down her thighs. She shivered as he knelt at her feet and helped her step out of the fabric.

While she scooted onto the bed, he stripped off his pants and underwear. As soon as it was free, his erection pointed straight at her. London reclined on the mattress, propping herself up on her elbows, her eyes gobbling him up.

Seeing that she had his full attention, she let her knees fall apart, opening herself to him. The sight of her so pink and wet and perfect made Harrison want to shout in jubilation. Grinning, he prowled onto the mattress.

"You are beautiful." He trailed his fingers across her skin, lingering over her neat strip of hair that led straight to where he longed to go. "Especially here."

"Really?" She stared at herself and frowned.

"You can't appreciate it the way I can." He grazed his finger through her slick folds and her eyes popped open as a throaty cry burst from her lips. "I love how you're so sensitive."

"You bring that out in me," she murmured, her words coming in soft pants.

Grinning, he lowered his face between her legs and stroked his tongue through her heat. Her hips bucked while a sharp curse escaped her.

"Warn a girl," she gasped, pressing toward his mouth.

His breath puffed out in a chuckle. "I'm going to put my mouth on you and drive you crazy before I let you come."

"Better." She moaned as he went back for a second taste.

Her scent and sweetness made him smile as he devoured her. Each movement of his tongue caused her to moan. Her fingers dived into his hair, digging into his scalp as he drew her pulsing clit between his lips and gently sucked. She gave a half shriek before calling his name. Her hips twisted as she took her pleasure against his mouth.

"Oh, Harrison," she cried, her voice raspy and broken. "That's so good."

He gathered her butt in his palms and opened his eyes to watch her every response as he continued to ply her with lips and tongue. As in everything she did, her body moved with perfect grace. Yet her usual reserve had vanished. She was completely caught up in the moment, her hips rotating like she was dancing for him. It was so incredibly sensual that he just knew he had to push her pleasure still higher.

Harrison redoubled his effort, plying her with every trick he knew. She wouldn't know what hit her when she climaxed. But first, he had to make sure she was thoroughly familiar with the joys he could bring her.

"Harrison, it's too..." She grabbed a handful of the quilt and pulled hard enough to cause her knuckles to go white.

"Touch your breasts," he commanded, wondering if she was too far gone to hear him. "Show me how I make you feel."

To his shock, she released his hair and the quilt and gathered her beautiful breasts into her hands, kneading and rolling her nipples through her fingers, displaying an abandon he never imagined he'd see.

"Oh," she groaned. "More. More. Yes."

Her impassioned cries made him harder than he'd ever been before. But this moment wasn't for him. At least not directly. He took great satisfaction in driving her wild. Recognizing how badly she wanted to come, he slid two fingers inside her. Her head came off the bed and an incoherent noise tore from her throat.

"That's it, baby. Give me all you've got." He squeezed her butt cheeks and drove his mouth hard against her clit, grinning as her body began to shudder. "Let go."

"It's...it's...incredible," she exclaimed and then, with one long keening cry, started to come apart.

Harrison watched it all unfold. There was nothing so perfect in the whole world as London McCaffrey so aroused she became utterly lost in her pleasure, rocking and arching as she drove herself against his mouth. A powerful orgasm moved through her and he savored each wave as it battered her.

When her body grew limp, he eased his mouth off her and tracked butterfly kisses across her pelvis and over her abdomen. Her chest heaved as she labored to recover her breath. She lay with her hands plastered over her eyes as a series of incoherent noises tumbled from her lips.

"You okay?" he asked, gliding his lips up her body and noting the glorious glow her skin had taken on in the wake of her climax.

"What did you do to me?" she mumbled, sounding shaken and utterly spent.

"I'm pretty sure I gave you an orgasm." He made no attempt to hide his smugness and hoped she wasn't feeling overly sensitive about how she'd let go. It had been sexy as hell and he didn't want her to retreat from him. "A big one."

She spread her fingers and peered at him. "What am I going to do with you?"

A second later she answered her own question by dropping her hand to his erection, making him moan. "Just give that a stroke or two." His voice became a croak as she followed his instructions, demonstrating that she was eager to please him in kind. "No need to be gentle. It's not going to break."

"Like that?"

A series of provocative strokes made him groan. "That works."

He bent and kissed her deep, showing her how much he liked having her hand on him.

"This is nice," she murmured when they broke apart. "But it would be better if you'd slide on a condom and make love to me."

He didn't need to be asked twice. In seconds he'd located the foil packet and rolled on protection. She watched his actions through half-lidded eyes, lower lip trapped between her teeth. He paused a second to appreciate her tousled blond hair and passion-bruised lips. Then sliding between her thighs, he guided himself to her tight entrance, the tip dipping in, testing her acceptance. The feel of her, so open and receptive, made him want the moment to be perfect for her.

Brushing a strand of hair off her flushed cheek, he kissed her softly. "You ready?"

"Do you really have to ask?"

It took all his concentration to take it slow and let her adjust to him. What he hadn't considered was his equal need to adjust to her. Her breath shuddered out in a long, slow exhalation as he filled her. It was as if she'd liberated something she'd been holding on to for a long time.

As the long, slow thrust came to an end, she opened her eyes and met his gaze. The trust he glimpsed there made him feel like the most powerful man alive.

"Babe, you feel incredible," he murmured, making good on his promise to talk. "So tight and hot. I love the way your muscles grab me. Like you want me there."

"I do." Her palms coasted down his back and over his butt. She gripped him with surprising strength, fingers digging into his muscles, pulling him hard against her. "I love having you inside me."

"It's not too much?"

She shook her head. "I think we're a perfect fit."

"So do I."

And then there was no further need for words. It was a blend of hands, lips, tongue, breath and skin as they rocked together, discovering each other on a whole new level. To say being inside her felt good was a massive understatement. She was all heat and hunger and intensity as she wrapped her legs around his waist and clung to him.

He thrust into her, finding a steady, pounding rhythm she seemed to like. Her hips moved in time with his, matching his intensity and even taking the wildness up a notch.

"Harrison, please," she begged, inner muscles clamping down on him. "Make me come again. Now. I need you."

Harrison had never been one to disappoint a lady. He slid his palm beneath her, lifting her off the mattress. Gripping her firmly, he went to work, watching her beautiful face for every nuance, adjusting his thrusts to bump her clit each time he plunged into her. And plunge he did. Over and over, gritting his teeth, a growl burning in his throat as he held back his own pleasure.

And then her back arched and a strained cry erupted from her lips. She drove her nails into his shoulder and summoned his name from some endless depth. Her body bucked against his, driving into his thrusts. Seconds later she was shuddering in a long series of ripples that drew him right over the edge after her.

With a final thrust, he collapsed onto his forearms, head falling to the mattress above her shoulder. She shifted so their sweaty cheeks pressed together. His chest heaved as he labored to draw breath into his lungs. It took effort for him to open his eyes. More still to lift his head. But he needed to look into her eyes to see for himself that the world-stopping sex had been just as amazing for her.

To his dismay, her eyes were closed. She was equally winded, but her features were relaxed into an expression of satisfaction.

"London?"

"That was way better than I expected." Her eyes flashed open. A possessive look blazed there for a moment before she let her lashes fall. "And I expected a lot."

He levered himself to one side, coming to rest beside her, his head propped on his hand. A strand of hair clung to her forehead. He brushed it off, delighting in the quiet moment. She lifted her hand and cupped his cheek. Her thumb grazed over his lower lip.

"Now I'm not just obsessed with your mouth," she said, sounding drowsy, "but with your dick, as well."

Harrison's jaw dropped. Had she really just said that? Did her society friends have any idea this woman existed? He didn't think so. In fact, if he had to guess, he'd say that London hadn't realized the depth of her wantonness until recently.

"It's happy to hear that," he murmured, sliding his arms around her and pulling her firmly against his body. "And so am I."

Nine

With her left hand firmly clasped in Harrison's right, London's heart picked up speed as he angled the Mercedes onto the driveway and streaked through the Crosby Motorsports entrance gate. Above them, the company logo flanked by the four Crosby team car numbers welcomed employees and fans alike.

London had been silent through most of the thirty-minute car ride, content to listen to Harrison narrate the history of his uncle's rise to being number three on the all-time winner's cup victories list for the racing league. And number two in modern-day wins. His teams had won at least one championship-level race each season since 2000 and Jack had ten owner's championships.

Tonight they were heading to an end-of-the-season party for the six hundred employees who'd assisted Crosby Motorsports in achieving its third-place cup finish. It was London's first official appearance as Harrison's girlfriend and all day she'd been queasy as she grappled with the potential repercussions of how far she'd let things go.

The flash drive Everly had given her was a psychological burden bearing down on her heart. Each day she didn't use it was another day she hadn't betrayed Harrison. The woman who'd agreed to take revenge on Tristan was someone she no longer identified with. And what did she really owe Everly and Zoe?

Fifteen buildings made up the four-hundred-thousand-square-foot state-of-the-art facility that supported four full-time Ford teams. Walking hand in hand, London and Harrison neared the company's heritage center. The site of the original race shop when the company was founded in 1990, the building housed Jack Crosby's extensive car collection.

The flow of guests swept them into the building and past several exhibits, which Harrison explained were popular fan destinations. Freestanding bars had been placed in strategic locations so the guests could get a drink ahead of the dinner being served in a giant tent erected outside.

"Some night I'll bring you back here and give you a proper tour," he promised as they strolled hand in hand past rare cars.

"What's wrong with now?" she asked him.

"I misspoke. I meant an improper tour. Have you ever wanted to make out in the back of a rare 1969 Chevy Camaro?" He hooked a thumb at the bright orange car beside them.

She shot him a droll look even as her cheeks heated. "Do I seem the sort of girl who'd ever have that sort of fantasy?"

Even as she spoke, however, the place between her thighs tingled. She imagined herself grinding on him in one of these vehicles, steaming up the windows and watching his face as he came. What was he doing to her? London shivered in pleasure while his fingers pulsed against hers as if he'd read her mind.

"I suspect you've already done things with me you never imagined."

He wasn't wrong and she gave a little shrug. Before she could figure out what to say, however, a young man approached them asking if Harrison would come meet his grandmother. She was a huge fan and hampered by arthritic knees.

"Go ahead," London said. "I'm going to find the ladies' room."

"Meet you back here?" He glanced toward the Camaro. "You can consider my offer while I'm gone."

"I'll be waiting," she replied.

Ten minutes later she returned to the spot to await Harrison, unsurprised that he hadn't made it back. From what she'd seen of him at the track and when they'd encountered his fans out and about, he was always happy to sign autographs and take photos.

The blend of adrenaline junkie, focused athlete and all-around good guy had slipped through London's defenses. His daring and honed reflexes were remarkably sexy, yet the fact that every second behind the wheel could result in disaster somehow made Harrison relaxed and calm.

His composure was a complete contrast to the emotional minefield London found herself in. Happiness. Guilt. Responsibility. Selfishness. She wanted to bask in the joy of her growing connection with Harrison, but worry and obligation tormented her. Allowing herself to blissfully date Harrison while Zoe waited in limbo for Tristan to suffer couldn't last much longer. Time was nearly up. She had to act even if that meant she would be compelled to end things with Harrison.

As if summoned by her thoughts, Tristan appeared in her line of sight. He strolled through the swarm of people as if he was the most important person in the room. He didn't radiate confidence as much as blare it. Several women and some men followed his progress and London couldn't blame them. The perfection of his strong, chiseled features, styled hair and powerful build made it hard to remain immune.

In his elegant charcoal suit, he looked broader-shouldered than Harrison, although she suspected his bulk wasn't all muscle. London knew firsthand the strength in Harrison's lean body. He was honed and sculpted by hours of mental and physical training.

Tristan looked less like a hungry cheetah and more like a sated lion. Either way he was dangerous. Which was why she felt that she'd been punched in the solar plexus when he caught her staring at him. Almost immediately he shifted direction and made a beeline for her. Cursing her lack of subtlety, she slapped a pleasant expression on her face as he neared.

"We meet again," Tristan said as he entered her space, eyeing her with an interest he hadn't shown during their first encounter. He held out his hand. "London, isn't it?"

"Yes." She gave him her hand and resisted the urge to yank it away as his fingers slid over hers in a way that was overly familiar. "I'm surprised you remembered me. We met so briefly at your aunt's charity function."

"You're a stunning woman." There was no mistaking the sensual glow in his eyes. "I remember thinking I'd like to get to know you better."

She doubted that. He'd barely given her the time of day before moving on to a woman with an impressive cleavage. So why the sudden interest now?

Confusion reigned as she forced a polite smile. "I'm flattered."

"You don't look as if you belong here any more than I do," Tristan said, echoing what would've been London's opinion a few short weeks earlier.

She glanced away from him and surveyed the party guests, noting the difference from the charity event where she'd first met Harrison and his brother. That evening the women had been dressed in expensive gowns and dripping with jewels. They'd navigated the room dispensing sugary phrases in droll tones.

Tonight's assembly wore jeans, team apparel and the occasional blazer or party dress. London recognized that she stood out in the leopard pumps she'd borrowed from Maribelle and her classic little black dress. As when she'd gone to the racetrack in Richmond, her styling choices highlighted that she didn't have much in common with these unpretentious people. No wonder Tristan had approached her. He wore a gorgeous custom suit in dark gray more appropriate to the yacht club than a tent.

"I have to admit this isn't exactly my regular crowd," London said, hating the way that sounded even though it was true. "I take it you don't have much to do with Crosby Motorsports?"

"Hardly." Tristan glanced around before leaning down as if to share a confidence with her. "My brother is the one who likes to get his hands dirty." His sneer made his contempt for Harrison clear and the contrast between the brothers grew starker. "The fact that he races cars has made him an embarrassment to our family."

London wondered if Tristan had any idea she and Harrison had been seeing each other. "He's quite successful at it."

"Successful…" Once again his gaze moved over her, this time lingering at her neckline. "Don't tell me you're one of those racing groupies. You appear to have a little too much class for that."

The man's prejudice was so blatant that London found herself momentarily speechless. And as she grappled with a response, it occurred to her that she'd been equally snobbish in the beginning, before she'd gotten to know Harrison. Shame brought heat to her cheeks.

"Feel like getting out of here?" Tristan's fingers curved over her hip, lingering for a few seconds as if to test her reaction. When shock kept her from pulling away, he must've taken that as encouragement because his palm slid over her backside and he gave her butt a suggestive squeeze. "My house is twenty minutes away."

London thought about the flash drive she'd taken to carrying in her purse. What excuse could she give Harrison that would let her slip away with Tristan and get the information off his computer? Her mind spun as she conceived and discarded a dozen justifications for leaving the party with Tristan. None of them made any sense.

"I—"

She never got to finish her refusal because Harrison emerged from the crowd and spied her standing with his brother. His brows came together in a frown that was half annoyance and half confusion as he noticed where Tristan's hand had gone.

With an inaudible gasp, London stepped away from Tristan and tried to catch Harrison's gaze as he approached them, but his attention was firmly fixed on his brother.

"What are you doing here?" Harrison demanded, his expression and tone unfriendly.

"I am the head of Crosby Automotive."

"That doesn't answer my question."

"This is a family business," Tristan pointed out.

"And you've made it pretty clear you want nothing to do with us." Harrison's eyes narrowed. "Or at least that's been your attitude before your profits started to dip. What? Are you hoping to convince Jack to help you out financially?"

Tristan's expression darkened. He obviously didn't appreciate his younger brother pointing out his shortcomings.

"I don't need his help or yours," Tristan said. "And this little shindig of yours is a complete bore. I've got better things to do." With an elaborate sigh, he glanced at London and gestured toward the door. "Shall we?"

Harrison turned stunned eyes her way and London opened her mouth to explain, but her scrambled brain produced no words. Why hadn't she come straight out and told Tristan she was dating Harrison? Scheming was not her forte.

"She's not going anywhere with you," Harrison said.

"Why don't you let the lady decide?"

"Ah, actually I came here with Harrison," London said, cringing as she realized it was too little, too late.

She now understood that balancing her growing affection for Harrison against taking down his brother wasn't possible. It was either one or the other and the moment for her to choose was now.

"You two are dating?" Tristan asked, laughter in his voice.

"Well..." she hedged.

Harrison suffered none of her hesitation. "Yes."

While Tristan laughed at their diverging answers, London stared at Harrison. She found herself short of breath as their gazes clashed. In his sea-glass eyes she saw her future. The beauty of it struck her and suddenly she wanted to cry. She'd ruined everything.

"Sounds like you two need to sort out what's going on." Tristan squeezed London's arm. "If you get tired of slumming, give me a call."

She remained silent, biting the inside of her lip as Harrison's brother walked away. Words gathered in her throat but a lump prevented them from escaping. On the heels of the realization that she'd let the encounter with Tristan get away from her came the recognition that by falling for Harrison, she'd put her emotions in direct conflict with her promise to help Zoe.

"I thought we were on the same page," Harrison said. "If we're not dating, then what are we doing?"

"I don't know." As much as she wanted to escape his questions, he deserved honesty and openness. "This wasn't supposed to get complicated."

He frowned. "Because I'm not the man you think you want?"

"What?"

She was starting to believe he was the only man for her. And she'd made a mess of things.

His eyes flicked in the direction his brother had departed. "Are you thinking he could make you happy? Because he is incapable of putting anyone's feelings above his own."

"I'm not interested in your brother." At least not in the way Harrison was insinuating. How could she defuse this argument without committing herself one way or another? "In fact, I was in the process of defending you when he hit on me. You interrupted us before I could react."

Harrison assessed her for a long moment and whatever he glimpsed in her expression caused him to relax. "I don't need you to defend me."

"I know." Yet she could see he appreciated it. She took his hand in both of hers and stepped into his space, waiting until the tension seeped from his body before she finished. "But there was no way I was going to stand by and let him criticize what you do."

"It seems to me that you felt the same a couple weeks ago." He snaked his arm around her waist and pulled her tight against him.

"All the more reason for me to have your back. I was ignorant and shortsighted. You're doing what you love and no one has the right to judge you for it. Not even your brother."

"Fine. I forgive you," he said, cupping her cheek while his lips dropped to hers.

His kiss was romantic and intoxicating. She threw herself into the embrace, shoving her worries aside for the moment. Later she would delve into the ever-deepening mess she was making of things.

How long they stood in the middle of the crowded party, lost in each other, London had no idea. But when Harrison eventually set her free, London returned to her body with a jolt.

What magic drove all thoughts of propriety and decorum from her mind whenever he took her in his arms? She'd never acted like this before and loved every second of it.

By contrast, her relationship with Linc had always been so proper. She'd certainly never thrown her arms around his neck and kissed him with utter abandon in a public place. She'd always been hyperaware of how things looked and who might be watching. With Harrison, even though he was also a celebrity, she never considered appearances before showing affection with him.

"I'm sorry," she murmured when he ended the kiss.

"For what?"

So many things. "The way I feel when I'm with you is thrilling and scary all at once and way more intense than anything I've known before."

He kissed her forehead. "For me it's the exact opposite. Being with you calms me down. When we're together, it feels right."

Tears burned London's eyes. The man was just too perfect

and she didn't deserve the happiness he brought her. Dabbing at the corner of her eye in what she hoped was a surreptitious manner, London took his hand in hers and exhaled heartily.

"You always say the right thing," she told him, wishing he'd demonstrate some of his brother's villainy. It would make using him to her advantage easier to swallow.

"Ready to go find our table?"

"Lead the way."

"This is quite a place," London remarked, taking in the state-of-the-art barn, paddocks, polo field and sprawling home with views that overlooked the horse pastures all belonging to Harrison's brother.

She'd started scoping out the house as soon as it had come into view, needing to find a way in so she could use the USB drive in her purse. The task terrified her. What if she was caught? Or the drive didn't work? Or the information they needed wasn't on his computer. So much could go wrong.

As Everly promised, Harrison had invited her to the charity polo event hosted at Tristan's property outside Charleston. She'd attended functions like this often with Linc. He'd loved giving back to the community. In fact, this particular charity was a pet project of his.

No doubt she could look forward to running into her ex. Would he be surprised that she was here with Harrison? Given what she'd heard about his relationship with his housekeeper, would he even care?

"I can't imagine how much it costs to maintain all this," she continued, anxiety making her remarks clumsy. "And he has a house in the historic district, as well? Crosby Automotive must be doing really well."

Harrison gave her an odd look.

Was she being too obvious in her interest again? "It's quite a bit of real estate," she added nervously.

"I guess. I've never really thought about it."

"And all these horses, it must cost a fortune to maintain them."

"Look, you really suck at beating around the bush," Harrison said, his tone slightly aggrieved. "Is there something you want to ask?"

"I'm being nosy, but I heard that his ex-wife ended up with next to nothing in the divorce settlement because Tristan wasn't doing all that well financially."

Harrison shrugged. "That might be what she's telling people. But what she got in the divorce might have more to do with something that triggered certain clauses in her prenuptial agreement."

"Oh."

London already knew what Harrison was referring to. Zoe had been accused of infidelity, a charge Tristan trumped up. There had been photos and hotel room charges. She'd disputed the accusation and proved her innocence, but the fight had racked up legal fees, eating up her small settlement. Meanwhile Tristan had cheated on her to his heart's content with no repercussions.

"You don't believe that?" Harrison asked, his ability to read her proving troublesome once again.

"I guess that makes sense."

All too aware she'd really put her foot in it, London cast around for a distraction and spied Everly in the crowd. Every encounter with the woman had driven London's anxiety higher and she tensed. Beside her, ever sensitive to her reactions, Harrison sent his palm skating up her spine in a soothing caress.

"Something wrong?" he asked, regarding her with concern in his sea-glass eyes.

What excuse could she give him? London's brain scrambled for anything that sounded reasonable but came up empty. At her lack of response, his gaze swept the crowd. Not far from Everly, Linc and his sister were strolling side by side through the crowd. He looked happy. Moving on had obviously been good for him.

In contrast, London's nerves were twisted into knots and her stomach felt as if she were on a small boat tossed by stormy seas. In the month since she and Harrison had first gone to dinner, the pain of her broken engagement had faded to a distant memory. She had Harrison to thank for that. Since that night at her condo, they'd been together almost every night. Sometimes at her place. Sometimes at his. Occasionally she wondered at her lack of interest in going out to dinner or in joining Maribelle and Beau for drinks. Having Harrison all to herself was addictive and she'd noticed herself almost constantly basking in the warm glow of contentment that he was in her life.

"Ah," Harrison said, bringing her back to the present. He'd noticed Linc and assumed that was why she was acting so strange. "Are you going to be okay?"

"Sure. Fine." London shook her head. "It's all good."

"Are you sure?"

Although he sounded concerned, his expression had gone flat. He'd obviously misinterpreted the reason for her dismay. London imagined how she'd feel if Harrison had an ex-fiancée and she was attending the same party. Not that Harrison could ever be described as insecure.

"Of course." London gave the declaration an extra punch to reassure him all was well. "It's water under the bridge."

"Is that why you're so tense?"

Damn the man for being so perceptive. London noticed her shoulders had started climbing toward her ears and made an effort to relax them. Usually only her mother had such a strong effect on her, but London had to admit Everly Briggs scared her.

"I haven't seen him since our engagement ended," London said. "It just takes a little getting used to." Pleasure suffused her at the concern in Harrison's eyes. As accustomed as she was to being strong all the time, it was a welcome change to lean on someone else. "Thank you for worrying about me."

And then, because actions spoke louder than words, she grabbed a handful of Harrison's bright blue blazer. Throwing propriety to the wind, she tugged him to her. Her high heels put her lips within kissing distance of his and Harrison obliged her by dipping his head. The kiss electrified her, sensation racing through her body with familiar and joyful results. She grew light-headed almost immediately and was glad for the strong arm he wrapped around her waist.

Thanks to him the kiss didn't spin out of control. If left up to her, London would have tugged him into a private corner and let her fingers find their way beneath his crisp white dress shirt. As it was, they were both breathing a little unsteadily when he lifted his head.

"Damn," he murmured in wonder. "You do surprise me sometimes."

"That's good, right?"

"Absolutely." He dropped a light kiss on her nose and relaxed his arm, letting her draw a deep breath. "Let's go claim some seats."

They found a spot near the center of the field and sat. Harrison hadn't relinquished her hand and London found herself having a difficult time concentrating on the match as he toyed with her fingers. It made her thoughts return to the morning and revisit how his caresses had danced over her skin until she'd begged him for release.

Her musings were interrupted by another glimpse of Everly. To London's dismay, the woman caught her eye and frowned at her. After she'd made her displeasure known, Everly glanced significantly in Linc's direction. London's ex-fiancé was chatting with several of his friends, but his attention was obviously not on the conversation. He was watching a slender brunette set up the picnic baskets for lunch.

London recognized Claire Robbins, Linc's housekeeper. All the gossip and speculation circulating about those two coalesced into reality and London felt…nothing. No regret. No jealousy. No shame. It was as if she'd gotten over Linc. Or she'd realized there wasn't anything to get over and that he'd been right to end their engagement.

Smiling, she glanced Harrison's way, but saw that his attention was on the polo match. As much as she wanted to share her epiphany with him, she kept silent. Everly's presence at the event reminded London that she had an ulterior motive for being here today.

The need to get into Tristan's house and plug the USB drive into his computer preoccupied London through the second match of the day and into the lunch break. The picnic-basket lunches for two that had been created by Claire were a delightful surprise to London. She had no idea how Linc's housekeeper had come to cater such a function or that she'd had any culinary leanings. The food was fantastic. There'd been a sandwich sampler made with beef, ham and salmon. The basket also contained an artisanal meat-and-cheese tray with a fabulous kale salad, fresh fruit, a bottle of Txakoli, and homemade aguas frescas made from melons, strawberry and mango.

London did little more than sample everything, but the sheer volume of food left her feeling thoroughly stuffed and a bit sleepy.

"That was amazing," she murmured, settling back in her chair with a groan.

"There's still dessert." Harrison gestured toward the food tent and the tables filled with trays of triple-layer chocolate cake, mini cheesecakes, tiny tortes, mousse and chocolate-covered strawberries.

"I couldn't possibly," London said, deciding this might be the opening she'd been looking for. "You go ahead. I'm going to take a quick walk and find a ladies' room."

With all the people milling around, it was surprisingly easy to gain entrance into Tristan's home. She was almost disappointed that the doors weren't locked because then she'd have a perfect excuse to turn around. What if someone caught her sneaking in? London lifted her chin and settled her nerves with a calming breath. The best thing to do would be to get it over with as quickly as possible.

It took her less than five minutes to locate Tristan's study. Heart pounding, London moved into the room and eased the door shut behind her. If she was caught in here, she had no explanation for sitting at his desk and perusing his laptop computer. This was madness. Was any of this worth the damage to her relationship with Harrison?

The question shocked London to her toes and made her chest ache. She craved more time with Harrison. More hours of conversation. More minutes holding his hand. More mornings sharing breakfast with him. More nights making love. More weeks to let their intimate connection grow and flourish. More years to build a life with him.

All of it was a foolish fantasy. There was no future with Harrison. The fact that she was standing in his brother's study on the verge of stealing the contents of Tristan's computer established where she'd placed her loyalty.

Fighting a sudden rush of helplessness, London pressed her back against the wall, letting her gaze roam the space. It was a typical masculine study with two of the walls lined in dark paneling, the others sporting hunting scenes and bookshelves. Heavy hunter green drapes framed the single window. An expensive Oriental rug stretched from her toes to a large, ornately carved wooden desk.

Move.

The longer she stayed in place, questioning her judgment, the more likely she was to get caught. Barely discernible above the thundering of her heart came the cheers from the crowd watching the polo match outside. She didn't have a lot of time. If she was gone too long, Harrison would start to wonder what was keeping her.

Tiptoeing across the rug to Tristan's desk seemed a bit ridiculous, but since London was breaking into the man's computer, she might as well act like a thief. Her hands shook as she rounded the enormous mahogany desk and approached his computer. She opened the laptop and the screen came to life. Unsurprisingly, the desktop displayed an image of Tristan on one of his polo ponies, looking suave and ruggedly masculine as he stared down the photographer.

Shivering with foreboding, London quickly found where to plug in the drive but hesitated before inserting it into the slot. Her heart raced, keeping pace with the rumble of hoof beats on the polo grounds. If she was going to do this, it needed to be now. Yet she continued to flounder.

And then the sound of approaching voices reached her: a woman's high-pitched laughter followed by a man's deep baritone. London jerked away from the computer, bumping into the desk chair and sending it thumping back against the wall. The noise seemed to explode in the quiet room and she glanced around wildly, looking for a place to hide before the couple entered. The long drapes caught her eye. In seconds she slipped behind the voluminous fabric, hoping she was out of sight.

Pulse jumping erratically, she waited. And waited. Expecting the door to open at any second, she tried to calm her rapid breathing but alarm had her firmly in its grasp. Had it been Tristan in the hallway? London recalled their encounter at the Crosby Motorsports end-of-season party. No doubt he had a string of women he entertained. The man's insatiable appetites weren't just gossip. He'd cheated on Zoe almost from the beginning of their marriage.

London wasn't sure how much time she spent behind the curtain before she realized no one was coming into the study. She eased out and glanced at the desk before making her way to the door. After straining to hear if anyone occupied the hall, she gathered a bracing breath and opened the door a crack. There was no one around, so she slipped out of Tristan's study and made her way back outside. Not until she reached sunlight and fresh air did she take a full breath. A second later the air whooshed out of her lungs in a squeak as someone spoke.

"Did you do it?"

London whirled around and spied Everly standing beside the side door. Her eyes gleamed with feral intensity.

"I couldn't."

"The program didn't work?"

London gripped the flash drive tighter. Would she have gone through with it if not for the near interruption? It was a question she'd be asking herself for a long time. How far was she planning to go to hurt someone she didn't know just to take revenge on Linc for ending their engagement? Especially when she no longer felt hurt and betrayed.

When she, Everly and Zoe had first concocted the plan, London had been reeling from the shock and hurt, and was feeling vengeful. But since Harrison had come along, she'd realized that Linc wasn't the only man in the world for her. Maybe he never was.

"I didn't try it," London admitted.

"Why not?"

"I'm not sure we're doing the right thing."

"Why? Because you're dating Harrison? Suddenly it's okay for you to back out on our agreement because you're happy? Is that fair to Zoe? She's living in the back room of the boutique she opened and can't pay her rent because the divorce lawyer got all her savings."

Because they weren't supposed to be in contact with each other, London hadn't had any idea Zoe's situation was so dire. "I'll give her some money to get by."

Everly ejected an exasperated snort. "You can't help her like that. The point of what we're doing is to not have any contact with each other."

"And yet you're here talking to me," London pointed out, glancing around and seeing that they were completely alone. "And apparently you've been keeping tabs on Zoe to know her current situation."

"I'm doing my part," Everly said, not responding to London's accusation. "If you don't do yours, then Zoe has no reason to go after Ryan. That man destroyed my sister and I intend to make him pay."

"I don't know," London hedged, unnerved by Everly's savagery. "This is all just so much more than I signed on for."

"Listen up," Everly said, leaning close, her manner intimidating. "We made a deal and you're going to see it through."

"Deals can be broken."

Abruptly, Everly's demeanor changed and she became cool and collected once again. "I wondered if this might happen with you. This is one deal you're not going to break."

"What are you going to do to stop me?" London asked, sounding more confident than she felt.

Everly's quicksilver mood change intensified London's concerns. What sort of unbalanced person had she gotten mixed up with?

"I've set things in motion that are going to ruin Linc's life. That was what I promised I would do. You need to do your part. You owe me and you owe Zoe."

"I'm out." London started to slide past Everly. To her surprise, the other woman grabbed her arm in a tight vise. "Let me go."

"If you don't go through with this, I will reveal to Harrison what you've been up to."

Panic flooded her and London scrambled for what to say to defuse the situation. The only way she knew to limit Everly's blackmail potential was to deny her feelings for Harrison.

"You'll only blow up this whole scheme if you do. I've used Harrison to get to Tristan. He means nothing to me except as a means to an end. If you tell him what I've been up to, we all go down."

That said, she yanked her arm from Everly's grasp, feeling the rake of the woman's nails against her skin as she pulled free. It wasn't in London to shove the woman before escaping, but if anyone deserved to be knocked around in that moment, it was Everly.

London walked away as swiftly as she dared, conscious that she'd already been away from Harrison for too long. Heat surged beneath her skin as her heart and lungs pumped adrenaline through her whole body. She couldn't go back to Harrison in this emotionally heightened state. He would want to know what was wrong. What could she tell him?

And then her gaze fell on a small group and the one individual who was utterly familiar to her. Lincoln faced Claire Robbins, and from her devastated expression and the anguish on his face, London realized whatever Everly had set in motion between Linc and the woman he loved had just come to a head.

Grief and rage hit her already raw nerves and London sped away from the crowds as her stomach pitched sickeningly. What had they done? What had she done? Linc didn't deserve to have his life ruined because he'd broken off their engagement. He'd been right that they didn't belong together. Only she'd been too busy wallowing in what she'd perceived as her failure to see it.

Tears blinded her as bile filled her mouth and anguish twisted her heart. She was well and truly stuck now that Everly had exacted London's revenge on Linc. Her chance to escape the situation long gone.

London made her way toward the refreshment tent where the lunches had been available earlier. She needed some water and a quiet moment to herself. What a fool she'd been to make such a terrible pact. Her fingers tightened over the flash drive. The moment to use it was gone. And London was relieved.

Everly's threat filled her mind. London had no doubt that Everly would tell Harrison what was going on even if it meant ruining everything for all of them. The woman was crazy. Or maybe it was London who'd lost it. She was still trying to figure out how she could get the incriminating information on Tristan and not let her actions destroy what she was building with Harrison. Talk about being stuck between a rock and a hard place.

* * *

Harrison had finished a full plate of desserts without London reappearing and wondered where she'd gotten herself off to.

The day had started out cloudless and warm for late November. Harrison's optimism had been sky-high. He'd considered their first appearance in Charleston society as a couple to be a statement about their relationship.

It had been.

Just not in the way he'd expected.

Ever since London had spied Linc Thurston, Harrison had noticed a nagging disquiet. No, that wasn't quite true. He'd been troubled since the first night he and London had slept together after she admitted her mother didn't believe Harrison was the sort of man London should date.

Normally he didn't care about anyone's opinions, but the closer he and London grew, the more he wondered when her mother would put pressure on her to find someone more suitable. Harrison had no idea if she'd fight for them or cave to her mother's will and that bothered him a lot.

Harrison had assumed he'd come to know London quite well during the last couple of weeks. And he believed he'd seen a change in her. Where she'd been reserved and even a bit prickly toward him at first, once he'd gotten to know the woman beneath the impeccable designer suits, he'd found complicated layers of ambition, passion and vulnerability that intrigued him but also made him leery of moving too fast.

Her walls went up and came down in ever-fluctuating responses to ways he behaved and how deeply he plumbed her emotions. Yet now as he wondered about London's views on the future of their relationship, Harrison accepted he couldn't walk away from what they'd begun. He wasn't a quitter. And she was a woman worth fighting for.

"There you are." London's overly bright smile couldn't hide the shadows darkening her gold-flecked blue eyes. "I've been looking all over for you."

"I'm glad you found me."

Harrison put out his hand and smiled as London slipped hers into it. Ten days earlier she would've resisted doing something this simple and profoundly intimate. Her level of comfort with him had come a long way in a short period of time. Yet he couldn't shake the feeling that things were ever on the verge of swinging back.

"Did you have fun?" he asked.

"I did. Makes me want to take up polo."

"Really?" He'd like to see her barreling down the field, mallet swinging. "Do you ride?"

"I used to when I was younger. My dad taught me. He loves to hunt." A girlish smile curved her lips. "You know, ride to the hounds."

"They still do that?"

"Tuesdays, Thursdays and Sundays during season."

Harrison shook his head in bemusement. "Who knew?"

"Can we get out of here?" she asked, catching him by surprise. "I want to be alone with you."

"Nothing would make me happier."

But a nagging thought in the back of his mind left him questioning whether she was eager to be with him or just looking to escape an event where her ex was with someone else.

It didn't help that she seemed unusually preoccupied during the return trip to Charleston.

"Anything in particular you want to do?" he asked, breaking the silence as the car rolled along King Street. "It's not too early to grab a drink."

"Sure. Where do you want to go?"

"The Gin Joint or Proof?"

"The Gin Joint, I think."

Fifteen minutes later they'd settled into one of the booths in the cozy bar and ordered two quintessential Gin Joint drinks. The bar prided itself on its craft cocktails, seasonally updated, with clever names like Gutter Sparrow, Whiplash, Whirly Bird and Lucky Luciano.

"Delicious," London commented after taking a sip of her Continental Army cocktail, featuring apple brandy, caraway orgeat, lime, Seville orange, falernum, sugar and muddled apple. "The perfect fall drink."

Silence fell between them as they sipped their cocktails and contemplated the snack menu. Harrison debated whether to bring up the topic of her ex and the issues bothering him.

"I'm just going to come out and ask," he said abruptly, causing London to look up from the menu in surprise. "Today after you saw Linc, you seemed distracted and upset."

Her eyes widened. "I wasn't."

She was a terrible liar, but he decided against pressing her. Instead, he turned to another burning question.

"Have you spoken with your mother about us?" Harrison winced at his blunt delivery. "I'm asking because I see a future for us." And he wanted to know what stood in the way.

"You do?" If it was possible, she looked even more stunned.

"I think about you all the time when we're not together and that's never happened to me before."

"But we barely know each other."

Concern lashed at him. Were they on the same page or not?

"I'm not saying I want to get married tomorrow, but I can't see an end to this thing between us and that's saying a lot." He leaned forward and fixed his eyes on her. "I need to know if you feel the same way."

"I...don't...know. That is..." She redirected her focus to the tabletop and an agonized expression passed over her features. "I do like you. A lot. But I haven't given any thought to the future."

Harrison sat back, unsatisfied by her answer. While he had to give her props for being honest, it wasn't the ringing endorsement of their connection he'd been hoping for.

"Then you'd be the first woman I've dated who hadn't," he

said, fighting annoyance that he'd opened up while she remained guarded. "Is it because of what I do?"

"You mean racing? No." When he snorted in disbelief, she reached both her hands across the table and laid them over his. "My engagement ended a couple months ago after I'd been with Linc for three years. I was just starting to figure out who I am when you came into my life."

"I think that's crap. You know exactly who you are. The question is whether or not that woman can see herself with a guy like me. I'm not someone your mother would approve of. I don't have any interest in making the rounds of Charleston society. Our daughter would never attend a single debutante event. But I can promise I wouldn't ever make you regret a single day of our life together."

"Harrison…" She blinked rapidly and heaved a sigh.

"You have to decide what's truly important to you."

"You make me sounds like such a snob," she murmured, her high color betraying her inner turmoil. "I know what people say about me. That I wasn't in love with Linc. And that's probably true. There's a good reason why we were engaged for two years without ever setting a wedding date. But then there's the part where I think he was cheating on me." London's voice shook as she finished, "What if I don't have what it takes to keep a man interested long-term?"

Her words flattened Harrison against the booth seat. Was that what was bothering her? That she believed herself undesirable? How was that possible when he'd shown her over and over how much he wanted her?

"You have what it takes to keep the right man interested long-term. You chose the wrong guy last time. Have faith in what you want and who you are." He turned his hands over so that their palms rested against each other. It wrenched his heart that she couldn't bring herself to meet his gaze. "You have what it takes to keep me interested forever."

Her breath caught. "You shouldn't say things like that."

"Why not? You don't think I'm being truthful?"

"I think you have a lot to learn about me and what you discover might change your mind."

He couldn't imagine what she was talking about and had no idea how to coax her out of this sudden funk she'd fallen into. "I guess that could be said of me, as well. All I'm asking is for you to be open to exploring who we could be to each other."

"I can do that." She gave his hands a brief hard squeeze and let go. After a large swallow of her cocktail, she fastened a bright smile on her face and said, "How about you and I go back to my place and do some of that exploring you were talking about."

Grinning, Harrison threw a hundred on the table and got to his feet, holding out his hand. "Let's go."

Harrison didn't know what to expect when they got to her condo. London had sent him smoking-hot glances the entire drive. Now the door was barely shut before she backed him toward the foyer wall and then gave a shove that sent the breath whooshing from his lungs. A second later she pressed her body against his, gripping his hair in a painful grasp while crushing her lips to his. She kissed him hard and rough, making his world go black and hot. Blood rushed through his veins, pounding in his ears as she ambushed his senses with teeth and tongue and ragged breath.

He was helpless to process the astonishing hunger that gripped her. All he could do was surrender to her feasting and let her set him on fire.

Sinking his fingers into her silky hair, he savored the soft texture while his other hand slid down her back and slipped over the curve of her butt, lifting her against his growing erection. The move caused her to shudder and suck his lower lip between her teeth. A searing nip, followed by the soothing flick of her tongue, made him groan.

"I'm going to make you come like you never have," she whispered in his ear while her fingers raked down his torso until they encountered his belt.

He was a fan of dirty talk, and her words slammed into him, sending blood rushing to his groin. He'd never expected to hear London speak so boldly or to want to be in charge. It turned him on.

"I look forward to it," he said, throwing her over his shoulder and heading to the bedroom so they could get the party started.

She squawked at the undignified carry, and from the expression on her face as he set her on her feet beside the bed, she intended to make him pay. Harrison stripped off his jacket and tie, and then went to work on his shirt buttons. He couldn't wait for her to do her worst.

By the time he'd kicked off his shoes, her clothes were in a neat pile on the dresser and she was naked. Hands on hips, she watched him drop his pants to the floor and step out of them. When her gaze dropped to the erection straining his boxer briefs, a little smile formed on her lips.

Harrison frowned as he tried to make out the significance of her expression. If he'd believed he had London all figured out, he'd been wrong. This was a new side of her. The woman who took charge when it came to her work was obviously capable of stepping up in the bedroom, as well. He found himself impatient to see what came next.

She stalked toward him and grabbed a handful of his boxers, tugging the cotton material over his jutting erection and down his thighs. He hissed as the cool air caressed his heated flesh, but the chill was short-lived as her fingers closed around him. The tight grip and firm stroke that followed felt out-of-this-world fantastic.

"On the bed, so I can get these the rest of the way off you."

"Yes, ma'am."

He did as she asked, admiring the way her breasts swayed as she stripped him bare. Like some sort of wild thing, she peered at him from between the glossy strands of hair that hung across her face as she tossed his briefs aside. Straightening, she put her hands on her hips, surveying him with a wicked half smile.

"Ready?" she asked, not waiting for his nod before bending over the bed.

"Drive me crazy with your delightful tongue," he growled, his voice a guttural rasp.

One corner of her lips kicked up in a smirk. She scraped her fingernails up his thighs and his mouth went dry. She obviously wanted to steer the ship and he was dying to see what happened next. Fortunately, he didn't have long to wait.

Lust blasted through him as her lips dropped toward the head of his erection, but instead of taking him into her mouth, she hovered millimeters above. The anticipation was almost too painful and it struck home that she intended to take her time with him.

A low curse passed his lips as she flicked her tongue out and swirled it over him. Harrison's hips came off the mattress as she followed that with a long stroke down his shaft and then back up. Placing her hands on his knees, she pushed them wider before crawling forward to set up between his thighs.

For a second his breath lodged in his throat as she gently cupped his balls and then her mouth swooped down again, sucking him into a hot, wet tunnel that made him groan and shudder. She swirled her tongue around his erection and pleasure detonated through him.

Speaking…was impossible.

Thinking… Incoherent chants filled his mind.

He was tumbling, falling into an upside-down world where his desire and pleasure were less important than the sheer bliss of catching her gaze and realizing she was enjoying watching his reaction.

Although he longed to close his eyes so he could better focus on the sensations pounding through him, the picture of her hair splayed over his stomach and thighs, her lips locked around him, was a sight to behold.

Her blue eyes sparkled as she glanced up at him. She was filled with naughty surprises. Tremors rolled through his body as he realized she was enjoying this as much as he was. He curved his fingers around her head as his stomach muscles tightened. Skin on fire, he fought to hold on, to make the moment last. But the flames licked him, spreading through his veins, consuming him. Her tongue swirled around his erection and the first shock wave washed over him. Then another. Her mouth felt so damned good.

"Coming." A curse ripped through his mind. "Coming hard."

And then a climax barreled through his body, crashing wildly into bone and muscle and nerves. The unleashed power of it obliterated words and stopped his heart. For several seconds he rocketed through supercharged joy while aftershocks jolted him.

He wasn't even aware that she'd released him until her lips trailed over his chest and slid into the hollow of his throat where his pulse slammed against his skin.

"Amazing." His voice cracked on the one word.

Enough strength had returned to his muscles to allow him to gather her naked body against his. He drifted kisses along her hairline as he slowly recovered.

"Damn, woman," he murmured, cupping her cheek in his palm and bringing their lips together. He kept the kiss light and romantic, showing his appreciation. "You're good as your word. I think I blacked out for a second."

"You're easy," she told him. "You seem to enjoy everything."

He lifted his head off the pillow and regarded her in bemusement. "If by 'everything' you mean your gorgeous mouth on me, then you have that right. You make me come like I never have before," he told her, echoing her earlier promise. "It's different with you."

She looked shell-shocked, and even as he watched, she began withdrawing behind her emotional walls. "You don't need to say that..."

"Do I strike you as someone who says things he doesn't mean?"

"No."

"Then believe me when I tell you I'm in over my head here. I don't know what you do to me, but I like it."

"You do things to me, too," she replied, her long lashes concealing her eyes. "And I like it."

As she spoke, she stretched her lean body, making him keenly aware of her silky skin, renewing his desire. Harrison rolled her beneath him and tangled their legs, his lips finding that spot on her neck that made her shiver.

"Good to hear," he murmured, "because I'm going to spend the rest of the night doing all sorts of things to you. And I think we'll both like that."

It was nearly two in the morning and Everly sat in her car outside a twenty-four-hour drugstore, tearing apart the packaging to get to the prepaid cell phone she'd just purchased. It was important that the call she was about to make couldn't be tracked back to her.

She'd been thinking about this step for two days, weighing the options and debating if such a radical move would be beneficial to their plans. In the end, she'd decided that London needed to be punished. Her failure to use the flash drive to pull the information off Tristan's computer proved that not only her priorities had shifted but also her loyalty.

How was Zoe supposed to get her revenge if London didn't do her part? More important, what was the motivation for Zoe to take down Ryan if nothing bad happened to Tristan? And Everly really needed Zoe to enact some truly devastating vengeance on Ryan for what he'd done to Kelly.

Everly had kept to her part of the bargain. Satisfaction lay curled like a sleeping house cat in her chest. She was nearly purring with pleasure at the damage she'd caused.

In the midst of the charity polo event, she'd ruined Linc Thurston's life by showing him the truth about his housekeeper, ending their ridiculous romance.

No doubt by now, with Claire's past catching up to her in a big way, exposing all her lies and deceptions, Linc was feeling devastated and more than a little stupid that he'd been taken in so easily by an obvious opportunist.

In some way, Everly had actually done him a favor. Not that he'd thank her if he knew she'd been the one who'd contacted Claire's family and let them know where she was.

The look on Linc's face when he'd realized that Claire had lied to him about everything had given Everly such a thrill. She'd planned and executed a flawless plan and the results had been better than she could have imagined.

But not everyone had the strength of will to follow through. That had become crystal clear with the way London had chosen her romance with Harrison over loyalty to the plan. And now she would pay.

Everly keyed the play button on her phone and London's voice rang out with clear conviction.

I've used Harrison to get to Tristan. He means nothing to me except as a means to an end.

Everly dialed a number on the burner phone and waited for the call to roll to voice mail. She'd chosen the late hour, knowing Harrison would be occupied with London. The two of them had been spending all their time together, and after watching them at the polo event, it was pretty clear Harrison was falling for the event planner. And she for him.

Well, falling in love hadn't been part of the plan. London should've kept her clothes on and her focus on what they were trying to achieve.

"You've reached Harrison. I'm not available right now, but leave me your name and a brief message and I'll get back to you."

Smiling, Everly hit Play.

Ten

London woke to a soft morning light stealing past the gauzy curtains of her bedroom. She loved that her windows faced east. Waking up to the sunrise always boosted her optimism. The soothing palette of peach, pink, lavender and soft gold offered a tranquil beginning to her day. She often took a cup of coffee onto her broad terrace and sucked in a heady lungful of river breezes.

Stretching out her hand to the far side of the bed, she found the space empty and the sheets cool. Sighing, she pushed to a sitting position and ran her fingers through her tangled hair. Usually she braided it at night, but Harrison said he loved the spill of her satiny locks over his skin and she adored the way he tunneled his fingers through it.

She slipped from bed and donned a silky robe before following her nose to the kitchen, where the smell of coffee promised a large mug of dark roast. But as she neared the kitchen, the sound of her own voice reached her ears.

I've used Harrison to get to Tristan. He means nothing to me except as a means to an end.

She stopped dead, a malignant lump of dread forming in her chest as she remembered when she'd made that declaration. What did Everly think she was doing?

In her kitchen, Harrison stood at the island, one hand braced on the marble countertop while he stared at the phone. He looked like he'd been told he could never race again.

It was the same devastated look Linc had worn at the polo event during the brutal incident with Claire.

A rushing noise filled her ears as the edges of her vision grew fuzzy. She must've made a sound because his gaze whipped in her direction.

"What is this about?" he demanded, holding up his phone. "Why did you say those things?"

Even if she could speak, she had no words to explain.

"Damn it, London." His voice broke on her name. "I thought we had something."

She had to reply. He deserved an explanation. But would he listen? London doubted she'd be open to it if their situation were reversed.

"It isn't like it sounds—"

"Don't lie to me. I want to know what's really going on."

Gathering a huge breath, she stepped up to the kitchen island and set her hands on it, leaning forward. "I'm trying to find out if your brother is hiding money."

"Why?"

She bit her lip. They'd promised not to tell anyone about what they were doing. Yet hadn't Everly broken their pact when she'd sent that audio clip to Harrison? What more could the woman do? Taint London's reputation? Bad-mouth ExcelEvent?

In the end, cowardice ruled. "I'm not at liberty to tell you."

For long, agonizing seconds he stared at her in silence, confusion and annoyance chasing across his features. "Why?"

"Because it's not my story to tell."

"So, us…?" The unformed question drained all animation from his eyes. "Was I a means to an end?"

She could try lying to him, but he knew her well enough by now to see right through it. "At first."

He took the hit without reacting. "I suppose you want me to believe that things changed."

"They did. I would never have…" She hesitated, unsure what came next. Thanks to the revenge bargain she'd become unrecognizable to herself.

"Never would have…?" He prompted. "Slept with me? Led me to believe your feelings for me were real?" Although his tone remained neutral, the tension around his eyes and the muscle jumping in his jaw displayed what was really going on inside him.

"I do have feelings for you."

But even as the claim left her lips, London saw it was too little and too late. Harrison's eyes hardened to flint, and her heart stopped.

"You don't understand," she protested.

He appeared impervious to her desperate plea. "Then tell me what's going on."

"I can't." Trapped between her mistakes and her longing to come clean, London closed her eyes and wished herself back in time to that fateful women's empowerment function. How had she believed that doing something wrong would make anything better?

"You mean you won't," Harrison countered.

"It's complicated."

The lame excuse bought her no sympathy. Harrison crossed his arms over his chest and regarded her in disgust.

"Can you at least explain to me why you're doing this?"

Maybe it would help if she did. She couldn't tell him everything, but she could say enough that maybe he'd understand.

"I'm helping a friend. Your brother hurt her and I'm trying to…" This is where her story got murky. London no longer believed that what she, Zoe and Everly were doing would make any of them any better off.

"Hurt him back?" Harrison guessed.

London found it hard to meet his gaze. "That's the way it started."

"And things are different now?"

"Yes and no. There's no question that Tristan is a bad guy who did bad things. I'm just not sure doing bad things to a bad guy is the answer. How is it helping anyone to get back at him?"

"I'll be the first one to admit that my brother has not always been a decent individual and I turned a blind eye to a lot of his behavior."

For a second London thought that maybe Harrison understood and could forgive her, but there was no sympathy in his eyes. Only regret.

"Your comments about his spending habits at the polo match got me thinking. I'm not sure if he's been engaged in questionable activities, and I sure as hell hope it has nothing to do with Crosby Automotive, but he's spending above and beyond his income." Harrison rubbed his hand over his eyes. "And I know he treated Zoe badly. She didn't deserve his abuse while they were married or to be discarded the way she was."

"She didn't have an affair. It was something Tristan trumped up to get out of paying her a fair settlement."

"I never believed she did and I should've spoken up on her behalf. She deserved better than she got."

London remained quiet as Harrison's eyes narrowed. His statements struck close to the heart of her motivation.

"Was Zoe the one you were helping?" Harrison asked after a long span of silence.

Her instincts urged her to trust him even as she doubted her purpose in doing so. Did she hope he'd forgive her if he knew what they'd been up to? And how would she feel about what Everly had done to Linc on London's behalf? And what if Everly got wind of the fact that she'd confided in Harrison? What insane stunt would she pull then?

"Talk to me," he said, softening his tone. "What the hell is going on?"

London chewed on her lip, fear of the consequences paralyzing her. At long last she sighed.

"All I can say is that I was trying to find out the truth about your brother's financial situation. It seems likely that he's hiding money because it's pretty common knowledge that Zoe didn't get anywhere near the settlement she should have."

"And how did you think you could do that?" Harrison asked.

"He has to keep track of things somehow. I thought by gaining access to his computer I could find everything I needed."

Harrison frowned. "That's absurd. Didn't you realize he'd have his computer and his files password protected?"

"I have something that's supposed to get past that."

"What?"

She went to her purse, pulled out the USB drive and held it up. "This. It's some kind of special program that was supposed to get me past his security."

Harrison came toward her, gaze fixed on the drive. "Where did you get it?"

With her eyes begging him to understand, London shook her head.

A muscle jumped in Harrison's jaw. "How does it work?"

She explained the process and he held out his hand.

"Give me the drive."

Meek as a lamb, London handed it over. "I'm sorry," she whispered. "Please don't tell Tristan. If he finds out, he'll make things worse for Zoe."

If her plea had any effect on him, nothing showed in his expression. He remained furious, but London hoped a shred of affection for her had survived and he wouldn't do anything to cause her harm.

Harrison turned the flash drive over and over in his hand, contemplating it. "My brother doesn't need to know about this. But I'm keeping this and you will stay away from him."

Relief flooded her. Nothing suited London more than backing away from the whole situation. Then she remembered that her problems weren't limited to Tristan. Everly had sent Harrison the snippet of their conversation as a warning shot. London still had to contend with her.

"What are you going to do with the drive?" she asked.

"I don't know." He dropped it into his pocket. "The only thing I'm sure of at the moment is that you and I are done."

Harrison drove the familiar roads to Crosby Motorsports, seeking comfort in what he knew and loved. Cars and racing had always been his go-to when things got hard. He'd lost track of how many hours he'd spent as a kid with a wrench in his hand, learning how to tear apart something and then putting it back together. There was security in the logic of how the pieces fit together, each with a particular purpose. As he'd reached an age when he spent more time behind the wheel than under the hood, his appreciation had grown for a perfectly functioning car.

Unfortunately, in the racing world, as much as they strove to have everything work smoothly, that rarely happened. Bolts loosened. Suspensions failed. Brakes gave out. Drivers trained for when things went wrong, when systems failed or other drivers made mistakes. Situations didn't always have to spin out of control.

The other side of the coin from preparation was luck. Harrison considered himself fortunate that during his career while he'd been involved in several wrecks, he'd walked away from all but one of them. Yet despite the danger inherent in his sport, he never questioned getting behind the wheel of number twenty-five.

Too bad life wasn't equally easy to prepare for and navigate. Nothing he'd ever experienced could've enabled Harrison to see the wreck between him and London coming. She'd completely blindsided him. One second he was in his lane, thinking that he had everything in hand, and the next he was spinning out of control on a trajectory that sent him crashing into the wall.

Ahead of him the entrance gate to Crosby Motorsports came into view. As he sped onto the property, the peace he'd always gathered from being there eluded him. The facility had been more than his home away from home for nearly two decades. It was the center of his world. Yet tonight as he pulled up in front of the engine shop, his heart wasn't here.

He expected the building to be empty. With the season done, the team had headed home for some much-needed rest and family time. Harrison used his keycard to access the engine shop and easily navigated the familiar space in the dim light. Of all the various components that went into the cars, he had a particular fondness for engines since his earliest memories were of working beside his uncle, learning how all the complicated parts came together to move the vehicle forward in breathtaking speeds.

Of course, the engines designed and built by the Crosby Motorsports team were far more sophisticated than the engines Harrison had learned on. These days the engines were customized each week for the particular racetrack based on the speed and throttle characteristics and even the driver.

"What are you doing here?"

Looking past the neat row of engines lined up along one wall, Harrison spied his uncle headed his way.

"Just clearing my head."

"How's London? Things going okay?"

"Why do you ask?"

"She's the first woman you've brought around in a long time. I figured she was someone special." Jack removed his ball cap and ran slender fingers through his thick gray hair. "And with the hangdog look about you right now, it stands to reason that something went wrong."

With the season over, Jack became a lot more approachable,

and Harrison decided to take advantage of his uncle's years of experience being married to a firecracker like Dixie.

"When London and I first started dating, I thought our biggest problem was going to be that she wouldn't give me a chance because I didn't have the sort of Charleston social connections she was looking to make."

"And now?" Jack asked, not looking a bit surprised.

"I think those issues are still there, but they aren't the biggest problem we have."

Jack shook his head in disgust and suddenly Harrison was an impulsive teenager again, eager to get behind the wheel of a car he couldn't handle.

"Do you think for one second if I hadn't fought for Dixie that we'd be together right now?" Jack asked. "Your dad and I had empty pockets and big dreams when I met your aunt."

"But she married you," Harrison reminded him.

"You say that like there was never any question she would. Her dad chased me off their property the first time I made her cry."

Harrison regarded his uncle in shock, intrigued by this glimpse into Jack's personal life. Usually his uncle stuck to tales about the business or racing and Harrison sensed there was a good story waiting to be told.

"You made her cry?" He couldn't imagine his tough-as-nails aunt reduced to tears. "Why? How?"

"I wasn't the smooth operator I am today."

Harrison snorted. His uncle often told stories, and the more dramatic the circumstances, the better. Not everything was 100 percent true, but there was enough reality to provide a moral. The key was discovering what exactly to believe.

"So, what happened?"

"She was debuting and wanted me as her escort for the ball. We'd been going out for only a few months at the time and I certainly wasn't her parents' first choice."

"Did you do something to embarrass her at the event?"

"I never made it to the ball."

"Why?"

"Stupid pride." Jack's expression turned sheepish. "I turned her down. She and I were from different worlds. I believed if we went together, she'd be the target of ridicule and I didn't want to put her through that."

Harrison winced. That same thought had crossed his mind at Richmond Raceway when he'd glimpsed London there. It had been so obvious that she didn't fit in. And later when he'd seen her with his brother at the Crosby Motorsports party, he'd briefly wondered if she'd prefer to be with someone who shared similar business and social connections.

"If that's what you believed," Harrison asked, "why did you start dating her in the first place?"

"Because she turned my world upside down. I could no more stay away from her than stop breathing. She was my heart and my reason for getting up every morning."

Jack's words hit closer to home than Harrison would've liked.

"So what happened after you turned down her invitation to attend the ball?"

"I'd underestimated how strong she was. And how determined. She didn't give a damn what other people thought. She was proud of me, of the man I was, and wanted everyone to know it." Jack raked his fingers through his hair as regret twisted his features. Even now, after more than three decades of wedded bliss, Harrison could see his uncle wished he'd behaved a different way. "My actions made it appear that I believed her choices were flawed. And that I didn't trust her."

"But she married you, so she must have gotten over it," Harrison said.

"It took a year."

Harrison could imagine what those months must've been like for his uncle. He was experiencing his own separation angst at the moment.

"You must have been really hung up on her to have stayed in the fight that long," he said.

"You know, at the beginning of the year I don't believe I understood what I was feeling. Plus, if I'd been truly in love or, more to the point, been willing to surrender my stubbornness and give in to my emotions, I might have saved myself a lot of pain."

Harrison didn't want to ponder an entire year away from London, so he asked, "Why did you keep going when she rejected you for a year?"

"Because to be without her hurt more than my foolish pride. I tried to stay away, but rarely lasted more than a week or two. Life got pretty bleak for me, pretty fast. It also made me more determined to be worthy of her. That's when Crosby Automotive really started to take off. I threw every bit of my frustration and fear and joy into making something I could be proud of. I thought if I was wealthy and successful that I could win her back."

"Did it work?"

Jack shook his head. "It made things worse. The better Crosby Automotive did, the more confident I became and the less she wanted to have anything to do with me."

Harrison wasn't liking where the story was going. "So what did it take?"

"She started dating someone perfect for her. A guy from a wealthy, well-connected family." Jack's expression hardened. "I fell into a dark well for a couple of weeks."

"How'd you come out of it?"

"I weighed being happy for the rest of my life against my pride."

"And?" Harrison didn't really need to ask. He saw where his uncle was going. "What did it take?"

"The most difficult conversation of my life. I had to completely open myself up to her. Fears, hopes, how she made my life better and that I wanted to be worthy of her love."

Strong emotion filled Jack's voice even after three and a half decades. The power of it drove Harrison's misery higher. His throat tightened, preventing him from speaking for a long moment.

Into the silence, his uncle spoke again. "Is what you feel for her worth fighting for?"

Could he live without London? Probably. Would it be any fun? Doubtful. For so long racing had been his purpose and passion. He'd never considered that he'd sacrificed anything to be at the top of his game. But was that true?

With London he'd started thinking in terms of family and kids, and there was no question that she'd pulled his focus away from racing. The telling part was that he didn't mind. In fact, he'd begun to think in terms of how he intended to make changes in his schedule next year to spend as much time with her as possible. He suspected that if this business with his brother hadn't gotten between them, he'd be well on his way to looking at engagement rings.

"For a long time I thought so." Harrison's chest tightened at the thought of letting her go, but he couldn't imagine how to get past the way she'd used him. He'd never been one to hold a grudge, but trusting her again seemed hopeless. "Now I'm not so sure."

Eleven

A subdued and thoroughly disgraced London entered the
Cocktail Club on King Street and searched the animated crowd
for her best friend. Maribelle had grabbed two seats at the bar.
As London made her way through the customers, Maribelle was
flashing her engagement ring at a persistent admirer.

These days because of the magic of Maribelle's true love
glow, members of both sexes flocked to her. By comparison,
London felt dull and sluggish. She couldn't sleep, wasn't eating
and couldn't remember the last time she'd exercised.

"Holy hell," Maribelle exclaimed as London slid onto the
bar stool beside her. "You look awful." She narrowed her eyes
and looked her friend up and down. "Are you ready to tell me
what happened?"

It had been ten days since that horrible morning when Harrison had received that damning audio clip from Everly.

As London filled her in, Maribelle's expression underwent
several transformations from shock to dismay and finally irritation, but she didn't interrupt until London's story wound to
its bitter finish.

"He's never going to speak to me again," London said, putting the final nail in the coffin that held the most amazing romance of her life.

"And well he shouldn't." Maribelle scowled. "I'm a little tempted never to speak to you again, either."

Knowing her friend didn't really mean that, London sat in rebuked silence while Maribelle signaled the bartender and ordered two shots of tequila.

"You know I can't drink that," London protested as the shots were delivered along with salt and limes. "Remember what happened the last time."

"I do and you are going to drink it until you're drunk enough to call Harrison and tell him the whole story, after which you're going to beg for his forgiveness. And then I'm going to take you home and hold your hair while you throw up." Maribelle handed her the shot. "Because that's what best friends do."

"I love you," London murmured, nearly blind from the grateful tears gathering in her eyes.

"I know. Now drink."

It took two shots in close succession and twenty minutes for London's dread to unravel. Two more and an hour before London found enough confidence to do the right thing.

"I'm going to regret this in the morning," London muttered, picking her phone up off the bar. The roiling in her stomach had nothing to do with the tequila she'd consumed. Yet.

"I know." Maribelle's voice was sympathetic, but she maintained the steely demeanor of a drill sergeant. "Now call."

Beneath Maribelle's watchful eye, London unlocked her phone and pulled up Harrison's contact information. With her heart trying to hammer its way out of her chest, she tapped on his name. As his handsome face lit up her screen, she almost chickened out. Maribelle must have sensed this because she made the same chastising sound she used to correct the new puppy she and Beau had just adopted.

London put the phone to her ear and reminded herself to

breathe. Facing Harrison after what she'd done to him ranked as the hardest thing she'd ever had to do. But she owed him the full truth and so much more.

"I didn't think I'd hear from you again."

She almost burst into ugly sobs as his deep voice filled her ear and suddenly her throat was too tight for her to speak.

"Hello? London, are you there?" He paused. "Or have you butt-dialed me while you're out having a good time? It sounds like you're at a party."

Someone behind her had a rowdy laugh that blasted through the bar right on cue.

"I'm not having fun." Not one bit. *I miss you.* "I have things to tell you. Can I come over so I can explain some things to you?"

He remained silent for so long, she expected him to turn her down.

"I'm home now."

"I can't tonight," she said, glancing at the line of empty shot glasses. "Tonight, I'm going to be very, very sick."

Again he paused before answering. "Tomorrow afternoon, then?"

"At two?"

"At two."

The line went dead and London clapped her hand over her mouth before making a beeline for the bathroom.

At a little after two the following afternoon, Harrison opened the door to his penthouse unit and immediately cursed the way his heart clenched at the sight of London. From her red-rimmed eyes to her pale skin and lopsided topknot, she looked as miserable as he felt.

To his dismay, instead of venting his irritation, his first impulse was to haul her into the foyer and wrap her in his arms. Her gaze clung to him as he stepped back and gestured her inside.

Due to the turn in the weather, she'd dressed in jeans, soft suede boots and a bulky sweater in sage green. From her pink cheeks and windblown hair, he suspected she'd walked over from her building along the waterside thoroughfare that ran beside the Cooper River.

With the front door closed, the spacious foyer seemed to narrow. Beneath the scent of wind and water that she'd brought into his home, her perfume tickled his nostrils. Abruptly, he was overwhelmed by memories. Of the joyful hours she'd spent here. The long nights they'd devoured each other. The lazy Sunday mornings when they'd talked over coffee, croissants and egg-white omelets.

"Thank you for letting me come over," she murmured.

Harrison shoved his hands into his pockets. He would not touch her or offer comfort of any kind, no matter how soft and sweet and vulnerable she looked. He would not let her off easy or tell her it was okay, because it wasn't.

"You said you wanted to explain about going after my brother," he growled. "So explain."

"I will, but first I need to say something to you." London's beautiful eyes clung to him. "When I'm with you, I feel... everything. I didn't expect all the things you make me want and need. I didn't understand that once we'd made love there would be no going back for me."

Harrison's muscles quivered and it took willpower to prevent his body from responding to what she was saying. Her every word echoed how he'd felt about her and the loss he'd experienced these last few days gripped him anew.

"All I want is to be with you." Her hands fluttered, graceful as a dancer's, opening and closing as she poured out her emotions. "You made me feel beautiful and fulfilled. You gave me a safe place to be open and vulnerable."

"That's not an explanation for why you used me," he said, his heart wrenching so hard it was difficult to keep a grip on his impatience.

Her expression was a study in consternation as she began

again. "I was afraid to tell you what I was doing for fear that you'd hate me."

Her declaration shook him to the core.

"I could never hate you."

He loved her.

The realization left him stunned and reeling. For days he'd ignored the part of him that had recognized the signs.

"Harrison, I'm sorry," London said, her voice sounding very far away even though she stood within reach. "I did a terrible thing."

He loved her?

How was that possible given what she'd done?

She'd used him to get to his brother. Didn't she know he would've done anything for her if only she'd asked? His soul ached as he resisted his heart's longing for her. She would always be his weakness.

Needing to put some distance between them before he succumbed to the urge to back her against the wall and lose himself in her, Harrison marched back toward his living room.

It wasn't until he threw himself onto the couch that he realized she hadn't left the foyer. With an impatient huff, he rose and went to find her. She stood where he'd left her, pulling down her sleeves to hide her hands.

"I'm so deeply sorry that what I did hurt you," she said, her voice tiny and choked with tears. "And I want to tell you everything."

"You might as well come in and tell me the whole story."

Losing the battle to avoid touching her, Harrison towed London into the living room and drew her to the couch. Once they were seated side by side, she began her tale.

"It all started when I met Zoe and another woman, Everly Briggs, at a networking event a few months ago. We were all strangers and each of us was in a bad place. Linc had just broken off our engagement. Zoe's divorce was going badly. And Everly claimed her sister had been wrongly imprisoned."

London's fingers clenched and flexed in her lap. "I don't know who first brought up the idea of getting back at the men who'd hurt us, but Everly jumped pretty hard on it and her enthusiasm swept up both Zoe and me."

Harrison hated that London's pain from her broken engagement had driven her to do something reckless.

"Zoe was pretty scared of Tristan and I didn't want to go after Linc and damage my reputation by appearing vindictive. So…" She blew out a big breath. "Since we were strangers who met by chance, we decided to take on each other's men. Everly went after Linc for me. I went after Tristan for Zoe. And she's supposed to take down Ryan Dailey for Everly."

Despite his dismay at her story, Harrison could see the logic in their approach. "So who sent me the audio clip of you?"

"Everly. She wanted to make you hate me." London peered at him anxiously. "She saw how important you were becoming to me."

His treacherous heart sang as some of his hurt and anger eased at her confession. The longing to take her in his arms grew more urgent, but he resisted. Although it was clear that no matter what she'd done or why, he couldn't stop wanting her, he required a full explanation before deciding what to do next.

"So where do things stand now?"

"I don't know. Obviously, I wasn't up to fulfilling my part of the bargain and you can see how Everly reacted to that." London made a face. "I feel terrible for Zoe. Among the three of us, what happened to her was the most damaging."

"Didn't you say Everly's sister went to jail?"

"Yes, but from what I've been able to find out, she did something illegal. Maybe Ryan Dailey didn't have to go so far as to press charges, but his company lost several million dollars because of her and he was well within his rights."

London lapsed into silence, her gaze fixed on his chest, her downcast expression battering the walls he'd erected against her. Her genuine remorse left him grappling with her decision to take revenge on her ex-fiancé. What did that say about her?

Yet after suffering his own heartbreak, he was better able to sympathize with the pain she'd experienced. Dark emotions had taken him to irrational places unlike any he'd visited before she entered his life.

Harrison reached around to the sofa table behind him and picked up a manila envelope. The information it held put him square in the middle of London's trouble.

"Here," he said, handing her the envelope.

"What is this?" London's gaze flickered from his face to the envelope and back again.

"Open it up and see."

London unfastened the clasp and flipped up the flap to peer inside. "It looks like banking information."

"My brother's banking information," Harrison clarified. "Turns out Tristan had secret offshore accounts and shell corporations that he used to move money to the States. I don't know if the information will help Zoe, but it wasn't fair that Tristan hid these accounts from her."

While he spoke, she pulled several pages out and scanned them. "Why did you do this?"

"Zoe got a raw deal."

It wasn't his only motivation, but Harrison wasn't ready to say more. He'd done a lot of soul-searching before he'd betrayed his brother by using the flash drive and stealing these files. Although he remained conflicted about his decision, seeing the questionable legality of what Tristan had been up to had eased his conscience somewhat.

"This is a lot of money," London said. "I mean a lot of money. Way more than he should have been able to put away by regular means. Where do you suppose it came from?"

The question had been keeping Harrison up at night. He had yet to figure out what to do with the information he'd gathered, but knew a conversation with his father and uncle was in order.

"I think he's been laundering money," he said.

"Laundering money for whom?"

"Drug dealers. Russian mob." The more he'd reviewed the information, the more extreme his speculation had become and the more concerned he'd grown about the potential repercussions for Crosby Automotive. "It's hard to say."

Her eyes went wide. "You don't seriously believe your brother is doing something illegal, do you? How could that be happening?"

"Crosby Automotive buys almost all its parts from overseas manufacturers and my brother is responsible for deciding which companies we buy from. It wouldn't be impossible for him to channel bribes into one of these offshore accounts."

"But does he need more money than he has?"

"You've seen his homes and his spending habits. Tristan likes to live the life of a billionaire. 'Act like you're worth a fortune and people will be inclined to believe it,'" he quoted in his brother's lofty tones. "Instead it looks like he just went deeper and deeper into debt."

"Is Crosby Automotive in danger from what he's been doing?"

"I don't think so." Harrison hoped not. It would be something he'd need to address in coming months.

London shoved the pages back into the envelope. "How can I thank you for this?"

"No need. What Tristan did to Zoe was wrong."

She set her hand on his. The move sent a zing of excitement through his body. He set his teeth against the urge to pull her onto his lap and sink his fingers into her tousled hair. His gaze slid to her full lips. One kiss and he'd be beneath her spell once more. But...

"I'm so sorry for what I did," she said, forcing Harrison to rein in his lust-filled thoughts.

"Look, I've started to understand your motives."

"My motives in the beginning," she corrected him, turning

his hand over so her fingers could trace evocative patterns on his palm. "Things changed when I got to know you."

Harrison's blood heated as she inched closer. The entreaty in her eyes undermined his willpower. "I get it, but I can't just go on as if none of this happened."

"I don't blame you." She peered at him from beneath her lashes. "But I just want you to know that you changed me in ways I never imagined possible."

"London..."

Before he knew it, Harrison found himself leaning in. Her feminine scent lured him closer still. He knew exactly where she applied her perfume. A dab on her neck, right over the madly throbbing pulse. Another behind her ear. The hollow of her elbow. Behind her knees.

"I know I have no right to ask, but could you ever...?" She bit her lip, unable to finish the question.

"Forgive you?" He was on the verge of forgetting everything except the driving need to delve into her heat as her palm coasted over his shoulder.

"I know it's not fair for me to ask. But if there's anything I can do." Her other hand found his thigh and Harrison almost groaned at the tornado of lust swirling in him. "If there's any way back to where we were," she continued. "Or forward to something better. All you need to do is tell me what you need me to do."

Harrison raked his fingers through his hair and blew out a giant breath while his craving for her warred with his shattered faith.

"My uncle told me a story about when he and Dixie were dating. He did something wrong and spent the following year trying to get back in her good graces."

"If you think it'll take a year for you to forgive me," London said, so close now that it took no effort at all for her to slide her lips over his ear, "I'm for doing whatever it takes."

Harrison shuddered as her husky voice vibrated through him.

"You'd make that pledge without knowing if I could ever trust you again?"

"I trust that the man you are will play fair with me." She tipped her head and let him see her conviction. "You are worth the risk."

With his ability to resist her unraveling, Harrison said, "You know, when we first started seeing each other I got the impression you didn't feel that way."

"That you were worth the risk?" She shook her head. "Maybe at the very beginning I judged you for what you did for a living. But you were willing to give me a chance anyway."

With a warm, willing woman sliding her hand farther up his thigh, Harrison couldn't figure out why he was still talking. But while his body was revving past safety limits, his heart hadn't yet recovered from crashing.

"You had great legs."

She shook her head at that. "I wasn't exactly your type, though, was I?"

"No. You were far too reserved."

They shared a grin at how much that had changed and more of Harrison's doubts began to fizzle and fade.

"If that was true, why did you approach me at the foundation event?" she asked, leaning more of her body against him.

"Truth?" He sighed as her soft breasts flattened against his arm. "Because you seemed interested in Tristan and I wanted to protect you from him."

"Seriously?" She eased back a fraction and shook her head in wonder. "So, if not for my ill-conceived plot against your brother, we never would've gone out."

"We might have." But he didn't really believe that.

"I don't think so," she said. "We were too different."

While she'd caught his eye at the event, he'd initially dismissed her as not his type. Odd that they'd both nearly let their prejudices get in the way of something amazing.

"That means," she continued, "in a fateful twist, the revenge plot brought us together."

Harrison considered that for a long moment. "I guess it did."

"I'm glad. I don't regret a single second of the time I spent falling in love with you."

"You what?" Her admission was unexpected.

She looked surprised that he didn't know this already. "I've fallen in love with you." Her voice gained confidence as she repeated herself. Drawing her feet under her, she got onto her knees and cupped his face. "I love you, Harrison Crosby. You are strong and thoughtful and sexy and just the best man I've ever known."

Abruptly, she stopped gushing compliments and scanned his face, gauging his reaction. As their gazes locked, the last of Harrison's doubts washed away. This was the woman he was meant to be with. The proof was in the thunderous pounding of his heart and the exquisite openness of her expression.

This time, the impulse to put his arms around her was too strong. Harrison hauled her against him.

"I adore you," he murmured, burying his face in her hair. "You've shown me what's been missing in my life and I know now that I'll never be happy without you."

As their mouths fused, he felt as well as heard a half sob escape her, and then she was pushing into the kiss, her tongue finding its way into his mouth. He let her take the lead, enjoying the way his brain short-circuited as her hunger set him on fire.

His fingers dived beneath her sweater, finding bare skin. They groaned in unison as his thumbs brushed her tight nipples. He shifted their positions until she was flat on her back, her thighs parted and legs tangled with his. For a moment he ignored the compelling ache in his groin and smoothed silky strands of her hair away from her flushed face.

"I want to marry you," he said.

Her surprise lasted less than a heartbeat. "I'd like to marry you, too."

"You don't want to think about it?" He looked for some hint of doubt or hesitation in her manner, but only love and trust blazed in her eyes.

"I'm a better person when I'm with you," she said. "Why would I ever want to give that up?" She smiled then and it was the most beautiful thing he'd ever seen. "You're stuck with me."

"I'd say we're stuck with each other."

"And I don't want a long engagement."

"Lots of planes go to Las Vegas every day from the Charleston airport."

His suggestion briefly caught her off guard but then the most mischievous smile formed. "I'm feeling like the luckiest woman alive at the moment, so that sounds like a great idea."

He'd only been partially serious, but seeing that she was game, he nodded. In truth, he'd expected her to want to spend months planning an elaborate wedding to rival her friend's. "Just you and me?"

"Would you be upset if I invited Maribelle and Beau? I think she'd kill me if I got married without her."

"Let's give her a call."

"Later." London's lips moved to his neck even as she gave his butt a suggestive squeeze, pulling him hard against her. "Right now I want to make love with you."

Harrison nodded as his lips swept over hers, tasting her deliciously sweet mouth. As he wedged his erection against her, he could feel her smile and grinned in return as she rocked against him, inflaming both their desires.

Eventually he knew they would take things to the bedroom, but for now he was content to fool around on his couch like they were a couple of teenagers.

* * * * *

Reining In The Billionaire

Dani Wade

Dani Wade astonished her local librarians as a teenager when she carried home ten books every week—and actually read them all. Now she writes her own characters, who clamor for attention in the midst of the chaos that is her life. Residing in the southern United States with a husband, two kids, two dogs and one grumpy cat, she stays busy until she can closet herself away with her characters once more.

Books by Dani Wade

Harlequin Desire

His by Design
Reining in the Billionaire

Mill Town Millionaires

A Bride's Tangled Vows
The Blackstone Heir
The Renegade Returns
Expecting His Secret Heir

Visit her Author Profile page at millsandboon.com.au, or daniwade.com, for more titles.

Dear Reader,

I grew up on a farm and had a horse as a teenager (along with goats, cows, chickens and various house pets). Nothing on the scale of my Desire characters, but there was a certain peacefulness in being out in nature that much, a certain connection that can only be felt when caring for an animal's very existence. The circle of life as you attend births, nurse them through illnesses, watch out the window as they play and bury them with lots of tears. It's a very different life from my current suburban one.

That's why I'm excited to visit horse-racing country with the Harrington brothers! These men know the land, the animals, and the women who can give them exactly what they (think!) they want. Too bad for them love doesn't always play fair...

I love to hear from my readers! You can email me at readdaniwade@gmail.com or follow me on Facebook. As always, news about my releases is easiest to find through my author newsletter, which you can sign up for through my website at www.daniwade.com.

Enjoy!

Dani

I'm very blessed in this life to have a wonderful mother-in-law, who I watch give herself tirelessly to those around her every day. Kay, thank you for all you do for us. These books would not happen without the love, encouragement and sheer physical support you gift to me and our family day after day. I love you.

One

Finding out that the old Hyatt estate was available for purchase immediately—cash buyers only—had to be the biggest triumph Mason Harrington had ever experienced. After all, how many people got to fulfill their life's goal of owning a horse farm and get the revenge they'd ached for—all in one unexpectedly easy move?

"The foreclosure was just approved and finalized through our corporate offices," the bank manager was saying from across the polished expanse of his desk. His worried expression made him look more like a concerned grandfather than a business-man. "The family hasn't even been notified yet. There simply hasn't been time—"

"I'll be happy to handle that part for you," Mason heard himself say. *Oops! Was that too much?* From the look on the manager's face, probably. The nudge from his brother confirmed it.

Mason subtly leaned out of reach from his brother's sharp elbow, ignoring the creak of his leather chair. Kane might resent Daulton Hyatt for his role in ruining their father's reputation in this town, but Mason had been at ground zero for the man's nuclear meltdown.

He'd never forget the humiliation Daulton had dished out with satisfaction...or the pain of having EvaMarie watch without defending him.

If the memories made him a little mouthy...

"I have to say that the foreclosure went through against my wishes. I'd hoped to help EvaMarie turn things around," the manager said with a frown that deepened the lines on his aged face.

"Why EvaMarie?" Kane asked. "Wouldn't it be Daulton Hyatt who needed the help?"

The man's eyes widened a little as he watched them from across the desk. After a moment, he said, "I'm sorry. I spoke out of turn. I didn't mean to discuss personal details about my customers." He lowered his gaze to the printed paper before him. Mason had found the foreclosure notice on a local website. The bank hadn't wasted any time trying to recoup its loss. "But I just don't feel comfortable—"

"That doesn't matter now. The bank has already listed the property," Mason cut in. "Look, we are offering more than the asking price, cash in hand. Do we need to contact someone at the corporate offices ourselves?" Surely they'd be happy to take the Harrington money.

Mason could tell by the look on the manager's face that he most certainly did not want that to happen. But Mason would if he had to...

"We can have the money transferred here by this afternoon," Kane added. "Our offer is good for only an hour at that price. Do we have a deal?"

Mason's body tightened, silently protesting the idea of walking away, but his brother knew exactly what he was doing. Still, the thought of losing this opportunity chafed. The waffling manager was obviously trying to look out for the family, as opposed to the strangers before him, but right now Mason didn't give a damn about the Hyatts.

He cared only about making them pay for striking out at Mason and his family all those years ago.

He couldn't help but wonder how EvaMarie would look when he told her to get out of her family home...

Slowly, reluctantly, the older man nodded. "Yes. I guess this really is out of my hands now." He stood, straightening his suit jacket and tie as if steadying himself for a particularly unpleasant task. "If you'll excuse me a moment, I'll get my secretary started on the paperwork."

And he would no doubt call corporate while he went outside the office, Mason suspected, but it wasn't going to do him any good. What the Harrington brothers wanted, they often got. Usually it was from sheer bullheadedness. This time, though, they had their inheritance to back them up.

Money did open doors, indeed.

Mason still missed his dad, who had passed away about six months ago. It had been just the three of them for most of Mason's life, and they'd all been really tight. Learning of their father's cancer had been hard.

But it had only been the first surprise.

The fact that their mother had been the debutante daughter in a very wealthy family in a neighboring state had never been a secret to the boys. She'd died of brain cancer when Mason was around seven. He remembered so little about her, except how good she'd smelled as she cuddled with him and the silky softness of her hair. He would brush it for her sometimes, after she got sick, because it soothed her and often got rid of the headaches she frequently had.

Still, she'd been gone a long time. It had never occurred to either of the boys that she had left something behind for them. Hell—something? This wasn't just *something*, it was a fortune. Their father's careful money management had paid off in big ways, and he'd grown their already substantial inheritance into a monumental sum. Mason couldn't even think of the money in real dollar amounts, it was so excessive.

After all, sometimes they'd had to scrape the bottom of the barrel growing up. Like when Mason had lost his job at the Hyatt estate. They'd had to move back to his mother's hometown. Times had already been tough. Little had he and Kane known, their dad had been going without while planning for their future.

And their future was now.

After the secret came out, Mason had asked his father why he hadn't used some of the money to make life easier for him, for them. He'd said he never wanted to prove their mother's parents right—they'd always said he'd married her for money.

The brothers had been around horses all their lives. Their father had been a horse trainer with an excellent reputation for creating winners. He'd taught them everything he knew. They'd also both learned a lot from working in some of the best stables in the area, along with raising their own horses and cattle. Now, finally, they had the capital to purchase and establish their very own racing stables.

Oh, and get back at EvaMarie Hyatt for almost ruining his family at the same time.

"That look on your face has me damn worried," Kane said, studying him hard.

Mason stood, pacing the space that was relatively generous for a bank office but still left Mason feeling cramped. "I can't believe this is finally happening."

"You know Dad wouldn't want us to get back at the Hyatts for what happened almost fifteen years ago, right?"

It may have been close to fifteen years ago, but to Mason, the wounds and anger were as fresh as yesterday. Kane thought of it as a teenage crush, but Mason knew he had loved EvaMarie with everything he had at the time. Otherwise, it wouldn't still hurt so damn much.

"Yep, I know." But he could live with that. Simply seeing the shock on EvaMarie's face—and that dictator daddy of hers—would be worth a little blackening on his soul.

Right?

"Are you saying you've changed your mind?" he asked Kane.

His brother was silent, thinking before he answered. Mason admired that about Kane—it was a trait he lacked. Mason jumped first and worried about the consequences later. But as a team, their differences worked in their favor...mostly.

Kane turned to meet his gaze, his expression harder than before. "Nah. I say, go for it. But just a little warning, Mason—"

Mason groaned. "Aren't we a little old for you to jump into big brother mode again?"

"I am your big brother, but that's not it." He gave Mason a level look. "You need to keep in mind that there might be a good reason that they've lost the estate. They may not care what happens to it or who has it. I haven't heard any rumors about them financially except that they were downsizing a while back."

He shrugged at Mason's raised brows. "So I kept tabs. But we're out of the loop, except for a few old friends." He shrugged, his suit still looking out of place to Mason. They were used to flannel shirts and sturdy jeans. Dressing up wasn't the norm... but considering where this inheritance was taking them, they'd better get used to it.

Kane shook his head. "I don't know. I just have a feeling this isn't going to play out like you want it to."

Mason thought back to his awed impression of the Hyatt estate when he was a know-it-all eighteen-year-old. The opulence, the care EvaMarie's mother had put into every little touch. That house had been her life. Not that Mason had been allowed to see it. Officially, he'd seen it only once. He'd been told to take some papers to Daulton Hyatt at the big house. EvaMarie's mother had trailed after him, anxious in case he tracked manure on her antique rugs.

As though he was too much of a heathen to know how to

wipe his feet. The only other time he'd been inside, there hadn't been a parent in sight.

"You may be right," Mason conceded, trying to shake the memories away. "But trust me, they care. I remember that much all too well." And he was gonna use what he knew about them to his every advantage.

It paid to know thine enemy.

EvaMarie Hyatt didn't have a clue who was driving up to the house in a luxury sedan followed by a shiny new pickup truck. But as she spied out her bedroom window on the second floor, she fervently wished that whoever it was would go back from whence they came.

After all, she was sweaty and gross after hanging insulation inside the old dressing room between her suite and the next. Plus, she had a headache pounding hard enough between her temples to rival a jackhammer. And she was the only one here willing to answer the door.

Still, she smiled with the satisfaction of knowing all of her hard work would be perfect for what she had in mind.

But this wasn't the time for lingering admiration of her handiwork. She had to get herself in gear and head their visitors off at the pass. She scurried down the back stairs, hyperaware of her parents' location. They'd be interested too, but she knew good and well they wouldn't come outside.

It was so sad to see her once social butterfly parents now housebound. Their secrecy and embarrassment made EvaMarie's responsibilities that much harder…and much more painful.

She made it to the side entrance just as the vehicles parked. Unexpected nerves tingled through her as she attempted to smooth her hair into some semblance of order. Maybe her parents were rubbing off on her…or the isolation of taking care of every last detail of their lives was turning her into a hermit.

To her surprise, the bank manager stepped out of the first vehicle, his pristine suit making her all too aware of her dust-covered T-shirt and sweatpants. But it was the driver of the truck who confounded her.

She studied him as the two men approached across the now cracking driveway. He was a stranger, yet familiar for some reason. There was something about the cocky set of his shoulders, the confidence of his stride. As he came closer, the realization struck her like lightning.

She hadn't seen Mason Harrington in nearly fifteen years. Oh, she'd wondered about him almost every day since then. But she'd refused to let her curiosity turn into anything more. After all, she imagined she was the last person Mason ever wanted to contact him.

It looked like the years had been good to him. Even at this distance, she could spot the telltale features she'd found so attractive: the dark blond hair cropped close at the sides, but leaving just enough length on the top to showcase its inherent wave; large hands rough from working but with long fingers that could play her like the most delicate of instruments; the square shape of his jaw that belied the soft curve of his full bottom lip.

He was even taller now, filled out and muscular in a way that made her uncomfortably aware of him. As did the piercing blue gaze that found her with unerring accuracy. But it was the signature black cowboy hat that he swung up onto his head that was the nail in her coffin, confirming that she faced the boy she had wronged.

And now he was every inch a man.

Mason Harrington was someone she certainly didn't want near the house…or within miles of her father. Rushing forward despite her nerves clenching her stomach, she ignored the bombshell and focused on the manager. "Clive," she said, "what can I do for you?"

"EvaMarie, I'm afraid I have some bad news."

She wanted to look at Mason, see if he knew what was going on. Which was silly. Of course he did or he wouldn't be here. "I thought we had everything straightened out last month?" Oh, goodness. Please let this not be what she feared most.

"Well, I'm afraid corporate overruled us. As I mentioned then, everything has to be approved through them."

Her breath caught for a moment, then she forced herself to speak. "But I thought you said you knew enough people up there to get them to listen."

"I know, honey. Apparently I wasn't quite persuasive enough. I was going to call today, but got—" he glanced at the silent man next to him "—sidetracked."

EvaMarie hugged herself as her heart pounded in her chest. Nausea washed through her. She'd been alone through a lot of hard times over the past five years, but right now she wondered if there was a person alive who wouldn't let her down. "What does that mean?"

Mason stepped forward, his boots scraping across the driveway. "It means I'm the new owner of the Hyatt estate."

His voice had deepened. This was a man speaking. A man taking away what he had to know meant the world to her. She couldn't even look him in the eye. Turning back to Clive, she struggled not to beg. "I just need a little more time—"

"Too late."

Mason's harsh words made her cringe, but she tried to focus only on Clive. Breathlessly she pushed the words out. "But the mares will foal—"

Clive stepped forward, cutting off her view of Mason with a hand on her shoulder. "You know it won't cover more than a few payments," he said, his voice low and firm, even though his touch was gentle. "Then you'll be behind again. You've done the best you could, EvaMarie, but we both know you're only delaying the inevitable. It's time. Time to let go."

She shook her head, the words ringing in her ears. Time to admit defeat—to Mason Harrington. Her father would rather die.

For a moment, she almost gave in to the tears that had

plagued her for the last six months. She glanced over at the quiet, still barn in the distance. The surrounding lush trees had sheltered her since she'd first walked. The lake in the distance had seen her learn to swim and fish. The rolling hills had been her playground in her youth, her solace as she'd gotten older. Her mind conjured up memories of a time long ago when the picture before her had been bustling with employees, and horses, and visitors.

Not anymore. *No matter how hard she tried.*

Every time she'd thought she was making progress, yet another setback would stomp on her efforts. But this one was the crowning glory.

Now she zeroed in on Mason, surprised by his smug *I won* look. Obviously, he could remember a lot about this place, too. Part of her ached that he still hated her enough to find taking her home from her a worthy challenge. But a part that she didn't want to acknowledge found a tiny bit of solace in the fact that she could still touch him in some way.

She'd never be able to admit all the ways he'd changed her, even after he'd been gone. The thought was enough to have her dragging her stoic expression back into place, covering her true emotions, all of the frustration and pain she'd dealt with since he'd left, since her father became ill.

She felt so alone.

"So when do we have to be out?" she murmured, struggling to be practical. She wouldn't think right now about how it would feel, leaving the only home she'd ever known. That would lead to the breakdown she wanted to avoid.

Mason stepped fully into view, muscling his way around the bank manager. How he'd heard her, she wasn't sure. "As soon as possible would be great. You can work that out with Clive here, but first, I'd like to look over my purchase, please."

If she hadn't been struggling already, his complete lack of compassion would have taken her breath away. EvaMarie looked at the smug man, seeing again the few traces of the boy she'd loved with all her heart, the boy she'd given her body to, even though she'd known she couldn't keep him—and wished she had the courage to punch him in the face.

Two

Mason's crude satisfaction at besting EvaMarie and her family quickly transformed to dismay as he followed her into the house.

Bare. That's the word that came to mind as he looked around the entryway and beyond. It was like a gorgeous painting stripped of all its details, all the way down to the first broad brushstrokes covering the canvas. The basic structure was still there. The silver-leafed cabinetry, the crystal doorknobs, the delicate ironwork. But a lot of the decorative china and porcelain figures and landscape paintings he remembered from that long ago day had disappeared, leaving behind bare shelves and walls that projected an air of sadness.

They had entered the house through a side door, the same one Mason had been let into fifteen years ago. The long hallway took them past the formal dining room and a parlor, then a couple of now empty rooms until they came to a sunken area facing the back of the house. Apparently the family used this as a cozier living room, if one could call the massive, hand-carved limestone fireplace and equally impressive Oriental carpeting "cozy."

Upon closer inspection, the once pristine furniture had a few worn corners. But weirdly enough, what impacted Mason the most was the flowers. Not the ones in the overrun garden outside the wall of windows, but the ones in the vase on the table behind the sofa as they entered the room.

He vividly remembered the large sprays of flowers in intricate vases from his first visit, impressed as he had been with their color and beauty. They'd been placed every few feet in the hall and several in each of the rooms he'd glanced into and entered. But this was the first flower vase he'd seen today: a simple cut-glass one. Inside was an arrangement of flowers that looked like they'd been cut from the wild gardens. Pretty, but they were obviously not the designer arrangements of hothouse blooms he remembered.

Boy, the privileged had truly come down in the world.

Glancing over to the couple seated near the fireplace, he recognized EvaMarie's parents, even though they'd aged. Mrs. Hyatt was dressed for visitors. Mason would expect nothing less, though her silk shirt and carefully quaffed hair denoted a woman who hadn't faced the reality of her situation.

The pearls were a nice touch though.

"What's going on?" Daulton asked, his booming voice still carrying enough to echo slightly on the eardrums. "Clive, why are you here?"

The bank manager shook hands with the couple, then stepped back a bit to allow EvaMarie closer. Mason had thought he'd want to see this part, to witness the lowering of the high-and-mighty Hyatts. After all, they'd orchestrated the moment that had brought his own family's downfall.

Yet somehow, he couldn't bring himself to close in, to gain an angle that allowed him to see EvaMarie's face as she gave her family the news that their lives were about to change. Afraid he was softening, he forced himself to stand tall, knees braced for the coming confrontation. He forced himself to remember how his father must have felt that day when he'd had to tell Mason and his brother that he was fired from the position he'd held for ten years at the insistence of Daulton Hyatt.

That hadn't been pretty either.

"Mom, Dad, um." EvaMarie's voice was so soft Mason almost couldn't hear it. Yet he could feel the vibration in his body. EvaMarie's voice was unique—even huskier than it had been when she was young. She'd grown into a classic Kathleen Turner voice that Mason was going to completely and totally ignore. "The bank has sold the estate."

Mrs. Hyatt's gasp was quickly drowned beneath Daulton's curse. "How is that possible?" he demanded. "Clive, explain yourself."

"Daddy, you know how this happened—"

"Nonsense. Clive..."

"Corporate took this account out of our hands, Mr. Hyatt. There's nothing I can do now."

"Of course there is. What's the point of knowing your banker if he can't help you now and again?"

"Daddy." At least EvaMarie had enough spirit to sound disapproving. "Clive has gone out of his way to help us on more than one occasion. We have to face that this is happening."

"Nonsense. I'm not going anywhere." A noise echoed through the room, like a cane banging on the wooden floor, though Mason couldn't see for sure. "Besides, who could buy something so expensive that quick?"

Clive turned sideways, giving Daulton a view of Mason where he stood. "This is Mason Harrington from Tennessee. He and his brother started the purchase proceedings this morning."

"Tennessee?" Daulton squinted in Mason's direction. Mason could feel his pulse pick up speed. "Why would someone from Tennessee want an estate in Kentucky?"

Rolling with that rush of adrenaline, Mason took a few strides into the center of the room. "I'm looking forward to establishing my own racing stables, and the Hyatt estate is perfect for our purposes, in my opinion."

Mason could see the realization of who he was as it dawned on Daulton's face, followed quickly by a thunderous rage. He was proud to see this glorious, momentous thing that Mason himself had ignited.

"I know you," Daulton growled, leaning forward in his chair despite his wife's delicate hand on his bicep. "You're that good-for-nothing stable boy who put your hands on my daughter."

It was more than just my hands. Maybe he should keep that thought to himself. *See, Kane, I do have control.* "Actually, I am good for something...as a matter of fact, several...million... somethings..." That little bit of emphasis felt oh, so good. "And I'm no longer just a stable boy."

Daulton turned his laser look on his daughter, who stepped back as if to hide. "I told you I would never allow a filthy Harrington in one of my beds. I'll never let that happen."

"Oh, I don't need one of your beds," Mason assured him. "I just bought a nice, expensive one of my own. I'll just take the room it belongs in."

"You aren't getting it from me," Daulton growled.

This time, Mason matched him tone for tone. "You sure about that?"

The other man's eyes widened, showing the whites as he processed that this Harrington wasn't a kid who was gonna meekly take his vitriol. "The likes of you could never handle these stables with success," he bellowed. "You'll fold in a year."

"Maybe. Maybe not. But that will be decided by *me*." Satisfaction built inside as he said it, and he let a grin slip free. "Not you."

He could tell by the red washing over Daulton's face that he got Mason's drift. The older man started to stand. Mason realized he was gripping the side of his chair with an unusually strong grip.

"Daulton," his wife whispered in warning.

But the old man was too stirred up to heed her, if he even heard her in the first place. Mason felt his exultation at besting the monster of his dreams drain to dismay as Daulton took a step forward...then collapsed to the floor.

A cry rang out, maybe from EvaMarie's mom. But everyone rushed forward except Mason, who stood frozen in confusion.

With Clive's help, the women got Daulton turned over and sitting upright, though he was still on the floor. Mason studied the droop of the man's head, even as his back remained turned to Mason.

Kneeling next to her father in dusty sweatpants and a T-shirt, hair thrown up into a messy bun, EvaMarie still had the look of a society princess when she glanced over at Mason. Her calm demeanor, cultivated through hours of cotillion classes, couldn't have been more sphinxlike. "Could you excuse us for a moment, please?" she said quietly. She didn't plead, but her gaze expected him to do as she asked.

He'd never been able to resist that dark blue, forget-me-not gaze, always so full of suppressed emotions that he wanted to mine.

Then she tilted her head in the direction of the door to the hallway. For once, he didn't have that unbidden urge to challenge that came over him when he was faced with authority. Especially Hyatt authority. Obviously there was more going on here than he was aware of.

Turning, he let himself back out into the hall, wondering if he'd be able to forget the impression that his brother had been right. This wasn't going how he pictured it...at all.

EvaMarie could feel her hands shaking as she finally left behind the drama in the living room to face Mason in the hall. Out of the frying pan and into the fire, as the old saying went. Her body felt like she'd been put in a time machine. All the devastating feelings from that long ago confrontation in the barn— the day her teenage world imploded—had come rushing back the minute her father had raised his voice at Mason.

She'd spent a lot of time throughout her life walking on eggshells, trying not to light her father's fuse. By the time she'd grown a semblance of a backbone, the angry man he'd been had mostly disappeared. He reappeared only during times of high stress, and it was all EvaMarie could do not to give in to her childhood fears.

Now she had to face Mason—with no time for deep breaths or wrapping herself in invisible armor. Just hunkering down, enduring—just like most of her days now. The fact that he was actually here, in this house with her right now, seemed completely surreal, but the derision on his face had been very real.

There had been no doubt in her mind how he felt about her after all these years. She should take solace in the fact that he hadn't completely forgotten her. But she had a feeling she wasn't gonna feel better about him, or this situation, any time soon.

Maybe a little diplomacy would smooth the way...

"Congratulations, Mason," she said as she approached him with measured steps, trying not to take stock of the new width of his shoulders beneath a fitted navy sports jacket that she never would have pictured him wearing, even if it was paired with a pair of dark jeans and cowboy boots. Talk about surreal...

He turned from his study of the formal dining room to face her, then raised a cool brow. How could he portray arrogance with just that simple movement? "For what?"

"Obviously, you done well to be able to afford—"

"—to no longer be pushed around by people, just because they have more money than me?"

Her entire self went very still. His words told her everything she needed to know—how Mason viewed his childhood, their breakup and her in this moment.

It told her one other thing: he was going to find a lot of satisfaction in this scenario.

Maybe it would be best to focus on business. "So, what can I do for you?" she asked, though she had a feeling he wasn't gonna make it easy...

"That tour I mentioned." He waved his hand in the direction of the stairs. "Lead the way."

EvaMarie simply could not catch a break. She could almost feel his gaze as she took deliberate steps down the rest of the hall, pointing out various rooms.

He wasn't even subtle in his gibes... "Can't say I'm loving what you've done with the place. This version has taken the concept of 'simplify' to a whole new level, I believe."

She couldn't even argue, because she agreed with him. The state of her family home was a drain on her emotional equilibrium every day. But having someone else point it out...well, it certainly hurt.

Should she admit she'd sold off all but her mother's family heirlooms to keep them afloat? Yeah, his reaction to that would be fun. Just one more thing to mock her with.

So she kept silent on that topic, instead launching into a knowledgeable diatribe on the parquet floor pattern, imported tile and other amenities her father had spared no expense on. All the little details she'd spent a lifetime learning that would be useless once she was driven away—but for now she could use them to keep herself from admitting the truth.

She'd done what she could, but the estate was going under, and there wasn't a whole heck of a lot she could do to stop it.

"You're getting a good deal," she said, trying to keep any emotion from her voice.

"A great deal," he conceded.

Color her shocked.

They stood at the top of the back landing, facing a large arch window that gave a clear view to the stables and beyond. It was a mirror of the front of the house, which looked out over the drive and the wooded property between the house and the highway.

Mason studied the view. "Gardener?"

"Um, no," she murmured. "Not anymore."

"That explains a lot," he replied.

Stiffening, she felt herself close off even more. Though she shouldn't be surprised that he just couldn't leave it with the question. From the first words out of his mouth, she had expected his judgment.

"My brother and I would like to offer anyone on staff a job," he said, surprising her. "No need for them to be worried about their incomes because the place has changed hands." He stepped back to the landing, studying the first floor from his higher vantage point. "And we're obviously going to need some help getting things in order."

Yeah, no need for the staff to worry...only her family worried about living on the street... She ignored the implication that the property would need a lot of work to whip it into shape. She'd done the best she could. "That's very generous of you," she said, struggling not to choke on the words and the sentiment. "Currently we only have one employee. Jim handles the stables."

Mason stared at her, wide-eyed. "And the rest?"

"Handled by me."

"Cooking? Cleaning?"

EvaMarie simply stared, not liking where this was headed. Sure enough...

"Well, someone has definitely grown up, haven't they? I can remember days of you being waited on and pampered..."

Unbidden, she flushed. "If that's a backhanded compliment, thank you." She turned away, breathing through her anger as she stepped over into an open area that branched off into hallways to the various rooms. "The rest of this floor is bedrooms and baths, except for this sitting area."

"Your parents occupy the master suite?" he asked, his voice calm and collected.

Of course it was. After all, he wasn't the one being typecast.

"No. The stairs are too much for my father anymore. There's a set of rooms behind the kitchen. They sleep there." They were originally staff quarters, but she left that unspoken.

"I'll see the master suite, then."

She gave a slow nod, then turned to the short hallway on the left.

"Your father's illness?" he asked, for the first time using a gentle tone she didn't trust at all.

"Multiple sclerosis, though he prefers not to speak of it," she said, keeping her explanation as matter-of-fact as possible. No point in exhibiting the grief and frustration that came with becoming a caretaker for an ill parent. "We've managed as well as we could, but the last two years he's steadily lost his mobility and physical stability."

Her mother had declined also, though hers was from losing the stimulation, social gaiety and status that she had fed off for most of her life.

The grandeur of the master suite swept over EvaMarie, just as it always did when she entered. It was actually two large rooms, joined into one. Both were lined and lightened by hand-carved, floor-to-ceiling white wooden panels strategically accented in silver-leafing, the same accent that was used throughout the house.

With thick crown molding and a crystal chandelier in each area, the space left an indelible impression. Even empty as it was now.

She stepped fully inside as Mason strolled the cavernous space, his boots announcing his progress on the wood flooring. "There are his-and-hers dressing areas and bathrooms on each end of the suite," she explained. "Though the baths haven't been updated in some time."

"I'm sure we will take care of that," he said, pausing to turn full circle in the middle of the sleeping area. One wall was dominated by an elaborate fireplace that EvaMarie could remember enjoying from her parents' bed as she and her mother savored hot chocolate on snowy days.

She thought of the ivory marble bathtub in her mother's bathroom, deep enough that EvaMarie had been able to swim in it when she was little. It didn't have jets in it like the latest and greatest, but it was a gorgeous piece that would probably be scrapped, if the latest and greatest was what Mason was looking to put in.

Unable to handle any more of memory lane, she turned back toward the door to the hallway.

"And your room?" Mason asked from far too close behind her.

"Still on… On the other side of the floor." She held her breath, waiting on him to insist on seeing her room. Between them was Chris's room—*please, no more.* She wasn't sure how much longer she could hold herself together.

In an attempt to distract them both, she went on. "The third floor has been empty for years. There're two baths up there. A couple of the bigger rooms have fireplaces. Oh, and the library, of course."

His pause was significant enough to catch her eye.

Did he remember the one time that she'd snuck him in to show him her favorite place in the house? Long ago, she could have spent entire days in the library, only emerging when her mother made her come to the table. Maybe Mason did remember, because he turned away, back to the stairs.

"Another day, perhaps," she murmured.

As they hurried down the stairs, he didn't look back until he reached the side entrance, his hand wrapped around the Swarovski crystal handle.

"If there are any problems, I'll have my lawyer contact you."

She let her head incline just a touch, feeling a deep crack in her tightly held veneer. "I'm sure."

"It was good to see you again." His sly grin told her why it had been—because it had served his purpose.

She wished she could say the same.

Three

"The signing date is set. The property is almost ours." Mason grinned at his brother, then turned back to the lawyer. "You've been great. We really appreciate it."

James Covey grinned back, looking almost as young as them, though Mason knew he was a contemporary of their father. "It's been my pleasure. I'm thrilled to be able to help y'all like this."

His smile dimmed a little, and Mason knew what he was thinking…what they were all thinking. That they wished their father hadn't had to die for this to happen. Kane's hand landed with heavy pressure on Mason's shoulder, and they shared a look.

It wasn't all a bed of roses, but they would honor their father's memory by establishing the best stables money could buy and talent could attain, using everything he'd ever taught them.

It was what he would have wanted.

"So are we going to be running into the Hyatts every time we turn around in this town?" Kane asked as they exited the lawyer's stylish brownstone in the upscale part of downtown that had been renovated several years back. Slowly they made their way down the steps.

Kane had been gone for a week and a half, starting the process of training their new ranch manager to take over their Tennessee stables. They weren't leaving behind their original property, though it wouldn't be their main residence any longer.

"I don't think so," Mason said.

"Good, because that would be awkward."

Mason rather thought he would enjoy rubbing their newfound success in Daulton Hyatt's face, but he preferred not to confirm his own suspicions that he was a bad person. "I'm not even sure what's going on out there," he said. "When I went to tour the stables, no one was there except the guy we're taking on, um, Jim. I haven't seen the Hyatts…or EvaMarie…around town."

"Well, don't look now."

Mason looked in the same direction as his brother, spotting EvaMarie immediately as she strolled up the wide sidewalk headed their way. The smart, sophisticated dress and heeled boots she wore were a definite step up from the sweatpants he'd seen her in, yet he almost got the feeling that she'd put on armor against him.

He wasn't that bad, was he? Okay, maybe he was…

She paused at the bottom of the steep concrete stairs, her dark hair falling away from her shoulders as she looked up at them. "The landlady told me where to find you."

"Um, why were you looking?" Mason asked, ignoring Kane's chuckle under the cover of his palm. He also tried to ignore the way his body perked up with just the sound of her husky voice.

EvaMarie ignored his question and nodded toward the office behind them. "He's good."

"I know." *So there's no getting out of the deal.*

EvaMarie was obviously not daunted by Mason's refusal to relent. She extended her hand in his brother's direction. "You must be Kane?"

His traitor brother went to the bottom of the stairs to shake her hand and properly introduce himself, then he glanced at

Mason over his shoulder. "Gotta go. I'll see you back at the town house tonight."

What a wimp! Though Mason knew Kane wasn't running; he was simply leaving Mason to deal with the awkward situation of his own creation. The odds of EvaMarie simply happening by here were quite small, even though the town was only moderately sized with a large population of stable owners in the area.

Sure enough, she waited only long enough for Kane to disappear around the corner before turning back to him. "Could I speak with you, please? There's a café nearby."

A tingling sense told him he was about to be asked for a favor. Not that the Hyatts deserved one. After all, Daulton had shown no mercy when he'd had Mason's father fired from his job and blacklisted at the other stables in the area. He hadn't cared at all that his father was the sole support of two children. He'd only wanted revenge on Mason for daring to touch his daughter.

Mason would do well to remember that, regardless of how sexy EvaMarie might look all grown up.

The café just down the street was locally owned, with a cool literary ambience that was obviously popular from the crowd gathered inside. Bookshelves lined a couple of walls, containing old books interspersed with teapots and mugs. Tables and ladder-back chairs shared the space with oversize, high-backed chairs covered in leather. He glanced at EvaMarie, only to see her gaze sweeping over the crowd in a kind of anxious scan.

Though he refused to admit it, seeing her do that gave him a little pang. It seemed as though things hadn't changed too much after all. She still couldn't stand to be seen with him in public.

Struggling to stuff down his fifteen-year-old resentments, Mason was a touch short when he snapped, "Grab a table. I'll order the coffee."

"Oh." She glanced his way, her smile tentative. "Could I just get an apple cider please?"

Apparently she hadn't chosen the place for the coffee. As he took his place in line, he couldn't help but think how strange this was. EvaMarie wasn't someone he'd had a typical relationship with—though she'd been the only woman he'd had more than just sex with. That was a first—and definitely a last.

But they'd never been on a real date, just his graduation party with his high-school friends. Never really out in public. Mostly they had gone on trail rides together, holed up in the old barn loft and talked, sneaking stolen moments here and there when no one was looking.

Once he returned with their drinks, she fiddled with the protective sleeve on the cup, moving it up and down as if she couldn't decide if she wanted to try the drink or not. But she'd requested this meeting, not him, so he waited her out in silence.

Which only made the fidgeting worse. Why did he have to feel such satisfaction over that?

"I found a place for my parents," she finally said. "They'll be moving tomorrow."

"That's nice—is something wrong?"

Just as he'd known it would, his question only made her more nervous. She started to slowly strip the outer layer off the corrugated paper sleeve.

"No," she said, then took a big swallow that was probably still very hot, considering the way she winced. "I'm fine. I just…well, I didn't realize there would be so many people here at this time of day."

"Still embarrassed to be seen with me?" he asked. Then wondered why in the hell those words came out of his mouth.

She must have wondered too, because her eyes widened, her gaze darting between her drink and his. "No, I mean, that isn't the issue at all."

"Could've fooled me." He wasn't buying it. Especially not with too many bad memories to back up his beliefs.

"And my father's reaction didn't teach you any differently?"

That gave him pause, almost coloring those memories with a new hue. But he refused to accept any excuses, so he shrugged.

"Anyway—" she drew in a deep breath "—they chose to

move into a senior living facility so my mother would have help with my dad. The cost of getting them settled is more than I anticipated. I wondered about an extension on the house?"

"Nope."

He caught just a glimpse of frustration before her calm mask slid back into place. "Mason, I can't afford first and last month's rent on a place to live and to pay someone to move all of our stuff."

"Don't you have friends? You know, the old standby—have a nice pizza party and pickup trucks? That's how normal people do it. Oh, right, you aren't familiar with normal people—just the high life."

She looked away. He could swear he saw a flush creep over her cheeks, but he certainly saw her lips tighten. That guilty satisfaction of getting under her skin flowed through him.

She turned back with a tight smile. Boy, she was certainly pushing to keep that classy demeanor, wasn't she? "Honestly, I've spent the last two years taking full-time care of my father. I don't have any—many close friends. And while I'd like to think of myself as capable, even I can't move the bed or couch on my own. I just need—"

He opened his mouth, ready to interrupt with a smart-ass answer, when a woman appeared at EvaMarie's side.

"Oh, EvaMarie, you simply must introduce me to your handsome friend."

"Must I?"

EvaMarie's disgruntled attitude made him smile and hold out his hand to the smiling blonde. "Mason Harrington."

"Liza Young," she said with a well-manicured hand laid strategically over her chest. "I don't believe I've heard of you—I would most certainly remember."

The woman's overt interest wasn't something Mason was comfortable with—he preferred women more natural than Liza—but rubbing EvaMarie the wrong way was worth encouraging it. Besides, he and his brother were gonna need contacts. Liza's expensive jewelry spoke to money, her confident demeanor to upper class breeding. "I'm new to the area." He glanced across the table so he could see EvaMarie's face. "Or rather, returning after a long absence."

"Oh? And what brings you here?" So far she had completely ignored EvaMarie beside her, but now she cast a quick glance down. "Surely not little EvaMarie Homebody."

Okay, this wasn't as fun. Mason narrowed his gaze but kept his smile in place. For some reason, it was perfectly acceptable for him to pick on EvaMarie—after all, Mason justified that he had a reason for his little barbs—but this woman's comment seemed uncalled for.

"The area's rich in racing history," he explained. "My brother and I are setting up our own stables."

"Oh, there's two of you?"

No substance, all flirt. Mason was getting bored. "Lovely to meet you, but if you'll excuse us, we were discussing business."

"Business?" She threw a sideways glance at EvaMarie, who looked a little surprised herself. "Well, that makes more sense."

Liza giggled, leaning forward in such a way to give Mason a good look into her not-so-modest cleavage. He couldn't help but compare the in-your-face sexuality and lack of subtlety in a woman he had just met with the image of soft womanhood sitting beside her. EvaMarie was smartly dressed, and yes, he detected a hint of cleavage, but she hadn't flashed it in his face in order to get what she wanted. Of course, that thought reminded him of just how much of her cleavage he'd seen…and how much he'd like to see it again. Sort of a compare-and-contrast thing. He remembered her as eager to learn anything he'd been willing to teach her—did she still need a teacher?

Mason quickly reined himself in. There was no point in going there, since he had no plans to revisit that old territory. No matter how tempting it might be. Besides, EvaMarie was looking stoic again. Maybe he should relent—a little.

He stood, then pulled a business card out of his inner jacket pocket. "Well, it was a pleasure to meet you, Liza," he said, handing the card over. "I hope I'll get to see you again soon."

Liza grinned, then reached into the clutch at her side for a pen, wrote on the card and handed it back. "So do I," she said, then flounced back to a table across the floor where several other women were waiting.

EvaMarie had turned to watch her go, then groaned as she caught sight of the other women seated at Liza's table, all of whom were craning their necks to get a good look. "Well, I hope you're ready to announce your presence, because it's gonna be all over town in about two hours."

"That's the plan," Mason murmured. A glance at the card revealed Liza's cell phone number. With a grin because he knew how much it would annoy EvaMarie, he slipped the card back into his pocket. "Now, where were we?"

The pained look that slipped over her face as she opened her mouth, probably to start from the beginning, made him feel like a jerk. So he broke in before she could speak.

"Let me see what I can do," he said. Not a concrete answer, but he needed time to think. And a few more days of worry wouldn't hurt her.

Dang it!

How come Mason Harrington had to show up every time she looked like a dusty mess? Here she was desperately trying to pack like a madwoman with only five days to move, and he was interrupting with his loud, insistent knocking.

She seriously considered leaving him there on the doorstep, especially since it was raining. Her nerves were strained from the physical labor, emotional stress and learning everything she needed to navigate while losing their home, but a lifetime of training had her opening the door.

But she only forced herself to produce a strained smile. After all, she was exhausted.

"Mason, what can I do for you?"

His lazy smile was way too tempting. "That's not very wel-coming."

It wasn't meant to be. And she refused to be lured in by his teasing—a long time ago it had been a surefire way to shake her out of a bad mood. Instead of saying what she thought, she sim-ply focused on keeping her smile in place. But she didn't move.

He didn't own the place yet.

"Come on, EvaMarie. Let me in," he added, a playful plead-ing look to his grin. "I have an offer that will make it worth your while."

She hesitated, then stepped back, because continuing to keep him out was bad manners. That was the only reason. Not that she should care, but a lifetime of parental admonishments kept her in check.

Mason took a good look around the high-ceilinged foyer with its slim crystal chandelier, then walked farther down to peek into a few other rooms on either side.

"Wow. You've made progress." His voice echoed in the now empty spaces.

That's because I'm working my tail off. But again, that was impolite to say, so she held her tongue. She didn't bite it, be-cause she had enough pain right now. Though she'd taken on a large amount of the physical work around the estate, it had not prepared her for all the lifting, dragging and pulling of pack-ing up her childhood home. Her muscles cried out every night for a soak in her mother's deep tub, but even that didn't relieve the now constant ache in her arms, thighs and back. Definitely hard on her back but great for weight loss.

He glanced down the hallway toward the back of the house. "Is your father here?"

She shook her head. "Why? Worried?"

"Nope." Again with the cute grin, which was making her suspicious. Why was he being so nice? "Just didn't figure it was good for him to get all riled up."

For some reason, she felt the need to defend her parent, even though Mason was right. "He hardly ever does anymore. Not like he used to. He had a heart episode about six years back that forcibly taught him the consequences of not controlling his temper." She gave him a saccharine smile. "I guess you're just special." Or inspired a special kind of hatred maybe.

"Always have been," he said. If he'd caught the insult, he let it roll off him.

His nonchalant handling of everything she said made her even angrier. Luckily, she was used to holding her emotions deep inside.

"Actually, I finished moving them to an assisted living facility yesterday."

Mason's raised eyebrow prompted her to explain. "I chose to put them there because at least I'll know there's someone to look out for them. Even though I feel that someone should be me." The place had cost a small fortune, but she was hoping being out from under the crippling mortgage payments would help. Now, what did she do about herself? Well, she hadn't figured that out yet.

Hopefully she'd find something soon, or she might just break down in a panic attack. She hadn't been kidding when she said the first and last month's rental deposits put most places out of her range. The fact that she didn't even have friends she could call on to let her sleep on their couch made her feel lost and alone.

"Do you work?" Mason asked.

The change in conversation came from out of the blue. "What?"

"A job. Do you have one?"

His tone implied she didn't even know what one was. She certainly wasn't going to tell him about the new career she was building. He would probably think she was crazy or arrogant to believe she could make a living off her unique voice.

"Taking care of my parents and this place was my job," she answered, even though most people didn't view it that way. Mason probably wouldn't either, even though it had been damn harder than a lot of things she could have done. And asking one of the families they knew in the area for a job would have meant exposing her parents' failure to their world. She'd chosen not to go against their wishes.

True to form, Mason asked, "How'd that work out for you?"

"I did the best I could," she said through gritted teeth.

"Think you could do better with a better boss and actual resources?"

Now she was really confused. "What?"

He turned away, once again inspecting the rooms. "My brother and I have plans—big plans. To establish our stables is a simple matter of quality stock, training and talent." He turned back, giving her a glimpse of his passion for this project. Guess buying this estate wasn't only about revenge.

"Establishing a reputation—that's a whole different story," he said, his gaze narrowing, "and we don't have the breeding to back it up."

She knew all too well how hard it was to keep and make contacts within society here—after all, her father had kept his illness a secret in order to protect his own social reputation. It took two things to break into the inner circle around here: breeding and money. Preferably both. But they'd accept just the money if someone was filthy rich.

"We can fast-track it—after all, money makes a big first impression."

A surreal feeling swept through EvaMarie. Honestly, she couldn't imagine she was talking to the same boy who'd held her so long ago. Sure, he'd talked horses and racing. She'd known he'd wanted to own his own stables one day—but money had never come up. Then.

They'd both been naïve to think it hadn't mattered.

"Which means we will be turning this into a showplace," Mason said, sweeping his hand to indicate the room.

"What does that have to do with me?"

He cocked his head to the side, a lock of his thick hair falling over his forehead. "You've lived here all your life?"

She nodded, afraid to speak. His sudden attention made her feel like a wild animal being lowered into a trap.

"I bet you know this place better than anyone."

"The house and the land," she said, feeling a pang of sadness she forced herself to ignore.

"So you could come to work for me. Help with the renovations. Prepare for the launch. I'll even give you more time to move everything."

Her heart started to pound as she studied him. "Why?" Revenge? Everything in her was saying to run. Why else could he possibly want this?

"I need a housekeeper. I'm assuming you need a job," Mason said with a nonchalant shrug. "You need time to figure this all out. That's what you were asking for, right?"

Regardless, working with him every day? Watching him take over her only home and never being able to show her true emotions for fear he would use them as a weapon against her? The last few encounters had been experience enough. *No, thank you.*

She shook her head. "I don't think that's a good idea."

"You don't?" He stepped closer. "Seems to me you're about to be out of a home, income... What's the matter? Afraid your friends will find out you have to get your hands dirty for money?"

That was the least of her worries. Her parents had feared that—yes—but not her.

He moved even closer, giving her a quick whiff of a spicy aftershave. Why was he doing that? Suddenly she couldn't breathe.

"I'll give you a job and a place to live. Sounds a whole lot better than the alternative, don't you think? And in return I get someone who can make this renovation move even faster."

Looking into his bright blue eyes, she wasn't so sure she agreed. There had to be a catch in there somewhere...but she truly wasn't in a position to turn him down.

Four

EvaMarie smoothed down her hair, wishing she could calm her insides just as easily when she heard Mason come through the side door. From the sound of other voices, he wasn't alone.

This time she was prepared.

Or so she thought. First she caught sight of Mason's brother, Kane, who had filled out just as much as his brother. The two men were like solid bookends; carbon copies with broad shoulders and muscles everywhere. If only Mason's shoulders were available for resting on. How incredible would it feel to have someone to rely on for a change? To lean against his back, feel his bare skin against hers, run her fingers down along those pecs—

Whoops. Not the direction she should let her mind wander down right now. Especially as the three men before her all turned their attention her way. The middle one—slighter than the brothers—looked vaguely familiar.

Kane stepped forward, intimidating in his size and intensity, until a smile split his serious look. "Hello, EvaMarie. I'm Kane."

"I remember," she murmured, and shook his hand. What a

surprise. No smart remarks. No ultimatums. Looked like at least one brother could be reasonable. "Mason didn't say when you'd be joining us." She could sure use a buffer from his brother.

"Oh, I won't be moving in right away. I'm still tying up some loose ends at our base camp, and we invested in a town house when we were scoping out the landscape." He shared a glance with his brother. "But I'll be here soon enough."

The thought of being here alone with Mason set off a firestorm of nerves inside her.

"After I get the chance to work my magic on this place. I've been waiting years," the slender man said as he moved forward. He didn't have the bulk of the other two, but she could tell he made up for it with loads of personality. The good kind.

"Hello, EvaMarie," he said, holding out his hand. "It's been years since we've seen each other, so I don't expect you to remember me. I'm Jeremy Blankenship."

"Oh, yes. I thought you looked familiar. It's good to see you again..."

Now that she had a name to go with the face, her memories clicked. Jeremy was a son of one of the active horse racing families who had decided to go completely against the grain and attend school for an interior design degree.

"Can we move past the pleasantries and get to work, please?" Mason groused.

"You'd better get used to pleasantries and small talk if you plan on socializing much in this town," Kane warned.

Jeremy nodded his agreement before turning his gaze back to EvaMarie with questions in his soft brown eyes that had her tensing. "When I heard the Harringtons had bought the estate, I didn't expect to find you still here."

Before she could answer, Mason cut in. "EvaMarie will be overseeing a lot of the daily work and details for me."

Jeremy looked between them for a moment. "Oh, so are y'all together?"

"No." Mason's voice was short, but EvaMarie wondered if

that was a hint of satisfaction she heard. "When I say she'll be working, I mean it literally. As in, for me."

There it was... EvaMarie felt her face flame, blood rushing to the surface as she wondered how many other people he would find satisfaction in telling her new status to. Part of her wanted to crawl away in defeat, but she forced her shoulders back, projecting a confidence she was far from feeling. With any luck, this job would be a gateway to a new life for her. One that wasn't going to be at the same level as she'd had growing up, but despite what a lot of people were probably gonna think, she was fine with that.

At least she'd be one step closer to this life being *hers*.

There was no point pouting over what she couldn't change... yet. That was one thing life had taught her. The key was to simply put her head down and power through. "Jeremy, would you like a look around?" she asked, assuming that's why he was here.

"Would love it. After all, I can't interior design if I haven't seen the interior, right?" He smiled big, as if to show her his approval, then linked his arm through hers and led her down the hallway.

She might just like having him here.

Most of the rooms were just going to need new wall treatments, updated lighting and furniture. Uncomfortable at first, EvaMarie soon put forth a few tentative ideas and received an accepting reaction from all but Mason, who remained aloof though not outwardly antagonistic. She directed the little party around the downstairs, then into the kitchen and family room.

"This would be a great place for a leather sofa and big screen television," Kane said. "Right next to the kitchen. Perfect hang out space."

The discussion devolved into name brands and types of electronic equipment that had EvaMarie yawning. Then Kane climbed the three steps to the main kitchen area. The rest of them followed. EvaMarie tried not to cringe. This room had been in desperate need of a makeover for years. Its mustard yellow appliances and farm motif dated it from the early eighties at the latest.

"I want more extensive work in here," Kane said. "Stainless-steel appliances, new granite countertops, the whole shebang."

"My brother," Mason interrupted, "in this area, I give you free rein."

"That's because you don't want to starve," Kane teased.

Mason winked, pointing at his brother. "You are correct, sir."

Without thought, EvaMarie said, "Well, looks like one of you learned to cook."

The men glanced her way. Once more she felt that telltale heat in her cheeks. Maybe she'd gotten a little too comfortable—the last thing she should have alluded to was her one and only trip to the Harrington household when she was a teenager. That's when she'd realized that the extent of Mason's cooking skills included opening a box and the microwave door. Of course, hers weren't comprehensive, but her mother had the housekeeper teach her the basics. She'd enjoyed it so much she'd taken home ec and some specialty classes once adulthood allowed her to pursue a small number of her own interests.

"Well, we will definitely coordinate these two spaces so they flow together," Jeremy said, smoothly glossing over her sudden embarrassed silence. He gestured back toward the living area beyond the bar that served as a divider between the two spaces. "Do you gentlemen want a true man cave here or something more subtle?"

"Man, too bad there isn't a place for a big game room," Mason said. "We can at least watch the Super Bowl on a big screen here, but something more intense would be a great addition."

Kane nodded. "Pinball machines, a poker table, a wine cellar. Wouldn't that be awesome?"

"What are the odds of us getting something that's awesome?" Mason asked Jeremy with a grin.

"Well, all of these first-floor rooms are open to the hallway. How true to the style of the house do you want to hold to?"

The guys bantered back and forth, Mason's smile breaking through full throttle. For the first time, EvaMarie caught a true glimpse of the Mason she remembered. Oh, he was older, more ruggedly handsome. But that smile showcased the fun-loving, friendly resonance of his youth.

She'd missed it, as much as the thought scared her.

As they talked more and more about what would make a really cool splash in the house, EvaMarie could feel her stomachache growing. Ideas sparked in her brain…as did the voice of her father calling her a traitor. The push and pull of what should be clear family loyalties confused her. After all, her family had had a difficult time with what life had thrown at them. While losing their home was just part of that life, losing it to the Harringtons was unforgivable to her father.

She shouldn't be helping them. But she needed to do a good job, right?

"What about the basement?" she asked, the words bursting forth before she'd actually made up her mind.

The three men shared a glance, then Jeremy asked, "What basement?"

EvaMarie offered the interior designer a tentative smile despite her guilt and led the way back out to the breezeway. On the far side of the stairwell was a regular door that opened to a fairly wide set of stairs. She could feel Kane as he leaned around the doorway. "Looks promising," he said.

"What it's gonna look is dusty," she said as she started down, flicking the light switch on as she went. "I can't even remember the last time anyone was down here."

She'd actually forgotten about the space, which was currently used for storage. Probably a good thing. Thinking about packing and moving all the stuff down here too might have thrown her over the edge of what sanity she had left.

Funny the things you could block out to protect your mind in a precarious state, she thought.

"Wow. This is incredible," Jeremy was saying as his dress shoes clicked on the concrete floor.

"The open space runs under this half of the house," Eva-Marie explained, relaxing a little in the face of his enthusiasm. "Since the house was built into the hill, they finished this portion for the square footage. But with only the three of us, there wasn't any need for it."

As Mason's expression darkened, she decided it was time to keep her mouth shut again. The men explored, brainstorming all the cool things they would do down here, sparing no expense on Mexican tile and glass block room dividers and yes, a place for pinball machines. Her input was no longer needed. Not wanting to get in the way, EvaMarie wandered back the other way to the one room on the other side of the stairway. A large open entryway framed the room beyond like a picture.

The long-mirrored wall reflected the ballet bar attached at a child's level. She could also see her elaborate doll house closed up in the corner. The few stuffed animals she'd kept were resting safely in the wooden toy chest. This had been her own space when she was a little girl—a safe haven from her father's unreasonably high expectations and her mother's silent pressure to conform.

A safe haven, until her mother had created the library on the third floor the year she turned twelve. It had been her birthday present.

"Havin' fun?"

Mason's voice right behind her head caused her to jump. Her heart thudded, even though there wasn't any danger. Was there?

She glanced over her shoulder to meet his gaze. "Sure."

"Just don't have too much fun. You're here to work, remember?"

I don't think you'll let me forget, will you? Probably not the most appropriate response to an employer...

Kane paused on his way to the stairs to pat Mason's shoulder. EvaMarie could hear Jeremy's shoes on the steps as he ascended.

"This is gonna be great," Kane said with a grin before he headed up.

EvaMarie had marveled at the camaraderie between the brothers. After all, she hadn't had a sibling in a long time. Certainly not as an adult. Would Chris have stood by her through thick and thin? He'd been extremely protective of her, so she had a feeling he would have.

Only he'd never gotten the chance.

"You're lucky. It's wonderful that you have a brother like that," she said, her gaze trained on the stairs though her eyes remained unfocused, wishing for something she couldn't have.

"Actually, it's wonderful to have someone at your back when the world turns on you."

The sharp tone penetrated her thoughts, the pain catching her attention. She glanced Mason's way to find his glare trained on her, close and uncomfortable.

"Yes," she whispered. "Yes, it is."

As if he knew he'd made his point, Mason walked away, leaving EvaMarie with the uncomfortable knowledge that she'd reminded him exactly why he was here...and why she was here too.

For a few minutes she'd forgotten, and that could be detrimental in a lot of ways.

Then he glanced over his shoulder to deliver another dictum. "The furniture for my bedroom will be here tomorrow. You'll set it up good for me, right?"

Sure. She had no problem performing what should be a perfectly normal task. So why did it feel so intimate to her?

A few very rough days later, EvaMarie bent from the waist and let her upper body hang toward the ground in an attempt to stretch her aching back. Since the work in the basement was scheduled to start simultaneously with the upstairs renovations, she had a week to get it completely emptied.

Which wasn't nearly long enough to handle the relics from two generations—all by herself. Regardless, she still had to be ready for the moving team in two days.

Faintly she heard something through the sound of her own exertions and the radio she'd turned on to help keep her mind off how lonely this job was. Standing up straight, she cocked her head to the side, trying to get her bearings as the blood rushed down from her brain. *Was that footsteps?*

Crossing the room, she cut off the radio just in time to hear her name coming from the direction of the stairs.

Great. Just what she needed—Mr. High-and-Mighty, probably showing up to give her just one more task to demean her pride and heritage. He'd been unbearable these last few days.

Even though it irked her no end, sometimes she could almost understand. Being at someone else's mercy wasn't fun. And knowing that person could control the fate of your entire family? Definitely scary. Mason must have been so angry and petrified when he'd left here as a teenage boy.

But the constant interruptions and subtle—or not so subtle—digs as he demanded she clean out the garbage disposal, bag up and carry out trash, and clean his toilet, all while he watched with a smug expression had worn out her patience long ago. Hell, her father wasn't even this obnoxious.

She hadn't realized when she agreed to take this job that she'd be serving as his whipping boy.

"I'm in here," she called as she heard him walk past her childhood playroom.

He stopped in the doorway with a hard step, back tight, frown firmly in place. "Why didn't you answer me?" he demanded.

"I didn't hear you."

"What do you expect when you shut yourself away down here with a radio on? Anyone could have waltzed right on in and made themselves at home."

She studied him for a minute, trying to figure out where this irritating attitude had come from. "You told me to come down here and clean it out so Jeremy could get work started," she said, keeping her voice calm but unable to control lifting an eyebrow. "That's what I'm doing."

"Part of working for me is being available."

Okay, she'd had about enough. "To do what? Kiss your feet?"

"What?" he asked, his head cocking to the side.

"Look, this high-and-mighty attitude is getting old—"

"You don't like the new me?"

Not really...if he just weren't so darn sexy.

"Ah, can't say anything nice, huh?"

If you can't say anything nice, don't say anything at all. How many times had her mother admonished her with those words? "It's just unnecessary. I know you hate my guts, but wouldn't it be more pleasant to be civil?"

"No," he said with a grin that was just as smug as it was sexy. "I'm enjoying this just fine."

"I'm sure you are."

He took a few steps closer, managing to appear menacing even though the grin never left his face. "If you have a problem with me, you're welcome to leave. I'll even give you a day to get all of your stuff, and your family's stuff, out."

Right. She just stared, feeling her mask of self-preservation fall into place. She'd let him see way too much of herself by arguing with him. It accomplished nothing other than giving him more ammunition for pushing her buttons.

"What can I do for you then, *boss*?"

Mason smirked. He knew he had her right where he wanted her. "Come with me. You're gonna love this."

Probably not, but what choice did she have just yet? Soon though. Soon she'd have enough savings and steady work in her new career lined up to make it on her own. Until then, she simply needed to keep her head down and endure.

Of course, it didn't stop her exhausted mind from questioning what task he had in store for her now—and whether her already taxed body was up to snuff for it.

The worry didn't set in good until they'd already traversed the length of the upstairs hallway. Then she followed him out the side door and across the parking area in front of the four-car garage. They passed the gleaming pickup truck he drove and her own much older sensible sedan. Then he turned onto the path to the stables.

This couldn't be good.

EvaMarie had taken on a lot of physical labor since her daddy had gotten sick, but one thing she'd never done was the heavy lifting in the stables. Feed the horses or brush and ride them—sure. But that was the extent of it.

Plus, she'd already worked all morning packing in the basement. And the day before that, and the day before that...

Mason finally paused beside the stall where EvaMarie's mare Lucy resided. The satisfaction marking his face told her his anticipation was high. Too bad it was all at her expense.

No matter what, she wouldn't cry in front of him.

"We're bringing in our best mare later today from the home farm. Kane should be here this evening. I'll be back in three hours to make sure this stall is cleaned and ready for her."

EvaMarie studied him for a minute. Surely he was joking, pulling a mean prank. "But Jim's not here."

"You are." His expression said he wasn't budging.

Stand up for yourself. Automatically, her stomach clenched, nerves going alert just as they had her entire life. Taking a stand did not come naturally to EvaMarie. Her daddy had squashed that tendency when she was knee high to a grasshopper. "I don't do stables."

"Says who? Is that written down somewhere that I missed?"

Her jaw clenched, but she forced the words out anyway. "You know it's not."

"Welcome to the world of manual labor." He skirted back around her, heading for the barn door. Even the sight of that high, tight butt in fitted jeans didn't lift her mood. "Have it done in three hours," he called over his shoulder.

"I can't!"

Mason turned back with a frown. "Princess, employees shouldn't try to get out of work. It doesn't look good on their evaluations."

"But I'm already working. In the house."

"Good. Then you won't mind getting dirty."

Five

This was gonna be so much fun...

Mason eyed the man in the dark suit who stood near the side door to the house, staring at it as if he could divine who was inside through the exalted abilities of his birthright alone. The tight clench of Mason's gut and surge of anticipation told him that his body remembered this man well...and the role he'd played in the destruction of Mason's family all those years ago.

He hadn't actually seen Laurence Weston since he and Kane had returned to town, but Mason had hoped he would have the chance to rub the snitch's nose in his success at some point.

He just hadn't planned on doing it here at the Hyatt estate.

"May I help you?" Mason's words were polite. His tone... not so much.

Laurence turned to face him with an expectant expression that reminded Mason of his own youthful expectation of having everything go his own way. Laurence had felt the same, only exponentially, and he'd made it a point to let those "beneath" him know their purpose was to serve—and not much else.

"I'm looking for EvaMarie."

"Right." Mason turned for the stables, leaving Laurence to follow if he wanted.

At least, Mason assumed she'd still be out here. Was she capable of cleaning out a stall in three hours? A month ago, Mason would have answered with an emphatic "no," but he grudgingly admitted that EvaMarie had changed a lot since he'd last seen her. Other than knowing how to saddle a horse, the teenage girl he'd fallen hard for wouldn't have known how to work the business end of a shovel, or pitchfork, or rake... Though he hadn't been there to see the actual work, the adult EvaMarie had made some impressive headway inside the house this week, without any help that he could tell.

Which just irritated him even more. Why was she working so hard, staying so loyal to a family who had obviously taken her hard work and obedience for granted? Which led him to do stupid things like put her to work in the barn...

A glance into the stall showed that she was indeed capable of cleaning one in a few hours. The straw bedding and buckets were fresh and clean. There wasn't even a hint of manure in the aisle for Laurence to step in, darn it—Mason would have loved to see those Italian loafers ruined.

Petty, he knew. Just like giving the princess the job of cleaning the stables. But this man—when he'd been a boy—had deliberately told EvaMarie's father where to find them together, simply because he'd wanted EvaMarie for himself. Considering they weren't married now, it must not have worked out the way Laurence had planned.

As they moved farther into the cool, dim depths of the stables, Mason heard the low hum of a husky voice. His entire body stood up to take notice. Man, that siren voice had played along every nerve he had when they were dating, lighting him up better than any drug. Sometimes just talking to EvaMarie on the phone was as good as seeing her in person. Now he felt the same physical charge—no other woman's voice had ever affected him like that.

More's the pity.

She'd grown into its depth though. As she came into view talking to one of the mares in a stall farther down, he compared the wealth of hair piled on her head and strong, curvy body to the delicacy she'd possessed as a young woman. His daddy had said she wouldn't stand up to one good birthing.

Then.

Now she was a strong woman capable of handling what life dished up to her—*so why was he piling on the manure?*

Before he could do something stupid like voice his thoughts, EvaMarie glanced up, spying him over the horse's back. Her features expressed the weight of her exhaustion, emphasized by the dirt smudging her cheeks and the pieces of hay sticking out at odd angles from her hair. But her words were as polite as always. "The stall is ready."

Which was what he'd wanted, right? He'd set out to demonstrate the hard work he'd done for her father once upon a time. Teaching her a lesson was his aim in keeping her here, wasn't it?

So why didn't seeing her like this, exhausted and dirty, make him happy?

"Why the hell are you cleaning stalls?"

As Laurence's voice exploded in his ear, EvaMarie looked to Mason's left with wide eyes. "Laurence?" she asked.

The other man stepped around Mason and got a good look at EvaMarie's disheveled state. "What is going on, EvaMarie? You don't answer the phone. You don't show up for this week's committee meeting. And now this?"

Mason could feel the hairs on the back of his neck lift, hackles rising as another male attempted to assert himself in Mason's territory. And he wasn't at Laurence's mercy like he'd been as a kid.

"Shouldn't you be asking me that?" Mason said, stepping around to take a stand between Laurence and the stall door. "After all, I'm the boss around here."

Laurence's incredulous glance between the two of them almost made Mason laugh. Obviously this was something he couldn't comprehend. Finally Laurence asked, "And who are you, exactly?"

Mason wanted to smirk so badly. In fact, it may have slipped out before he caught it. "I'm Mason Harrington."

It took a minute for the name to register. After all, what need would Laurence have had for that nugget of information all these years? Then his eyes widened, his gaze cataloging the adult Mason. "And you're the boss, how?"

Behind him, Mason heard the stall door open, but he wasn't about to let EvaMarie deprive him of the joy of putting Laurence in his place. "I'm the new owner of the Hyatt Estate."

Laurence trained his hard gaze on EvaMarie. "How is that even possible?"

The rich never wanted to believe that one of their own could fall…unless the fall worked to their advantage somehow.

"The estate went into foreclosure, Laurence," EvaMarie said in a hushed tone. "We were forced to sell."

Mason braced his legs, arms crossing firmly over his chest. "And I simply couldn't wait to buy."

"Wasn't your dad just a jockey? A trainer of some kind?"

If anything, Mason's spine stiffened even more. "He was a one-of-a-kind trainer whose career you ruined with your little disclosure to EvaMarie's father all those years ago."

Laurence's gaze narrowed, but Mason wasn't about to let him get away without hearing the facts. "But it didn't matter in the end. Upon his death, my father left Kane and I enough money to buy this estate and start our own stables. Probably five times over." He took a step closer, edging the other man back. "We may have been easy targets back then, but threatening us now would be an unwise move…for anyone."

Laurence stood his ground for a minute more, though Mason was close enough to see the staggering effect his current situation had on Laurence. "How is that even possible?" he asked.

"I know it's hard to imagine someone bettering their circumstances through hard work—" and a lot of deprivation "—but the truth is, I earned it."

I earned it.

Those words rang in EvaMarie's ears as she ushered Laurence back toward his Lincoln. Mason was right—he'd always worked hard. Since she'd been working for them, it had become very obvious he and Kane had no plans to rest on their laurels and simply enjoy their money.

She couldn't help comparing Mason to Laurence, who had gone to a good school thanks to his daddy's money, coasted by and gotten a job in his daddy's real-estate business where he sold off of his personality when he actually tried, and let someone else handle the paperwork for minimum wage.

She wasn't immune to his faults, but he was the one friend who had stuck with her all this time, despite knowing some of the realities of the Hyatts' situation. He was also the only one her parents had let see what was really happening to them. Even though they were holding out hope she'd eventually give in and marry him, this was the one area of her life where she'd built a wall of resistance.

"How could you let this happen, EvaMarie?" Laurence asked, digging his expensive heels into the driveway to bring them to a halt. "All you had to do was call me. I could make all of this go away. Easily."

Only if she accepted his conditions. In that, he and Mason were very similar—every offer came with strings. Why Laurence was so insistent that he wanted her, she couldn't fathom. With his uninspired track record when it came to work, he should have given up long ago.

"I told you I can handle myself."

"By losing the family estate? Great job."

That stung.

"Why didn't you call me?" he went on. "Tell me you were in this much trouble?"

"It was my dad's decision whether or not to share. You know how careful he is. He didn't want word to get around."

Laurence shook his head, hands on his hips. "He's not gonna be able to hide it for long with those yahoos horning in."

That sounded like sour grapes to EvaMarie. "Regardless," she said, "I'm simply staying until everything is up to standards. By then, my plans will allow me to support myself."

"Plans to do what? Work yourself to death?" He grabbed her forearm. "Spend your days dirty?" He used his hold to give her a good shake. Her irritation shot through the roof. Laurence's voice rose to match. "Where do I stand in those plans?"

EvaMarie felt her backbone snap straight despite her fatigue. "Don't. Start."

His grip tightened, as if he was afraid she'd escape. He crowded in close, giving her an uncomfortable view of his frustration. Memories of several such confrontations with her father caused her stomach to knot.

"You know I can give you the life you deserve," Laurence insisted, his breath hot on her face. "Pampered and taken care of instead of cleaning up after your parents and that guy." His expression tightened with disgust as he assessed her with a sharp glance. "I mean, look at you."

Yes, look at me.

For a moment, just a brief moment, she was tempted to stop fighting and let someone handle life for her for a change. Tears of exhaustion pushed their way to the fore.

"It's what our parents always wanted," Laurence said, his voice deepening. It was low and husky in a way that left her cold. It shouldn't…but it did. But he was insisting… "We'd be perfect together."

Until the thrill of getting what he wanted wore off. Through years of dealing with Laurence, EvaMarie had learned he was like a big child who wanted a toy to entertain him and an adult to handle all the hard stuff. After the goal was accomplished, EvaMarie would simply be left taking care of Laurence, just as she did everyone else, and be expected to make his life as easy as possible.

Hers would be just as hard. Just as lonely. But he didn't see it that way.

"Everything okay?"

EvaMarie glanced to the side and saw Mason eyeing Laurence's hand on her arm.

Laurence glared, refusing to budge. "Yes," he insisted.

Ever the diplomat, EvaMarie reached up to pat his hand with hers, wincing at the unexpected pain in her palms. "Everything's fine," she agreed. Then she gave Laurence a hard look. "Goodbye, Laurence. I'll see you at the library committee meeting next week."

He looked ready to protest, but then adopted a petulant expression and let go of her arm. Because it was easier. Because in the end, he was still an overgrown child.

Which was evidenced by his defiant gunning of his engine on the way out. EvaMarie rubbed her arm, once again feeling that sharp pain in her palm. She glanced down, but one quick peek at the red, raw patches on her skin had her hiding her hands by her sides.

"Seriously?" Mason asked. "That guy is still around?"

EvaMarie tried to hide the exhaustion that was now starting to weigh her down like a heavy blanket. She just wanted a shower and her bed. If she didn't get inside soon, the shower wasn't happening. "Laurence is a friend of the family."

"But not part of the family? Bet that's a disappointment to your father."

He had no idea. The only thing her father continued to badger her about these days was Laurence. Though he wouldn't say it explicitly, Daulton saw Laurence as the answer to all of his problems. No matter where that left EvaMarie.

Too tired for more politeness, she headed for the door. Mason could follow or not. "There's a great many things I do that are a deep disappointment to my father," she mumbled.

Her choices had always been wrong—ever since her brother had died. The smiling, applauding father had long ago turned into the disapproving dictator. Illness and age had quieted him, but not mellowed him. "Anyway, Laurence is just looking out for me."

"Don't you mean looking out for his investment?"

She skidded to a stop on the tile in the foyer. "What?"

"Well, he's put a lot of years into pursuing you. Wouldn't want all of that effort to go to waste."

"Effort isn't even a word in his vocabulary." If Mason thought any different, he didn't know Laurence at all.

But she might have underestimated Mason. He quirked a brow as he said, "Ah, I see you've gotten to know him quite well. Took you a while."

No, she'd always known how Laurence was. Only no one had trusted her to make the right choices, only the easy ones. They'd expected her to give in to her parents' demands and marry the man they wanted for her. She might have given up a lot in her lifetime, but that choice was not one she was willing to let go of. She did have boundaries, even if no one else bothered to see them.

Or respect them.

Wearily she made her way up the stairs, her feet feeling like lead weights. If only she could pull on the banister for support, but she had a feeling her hands wouldn't appreciate the pressure. "Good night, Mason."

"Wait. Why are you stopping for the night?"

Because I can. She didn't answer at first, just kept on going with all the energy left inside her.

When she reached the landing, she finally repeated, "Good night, Mason," and dragged herself to her room.

That man was like arguing with a brick wall.

Six

Mason winced as he bumped into the banister in the dark, then wondered why on earth he didn't turn on the lights before he fell down the back staircase.

Nightlights were placed at intervals along the hallway, but didn't help him with the unfamiliar spaces and shadows. Lightning from the thunderstorm beating the house from outside lit up the nearby arched window, giving him a chance to locate the light switch. The hanging chandelier lent its glow upstairs and down, allowing him to make better progress on the stairs and in the hallway.

As he approached the family room, he heard a noise. Looked like it was time for a little midnight tête-à-tête with his roomie.

As he made his way through the darkened family room into the kitchen, with only a faint light burning above the stove, the muffled sounds he'd heard morphed into husky curse words that were creative enough to raise his brows. Apparently the princess had gotten herself an education while he'd been gone.

This should be interesting.

Flicking on the overhead lights, the first thing he noticed was legs. Bare legs.

EvaMarie stood next to the bar in a nightgown that barely reached midthigh. Beside her were open packages and what looked like trash strewed across the counter. She blinked at him in surprise...or maybe it was just the bright lights.

Mason stepped closer. "Problem?" he asked, unable to keep the amusement from his voice.

If she'd been a kid caught with her hand in the candy jar, she couldn't have turned redder. Her body straightened; her hands slid behind her back.

"Nope. Everything's fine."

Right. Her shifting gaze said she had a problem, just one she didn't want him to know about.

He stalked to her, even though he knew being close to all that bare skin wasn't the best idea he'd ever had. But seeing the first-aid kit in the midst of all the wrappers, he realized this wasn't the time to play.

"All right. Let's see it," he said, his tone no nonsense. "After all, we don't have time for you to be off duty."

Those dark blue eyes, so thickly lashed, couldn't hide the wash of tears that filled them. Alarm slammed through his chest. He could handle a lot of things, power through just about every situation. But put him in the vicinity of a woman's tears, and he was hopeless.

Luckily she blinked them back, but then murmured, "It'll be fine." Her lashes fell and skimmed the flushed apples of her cheeks. "I'll be fine by morning. Just go back to bed."

Even Mason wasn't that self-centered. Gentling his voice, he said, "Just let me have a look, Evie. Okay?"

Her eyes connected with his. He saw his own surprise reflected there. He hadn't called her that name in too many years. But it worked, because her hands slipped from behind her back, as though she instinctively trusted that connection.

For once, he refused to use it against her. She didn't need that right now.

Or ever, his conscience chastised him.

Pushing his conscience aside to deal with later, he cupped her hands in his and turned them over so he could see the palms. "Holy smokes, EvaMarie. Why didn't you wear gloves?"

He could feel her stiffen and try to pull back. Her fingers curled as if to protect the wounds from his judgment. "I did," she insisted. "The only pairs I could find were all too big. They kept slipping against my skin."

Alarm mixed with a darker emotion, deepening his voice. "I can see that. Looks almost like you have carpet burn on your palms. Let me have a better look."

As he led her over to the stove so he could get some direct light, she said, "I cleaned them as best I could in the shower, but the soap burned—"

"I bet."

"My wounds weren't that dirty. The gloves kept the dirt out for the most part. But I think they need to be wrapped." She glanced over her shoulder at the mess on the bar. "Only it's kind of hard to do one-handed."

And it hadn't occurred to her that there was now someone else in the house she could ask to help her. Why should it? His conscience flared up again. He'd proved pretty well so far that his job was to make her life harder, not better.

He cradled one of her hands in both of his, bending closer for a good look. Memories of holding her hand abounded, but he couldn't remember if he'd ever examined her there in this much detail. He was pretty sure those calluses on her palms and fingertips hadn't been there before. The skin along the back still felt silky smooth and smelled faintly of lilacs. Was that still her favorite scent?

And when he noticed the faint outline of curvy, muscled legs down below the bar, his body went a little haywire. The mix of past and present was throwing him off balance.

For a moment, he could almost understand her father's protective nature, the desire to shelter her from harsh reality—though Mason could never forgive the lengths her father had gone to achieve that aim. No one deserved to have their life ruined like that, not Mason, not his father.

As he surveyed the abraded skin, the damage done by his own selfishness, a strange compassion kicked in. One he almost resisted, almost ignored. Man, it sucked to realize his brother had been right. They'd been joking with each other, but Mason *had* done a bad thing.

"Let's get these wrapped up so they don't get dirty. I think they'll heal in a few days, but we don't want infection getting in where the skin is broken." He turned back to the bar, breaking their physical connection. The cool air he drew into his lungs cleared his head. The sound of the rain outside ignited thoughts of starting over.

As long as he didn't let himself get too close, get drawn into the attraction that flirted behind the edges of his resentment. Therein lay the real danger he needed to protect himself from.

"Then how about I make some hot chocolate?" he asked, remembering it as her favorite drink. "That'll warm us up before trying to sleep."

"So you have learned to cook?" she asked, cautious surprise lightening her voice.

"No, but I make a mean microwave version."

EvaMarie held herself perfectly still.

Her insides jumped and shivered with every touch of Mason's fingers against hers, but she refused to let it show. Part of her wanted to relax into his newfound compassion. After all, she remembered an all-too-nice version of Mason that she wished would come back.

But the bigger part of her couldn't forget his behavior since his return. Better not to trust that this version would last longer than it took to feed her hot chocolate and send her to bed like a child.

Maybe that was the key—treating her like a child. After all, he didn't seem to care for the grown-up version of her too much.

His touch was amazingly gentle as he applied a thin coating of antibacterial ointment to each palm, then set about wrapping her hands in gauze and tape. Memories of other times he was gentle, like the night she offered him her virginity, pushed against the barriers she had erected to block them out of her brain. What good would it do to relive those times? After all, he hated her now. Thinking about it would get her nothing but grief.

But she'd pulled out the memories of their loving often over the years. Mason had been her first, and best, lover. Her one experiment in college to replace those memories had proved a disappointment. So her time with Mason was all she had to live on during the long, lonely nights of her adulthood. But she had learned one lesson from that lackluster experience in college: settling for something less than what she'd experienced with Mason wasn't worth the trouble.

Which had kept her from making several stupid choices that would have easily gotten her out of this house years ago. Like marrying the man who had pestered her to do so since she'd turned eighteen.

EvaMarie's suspicions grew as Mason deposited her at the nearby table, cleaned up all the wrappers and discarded bandages, then went to search in the pantry. Some food had been delivered on the same day as his furnishings and personal items, but she didn't remember any hot chocolate mix. But sure enough, he pulled out a round brown canister with gold lettering: a specialty chocolate mix, her one indulgence.

The awkward silence in the room, broken only by the sounds of Mason and the rain outside, urged her to do the polite thing and speak. But what subject wouldn't be fraught with unexploded land mines? As she studied the expert wrapping on her hands, she knew she had to try.

"So I suspect that your purchase of the estate is the talk of the town, or will be soon," she said, her voice hushed in deference to the night and the storm outside. For some reason it just seemed appropriate, even if a touch too intimate. "It's really incredible, Mason. I'm proud of you and Kane for being so successful."

And she was. Her one visit to the Harrington farm when they were dating had shown her just how different their lifestyles were. Mason's family hadn't lived in poverty, but their situation had probably been what EvaMarie now knew as living paycheck to paycheck. Mason's dad had cooked her a simple meal of homemade fried chicken, and macaroni and cheese from a box. It had been good, and the atmosphere around the table had been friendly and welcoming.

Mason hadn't been able to understand when she said it was the most comforting night of her life. He hadn't understood what life was really like for her...and she hadn't wanted him to know the truth.

"I know your dad must be too," she added.

Mason turned away from her as the microwave dinged. "Actually, my father's dead."

"Oh, Mason. I'm so sorry."

He was silent for a moment before he asked, his voice tight, "Are you?"

"Yes. He seemed like a nice man."

"He was. He didn't deserve the lot he had in life. Constantly undermined and unjustly ridiculed by people who didn't even know him, but who had all the power."

The spoon Mason used to stir the hot chocolate clanked against the side of the cup with a touch more force than necessary. EvaMarie winced, knowing that he was talking about her father, and his father's former employers. She held her breath, awaiting a return of the snarky, condescending man he'd shown her since his return. Instead, he crossed the kitchen and set the mug before her without comment.

She wasn't sure how to respond, so she remained quiet. The steam from the cup drew her. She wrapped her aching hands around the outside, letting the heat slip over her palms into the joints, then up her arms. So soothing… "So he left you an inheritance?" she asked, hoping to steer him away from the touchy subject.

"Actually, it was my mother."

EvaMarie nodded, though she'd never heard much about the woman before. Lifting the cup close, she breathed in the rich chocolate scent. The comforting familiarity cloaked her in the very place where familiarity seemed to have gone out the window. This was her kitchen, the one she'd drunk hot chocolate in all her life, but it wasn't hers anymore. And the man next to her wasn't hers either.

"We moved back to Tennessee where she was from, though my grandparents on her side wouldn't have anything to do with us for the longest time. My grandfather never did come around."

"Why?" She couldn't get out more than a whisper and found herself grasping the mug just a little tighter.

"They were high society, lots of money." His glance her way said *sound familiar?* "They never approved of the marriage, or the fact that their daughter died after he took her away."

The level of Mason's resentment after all these years was starting to make a little more sense. "They wouldn't come see her?"

Mason shook his head, his hands clenching where they lay on the table. "My father even sent a letter after receiving her diagnosis. He knew it was bad. My grandmother later told him her husband refused to allow her to open it. They didn't see her before she died."

A stone-like weight formed in EvaMarie's chest. "How awful."

"My mother had a sizable trust fund created for us. Over time, my father managed to grow it out of proportion to what she left us. But he never touched it."

Considering how much they had struggled after his father lost his job, EvaMarie couldn't imagine that kind of sacrifice. But she daren't mention it for fear it would make Mason angry again. This small moment of civil conversation was a gift she didn't want to squander.

"He told us about it after his first heart attack. Helped us decide what to do and taught us how to manage it. It was—" he paused, shaking his head "—*is* still amazing to me."

"That's an incredible gift," she said.

"Yes. And he was an incredible man."

Indeed. To have taken such care with his wife's gift for her sons, even when it made his own life harder than it had to be—that was a true father. EvaMarie struggled not to make a comparison to her own father, to the lack of foresight he'd exercised, but her heart remained heavy.

As she sipped, the downpour outside quieted to a light, steady rain, soothing instead of boisterous. The ache in her palms had subsided some beneath the warmth and care of her bandages. And Mason had surprised her. They hadn't talked, truly talked, in many years. She shouldn't be enjoying it this much.

Her eyelids drooped. The day had been a long, hard one. And she'd start an even busier one tomorrow on even less sleep. As much as she wanted to savor this truce while it lasted, it was time she headed back to bed.

Standing, she glanced across at Mason, only to catch him surveying her bare legs. Almost as quickly he looked up, but she pretended not to notice. "Um, I think it's time I headed back upstairs," she said. Then trying to smooth over the awkwardness, she asked, "Is your room set up all right?"

"Yes, thank you, EvaMarie."

She tried to squash the glow that blossomed at his words, but couldn't. Tomorrow, he'd kill the glow soon enough.

"Well, good night. Thank you for the hot chocolate and, well..." She nodded toward her hands.

Mason stood, as well. "It's the least I can do, EvaMarie."

She took a few steps back, then paused. "Until tomorrow." She turned and made quick progress toward the hall. She'd almost made it when she heard him behind her.

"EvaMarie."

Heart pounding, though she knew it shouldn't, she glanced back. "Yes?"

"You have a storage building already, correct?"

And just like that, they were back to boss and employee. Why did tears feel close all of a sudden? "Yes. I promise all arrangements have been made and the moving guys will be here on Wednesday to have everything out in time for the renovations to start."

He stepped closer, looking mysterious as the darkness hid his expression. "Actually, a moving crew will be here tomorrow to help you. All you have to do is direct."

The bottom dropped out of her stomach like she'd taken a fast-moving elevator. "What?"

He didn't move, didn't speak for a moment. Then he let out a deep sigh…one she'd almost mistake for regret. "Just consider it hazard pay."

Seven

"I'll be on the second floor if you guys need me for anything, okay?" EvaMarie said.

"No problem. Thanks, Miss Hyatt."

With a deep breath, EvaMarie headed up the stairs from the basement, skirting the carpenters already measuring for their plans to widen the entryway. Sad to say, but she'd rather be down there helping with the packing, even with her sore palms. But she had another job waiting for her.

With the extra help, her family's belongings were going into storage a lot quicker than she'd anticipated. Which meant she had to get her brother Chris's room cleaned out ASAP. She was surprised Mason hadn't asked about the other empty room on this floor, but she was grateful. She didn't want movers in there.

Yet cleaning it out herself wasn't a task she was looking forward to.

Her hand trembled as she reached for the doorknob. As if this wasn't gonna be hard enough.

"Is this where you'd like the boxes, Miss Hyatt?"

EvaMarie almost jumped, but caught herself before turning

back to the young man. "Yes, please." After he set them and some tape down in a neat pile, she added, "Thank you so much for bringing those upstairs."

"No problem."

His gaze flicked to the still-closed door before he turned back toward the stairs. He might be curious, but he wasn't going inside. No one had been inside that room except her and her mother for over twenty years. Not even her father.

Turning back, she took a deep breath and forced herself through the door. A quick glance told her everything was the same. A small part of her had wondered if her mother would take something from the room with her when she left, but it didn't look like she had.

In fact, the room remained exactly as it had been when Chris had died in a tragic car accident here on Hyatt land. He'd been fifteen. The emotions of that day stood out so vividly in EvaMarie's mind, though the actual images were mere shadows now. She'd been angry with her brother because it was one of those rare times he'd refused to let her tag along on his adventure. It was one of the few times he'd disobeyed their father. He wasn't supposed to be in the vehicle unsupervised.

While he was out, he'd lost control of the truck, and it plunged headfirst into a ravine. His chest had been crushed against the steering wheel. By the time anyone found him, he was gone from her forever.

But his room remained full of old-school video games and a huge television, the best model from that time. Horses were everywhere, whether it was pictures or his collection of carved wooden figures. While Chris had been a typical teenage boy, he'd loved the family's animals and looked forward to taking over from their father someday.

A Tennessee football bedspread and pillowcases. A BB gun and his very first rifle on the gun rack above the bookcase. Even a pair of discarded cowboy boots peeking out of the barely open closet door. How did she even begin to pack away the life of someone she loved and missed so much—even to this day?

She picked up the photo box she'd brought in the other day, along with some trunks to pack away the more valuable keepsakes, and walked over to the wall beside the bed. Pictures of Chris at various sporting events and horse shows, some of him alone, some with her or their parents, were barely hanging onto the wall. The tape had deteriorated over time. One by one she took them down, removed what adhesive was left and packed them away in the box. Her mom might not want them now, but eventually she might. EvaMarie had long ago made secret copies of the originals for the scrapbook she kept in her room.

"Whatchya doing?"

Whirling, EvaMarie tilted off balance before righting herself for a good look at Mason. "Oh, I thought you were gone for the day."

He shrugged, but his gaze steadily cataloged the room around them. Her hands tightened on the box until the edges cut into her bandaged palms. She didn't hide her wince soon enough.

"I took care of some stuff in town," he finally said. "Then I came back to see how things were going. Looks like they are making steady progress in the basement."

Her voice was breathless as she tried to justify herself. "Yes, I planned to get back down there—"

Again that nonchalant shrug. "You did fine. They were very clear on what you wanted done. You've gotten everything pretty organized."

"I try," she murmured. It felt weird to acknowledge the compliment, as if she needed to search for some hidden insult. After last night, she wasn't sure what to expect.

Or quite how to react.

"How're the hands?"

"Better." She gestured with the box. "Awkward."

"I'm sure. Let me know when you need some new bandages."

Which just reminded her of the two of them in a dimly lit

kitchen and how she had been half-dressed. That had been an ill-timed choice, but when your hands were on fire and you needed to get to the first-aid kit, putting on pants moved low on the priority list. At least he hadn't seemed to mind...

A flush swept up her body and bloomed in her cheeks. She nodded and turned away, anxious to hide her reaction.

Behind her, she heard him moving, prowling the space. She bit her lip. Though she knew the reaction was unfounded, part of her ached to stop him. Her mother wasn't here to care that there was a stranger in Chris's room, but it still felt wrong.

"Can I ask whose room this is?"

Despite his gentle tone, despite last night, she was still afraid to say. Afraid of the condemnation or judgment that might come from the revelation. But it wasn't as though she could hide it with him standing right behind her.

Gathering the last of the pictures into the box, she carefully put the lid on top and laid it on the desk near the door. "This room belonged to my brother, Chris."

Mason's slow nod didn't give her a clue as to his thoughts. "You've never mentioned him before."

No, she hadn't. Not even when she and Mason had been close. So his accusing tone was justified—this time.

How did she begin to explain that it was a barrier her parents had put up that she was almost afraid to cross? Especially since her own grief, never properly expressed, might have broken through the dam if a crack had ever appeared. Even now, she wasn't sure what openly experiencing her grief would have been like.

"My parents—" she cleared her throat, trying to loosen the constriction "—they never talked about him."

He shook his head. "How is that even possible? Not to talk about your own child?"

Now it was her turn to shrug, because she didn't understand it as well as she wished she did. Even now, she couldn't explain her tight throat or pounding heart. It made no logical sense, but the sensations were there, nonetheless.

Still, she forced herself to speak. "Once we came home from the funeral, he wasn't ever talked about again. Everything about him disappeared, except this room," she said, glancing around with a covetous look. "As if he didn't exist—at least, it felt that way."

She stroked a finger down a picture of Chris on his favorite horse that sat framed atop the desk. "Only I know that wasn't true. At least, not for my mom."

"How?"

She pursed her lips before she spoke. "Because mine is the next room over. I could hear her crying in here some nights." She took a shuddering breath, remembering the eerie, sad sounds. "But no one mentioned it in the morning."

Behind her, she could hear him moving but was too caught up in her emotions to turn around.

He asked, "So you were old enough to know him, to remember it?"

EvaMarie turned around and nodded. "He was quite a bit older than me, but the age gap didn't keep us apart. Chris took me everywhere with him. Taught me to ride horses, swim. We were rarely apart. He was my champion." Her voice trailed to a whisper. "My protector."

He'd protected her from their father and his demands for perfection, even at her young age. After Chris's death, her father had become her jailer. For a long time, she'd understood the need to keep his only living child safe. Until Mason. Until she'd become desperate to finally live.

"I don't remember hearing about his death, but then I'm only a couple of years older than you."

"It was sudden, a car accident here on the estate. When something isn't talked about by the family, and no one dares ask, it becomes a matter of out of sight, out of mind."

A few steps brought him closer, almost to within arm's

length. EvaMarie was amazed at how desperately she wanted him to close that distance, to hold her against him until the sad memories dissolved.

"But why would *you* never tell me?"

Her gaze snapped up to meet his. Unnerved by the intensity of his stare, she swallowed. For a moment, she considered giving some kind of flippant, casual answer. But something about that intensity demanded a true reason.

So she gave it. "You'd be amazed, I'm sure, at how deeply a family's darkest moments can be buried. When something makes you happy, the last thing you want to do is remember the bad times."

Which was why she'd never been completely honest with him about her father, even. Yes, she'd warned him they needed to be careful. That she wasn't allowed to date. That her father would probably run Mason over with his truck if he caught them together—if he didn't get his gun first. But she'd never told him that her father scared her. That he controlled every last second of her life, demanding that she be the perfect, compliant child.

Because she didn't want to taint their time together with the darkness she lived with every day.

Her chest tightened, threatening to cut off her air supply. Time to change the subject. "Thank you, Mason."

"For what?" he asked with a slight tilt of his head.

"For listening, letting me talk about him." The words were rushed, but if she didn't get them out quick, they wouldn't come at all. "Though I wish I'd had more years with him, I try to remember how he lived while he was with me."

His slight smile told her he could relate. "My father always said, the least we could do to honor my mother was to keep her alive through our memories, to keep her a part of our family. He talked about her until the day he died."

"I wish we had." EvaMarie's heart ached as she looked over her brother's possessions. "I'm so out of the habit now…it feels weird." She lifted her head. "And it shouldn't."

And somehow, she'd find a way to change this…just like she was changing a whole lot of other things in her life. So with a deep breath, she got started packing.

Mason followed his brother into Brenner's, breathing in the smell of grilled meats and a real wood-burning fire. This wasn't a touristy place but had a huge local following—off the beaten path.

Though they had a varied menu, their steaks and Kentucky microbrewed beers were a superb version of man food.

Kane stretched in the booth, taking in the roaring fire nearby and the authentic aged brick walls. "Can you believe we're here and eating at a place like this?"

"As opposed to the cheap burgers that were a treat growing up?" Mason shook his head. "Kinda hard to believe, even now. But dad would have loved this."

Mason thought of the man who had worked so hard, taught them so much, and had still laughed and had a beer with them… He shifted, uncomfortable comparisons with what he now knew of EvaMarie's childhood rising up in this mind. But before he could mention anything to Kane, the waitress appeared.

By the time their orders went in and their foam-topped beers had come out, Mason thought better of sharing. After all, it really wasn't his story to share. Since EvaMarie would be working with Kane some too, he didn't want her to be uncomfortable if Kane let his knowledge slip.

While he and his brother both sat in thoughtful silence, Mason couldn't help but think about the changes in their circumstances that were so unexpected, so welcome, and yet made him long for the man who had made it all possible. Their lives could have been very different if their father had been a different kind of man.

As if on the same wavelength, Kane raised his mug. "To the man who sacrificed so we could have all this."

They tapped beers and drank. The smooth amber liquid had

just enough bite for Mason's satisfaction. "Dad loved us," he said. "That much is clear."

"Was always clear," Kane agreed.

Again Mason came back to EvaMarie, her childhood, her family. He'd had something she'd never had for all her privilege: the unconditional love of a parent.

Kane went on, "I'd like to think he'll be happy with us naming the stables after him. He was so excited when we told him what we wanted to do."

But not about them moving back here. The one and only time Mason had mentioned that idea, his father had become visibly upset. Maybe through the years he'd realized just how hard the persecution had been on Mason, and had probably known that if he got within a hundred miles of the Hyatt family, revenge would be the only thing on his mind.

"You okay, Mason?" his brother asked.

Suddenly he realized he'd been staring into his drink. But the last thing they needed right now was his confused thoughts on the Hyatts complicating their vision for their racing stables. "Yeah," he said. "Harringtons. Quite an upscale ring to it, I'd say."

They shared a grin before Mason raised his glass once more. "We'll make it everything he would have wanted." If he could have had what he wanted in life…or rather taken their money to build what he'd wanted. "He was a selfless man, you know," Mason said, preaching to the choir. "Makes me wonder if I can even attempt to live up to the man he was."

Kane raised a brow in query at the sudden turn of the conversation. "Living in the same house with EvaMarie got you thinking a little differently?"

"How'd you guess?" Mason hated a know-it-all.

"Brother, there's a reason I opted to oversee the transition at the home farm when we decided to buy the Hyatt estate. You need time to work through things, good or bad."

"I didn't expect it to be good. Didn't expect…" *Her.* He shook his head. "This isn't going how I planned."

"Told ya so."

Mason had a suspicion his brother was making fun of him. Now the smirk made it obvious. "I'm glad you're enjoying this."

"Then we're both happy."

"Smart-ass."

"And practical." Kane winked. "EvaMarie seems like a nice, capable, intelligent woman. How can she possibly complicate your life that much?"

"You'd be surprised," Mason mumbled.

"Then I guess you shouldn't have hired her then, huh?"

Mason hated it when his brother had a point. Luckily the waitress brought their food just then, filling the table with enough plates of steaks and sides and bread to keep them busy for quite a while. Then she headed back for another round of beer.

Mason was savoring his first bite of succulent meat when Kane's grunt drew his attention. Kane's gaze followed the activity over Mason's shoulder.

A quick glance and Mason wanted to grunt himself. Daulton and Bev Hyatt were making slow progress across the main part of the restaurant floor, patiently accompanied by the friendly hostess who was chatting with the one and only Laurence Weston. Mason's very own kryptonite, all at one table.

He turned back to his food. "Well, that's great."

And it only got worse. The hostess was making for a table not too far away. In fact, it was directly across the fireplace from the booth Mason and Kane occupied. Right on the edge of Mason's peripheral vision.

So much for enjoying dinner.

He pushed back, wiping his mouth with a few rough strokes of his cloth napkin. "I'm done."

"Admitting defeat already?" Kane asked with an arched brow.

Why did his brother have to be such a voice of wisdom? "Are you thirty-two or eighty-two?"

Kane shrugged, that trademark Harrington grin making another appearance. "Not my fault someone has to be the adult."

He wasn't joking, no matter what that smile said. Only two years Mason's senior, somehow Kane always played the adult role. He wasn't prone to the same emotional outbursts as Mason. Very few people had seen his serious side—and they definitely regretted it when they did. When crossed, snarky, joking Kane turned cold and calculating.

A scary thing to see, even for Mason.

So he acknowledged his brother's point with a short nod and returned to his food. No reason why the other family had to impact his and Kane's dinner, which had started on such a bright note.

The brothers' conversation turned desultory before they regained their normal rhythm. Their refreshed beers helped.

But it wasn't long before the weight of unwanted attention settled on Mason. He considered ignoring it, but he just wasn't that kind of person. A casual glance to his right showed him that, sure enough, the Hyatts were staring. Laurence had his gaze trained almost defiantly on the couple, as if he refused to lower himself to looking Mason's way.

Mason dipped his chin in a single nod of acknowledgment, then returned his attention to Kane. "Was that adult enough?" he asked, hoping to lighten the mood.

Kane grinned. "Sure."

But apparently it wasn't enough for Daulton. Within minutes, snippets of the conversation across the fireplace struck them like pellets from a BB gun.

"—just a shame, in this day and age, people like that can come in and steal everything you've worked for."

The low rumble of other voices answered. Mason met Kane's look across their table. His brother sighed. "This is going to be interesting."

Mason tried to ignore it. He really did. But Daulton Hyatt had no compunction about slandering the Harringtons in a public restaurant. At all.

"In my opinion, there's a reason God lets people be born with no money. Everyone has a station in life. That's an indicator. And a predictor of future behavior."

The bright flush radiating from Bev Hyatt's cheeks was almost painful to see, but Mason noticed she never made an attempt to quiet her husband. She simply worried the edges of the cloth napkin beside her plate. Laurence's remarks must have been more moderate in tone, since Mason couldn't make out the words, but whatever he said seemed to spur Daulton along.

"Those Harringtons don't even know what to do with a horse, much less a stable of them," he said loudly enough to turn a few heads from the tables around him. "You mark my words," he said, adding emphasis by shaking his steak knife, "they'll be a complete failure within a year."

Kane was on his feet two seconds quicker than Mason expected. He followed, eager to provide backup.

"I'm not sure I heard you correctly," Kane said. "Did you mean we'd be as much of a failure as you were?"

The older man straightened, obviously unused to being challenged. "I am not a failure."

"Really?" Kane wasn't backing down…and he chose not to lower his voice either. "Because your stables were in bankruptcy when we bought it. Was that from mismanagement? Lack of knowledge? Or sheer laziness?"

Oh boy. Kane was dangerously calm as he went on. "You mark *my* words, old man. We aren't afraid to fight dirty, so I'd pull my punches if I were you."

Daulton Hyatt turned to his companions. "Listen to how they talk to me. Guess their father was as inept a parent as he was a businessman."

Mason quickly sidestepped to force his body between Kane and the table. Otherwise, Mr. Hyatt would have been counting his broken teeth. Unconsciously, he reached for his own form of ammunition.

"That's a strange attitude for you to have, considering your daughter is working for me now," Mason said with a deadly quiet reserve that he knew wouldn't last for long. Unlike Kane, he enjoyed yelling.

He could see the surprise knock Daulton back a little, but he never looked away. Bev glanced across at Laurence with wide eyes. Whatever she saw there made her swallow hard.

"My daughter would never betray me by working for you," Daulton blustered. "She got a job at the library."

"Sure about that?"

Daulton must not have liked what he saw in Mason's eyes. "EvaMarie is a good girl. Too good for the likes of you. Or did you somehow trick her into doing this like you tricked us out of our house?"

Now it was Kane's turn to restrain his brother. His hand on Mason's arm was the only thing that kept Mason from slamming his palms on the Hyatts' dinner table. "You know, Eva-Marie is a good person, a good *woman.*"

His emphasis on the last word did not sit well with EvaMarie's parents. Their eyes widened, full of questions. Questions that Mason would never stoop to answering.

"It's amazing that she's turned out as well as she has," he went on, "considering the overbearing, manipulative father she's put up with all her life."

"Overbearing? Dear boy, that's the last thing I am." Daulton's chest puffed out. "I made sure my child learned right from wrong, how to be a true lady and how to conduct herself with respect. Which is more than your father ever taught you."

Kane's deliberate removal of his hand from his brother's arm signaled exactly how hard that blow hit. But this time, Mason used words instead of fists. He leaned onto the table, getting close to Daulton's face even though he didn't lower his voice. "My father was more of a man than you'll ever be. He

cared for his family instead of browbeating them." He shook
his head, driven to break through the man's steely facade. "He
would never have completely erased a son from his life simply
because he had the gall to die on him."

"Mason!"

Jerking around, Mason found himself facing EvaMarie. The
flush of her cheeks and slight sob to her breath told him if she
hadn't heard everything, she'd heard more than enough. But it
was the accusation in her eyes, the betrayal in that look that
cut past his defenses.

For once, it was more than deserved.

Eight

"How could you disgrace us by working for that man?"

The Harringtons were barely out the exit before the interrogation started. A quick glance around at their fellow diners only reinforced EvaMarie's wish that her father would lower his voice. After all, she was only across the table from him.

With few other options, she modeled a lower tone. "That man and the job he offered me—a great paying job along with room and board—are helping us get through our…situation," she insisted.

"I don't see how," Daulton said, leaning back in his chair and crossing his arms over his chest. It was a stubborn pose if ever she saw one. A pose she'd seen him adopt often in her lifetime.

She knew, just looking at her father, that Mason's outburst wasn't his fault alone. Her father could provoke the calmest of people. And right now, her own anger was rising hot. Anger at Mason. Anger at her father. It was threatening to crackle the paint off her inner walls, walls that had locked away years' worth of emotions and kept her calm and collected for far too long.

She leaned forward, crowding over the table. "*You* can't afford to live in that facility, Dad. I know you'd rather not face it, but that's the reality." Her heavy sigh might seem mild to most people, but was a risky move with her father. "When are you gonna face how life really is, Dad—for you and for me?"

As her father's expression closed off even more, her mother joined the conversation for once. "But to tell Mason those things—personal things about us…"

Sadness and guilt mingled within EvaMarie as she watched her mother clutch her cardigan together at the vulnerable hollow of her throat. Compassion softened her response. "I'm sorry, Mother. Mason found me clearing out—" she choked slightly, still unable to speak her brother's name in front of them "—the room. I gave an explanation. It never occurred to me—"

"That he'd use it as ammunition?" her father interjected. "How naïve are you, EvaMarie? That's the kind of man he is."

Laurence nodded. As much as EvaMarie wanted to argue that Mason wasn't like that, that she'd seen him laugh with and support his family, show compassion even to her when he probably didn't feel like she deserved it, she'd heard his accusation herself.

"How could you lie to us, darling?" her mother asked. "We thought you were working at the library?"

"Shocked me too," Laurence added.

With a quick sideways glance, EvaMarie mumbled, "You aren't helping."

But Laurence wasn't backing down. He loved stirring the pot. "Honey, you weren't born to clean barn stalls."

The surround sound gasps told her he'd gotten his point across. That was the problem with Laurence…always had been. He was only willing to further his own agenda.

"No daughter of mine—" her father started.

The smack of her palm on the table sounded impossibly loud to EvaMarie. No one else in the restaurant even looked in their direction, but she felt like she suddenly had a 1000 kilowatt light shining right on her.

It was always that way when she dared defy her father.

"Yes, I will." She enunciated clearly, hoping she could get her point across in one try. The quiver in her stomach told her the chances were iffy, but at least a numbness was starting to creep over her raw emotions, giving her a touch of distance as she delivered what was most likely her long-needed declaration of independence.

"I will do whatever I'm told by Mason. I'm not a princess, not anymore—face it, Dad. I'm a worker bee."

The breath she drew in was shaky, fragile. "This is my life. One I am struggling to resurrect out of the gutter after years of trying to keep us afloat. What did you think would happen when you left me to clean up the mess you left behind? I'm doing the best I can with what I have to work with here."

Shocked silence was a new response from her parents. A novel one, in fact. Thank goodness, because she wasn't sure she'd have been able to withstand any dictums to sit down and shut up. Instead EvaMarie stood, palms firm on the table to keep her steady. "I thought you'd be proud of me, Daddy. After all, you're the one who taught me not to argue with authority."

The reality of what she'd said didn't honestly hit EvaMarie until she was on her way home. Then she had to pull the car over until she could get her shaking limbs under control. How could she have talked to her parents like that? But then again, every word had been honest.

Though her father regularly wielded his honesty like a sword, EvaMarie had never been allowed to own hers.

Her emotions were in turmoil, overflowing until she didn't know how to contain them. Especially when she ran into Mason on the upstairs landing. Suddenly she had a target for her deepest emotion: anger.

"How dare you," she demanded, stomping across the landing to crowd into his space.

He straightened, withdrawing only an inch before staring down at her intently. EvaMarie felt her emotions go from hot to supernova.

"Your dad was deliberately pushing my buttons," Mason said, for once the calm one in the situation. "You should have heard what he said before you got there."

She shook her head, her mind a jumble of thoughts and questions, but one stood out from the rest. "Why would you talk to him in the first place?"

His incredulous look didn't help matters. "How could I not? He made sure he spoke loud enough for the whole restaurant to hear."

Well, that did sound like her father. "That's no excuse."

"Actually, it's enough of an excuse. I'm not gonna sit by and let him malign my family and keep my mouth shut."

"But it's okay to retaliate by throwing his dead son in his face?" She stomped closer, close enough to feel Mason's body heat. "I trusted you with that information—something I've never done with another living soul. Why would you turn around and tell it to anyone? Much less use it as a weapon against my father?"

"I got angry," he said with a shrug. "Kinda like you are right now, only you're much cuter."

EvaMarie wasn't sure what happened. One minute they were facing off. The next the knuckles on her right hand burned and Mason gripped his left arm. She'd...oh man, she'd hit him. Her whole body flushed.

When Mason pushed forward, she instantly retreated. Standing her ground wasn't something she'd ever been good at, especially when she was afraid. If he decided to retaliate, she certainly deserved it.

Then her back met the wall. His body boxed her in. She looked up into his face, fear gripping her stomach, only to have his lips cover hers.

This wasn't a teenage kiss. It was rough, powerful, and had

EvaMarie's body lighting up all on its own. Leaving anger far behind, she wanted nothing more than to drown in the hot rush of need that overtook her in that moment.

Suddenly his teeth nipped the sensitive fullness of her mouth. Her gasp gave him free access. He pressed in, those vaguely familiar lips giving her a good taste of what he was capable of as an adult. This was no innocent exploring. Instead he conquered. With every brush of those lips, every stroke of his tongue, her body bowed into his without compunction.

Without thought, she pressed her palms against his sides, her fingers digging into his rib cage to urge him closer. Images of his body covering hers forced tiny mewling sounds from her throat. How had she lived this long without having him again?

Suddenly he pulled back. Bracing his hands over her head on the wall, he rested his forehead against hers. The sound of their rapid breathing was loud in her ears. *No, please don't leave.*

She should be embarrassed by her need, ashamed to want a man who had set out to make her life miserable. But she couldn't find the self-preservation to care. It was hidden somewhere beneath the desire that had lain dormant in her body for fifteen years—and was now clamoring for fulfillment.

Then his hand pressed up on her chin, forcing her to face him. By sheer will, forcing her to open her eyes and see the man behind the touch.

"I know I'm a safe outlet for your anger, EvaMarie. Much safer than your family," he said, still struggling to get his own breath under control. That gave her more than a hint of satisfaction. As did the deep timbre of promise that resonated in his words.

"But remember, that doesn't mean I won't retaliate."

Mason awoke the next morning with the taste of EvaMarie on his lips and the scent of her in his head.

Still.

That fresh taste of guilelessness with a dark undertone of desire was like rich chocolate, igniting Mason's hunger for more. But there was too much history. Too many complications.

Yeah, he just needed to keep telling himself that—no matter how many times his body reminded him just how soft she'd felt, how much fuller she was as a woman, with intriguing curves that he ached to spend a night exploring.

Nope. Not gonna happen.

Grabbing a pair of jeans, Mason dressed quickly and headed downstairs. He could hear the faint sound of workmen from the basement. But there was no EvaMarie in the dining room, family room or kitchen, and no fresh coffee either. He made quick work of getting it set to brew, and stared broodingly out the window.

He shouldn't want to see her, but here he was searching around every corner. What was his problem?

Jeremy called to him from the hall. "Morning, Mason. Hope we didn't wake you."

"Nope. That basement has great soundproofing."

His friend grinned. "Good thing, considering the sound system you guys want installed."

"Oh yeah." That was gonna be fun.

Jeremy nodded toward the hallway. "Wanna take a look at the wall treatment going in the formal dining room? It's about halfway done."

"Sure." Mason paused long enough to fill a coffee mug, then followed. "When are the new floors going down?"

"Two weeks."

He grinned. "I'll make sure I'm absent that week."

"I don't blame you," Jeremy said, then presented the room under construction with a hand flourish worthy of Vanna White.

After admiring all the improvements Jeremy had gotten done in a very short amount of time, Mason finally got down to what he really wanted to know. "Have you seen EvaMarie this morning?"

Jeremy nodded. "Sure. She was in the barn when we got

here this morning. She came over to let us in, then she went back." A frown marred his young face. "Looked like she'd had a rough night. You haven't been making her clean out more stalls, have you?"

Mason paused, eyeing his friend over the rim of his coffee mug. "Told you about that, did she?"

Jeremy eyed him back. "That was not nice."

And Mason wouldn't be allowed to forget it. "I know. Of course it won't happen again."

Jeremy looked skeptical but let his line of questioning dry up.

As soon as he could escape, Mason dragged on his boots and headed for the barn. Jim's truck was in the drive, which made EvaMarie's presence in the stables that much more of a mystery.

As he stepped into the cool darkness of the large building, he heard the faint murmur of EvaMarie's voice. Just like the other day, all his senses stood up and took notice. The farther he walked, the clearer the words became until he realized she was singing a lullaby. As he walked past Ruby's stall, the mare had her head out of the box, ears pricked forward as she stared down the aisle toward the source of the soothing tones. Apparently Mason wasn't the only one entranced.

The sound originated from the double stall down on the far left. As he reached the half-door, Mason couldn't see EvaMarie's upper body because the mare had crowded over the half-door to her stall to rest against EvaMarie's shoulder as she sang. He could see a delicate hand resting on the horse's neck, the flash of blunt-cut nails as she lightly scratched in time with her song.

An ache shot through him, so strong his knees went weak.

Swallowing hard, Mason watched that hand—so graceful yet so capable—until the horse pulled back to glance into the stall behind her.

Jeremy had been right—EvaMarie was a mess. He'd go so far as to say she looked worse than when she'd cleaned the stall. Almost as if she'd slept all night on the barn floor.

"Yes," she crooned at the animal, unaware of his observance. "You have a pretty, pretty baby."

"That she does," Jim said, appearing from the other side of the stall door. "Very pretty indeed."

A baby. The mare had foaled during the night...which explained a lot about EvaMarie's appearance. Jim grinned when he saw Mason standing there.

"She delivered about two hours ago," he said, bringing Eva-Marie's attention his way. Mason wanted to grin as she suddenly smoothed a hand over her hair, then plucked out a piece of straw, but figured she might not appreciate that he found her disheveled state cute.

"Why didn't you come get me?" he asked instead. "I could have helped."

"She's not your horse," EvaMarie replied, quiet but firm. "Besides, Lucy did the work. We were just here in case of trouble."

The reserve he heard in her voice was clear. Mason just wasn't sure if she was still angry with him, or embarrassed by their confrontation the night before. He couldn't resist teasing her to find out.

"Sure looks like you worked hard to me...all night long." He let that grin slip out. "Jeremy accused me of making you clean out stalls again."

Her cheeks flushed pink. He would swear he heard her mumble as she turned away, "You'd think they'd never seen a woman get dirty before..."

Oh, Mason hadn't...at least not in the way he wanted.

Funny how EvaMarie could do the simplest of things and it would crack his resistance like a sledgehammer—like laugh with Jeremy, blow across a cup of hot chocolate, bristle at Mason's comments. Every move was way sexier than it should be—or maybe he just had a really dirty mind.

As she disappeared from his range of sight, Jim inched closer. "She told me about the argument with her father."

"Yes?"

Jim didn't look angry, so maybe Mason wasn't in too much trouble.

"Well, there's lots of time to talk while you're waiting and watching for a birth to happen. Anyway, Mr. Hyatt has always been a difficult man. I almost quit more than once."

"Been here long?" Mason didn't remember the older man from his brief stint here as a teenager.

Jim nodded. "I was here for a while, then moved to Florida for several years to care for my wife's parents. We moved back after they both passed away."

Mason knew he shouldn't ask, didn't have the right to, but he heard himself asking anyway. "Were you here when Chris died?"

"Yes," Jim said, his tone low as he glanced toward the stable entrance as if seeing something that wasn't there. "I watched Mr. Hyatt carry that boy's body out of the woods himself. It was a tough time for everyone, but especially for EvaMarie."

"Losing a brother must have been hard, especially at that age." Mason couldn't imagine a tiny EvaMarie with no one to hold her, comfort her in her grief.

"It was." Jim met his gaze. "Losing her parents right along with him was even harder."

Mason zeroed his attention in on the other man. "What do you mean?"

"He wasn't always like this, you know. Mr. Hyatt was tough, and had a quick temper, but he loved his kids. Spent loads of time with them...until the day they lost Chris."

Mason instinctively glanced toward EvaMarie but couldn't see her anymore. How confusing must the change in her father have been? On top of never being able to mention the brother she'd idolized...

"It rocked her entire world," Jim murmured, seeming lost in his own memories of that time.

No doubt it had lasting repercussions for her... Mason's own loss at a young age had hit him hard, left lasting scars, and he'd had his brother and father to lean on.

EvaMarie had been all alone.

Suddenly Mason was hit with the realization of how long they'd been standing there talking…and how quiet EvaMarie was. He glanced over Jim's shoulder again but didn't see her.

Taking his lead, Jim moved away to look behind the open part of the door, then he gestured Mason in with a smile.

Some internal instinct had Mason entering with quiet steps. As EvaMarie came into view, Mason's heart melted. She sat curled against the barn wall in a thick pile of hay, fast asleep. He remembered how she could sleep anywhere, but this had to be a first.

As much as he didn't want to, as much as he wanted to hang on to the distance and anger, Mason couldn't look at her without seeing a gorgeous woman, grime and all. Not only that, he saw a woman who had endured a lot, who had stood on her own two feet without a hell of a lot of support, possibly none.

A woman he wanted the chance to know, even if it was complicated. But he doubted he'd ever be able to see her as the enemy anymore.

Mason glanced toward the stall, listening to the soft sounds of the horses as mama and baby got to know each other. "Everything good here?" he asked.

Jim nodded. "The mare's a pro, and she handled the birth like one." He eyed Mason a moment, then looked over at the sleeping beauty. "I think EvaMarie already has a buyer. The stables will be cleared soon enough. She's gonna miss them though, and vice versa."

Thinking back to what he'd seen when he entered the barn, Mason completely understood. "Once you get the mare settled, text me, then go home."

Jim's eyes widened. "But boss—"

"No." Mason's voice was firm, carrying through the aisle. "You've been here all night. I'm more than capable of watching her." *Both of them*. "Go get some rest. There's nothing here that can't wait until tomorrow. I'll get EvaMarie inside."

"Poor thing is exhausted. When she's devoted, she's all in—and she wasn't leaving until they were both okay."

From what Mason had learned, that sounded about right.

Nine

Carrying a sleeping woman was a unique experience for Mason. He hadn't expected it to be quite so emotional—and it wasn't, not in a soft, mushy way. The feelings rushing through him were fierce, protective and full of demanding need. Add in yesterday's ups and downs and a fitful night's sleep dreaming of this woman's lips, and he had a feeling he was about to be in a very tough spot.

He skirted by the dining room without being noticed by anyone inside. As he climbed the stairs, EvaMarie began to stir, but didn't open her eyes until they reached the landing.

Even then, a sleepy haze covered her baby blues. They barely opened as he watched her fight her body's normally heavy sleep mode to handle whatever trouble she'd landed herself in now.

If her habit had stayed the same all these years, EvaMarie slept like the dead once she got going.

He carried her to her room, smiling at the feminine touches and soothing green color on the way through to her bath. Once inside, he eased her down onto a little padded bench and kneeled before her, slightly uncomfortable when the comparison to a prince before a princess came to mind.

"EvaMarie, honey, you need to wake up."

Her brow furrowed, but those sleepy blues cracked open once more. "I'm sorry," she murmured, "I'm just so tired."

"Not sleeping will do that to you. But you're also dirty."

Her eyes widened, and she looked down at her dusty clothes. Then he heard a soft sigh. "I almost don't care," she said.

Mason wasn't falling for that. "But you'll blame me when you wake up in dirty sheets, so let's go."

"Go where?" Her lids slid closed, and she slumped toward the wall.

"Oh, no, you don't." Mason pulled her forward with a tiny shake. "EvaMarie, you have to shower."

"With you?"

Mason's world stopped. "What, Evie?"

He saw her eyelids flicker, but it took a minute for her to brave opening them.

"Will you stay with me?" she finally whispered.

His hands tightened, his need to tear through their boundaries seriously compromising his resolve. "That's not a good idea," he managed to say. "For a lot of reasons."

The barest sheen of tears made her eyes look like damp blue flowers, catching him off guard before she closed them once more. "You're right. I'll be fine."

But *he* wouldn't be.

He hadn't been fine since Evie had come back into his life—and for just a little while, he wanted a taste of what they could be together once more.

Slow but sure, he reached out and started working on the buttons down the front of her flannel shirt.

"What are you doing?"

The simplest answer was the best, because he wasn't entirely sure what he was doing. Going out of his mind, maybe? "Undressing you."

Her breath caught, then she said, "You don't have to do this."

Just as he had yesterday, he reached out and lifted her chin with his knuckles until there was nowhere else for her to look but at him. "No, I don't have to. I want to."

I want you.

Layer by layer he peeled away her clothes; she'd bundled up to keep herself warm. Pulling that last T-shirt over her head to reveal skin and lingerie had him sucking in his breath. Blood and heat pooled low. EvaMarie had filled out into some serious feminine curves. The combination of creamy skin, pink lace and the scent that was uniquely hers sent his heartbeat into overdrive.

This was really happening.

And it looked like he'd found the perfect thing to wake Eva-Marie. Though her lashes were lowered, she still watched him. The throb of her pulse at the base of her neck served as a barometer for her response. As did the quiver of her bottom lip.

He eased her to her feet, eager for more. One thing about Mason, once he committed to a cause, he was all in. This time, his entire body agreed.

Before he could get carried away, he turned on the shower to let the hot water work its way up to the second floor. Then he stripped off his own sweatshirt and thermal undershirt. Her eyes drank in every inch of flesh, giving Mason an unaccustomed feeling of pride. He worked hard. His body showed it.

And he was more than happy for EvaMarie to enjoy the results.

Stepping closer, he reached for one of her hands, lifted it for a light kiss, then rested it right over his heart. Suddenly she curled her fingers, scraping her blunt nails against his skin. Just as he'd ached for in the stables.

His body flooded with desire, hardening with need. Soon. Soon.

Without preamble, he unzipped EvaMarie's jeans and shoved every layer beneath down to her upper thighs. He didn't give her time to object, but guided her back down onto the bench and made short work baring her legs and feet. She had shapely muscles—obviously he wasn't the only one who worked out. And painted toenails—just like always. He grinned at the burgundy polish with gold flecks. A sexy mature choice compared to the neon pinks she'd been into when she was young.

As he lifted her to her feet again, he kissed each of her flushed cheeks. "There's no need to be embarrassed, Evie," he murmured against the smooth slope of her jaw. "This is just you and me."

She curved her fingers over the front of his waistband as if holding on for dear life. "It's been a long time, Mason...you might not like—"

He cut her off with a kiss, tasting her with lips, tongue and purpose. Just as he had last night. Only this time he let the rest of his body join in the game. He tilted slightly, rubbing his chest against lace and skin. The friction drove him crazy. So did the clutch of her hands around his biceps, urging him closer.

He made quick work of his own jeans, but he couldn't bring naked skin to naked skin soon enough. Evie's gasps and groans filled the air. Reaching around her, he placed a hot and heavy palm on each of her butt cheeks to pull her flush against him. The breath seemed to stop in her chest. She held herself perfectly still. His body throbbed hard, demanding more.

"I'm scared, Mason," she murmured.

He knew she spoke the truth, and was probably asking for reassurance at the same time. But this was something she needed to choose willingly.

Stepping back, he retreated out of her reach. Her expression shattered, but he refused to be swayed. Sliding back the glass door, he stepped into the shower, fighting a shiver when the hot water hit his back, adding to the overload of sensations.

"Join me, Evie," he said, and held out his hand.

Her choice. His chance. His only thought as she took his hand was *hell, yes*.

* * *

The last vestige of sleepiness fled as EvaMarie stepped beneath the onslaught of hot water. She'd thought taking off her bra had been hard. But in the steamy space her skin went tight, her nipples even tighter.

How could she want him this much and be so afraid at the same time?

Her desire was dampened by her fear, her self-conscious awareness of the changes in her body and her life. She wasn't a teenager anymore, but she barely had more experience than all those years ago. Would she disappoint him? Would he find her boring?

Still she couldn't walk away from this chance to have Mason one more time. Tears flooded her eyes, forcing her to blink. She needed this. Needed him. He waited patiently, quietly. Though tentative, she reached out her hand to his chest, her eyes closing as she savored the textures of skin and water together.

This was new, exciting. Her heart pounded in her chest; her blood pounded lower. No matter what happened later, she simply couldn't stop.

A step closer, and she couldn't resist glancing up. Mason watched her with a hooded gaze. His body told her he was more than interested. And that look—it conveyed the primal need of an adult male. She was more than happy for him to take what he wanted…so why didn't he?

She caught her bottom lip between her teeth. "Mason?"

"Come to me, sweetheart. Show me what you want."

But that wasn't what she wanted. She needed him to direct, to take…to overpower her so she could stop thinking for once and just feel.

Again he tilted her chin up with his knuckles. She should hate that, resent being manhandled. Instead the gesture made her feel cherished, seen.

"We're gonna do this together, okay, Evie?"

Mesmerized by the intensity in his blue eyes, she nodded.

"Then touch me however you want. Learn whatever you like."

Somehow, his permission loosened her inhibitions. She pressed close, gasping as every inch of her met every inch of him. Slick, steamy, sexy. She explored his body with her own until the friction had her parting her thighs.

Mason took full advantage to thrust his leg between hers. She rose against him, entranced by the feel of hard masculine muscle against her most sensitive skin. Again and again she lifted against him, dragging out the sensations, aided by the guidance of Mason's hands pulling and pushing her hips. His touch added just enough force, and a ton of excitement.

Her whimpers echoed around them. Her body flushed hot as she rode him. With each glide, the friction of his body against her core made her insides tighten with delicious anticipation. Little mini-explosions prepared her for the fireworks to come. Somehow her nails were digging into Mason's shoulders. She should stop, but she couldn't. He wouldn't let her.

Then his hot, open mouth covered the side of her neck, sucking, drawing her orgasm to the surface until she exploded with a cry she couldn't hold inside. His hands pinned her hard against his thigh. His masculine growl vibrated against her sensitive skin, prolonging the ecstasy.

And Mason wasn't about to let that be the end.

He switched places so that her back slammed flush against the tile wall. He rubbed against her, his movements rough, urgent. "Oh, Evie, yes."

Every nerve ending seemed to answer his call. She arched against him, needing, demanding. Lost in sensation, she somehow managed to open her eyes to find his damp drenched blue eyes cataloging her every expression.

"Mason, please," she begged.

His trademark grin made an appearance. "With pleasure." He ripped open the condom packet he'd pulled from his jeans earlier and made quick work of covering himself. His groan as he pulled away for mere seconds made her body soften that much more. He didn't ask, didn't wait for her to comply.

He simply did what he wanted with her. All of her.

Lifting one of her legs at the knee, he hooked his arm beneath it. Opened her wide. Left her vulnerable to whatever he needed of her. The wall and her hands on his shoulders gave her leverage, but Mason wasn't about to let her fall.

Bending his knees, he made a place for himself right where she wanted him. He eased himself barely inside her. She gasped, tilting her hips in an attempt to accommodate his size. It had been too long. She was embarrassed at how long.

"Easy, baby," he murmured. "Let me make it good."

Just like that, she relaxed. Mason worked his hips, opening her little by little, filling her. The sounds he made lit sparks inside her. His groans, grunts and masculine cries carried the wordless emotions straight to her heart. She pushed her hips toward him, her body now more than eager for his full possession.

As he slid in to the hilt, he moaned through gritted teeth. With a shudder, his whole body strained, his head falling back in a kind of ecstasy that mesmerized her. The pressure between her thighs anchored her to him, to this experience. She thought he would make quick work of it now, driving himself to oblivion.

Instead he paused. Those big hands left her hips to cup her face, and she felt her soul crack a little as his mouth covered hers in a soft, sensual taste that belied the strain of his lower body. His eyes remained open, creating a connection that Eva-Marie vaguely thought she might regret later but couldn't turn away from in this moment.

Then he trailed his hands back down, tweaking every sensitive spot along the journey. When he regained his hold, she braced herself for the ride. Sure enough, his body took over, demanding its due.

Every thrust forced her up on her toes, but she didn't notice as sparks flew through her body. She strained with him. Eager.

Tense. They both moved on instinct alone until Mason pinned her hip to hip. As their cries mingled in the steam, EvaMarie knew she'd never be the same.

Ten

Horse—check. Workers—check. Food—check.

Mason balanced the tray with care as he made his way back upstairs. The house was not only quiet, it was empty. He'd sent everyone home a couple of hours early tonight, eager to have the place to himself.

What awaited him in EvaMarie's bedroom would be a challenge. He had no doubt.

She'd been asleep before he could get her head on the pillow. So Mason left her to rest while he took care of the work crew and checked a couple of times to make sure Lucy and her foal were getting along well. He knew EvaMarie would want an update when she woke. And hopefully she'd want other things, as well.

But he had a feeling his little filly would be having second thoughts the minute her eyes opened.

He let himself into the darkened room and stood for a moment, soaking in the stillness and the sound of Evie's breathing as she slept. He should be having second thoughts, too. Way more than EvaMarie. So why wasn't he shaking in his boots?

Instead he was bringing replenishment to the woman so he could—hopefully—have his way with her again.

God, being with EvaMarie had been nothing like when they were teenagers. Before she'd been tentative, untried. Her hesitation this morning had made him think she'd be the same, but soon she'd been as hot as the water and as responsive as hell. He could still hear her cries echoing off the tiles in the bathroom.

He wanted to hear them again.

Setting the tray on the chaise in her room, he shucked his jeans before easing back the comforter. Suddenly EvaMarie sat straight up. "What are you doing?" she gasped.

Distracted by more bare skin than he'd hoped to see this soon, Mason spent a moment trying to pry his tongue from the roof of his mouth. Noticing the direction of his gaze, Evie gasped again, this time jerking the comforter up over her nakedness. Which was a shame.

He tried to tease her with a grin. "I'm coming back to bed," he said, his voice gravelly with the desire evoked by just the thought of being with her again. "But we can go to my bed if you'd prefer. It's a little bigger. More space for rolling around."

Her eyes widened, and he could just see the images she was tossing around in her mind before she blinked. With innocence overlaying a deep river of sensuality, she was so damn intriguing.

But then panic engulfed her expression. She scrambled back to sit against the padded headboard. "Mason, look, I'm so sorry."

Hmm… Was she sorry she'd slept with him? Because he'd never push her for more than she was willing to give. Or was it something else? This time, her expression wasn't telling the whole story. He let a raised brow speak on his end.

EvaMarie swallowed hard. "I realize you're my employer, and I did not mean to throw myself at you."

Ah, this he could answer. "You didn't."

"I remember asking—" The blush that bloomed over her cheeks was bright enough for him to see in the dim light coming from behind the pulled curtains. Luckily she looked away and didn't notice his smile. He didn't want her to think he was making fun of her. He was simply, well, to his surprise, he was simply enjoying the ins and outs of being with her again.

"And I remember accepting," he finished for her. "I consented way before any clothes came off." He crawled onto the bed to get closer, though he left her with the protection of the comforter. "And I'm really glad I did."

A quick cut of her gaze his way showed him her surprise. "Um. Thank you?"

He chuckled, easing the tension enough for her to meet him face-to-face again.

"Is this gonna be awkward?" she asked.

"Depends."

When she tilted her head to the side, a waterfall of tangled hair spread over her bare shoulder. As the image of burying his face in that silky mass came over Mason, he almost groaned.

But she wasn't done asking questions. "Depends on what?"

"On where this goes now." He flicked his tongue over his suddenly dry lips. "I know what I want, but I'm not gonna push you into anything you don't want to do. Anything that makes you uncomfortable."

"What do you want?" she whispered.

Which only made him think of what other words he wanted her to whisper to him.

"I want the chance to take you to bed."

It wasn't romantic, he knew that. But it was honest. Besides, "romance" and "relationships" came with a lot of complications—especially with EvaMarie.

To his surprise, she said, "On one condition."

This was new. "What's that?"

"That there're no obligations in the end. And no rules as we go."

To Mason's surprise, a trickle of disappointment wiggled through his gut. Why in the world would he be disappointed?

EvaMarie was offering him every man's dream—unattached sex with a sensual, beautiful, responsive woman living right in the same house with him. "That's not anything like dating, you know."

She shrugged. "That's not what I'm looking for."

Me, neither. He crawled toward her on all fours, enjoying the widening of her eyes as he stalked her. "But that's two rules, not one."

Her giggle was spontaneous and went straight to his nether regions. He buried his face against her neck. "Then I guess we can have dessert before dinner, right?"

EvaMarie plopped down on the staircase a couple steps up from the bottom. Long minutes of pacing had worn her out, yet parts of her still felt all jittery. The nerves were getting to her.

Mason had left this afternoon to meet with Kane and their lawyer, who had then taken them to dinner. Which was perfectly fine. A weekend in bed together couldn't last forever—nor should she want it to.

She was simply eager for him to see the storage system that had been added to the wine cellar today. That's all.

Oh, who was she kidding? Sure, Mason had been happy to take her up on what she'd offered, and the memory of her request had her face flaming hot. He'd even been complimentary, patient and enthusiastic, which had led to the most incredible two days of her life and done wonders for her ego.

But the minute he'd walked out the door this afternoon, doubt had set in. Her impulsive actions had been the result of a whopper of a few days—the argument with her father, then Mason, then lack of sleep and seeing the foal being born. She certainly hadn't been thinking straight, but couldn't bring herself to regret it.

She simply wasn't ready for it to end.

Since there were no rules, she wasn't sure what to expect. Then tonight, he hadn't come home…no phone call or even a text to let her know where he was after ample time for dinner. Her fingers were crossed Mason wasn't simply avoiding her because he'd had his fill and now he was done.

She shifted on the hard stair. Wouldn't that be a humiliating conversation?

Yes, asking him for some no-strings-attached time had been unprecedented, as well as unpremeditated. But she'd realized that she wanted Mason, without the complications that had come before—and now she could have him.

But for how long?

Mason had agreed...but did he regret his decision the minute he'd left her? Had he told Kane? Were they even now trying to figure out a way to fire her...to get her to leave without angering her enough to file a sexual harassment suit?

Just as her panic reached fever pitch, she heard a key in the front lock. Her stomach clenched hard enough to force her to swallow, but she couldn't tell if it was fear or anticipation. Then she heard—wait, was that a woman?

The wave of nausea rushing over her kept her immobile, so when the door opened she stood and continued to stand there like a scared rabbit, shaking in her sweatpants. *Busted.*

The wave of relief to find herself facing a group of people, and not just Mason with some woman he'd brought home, was short-lived. Because she knew these people. Mason. Kane. John Roberts. And Liza Young.

Liza's gaze swept up the stairs and right to EvaMarie with her bare feet, baggy sweats and T-shirt. A wave of heat followed that look, lighting EvaMarie with embarrassment everywhere it touched.

"Wow, EvaMarie," the other woman said in an exaggerated drawl. "Whatever are you doing here?"

The heat and nausea combined caused EvaMarie to break out in a sweat. She glanced at Mason, hoping for a little help, but he remained silent, his expression a touch perplexed. Her smile felt sickly, but she offered it to the rest of the group anyway. "Could you all excuse us a moment?"

Surely Mason got her point, but he only went as far as the stairs, even when she moved as if to go farther down the hallway. His frown didn't bode well. Kane and John spoke in a low murmur, but Liza never looked away. With the uncomfortable feeling that her oversized T didn't cover nearly enough, EvaMarie pulled at the hem.

She returned her attention to Mason, and her nerves flared. "Couldn't you have let me know you were bringing people home?" she snapped.

His right brow shot up. He'd gotten pretty good at the haughty look for someone who hadn't grown up using it. "I didn't realize I needed permission to bring people to *my* house."

Nerves gave way to pain as the remark hit her like a slap to the face. Then a giggle came from right behind Mason's shoulder. They both turned to find Liza listening, her overly mascaraed eyes wide, taking it all in. Her grin turned EvaMarie's stomach, because she'd seen it before—whenever Liza knew she'd just landed a juicy bit of gossip that she could use to her advantage.

"Well, Mason, I thought this was your place now," she said, blinking as if her remark was innocence itself. "But that does make me curious as to what she's doing here…"

Mason glanced back at EvaMarie with a look that said since this situation was all her fault, she could get her own self out of it. Quelling the unexpected urge to smack him, she quietly filled the silence. "I work here."

Liza's exaggerated gasp made EvaMarie want to cringe, but she maintained her stoic expression with the last ounce of her strength.

"Whoa," Liza said, throwing a look around the room as if to include everyone there. "Did y'all hear that? From princess to pauper. Bet that's a big change."

Mason's frown deepened. Luckily this time it wasn't directed at EvaMarie. He turned to face Liza. "Nonsense. EvaMarie knows this place better than anyone," he said. "And she's quite talented with organization and interior decorating."

Kane chimed in too. "She's doing a great job overseeing the renovations. Let's go look. After all, that's why you're here."

Mason led the way. John Roberts was quick to cross the foyer and offer his arm to Liza, but she was just as quick to get in her parting shot. "Well, she's dressing the part, isn't she?" The words were whispered to her partner, but echoed off the walls of the cylindrical room.

The hitch in Kane's stride said he'd heard, but still he paused right below EvaMarie. "Join us?" he asked.

Words wouldn't come right now. As much as EvaMarie knew she'd be the object of ridicule every time she met someone of Liza's caliber in the future, that didn't mean it didn't hurt. She was too soft-hearted, her daddy had always said. But truly, it was Mason's response that had hurt her more. If she went with them, she'd probably do something stupid like cry. So she simply shook her head.

The pity in Kane's look quickened her getaway. Her hope to witness the excitement on Mason's face when he saw the new wine cellar pieces didn't matter anymore. Climbing the stairs proved tortuous, as did the whirl of her thoughts. She could go to bed, but Mason would just find her there later—probably crying. Or maybe not.

After all, he didn't seem very interested in her at the moment.

There was only one thing she could think of to soothe herself. A deep breath helped her pull on her big girl panties…along with jeans and a pair of boots. She'd known she was naïve, but not how much until this very moment.

Now she knew. When Mason said this wouldn't be like dating, he hadn't been lying. This definitely wasn't dating…it wasn't even friendship.

Eleven

Mason gritted his teeth against Liza's inane chatter as he walked their little party back down the promenade to the foyer.

"What, no EvaMarie to see us out like a good girl?" she asked, her giggle scraping Mason's nerves. The glasses of wine she'd had at dinner had combined with the sampling they'd had downstairs to celebrate their renovations, pushing her into the just-inebriated-enough-to-lose-any-claim-to-class stage of drunkenness.

She'd been an unfortunate discovery as John Roberts's dinner companion when their lawyer had introduced them to the stable owner who was also a fellow lawyer. About ten minutes ago, Mason had reached his utmost capacity for stupid and catty remarks for the evening—even if they had learned quite a lot about a few key players in the local upper echelons tonight.

From his increasingly stoic expression, it looked as though Kane felt the same.

"I can't wait to tell the girls that juicy story," the woman rattled on.

"Liza." John Roberts's soft rebuke didn't have any back-bone to it.

Mason didn't have the patience to be that soft. His voice came out a low growl. "Excuse me?"

"You know, the whole privileged-daughter-is-now-the-hired-help story," Liza gushed.

Mason had to wonder how long she'd been holding this in. Maybe she'd taken his silence earlier this evening as permission.

"She's always been such a Goody Two-shoes." Liza threw a sly glance at Mason. "At first, I thought maybe she had a to-tally different reason for being here, but she certainly wasn't dressing to entice anyone, was she?"

Like you would have? Clenching his jaw to keep the words inside, Mason had a sudden epiphany. EvaMarie hadn't been dressed to entice, but she'd definitely been waiting for some-one. Crap. That's why she'd been upset that he'd brought peo-ple home. She didn't want advanced warning because she felt any kind of ownership over the house or him. She'd wanted the common courtesy of being able to prepare herself before some-one came in—something Mason wasn't used to dealing with, so it hadn't occurred to him.

Man, he'd better get these two out of here before he said something he shouldn't…and gave away more than EvaMarie would appreciate.

Aiming for a distraction, Mason ushered them out the door, then watched as John Roberts gallantly helped Liza down the stairs and out to his car. Halfway across the driveway she ditched her heels, leaving her date to pick up the pieces.

"That woman's laugh could be used as a torture device," Kane said from beside him.

Mason allowed himself a chuckle before turning away from the departing couple. He faced Kane, the man he'd always been honest with. "I screwed up, didn't I?"

"I believe so."

He'd just seen EvaMarie's haughty expression, heard her

irritated tone and snapped back in kind. And reacted like the moody teenager he used to be.

Mason stared out into the night as he thought about the implications of tonight's encounter. "Do you think she's told anyone that she's here, working for us?"

"I doubt it." Kane rocked back on the heels of his cowboy boots. "Her parents have taught her the exaggerated importance of preserving her privacy."

"Yeah."

"Did you see her face when Liza made that snide remark about her clothes?"

"No." He hadn't even heard the remark. He'd been too intent on showing off, which meant getting the others downstairs and away from a situation he wasn't sure how to handle.

"Don't think I've ever seen a face go that blank."

EvaMarie's parents had drilled their version of acceptable behavior into her so thoroughly that making a scene or standing up for herself never would have occurred to her. She'd taken what Liza dished out without a complaint, though he noticed she hadn't joined them downstairs.

"I'd better go check on her," Mason said.

The brothers parted with a quick hand slap, and Kane headed for his truck. Mason went to EvaMarie's room, but she wasn't there. Stumped, he stood on the threshold for a moment.

Maybe she was in Chris's room? After all, he'd bet she was more than upset. But no. She wasn't there either.

You're a smart boy, Mason. Figure it out.

A sudden memory rose of watching a young EvaMarie saddle her horse with tears flowing down her rounded cheeks after yet another dressing down from her father. Did she still love to ride to clear her head? Did she still sit by her favorite tree on the side of the stream that flowed through the middle of the estate into the lake?

He bet she did.

After a quick change into jeans and boots, Mason confirmed

his suspicions when he found one of the mares' stalls empty. He quickly saddled up Ruby, groaning as he swung into the saddle. It had been too many days since he'd been on a horse. His growing business activities here cut into his riding time.

He needed to change that.

The ride felt good, free. He moved with the horse, limbering up and clearing his head as he gained speed, though he didn't push the mare too hard in the dark. Since he hadn't been back in the wooded area along the creek as an adult, Mason dismounted and led the horse down the still-clear path he remembered from all those years ago.

The soft whinny of EvaMarie's horse corrected his course just a little. She didn't glance his way as he broke from the tree line. He tied Ruby near Lucy and cautiously approached the blanket EvaMarie was reclining on. "Hey," he said softly, not wanting to startle her if she'd slept through his arrival.

"Hey," she replied.

Which gave him nothing to go on. After all, EvaMarie had evolved into a master at hiding her emotions. Unsure what else to say, Mason lay down next to her in the darkness. The blanket provided a thick barrier over the mixture of bare dirt and clumps of grass beneath them. The trickle of water from the stream reminded him of the soothing sound when they'd lain here and held each other so long ago. The sky showcased an array of bright stars framed by tree limbs that he didn't remember from his last visit here.

Of course, they hadn't come here for the stargazing back then.

"I wasn't demanding anything from you, Mason," she finally said, her voice sounding huskier, deeper than before. "I don't think I should have to demand the common courtesy afforded to anyone living in the same house—like normal roommates."

Whoa. Though she'd spoken quietly, Mason recognized an unfamiliar tone in EvaMarie's voice. It wasn't even the same tone she'd used when she'd spoken to him in anger the other day. Instead, it was the simple assurance that the facts were in her favor—the facts that called him an overreacting idiot.

Before he could formulate his thoughts, she went on. "I realize that might not be a courtesy given to paid employees—"

"Shush, will ya?"

Leaning up on his elbow, Mason stared at the oval shape of her face, but had trouble making out the details in the dark. "There's no need to play the martyr, EvaMarie."

He rushed on when she opened her mouth to parry with him. "It was thoughtless of me to bring people home without letting you know. Hell, it was thoughtless not to tell you we'd gone to dinner after our meeting, then had drinks. I'm sorry."

She must have been as surprised as he was, because she didn't speak.

"I'm not used to having to think about those things, about other people. Kane and I never had company much except our weekly poker game with the guys. And half of them were stable hands. They just walked in off the job for dinner."

"Thus the poker room, huh?"

Smart girl. "You got it."

He heard her take a deep breath. "I'm sorry, Mason. I was just embarrassed, I guess."

Should he warn her she'd be even more so if Liza had her way? He'd face that tomorrow. For better or worse, Mason didn't want to shatter the now lighter mood.

But it seemed as though she was going to do it for him. "I don't think this is gonna work, Mason," she said, what sounded like regret weighing down her voice.

Was that the same emotion sinking like a rock into his stomach?

He didn't want it to be. Still he asked, "Why?"

She stood, presenting her back. "I know I asked for this, but honestly I don't know how—"

The strangled sound that choked off her words resonated with him—because he didn't know either. His history of plenty of one-night stands and a couple of longer stretches with the same woman didn't match anything in his situation with Eva-Marie. Here, he was with a woman he knew, but didn't know just the same. He suspected she didn't know this side of herself very well either.

But he wanted to know her, every part of her, with a desire that was more than likely dangerous.

"Haven't you ever wanted to make your own rules?"

What prompted his question, he wasn't sure. But he sensed that something inside Evie was changing, breaking free, and he wanted to encourage it.

She responded with a huff of a laugh. "Only forever."

With a firm hand, he reached for her arm and turned her to face him. "Then we'll do that here. Together."

"Why are you doing this?"

He hadn't expected the question or the aching sadness in her voice. But he couldn't ignore it. "We were friends once, long before—" He cleared his throat. "We were friends first. Let's remember that." Especially in this place that had seen so much of that young love—not just the sex, but talking, laughing and the sharing of dreams. He owed that time something.

"Like friends with benefits?" she asked with a giggle.

"Oh, I definitely hope so."

She seemed to sober, though he couldn't see her features really well. "How?"

Good question. "One day at a time."

"That simple?"

"That simple. And the first rule should be that common courtesy rules the show. Agreed?"

She didn't speak but simply nodded.

"And rule number two…" He pushed forward, meeting her chest with his, combining their body heat with explosive results. Her gasp said she felt it too.

Breathlessly she asked, "Rule number two?"

"Let me show you."

* * *

And boy did he.

Drawing her up to her knees, Mason moved in close before she could catch her breath, leaving just enough room for his hands. Very busy hands. All too soon he'd taken her shirt off, and the cool night air kissed her bare skin. The brush of his shirt against the tips of her breasts had her gasping for air.

Then he efficiently removed that final barrier, and heated skin pressed to heated skin. If EvaMarie remembered nothing else from their time together, she knew that first moment of full body touch would stand out above all else.

But she wasn't content to wait on him this time. Her own urgency pushed her to grasp his muscled shoulders, to pull him as close as possible. One of his knees slid between hers, the length of his thigh pressing her jeans roughly against her feminine core. Her moans mingled with the sound of the water nearby and the rush of the wind, all intertwining to heighten EvaMarie's acute senses.

Reaching around, Mason cupped her jeans-clad bottom with his large hands, pulling her up along his leg, then pushing her down until her knees once more touched the ground. The force of his touch and the strain of his body told her this was happening quickly.

His breath deepened, the sound accelerating with the beat of her heart in her ears. His urgency fed her own. Her grip tightened. Her core ached. And her brain short-circuited in her pursuit of making any sense of what was happening.

Better to just feel. Thinking was overrated.

His mouth devoured hers. Nibbling, sucking, exploring. EvaMarie was ready to do a little exploring of her own. Her hands traveled down his back, laying claim to the smooth territory below his waistband. More than enough to overflow her palms, his butt cheeks were squeezable and oh, so sexy. The muscles flexed as he did what he wanted with her body, previewing the dance they would indulge in all too soon.

Suddenly he sucked at her neck, causing everything inside her to tighten—including her fingers. Her nails dug against his skin. In return, he set his teeth against the tendons running along her throat. Their groans filled the air.

"Again," he gasped.

The combined tension and need left EvaMarie light-headed on a runaway train. And she wouldn't have had it any other way.

The same need had Mason fumbling with the button of her jeans. His combined chuckle and growl of frustration floated over her nerve endings like an electrical current. The sheer sensations of being with him like this pulsed beneath her skin.

Within minutes of getting naked, Mason lay back on the blanket. "Take what you want, Evie," he gasped.

To her surprise, the idea inspired her, though her natural hesitation still reared its ugly head.

"Now, Evie."

The force of his words unlocked her barriers. Instead of the slow and careful advance she would have expected, her body leaped into movement. Crawling over him, relief spread through her as she straddled his thighs. Relief, and a rush of desire so strong it was almost a cramp.

Mason was ready for her, but he didn't reach out to help. He positioned himself like a platter on display, eager for her to avail herself of his bounty. So she did. With a single swift move, she made them one. Her entire body gasped at the intrusion, her mind overtaken with the sensation of fullness. Her muscles clasped down in ecstasy.

Mason's moan played over her ears, heightening her experience.

In fact, every response to her movements held her breathless. Never had she felt such a sense of power or responsibility—she could do whatever she wanted with his permission, yet what she wanted was to make it good for him too.

Her body adopted a natural rhythm, one learned through a lifetime of riding. Mason grasped her hands in his, leveraging her up yet keeping them connected. She could watch his face as she moved, learning what entranced him, what ramped up his need and what sent him over the moon.

Before long they were both gasping, playing along the edges of ecstasy without falling over. All too soon, EvaMarie couldn't hold back. She thrust hard. Once. Twice. The explosion catapulted her into a feeling of flight.

Mason reared up, wrapping his arms tightly around her. His guttural cries against her skin sparked shock waves in the aftermath. A sound EvaMarie knew she'd never forget.

An experience she'd carry with her for a lifetime.

Twelve

"Jeremy, do you know where EvaMarie went?" Mason asked as he stepped into his bedroom.

The crew had repainted the room the day before and was now addressing the crown molding, among other upgrades to the dressing area and adjoining bath.

Jeremy glanced up from his clipboard and blinked, but didn't answer.

"I saw her car leave as I headed back from the barn," Mason prompted.

"Ah, EvaMarie, yes," Jeremy said. "She headed over to the library, I believe."

The library? She'd always been a reader, but—suddenly her father's voice came back to him, *"She got a job at the library."*

Mason tried to continue the conversation casually, but in the back of his mind, unease grew. More than that, his worry unsettled him.

Within twenty minutes he hit the road. The main branch of the town's library wasn't too far from the house. When he entered the building, two librarians eyed him as he walked past, but he continued on his hunt. Finally, a husky, resonating voice led him to…the children's room?

The door to the glassed-in room remained open, but Mason didn't need to stand right on the threshold. EvaMarie's voice carried, so he stood to the right so he could watch her from outside her line of sight. Mason let go of the words and simply focused on the cadence of her voice. As much as he adored that sound, what struck him the most was her expression. Calm. Happy.

She's enjoying herself.

Since his return, the closest he'd seen EvaMarie to happy had been during their discussions about the house, and with the horses. Their most intimate moments together were about a different kind of enjoyment. And he'd seen all too many instances of the blank mask she used to hide her emotions. But this, he could only describe as carefree.

Her guarded look returned as soon as story time ended. Their gazes met through the glass, and Mason could almost see the barriers go up, which told him more than she probably wanted. It meant this place, this time, meant something special to her. Remembering how much she'd loved books when he'd known her before, seeing all the books around her rooms since his return, and her joy in being among these children, he'd have to be completely clueless not to have figured it out.

And he was glad she'd taken steps to create something meaningful in her life.

But her cautious approach said she might not have been ready to share it with him. "Hey. What are you doing here?"

The tone wasn't exactly accusatory. He couldn't put his finger on it, but definitely the caution was there. And for once he wasn't quite sure how to answer…because saying he'd rushed down here because he was afraid she was interviewing for another position would make him more vulnerable than he was ready for.

"Miss Marie?"

Mason looked down to find a little blonde sprite between

them. Her arm wrapped around EvaMarie's thigh, as if to claim her in the face of the big bad man across from them. He glanced up at EvaMarie with a questioning look.

"My full name is too much for some of the younger ones to pronounce," she said with a rueful grin.

"Is he your daddy?" the little girl persisted.

"What?" Mason's tone conveyed a wealth of *hell no*.

He immediately recognized his response as a bit too much when a slight wash of tears filled the wide eyes watching him. Unlike him, EvaMarie knew exactly how to handle the situation. With natural ease, she bent down. "He's my friend," she said in a soothing tone. "Like Joshua is your friend."

"Do you play together?"

This one Mason had an answer for... "All the time."

EvaMarie shot him a glare, even as her face flamed.

But the little miss wasn't done yet. "Sometimes Josh will pull my hair."

Mason choked back his laugh as best he could. EvaMarie's skin almost glowed in her embarrassment. But this time Mason bent to the little girl's level. "Well, you tell him that's not how girls like to be treated. He needs to be a gentleman and treat you like a lady."

The little girl preened, her smile saying she liked that idea. Then her mother called from across the room, so she hugged EvaMarie quickly and left them with a cute little smile.

"Whew," Mason said, "that was getting tricky."

EvaMarie raised her brow in a nice impression of a Southern belle. "You brought it on yourself."

He had to concede with a grin. After all, he was fully aware of his shortcomings. Instead, he waved a hand toward the rapidly emptying room. "Why this?" he asked.

"My degree is in early education, and this is a helpful way to put it to use," she said as she started straightening up the room.

"Degree?"

Her grin was self-deprecating, but there was also disbelief

mixed in over his surprise. "Yes—believe it or not, I did go to college."

"Oh, I believe it. You always liked to learn." Which reminded him of his one unauthorized visit inside the Hyatt house as a teen. "Is the library still in the turret tower?"

He caught a glimpse of sadness crossing her face right before she turned away to fit the book she'd read back on the shelf. "The room is there, but the movers helped me pack away the books and store them."

She didn't have to tell him she missed it. The turret library had been her favorite room when he'd known her. Her escape, other than the horses.

She turned back to face him, more questions in her eyes, but then her expression changed. "Hello, Laurence," she said, looking over Mason's left shoulder.

"EvaMarie," the other man said, offering Mason a short nod but keeping his gaze on EvaMarie. "I was just down here discussing the Derby festivities for the children's festival." His eyes narrowed. "Could I speak with you, please?"

Mason wasn't sure what came over him exactly. Masculine pride? The burn of competition? But he couldn't stop himself from saying, "Actually we're on our way to lunch. You can call her later." He didn't even look at EvaMarie to see what she thought.

Of course, Laurence wouldn't be a worthy opponent if he didn't protest. "I prefer—"

"Is it urgent?" Mason asked.

"Well, no."

"Then call later." *Or not at all.* Mason hooked his arm through EvaMarie's. "See ya."

Then he ushered her outside.

They were almost to her car when she asked, "Was that really necessary?" Instead of the angry tone he expected after his interference, she sounded almost giggly. He glanced over to see her suppressing a smile.

"Got a problem?" he asked playfully. "Because I can take you back in."

"Right, like I'm looking forward to the lecture I was in for for associating with the... No way." She shot him a look that arrowed straight to his groin—sassy, sexy and something he'd never expected to see from EvaMarie in public. "But I guess this means you owe me lunch."

If this was punishment for opening his big mouth, he'd do it every time. "I'd never dream of going back on my word."

Mason parked on one side of the historic square downtown, and EvaMarie was able to pull into the spot right next to his. They didn't touch as they walked along the sidewalk, but their connection felt almost tangible to EvaMarie. She didn't need his touch to know that he was aware of her, which was an empowering, heady experience.

After last night, she'd felt almost revived, set on a new course, a better course. But she didn't have the overall plan yet.

As they strolled past Mr. Petty's antique shop, something she glimpsed through the window made EvaMarie pause. Her instincts urged her to look closer, check it out, but maybe it wasn't her place to do so. Only she hesitated a moment too long.

Mason joined her. "What is it?" he asked.

So far Mason and Jeremy had been the driving forces behind the renovations. EvaMarie had been present at most of the discussions and had offered her opinion, but never had she taken the initiative. She worried her lip with her teeth for a moment, trying to decide. Finally she offered a small smile. "Let's go inside."

He nodded and held the door for her. Stepping across the threshold to the jingle of the doorbell, EvaMarie made her way straight to the piece she'd seen through the window: an old-fashioned sign for a gentleman's sports lodge, weathered with age, but in good repair. She pointed to the sign. "Mason, wouldn't that be great in the poker room?"

"Hell, yeah." He grinned up at the sign. "This is perfect. Good eye."

She tried to ignore the glow of pleasure blooming in her belly. "We could carry the dark wood theme from the wine cellar into the game room, kind of give it a hunting lodge-type feel."

"I've got more where that came from, if you're interested."

EvaMarie turned to see the proprietor had found them. "We're decorating a game room. What did you have in mind?"

Half an hour later, they had purchased the sign, wall rack, poker table and wine rack in varying degrees of restoration. It was a job well done. It felt good, and Mason's deference to her opinion left EvaMarie glowing.

They continued down the sidewalk to a popular corner café at a casual stroll. "So where did you go to college?" Mason asked.

"An exclusive women's liberal arts college in Tennessee. Father wanted me to study so I would be articulate and ladylike, but he didn't really care what else I actually learned there, so I decided on something I thought I would enjoy doing one day." How different she'd dreamed her life would be, even then. "By the time things went downhill and I needed to get a job, my degree was years old. I'd need some updating and to pass my teaching certification exam. There was always so much to do, I just never seemed to find the time to enroll."

Many people, Mason included, saw her from the outside and expected days filled with directing staff and having her nails done. When the actuality of running a household, caring for a sick parent, and bolstering up another weak parent were like two full time jobs in only one twenty-four-hour period. "What about you?" she asked, curious about Mason's life after he'd moved away.

"I majored in business management. Dad insisted, even though I didn't see the point in a full four-year degree. We always knew we wanted to run our own stables, and had plenty of hands-on knowledge, so I thought shorter, more specific studies would be more appropriate."

He smiled at the hostess as she seated them. To EvaMarie's surprise, he took the chair right next to her instead of the one across from her, bringing them closer, creating a more intimate atmosphere that matched their conversation. She forced herself not to acknowledge the tingles low in her core at his nearness, his attention.

Seemingly unaware, Mason went on. "Now I know why he did so many things I didn't understand. Kane and I both needed the knowledge, ways of thinking and maturity that came from college to not only maintain our own businesses, but build the reputation that will help sustain us in such a public arena."

"And then you cut your teeth on the stables back home."

Mason nodded, then smiled at the waitress as she delivered their drinks and an appetizer of fried green tomatoes with corn-bread muffins. He waited until she'd taken their lunch orders to answer. "We started those stables with our dad. There's also some cattle ranching, but it's not a huge herd because the property isn't big enough to sustain it. Our big focus there is horse breeding. As we developed those lines, we were on the lookout for stock that would be our start into racing. I'm proud to say our dad helped us pick out our first mare and stud."

The smile they shared felt like more—more personal, even intimate in the midst of a crowd. What they were discussing might have seemed mundane, but EvaMarie knew how much it meant to Mason. She remembered him talking about running his own stables when he was a teenager, and had watched him soak in everything the other stable hands and manager had been willing to teach him.

As much as it saddened her to leave her home, she could actually see that it would be in good hands with the Harrington boys. "You're gonna do great," she murmured.

Surprise lit up his eyes. "Your dad would call that kind of talk sacrilege."

"Of course he would. That doesn't make it any less true."

His gaze held hers. "Thank you. That means a lot to me."

The very air between them seemed to grow heavy, leaving EvaMarie breathless and a little confused. Mason blinked, then focused on the plate in front of them. He snagged one of the tomatoes and lifted it toward her lips. "Taste this. I had some the other day, and they're great."

She wasn't about to tell him the treat was nothing new to her. Instead, she clamped down on her surge of need as he fed her the crispy tart bite, then took one of his own. Definitely not the kind of response she should be having in public.

"Well, this doesn't look much like business. Now does it?"

Liza's cutting, accusatory tone belied the saccharine smile plastered on her face as she stood beside their table. How long she'd been there, EvaMarie couldn't have said. She'd been too caught up in the magic of Mason's attention.

Silence reigned for a moment. After last night, Mason was probably afraid to touch the remark with a ten-foot pole, so EvaMarie adopted a closed expression and answered just loud enough for the group of women watching from a few feet away to hear her. "We just finished buying the decor for the new game room at the shop next door. Antiques will give the room real depth, I believe. Don't you agree?"

Liza's eyes widened, as if she didn't know how to take this polite response to her tasteless interruption.

"I agree," Mason finally chimed in. "Mr. Petty has some unique pieces in his store. I'll probably go back for other things for the house, but what we ordered today is perfect for that room." The grin he offered Liza sparked some nasty jealousy, but EvaMarie ignored it. Because Mason wasn't hers to be jealous over.

"Still a man cave," he went on, "but with class."

The attention helped Liza recover. She offered him a smile seemingly loaded with double meaning. "As if you could be anything but classy." Stepping a little closer, she rested her hand on Mason's shoulder. Her red nails seemed to dig just a touch. EvaMarie might have been imagining that from this angle. But she wasn't imagining the husky quality that colored Liza's voice. "I had such a good time last night."

I'm amazed she remembered it...

Meeting Mason's gaze with her own, EvaMarie could have sworn she saw the same thought reflected there. He gave a slight nod and her heart pounded. Being on the same wavelength with him was certainly a heady experience. Then he turned back to look up at Liza.

"How's John Roberts?" he asked.

Liza frowned. "How should I know? He dropped me off after a lecture on—" Stopping abruptly, she flicked her gaze between Mason and EvaMarie, then shook her head. "Anyway, I haven't seen him today. The girls and I are just out for some shoppin' and strollin'."

"Well, I see the waitress headed this way with our lunch," Mason said, "so if you don't mind..."

Sigh. What woman couldn't see that Mason wasn't interested? Of course, just the thought made EvaMarie worried that she was also the type of woman who read more into what was happening between her and Mason than what was really there. Things she really shouldn't want but couldn't quite turn away from.

"Of course," Liza said, never taking her eyes from him. "But I do hope you'll remember that preseason party we're having. It's gonna be the biggest thing around here. Anyone who is anyone will be there. Please tell me you'll come."

"You said you hadn't even sent out the invites yet."

The other woman's sweet smile made EvaMarie slightly sick.

"Mason, dear, you don't need an official invite. You're welcome anytime."

After her parting salvo, Liza turned without a goodbye and headed for the table her shopping companions had claimed... right within line of sight. Mason ignored the final part of the conversation and dug into his food with the gusto of a hardworking man.

But EvaMarie was left with the knowledge of the role reversal between them. For the first time, he was invited to the party she wouldn't be considered good enough to attend.

Thirteen

"Girl, aren't you about done with all this work for the day?"

EvaMarie gasped, her heart automatically jumping at the sound of a man's voice despite knowing Mason was out of town. "Don't scare me like that!" she scolded Jeremy.

He leaned against the threshold to what used to be the walk-in closet off her dressing room—now her sound studio. "You know you're too protective of this," he said. "If you'd just tell Mason, he'd fix it so you could continue to work here."

She looked around the surprisingly roomy space. At least, it was roomy for what she needed. When she'd started creating the studio, she'd given away and stored tons of clothes that she'd held on to since she was a little girl. Her current wardrobe resided on a portable rack in her dressing room.

In here, she'd stripped the walls down to the Sheetrock and installed a layer of insulation. She'd planned to refinish the walls, but then Mason had bought the estate. The space left provided enough room for a small desk that held her recording equipment, scripts, a small lamp and office supplies.

Just what she needed to build her career narrating audiobooks.

She'd never brought Mason in here, and he'd never asked.

What she was trying to do here, and the hope it represented for a new life, a new independence, felt fragile to her. Mason had always gone after whatever he wanted and damn the consequences. He'd probably see her efforts as weak, shadows of his own mighty conquests. Hopefully she could finish out her time in her childhood home without having to expose this part of herself.

It was the very first thing that was all her own. Her parents didn't know. Neither Laurence nor any of her friends knew. Jeremy had only divined the truth after wiggling his way in. To her surprise, he'd become her fiercest cheerleader. She simply hadn't been able to share it with Mason yet. It was too personal, too risky. If she failed, she wasn't gonna do it in front of an audience. "I know things aren't going to end well with him," she argued. "They can't. This, I mean, I haven't even told my parents about this. How could I—"

"You gotta have positive thoughts, girlie."

"No." She turned his way, giving him a hard glare. "No positive thoughts. Not in this. My father almost ruined Mason's family. No matter how much of a good time we're having…" She stumbled over the words.

Jeremy gave her a knowing grin. "And a very good time it is, indeed."

"Shush. It won't last." She glanced around the small room. "This—I need in my life. I need to accomplish this, to support myself, okay?"

"So if this thing with Mason isn't gonna last, why do you have this out?"

From the rack beside the door, Jeremy lifted up a formal dress in a garment bag. EvaMarie's heart thudded. Jeremy knew what the dress was—they'd discussed it when the movers were cleaning out a storage room downstairs. She should have sent it to the storage unit, but she hadn't been able to. She shouldn't have tried it on, but she hadn't been able to resist. She shouldn't have had it cleaned this week, but she hadn't been able to quiet the hopeful voice inside that said Mason would ask her to go to Liza's family's ball the day after he returned.

She knew he had a new suit. She'd taken delivery on it when it had arrived.

"I don't even know why I have it out. He hasn't mentioned taking me." She slumped into her chair, disgust rolling through her to wash all the starch from her posture. "Why am I torturing myself like this?"

Because this had been the best few weeks of her life. No parents to judge or criticize her. Purpose and meaning in her work. And a man who made her feel sexy and wanted.

Even if he didn't really want her for the long term.

"So just go yourself and show him what he's missing," Jeremy said.

Her grin was rueful. "Can't. I didn't get an invitation. Except—"

"Except what?"

"Laurence has asked me to go with him, as a friend."

Jeremy was already shaking his head. "Don't do it."

"I'm not." But she wasn't sure that she wouldn't. The thought of Mason being there without her, not even realizing he could have invited her, stung. She might just be selfish enough to give in to Laurence.

Jeremy lifted the bag once more. "This would fit you perfectly. And there's nothing wrong with hoping, EvaMarie."

"Except feeling shattered when your dreams don't come true," she replied, but her tone held little heat. Deep inside, a small part of her was already resigned to never finding someone who would accept all of her, including her family obligations and who she truly was and wanted to be as a person. Those guys seemed few and far between.

But it was the dream dress—her mother's from her "debut"

on the local scene. It fit EvaMarie perfectly... Who was she kidding? She wasn't going to any stupid dance, so she should stop mooning around about it like a teenage girl from an after-school special.

"Did you need me?" she finally asked, doing her best to forget the complications and focus on reality.

"Do you have time to show me where the furniture needs to be placed in the study?"

"Yeah. I've got about an hour's worth of recording left, but I need to give my voice a break first."

Her current project was a blessing in many ways. It had come in the same day Mason had left to go out of town—it was also her longest project to date, by an author she'd never worked with before, so she hadn't been entirely certain how many hours would be involved. But the author was a bestseller with lots of connections. If she liked EvaMarie's work, this could lead to some good things for her budding career.

But she'd delayed jumping into the project because she'd been nervous about doing a good job. A few false starts, though, and she'd been ready to go.

Jeremy glanced over the equipment she'd painstakingly paid for, piece by piece, and treated like the most delicate of babies. "I think this is so cool," he said. "With your voice and attention to detail, you're gonna be a star."

"I'll settle for financially stable, but thank you."

She was gonna miss the little studio when she was forced to move. Despite the half-finished walls and need for secrecy, the alternative would likely be a tiny closet or bathroom in an apartment complex, with all the noise complications that came with it, so—

"You should still tell him," Jeremy said, nagging her. "I thought you were moving into a whole I'm-going-after-what-I-want stage of life?"

The reminder had her standing up straighter, but she knew the minute she looked into Mason's eyes, her words would die unspoken. She enjoyed having sex with him—hell, that was an understatement. And not just the physical part, but the exploration and intimacy of being with Mason. She even enjoyed living with him—his smart, funny approach to life kept her guessing and on her toes.

But she refused to use the L word. Because if she couldn't trust Mason with the most important things in her life, like the career she was struggling to build book by book, then he wasn't truly the man she wanted for forever.

Was he?

EvaMarie took a deep breath and braced herself before she even stepped out of her car. The doors of the assisted living center where her parents now resided weren't quite far enough away for her liking. She hadn't seen her parents since the blowup at the restaurant. Heck, she'd barely even talked to her mom, and not at all with her dad.

Maybe she should put this off for another day?

But her mother had needed a few things from storage and given her a few niggling reminders that EvaMarie hadn't been to see the place since they'd gotten settled and—boom! Here she was...

I'm such a sucker.

Trying for a positive attitude, she pushed through the door with purpose and smiled at the girl behind the reception desk who directed her to the Florida room. According to her mother, their new afternoon routine included cool drinks with friends before dressing for dinner. Her parents were happy. Settling in. Her job was done.

Except walking through the spacious rooms with their lush, real plants and unique pieces of artwork only heightened the sense of pressure to perform. Her parents couldn't truly afford to live here without digging deep into the savings that needed to stay untouched in case of a rapid decline in her father's health. So EvaMarie was supplementing his disability checks.

Something she'd need to continue doing, which meant achieving her goal of becoming a successful voice artist was of the utmost importance. And after her time with Mason was done, she'd probably have to take another part-time job, as well. Some days she thought she would never know what it was like to live without the performance pressure.

"EvaMarie, there you are," her mother said as soon as she reached the door. Her mother met her halfway with a kiss. "Darling," she murmured, "you couldn't have dressed up a bit more?"

Since when was she required to "dress" to visit her parents? She'd thought her jeans and nice shirt were perfectly presentable.

They approached a table where several other residents were seated. As soon as her mother started to introduce everyone, EvaMarie changed her mind. Maybe dressing up would have bolstered her confidence in the face of so many people. Her father rose to stand beside her, an arm around her shoulders. It was a pose they'd adopted many times through the years. The picture of the perfect family.

To EvaMarie, it only reminded her just how far from perfect they were.

"If you all will excuse us a moment," her mother said, "I wanted to introduce EvaMarie to Mrs. Robinson."

EvaMarie moved along with a smile, then said, "Mother, I really need to bring in your clothes and stuff—"

"Nonsense. There's plenty of time for that."

They came to a table closer to the floor-to-ceiling windows occupied by an elderly woman. She appeared awfully frail, but her expression was alight with intelligence when she turned to them. At her direction, they were seated and her father flagged down a waiter for a round of iced sweet tea.

"You were absolutely right, Bev," Mrs. Robinson said. "Your daughter is beautiful."

EvaMarie murmured her thanks, while her mother beamed. Though it made EvaMarie feel like she was three, the compli-

ment pleased her mother. After chatting for a few minutes, her
father stood. "Bev, let's go arrange to move your things to our
apartment."

But when EvaMarie started to rise, he waved her back. "We
can take care of it. You stay and chat."

"Um..." Her parents seemed all too happy to make a hasty
retreat. But the silence wasn't awkward for long.

Mrs. Robinson chuckled. "They aren't subtle, those two,
that's for sure."

"I'm so sorry."

"Don't be, child. I did actually want to meet you, and now
that I have, I'm very glad." Her smile softened the angular
edges age had added to her face. "In this instance, I think your
mother was dead right."

"About what?" EvaMarie asked, caution leaking into her
voice.

"Why, I'm looking for someone to hire to take care of my
place."

Surprised, EvaMarie stared for a moment. "Your place?"

"Yes, child. I had to move here about six months or so ago
when I started having some bad back issues. My nephew has
been staying at my home since then. Keeping everything in
good repair and making sure no one starts thinking it's empty."

"That's nice of him."

Mrs. Robinson laughed again. "Well, I paid him to do it. I
don't expect anyone to uproot themselves out of the goodness of
their hearts. Plus, the house is a good enough size and filled to
the brim with antiques, so there's always something that needs
looking after. But now he's been offered a really good job in
Nashville, and I need someone to take his place."

EvaMarie stilled. "You want to pay me to watch over your
house?"

"Well, you'd need to live there. Your parents mentioned you
would need to move out of your own situation posthaste. That's
perfect for me. Not that I expect you to give up your normal

activities. Just stay on top of things and come out here once a week for us to go over what's happening and any expenditures."

Mrs. Robinson glanced over EvaMarie's shoulder. "Ah, I see your parents heading this way, so I'll hurry. Despite what they may say, dear child, there's no pressure. But if you think you'll be interested, please let me know soon. You can call the front desk and ask them to transfer your call to my suite."

She reached across the table with one frail hand, prompting EvaMarie to take it. "You let me know. All right?"

EvaMarie had to clear her throat to get her words out. "Thank you, ma'am."

"My pleasure," the elderly woman said just as EvaMarie's glowing parents returned.

Another fifteen minutes of casual conversation was punctuated by her parents casting pointed glances her way. Somehow EvaMarie managed to ignore them, and Mrs. Robinson gave her a pleased nod as they left. They didn't even make it around the corner before her mother started in.

"Isn't it a wonderful opportunity?" she gushed. "The old Robinson place is one of those gorgeous antebellum homes in the historic district. Very prestigious looking. You couldn't ask for a better situation."

"I thought you didn't want me taking care of other people's homes," EvaMarie asked, the dry question going right over her mother's head.

"Don't be silly, dear. We'd just prefer for you to work for someone whose reputation would enhance your own. Why, this would hardly be work at all."

"But I do have obligations right now—"

"Nonsense," her father barked. "You don't owe anything to a cheater. He manipulated you into taking that job."

Maybe, but still… "But it was a job that I needed. And I'm grateful for it."

Her mother, always eager to soothe over what might turn into an argument, said, "But this would be much less awkward. And you'd start right away. Mrs. Robinson is a lovely lady. This is perfect for you, dear."

"What idiot would turn it down?" her father added, probably to combat the resistance he could sense was growing inside her. Or maybe he was just mad that she hadn't automatically poured gratitude all over Mrs. Robinson and them for the opportunity they'd handed her.

Take what you want, EvaMarie.

"I'll discuss it with her a little more before I decide," she hedged, a little ashamed that she wasn't truer to the memory of Mason's words echoing in her head.

"What's to discuss?"

She tuned out the rest of whatever her father said, a skill she'd long ago perfected.

Twenty minutes later, when she managed to escape to her car, her ears rang with her parents' strident insistence that she contact Mrs. Robinson tonight and accept her offer. And even though it smacked of giving in, EvaMarie had to admit that they had a point.

It would be an easy job that she'd be paid for—a lot easier than overseeing the renovations. She'd have the space and privacy to build her career without interference or worry. And she could put an early end to the probably unhealthy reliance she was developing on Mason's touch, Mason's presence.

So why did the very thought of accepting make her so sad?

Fourteen

Mason frowned as he waited one more time for EvaMarie to answer her phone. He'd called twice already—once at dinnertime, then again a couple of hours later. Both calls had gone straight to voice mail.

If everything hadn't been just fine when he'd left, he'd think she was avoiding him.

"Hello?"

Boy, one breathless word and Mason was wishing away the hundreds of miles between them. How had he become addicted this hard this fast? "Hey," he replied, his own voice deepening with his desire.

She didn't speak, and her very hesitation magnified his uneasiness from earlier. He focused on the sound of her breathing. "How has your day been?" he finally asked.

Oh, that deep sigh could mean so many things.

"Well, Jeremy's crew completed the first-floor tiles."

Mason had known the job was next on the list, but he hadn't expected them to get to it this quickly. "That's great."

"Yes. But I finally had to leave," she said with a soft chuckle.

"I couldn't handle the sound of them cutting. No matter where I hid, that high-pitched whine chased me down."

The noise could be piercing. Not to mention the commotion caused by the extra crew Jeremy had brought in to get the entire floor done quickly. Good thing Mason had been out of town. "So did you ride out to the stream so you could fantasize about me?"

His little joke didn't garner him the laugh he was looking for. "Actually, I went to visit my parents."

"Bummer."

"Mason."

How could even her preschool teacher voice sound sexy? "Hey, you know you need someone to brighten your day. I'm just trying to help that along."

Her huffy sigh expressed a depth of exasperation that told him his playful mood was not winning him any points. He probably shouldn't ask if they'd spent the entire time lecturing her on quitting her job. Maybe he'd try a different tactic.

"I actually did want to talk to you about something."

"Really?"

He grinned as excitement entered her voice, softening the irritation.

"Yep. Kane and I have a new job for you."

"Oh."

Mason rushed on, his enthusiasm for their idea pushing to the surface. "We've decided to host a big bash at the house. After all, there will be a lot to show off, right? Introduce ourselves to the racing community, entertain in the new spaces downstairs, have a buffet in the formal dining room..." It took a while for him to realize that EvaMarie wasn't responding. "What do you think?" he demanded.

"If being seen is what you want, that will make a big splash."

"We need to be seen and make contacts...it's good for business."

"This will definitely be good for business."

So why didn't she sound excited? "We want you to put it to-gether for us. I told Kane that no one would know better what to have and who to invite. You'll do great."

"Sure."

Maybe she was simply overwhelmed. "I know you've got a lot going on with the renovations, but this will be fun. And great for us."

"It will be my pleasure to organize a party for you."

But it didn't sound like a pleasure. Her voice was stiff, not husky and molten like when he usually spoke with her. Maybe he should change tactics. "I think I'll be back by Thursday."

She was silent so long he wondered if they'd been discon-nected. "EvaMarie, are you okay?"

"Sure." She still didn't sound convincing, but at least she was talking. "I'm just tired, I guess. A lot on my mind."

"Anything I can help with?"

"I doubt it."

He wasn't sure, but he had a good guess what the problem was. After all, in twenty minutes her parents had totally screwed up his head. He could only imagine what they could do to hers in an afternoon. "Did you spend all day fighting off new suit-ors or better job offers?"

"No," she snapped back. "Nothing like that."

"Come on...work with me here," he crooned. He'd never seen her in this kind of mood, but he was more than up for the chal-lenge. "I'm very good at distraction."

"And that's helping, how?"

"Do I look like Dr. Freud? Don't kill the messenger. I'm not the obsessive worrier here, am I?"

Now he garnered a laugh, small one though it was. "Well, I can't deny it, as much as I'd like to."

"See?" It felt good to make her feel good, even over the phone. Almost as good as making her feel awesome in person.

And she wasn't letting him off the hook. "Well, if you want to help, you may need to work a little harder."

"Oh, I'm perfectly capable of working it hard if you need me to." He let his voice deepen into a playful growl.

"Mason!"

There we go. Time to have some fun. "Well, maybe not from this far away…but I can make it work for you."

"What did you have in mind?" That breathlessness from earlier had returned. Even though they were only connected by phone, her husky voice worked its way along his nerve endings to set them all abuzz.

"Just talking. You like talking to me, right?"

"Of course."

Her response was too matter-of-fact. He needed to shake her up. "Then tell me your favorite part of what we do together."

"Um, what?"

She sounded so innocently shocked he wanted to laugh…or kiss her thoroughly. "Come on, baby. Tell me what you like." His body throbbed as he waited for her answer.

"I don't know," she whispered, leaving silence to hang between them.

"I'm waiting."

"When you…" He heard her clear her throat. "When you kiss and suck at my neck," she finally murmured.

Mason's mind conjured up explicit details of him doing just that. "And I love how you respond. Moaning. Nails digging in. Your hips lifting to mine."

Every word brought a new picture. His body tightened, and he desperately wished she were there for him to hold close right now.

She felt it too. He could tell by the acceleration in her breath. Was she eager to play? "Now tell me how you like to be touched."

"With hands…" she said, quicker now to respond, "hands that are rough, calluses on them."

Just like his.

"Firm. Guiding me. Supporting me."

Just like he wanted to.

"Digging in." Her voice was almost deep enough to be a moan. "Not to hurt, but in the excitement of the moment."

Just like his did when he felt her climax around him.

Mason broke out in a sweat, hands clenching into tight fists. Not from the images she was conjuring. But from the fear that after playing with fire, he'd never again be free of his need for EvaMarie.

"I thought we agreed you wouldn't go to the ball with Laurence?"

EvaMarie paused in her attempt to work one of her amethyst earrings into the hole in her ear. She hadn't worn them in forever. There wasn't any need for fancy jewelry at the few places she went. But they went perfectly with her mother's debutante dress, so EvaMarie hadn't been able to resist.

"I'm not, actually," she replied to Jeremy. The frown that appeared on her face in the mirror didn't go with the filmy cream layers of her dress or the elegant upsweep of her hair. Why did he have to ruin her anticipation? She was having a hard enough time hanging on to her composure as it was.

She caught the pointed look he directed her way via the hall mirror. "I'm going on my parents' invite, okay? They insisted. I might be meeting Laurence there, just as friends."

After all, how pathetic would she look without a date? And the fact that she had to worry about that, when she had a man who had no problem climbing into her bed every night, ticked her off.

"But you're really going to be spying."

"I don't know," EvaMarie said. Her frustration from the past week boiled over. "He didn't say if he was going, okay? Didn't say if he was coming home tonight. Didn't give me any indication whether me going with him was even an option at all." She huffed, blinking back tears. After all, she didn't want to ruin her mascara.

At least, that's what she told herself.

"Why didn't you ask?" Jeremy said.

Ask? "Why didn't I ask? Because wouldn't that leave me looking pathetic when he said no?"

"So it was easier not to ask than it was not to know?"

"I..." Maybe so. Maybe not. "I'm just confused."

Jeremy moved in close, looking suave and elegant in the mirror in spite of the casual clothes he wore for working on the estate. He settled warm hands on her bare shoulders. "Sweetheart, you are worthy of an answer. If you don't get one, you have to demand one."

"But—I can't..." In her world, demands were always punished. "That's just not me."

"Isn't it? Isn't that what this is all about?" He waved a hand over her dress. "A way to demand Mason answer your unspoken questions without having to come right out and ask them?"

Her hands clenched into the gown at her sides, as if fearful someone would try to tear it from her. "Are you saying this is wrong?" she asked.

"Absolutely not," Jeremy said, meeting her gaze in the mirror. "I just don't want you to sell yourself short. Have some self-respect, EvaMarie. You've earned it the hard way. But you'll never build up your stockpile if you keep letting people steal it from you..."

The image that statement created in her mind held her in awe for a moment. She could literally picture a pile of gold bars that her father and mother and Mason and Liza all kept stealing from...and she did nothing to stop them.

"All right," she said, a glimmer of understanding rapidly expanding in her mind. "I just want to see if something happens... if he responds. Wouldn't you?"

Her restlessness this week had coalesced into a fierce curiosity to see just how Mason would react to her in a public setting. After all, they weren't dating. But somehow, some way, she'd still thought he would invite her to go to Liza's ball with him.

She'd been sorely disappointed.

But she didn't know the why of it—at least, a why that she could accept. That's what was eating at her. Along with the job offer she'd had. She hadn't been able to bring it up with Mason...but she needed to make a decision before the opportunity slipped through her fingers.

Jeremy kissed her on her temple. "Girl, yes, I would." He squeezed her arms to encourage her. "You look beautiful, sweetheart. I just don't understand why you think things couldn't work out with Mason. Any man would be lucky to have you."

EvaMarie shook her head, blinking back tears. "It can't work. There's too much history, too much—"

"Seems to me like it's working now. I don't see what the past has to do with anything."

She met his gaze straight up. "Can you honestly see my father walking me down the aisle to meet Mason? I'm not ready to spend a lifetime separated from the parents I still love."

Like Mason's mother. Had it been wrong of her to walk away from her family for love? Had she regretted it? EvaMarie knew her parents would be the same, forever condemning her for that choice. But then again, they might not cut her off completely. They'd become quite dependent on her these past few years.

If her parents weren't an issue, would she make a different choice?

"I'll see you at the party," Jeremy said, turning to go as if he knew he'd said enough.

She nibbled on her lip as Jeremy's footsteps echoed down the hallway and then down the flight of steps to the basement.

She could tell herself she was going because she wanted to, but deep down, she knew what she really wanted was to see Mason there—and be seen by him. But she did have some pride. If he ignored her, she would not push the matter.

To make her nerves worse, Mason hadn't made it home the day before as planned. She knew he was heading out sometime today, but he hadn't said when, hadn't called her when he left, nothing. So this was probably just a tournament of nervous tension for nothing.

Stop mooning and go if you're going.

So she did. Only stepping out of her car was a bit more difficult than she'd anticipated. After all, she'd always come to these events *with* her parents or *with* Laurence. Never on her own. And people could talk about lifting your chin and storming a room with pride...but it was actually a damn hard thing to do.

But she pictured that pile of gold bars and knew she didn't ever want to be with someone who wouldn't add to that pile. Which meant, if she were to continue living with herself, she better get to work.

Because she was worthy of way more than a pile of gold. She was worthy of respect—and tonight she would demand it.

Fifteen

Mason stumbled, exhausted, into the side entrance when he got home around seven on Friday. Over twenty-four hours after he should have been here. He hadn't even been sure he'd make it in tonight. The long drive over, after some last-minute meetings this morning, had about done him in. But as much as he wanted to hole up underneath EvaMarie's cozy down comforter, he needed to put in an appearance at Liza's party.

Kane hadn't been able to leave at all, making it all the more imperative that Mason serve as the lone rep for their debut tonight in Kentucky racing circles. Liza's family was both prominent and well-connected in the local racing scene. Mason needed to get his name—and even better, his face—circulating.

But first, he wanted to see EvaMarie. She hadn't sounded right when he talked to her on the phone yesterday, and something told him she was upset. Hopefully not with him, but she hadn't wanted to talk about it. He could tell by the hesitation in her responses and how distracted she'd sounded.

EvaMarie wasn't the type to spill her guts, even after all they'd shared. If Mason wanted to know, he'd have to coax it out—something he hadn't wanted to do over the phone. He was much better at it in person.

He looked around the downstairs, noting the sleek elegance of the new tiled floors and the finished dining room. No sounds came from the basement, so Mason assumed they were done for the day, though Jeremy's car was still in the drive.

Mason took the stairs two at a time, hoping to find EvaMarie in her room, but all was quiet. As he searched, the ticktock of time passing niggled in his brain.

No EvaMarie. Maybe she was in the barn. Would she be able to shower quickly and throw on a dress? Did she even own a formal dress? Surely she did, but he wasn't sure how long it had been since she'd worn one.

He'd spent years dreaming of her living the high life on her parents' money. But in actuality, her life had been very different.

In clear detail, Mason now saw the drawbacks to his decision not to mention the party to EvaMarie. He might have been worried he wouldn't make it home, but if she was here somewhere, he hadn't left her a lot of time to get ready.

Of course, he'd also felt some confusion over whether he should ask her at all. Despite the incredible intimacy they shared, they weren't technically dating. They'd agreed on that. Mason didn't want her to feel like she had to go with him if she wasn't comfortable making a public appearance on his arm.

But by God, he wanted her with him tonight.

He reached into his pocket for his phone to call her, all while stomping across her rug to the dressing room he knew was on the other side of her bathroom. As he entered the room, he saw a rack of clothes to one side, which seemed odd. No formal dresses there, though. He reached for the door to the closet. Maybe she kept things she didn't wear much in here.

But what he found inside had nothing to do with clothes. What the hell?

"Girl, why are you back already? Did you forget something?"

Jeremy called from the bedroom. "Or did the thought of facing an evening with dull Laurence make you change your mind?"

Ducking back out of the closet, Mason came face-to-face with the other man.

"Oh, snap," Jeremy said. He swallowed hard. "I don't think you're supposed to be in there."

"It's my house," Mason said, stalking closer. His exhaustion faded in the face of his growing anger. "I can be wherever I want."

Jeremy inclined his head, holding his hands up in surrender. "Also true."

"What's this?" Mason asked, jerking his head back toward the closet.

The walls had been covered in insulation, and the shelves were empty of clothes. A table and a filing cabinet had replaced the closet's usual function. If he had to guess, what looked like sound equipment was the key to the mystery.

Jeremy worried his lip as his averted gaze told Mason he didn't want to answer.

"You obviously know," Mason said. "Spill it. Does princess have a ham radio obsession I'm not aware of?"

Jeremy laughed, then slapped a hand over his mouth. When he finally removed it, he was sober under Mason's glare. "Well, she has an incredible voice, right?"

Mason couldn't argue that. "What does that have to do with—"

"She needs a way to support herself," Jeremy rushed to say. "A mutual friend of ours is an author, and she put EvaMarie in touch with some people in the audiobook industry. She's been working very hard to build a foundation..."

Jeremy's voice trailed off as he noticed Mason staring. Mason couldn't help it. His brain had short-circuited the minute he'd realized EvaMarie was building a career. Not a job, not a hobby. A career. One she hadn't bothered to mention to him—at all.

"Where is she?" he demanded, not caring that his voice had roughened.

He could tell from Jeremy's face he wasn't going to like this answer either.

"She left about forty-five minutes ago for Liza's party."

Liza's party. Without him. Yet another thing she hadn't mentioned. "With dull Laurence?"

Jeremy shook his head but paused under Mason's look. "Well, she drove herself, but she was meeting him there. As friends."

Mason gave a sound of frustration and anger all mingled together.

For once, Jeremy didn't pause. "Well, what did you expect, man? *You* certainly didn't invite her."

No. No, he hadn't. He'd thought to keep everything separated into neat little compartments. But that didn't mean he wanted to hear about it from someone else. "I don't think I need you to tell me how to handle this—" He'd almost said relationship, but that wasn't what he had with EvaMarie, was it? Not really.

"Well, you certainly need someone to tell you," Jeremy said, gaining bravado and not backing down beneath Mason's glare. "She's not just your housekeeper, now, is she? She's your woman…or is she just convenient?"

Shock jolted through Mason. "Is that what she thinks?"

"Should she?"

"Should I?" Mason demanded, gesturing back toward the modified closet.

Jeremy frowned. "I'm sure she has her reasons for keeping certain things private, but I think EvaMarie isn't the only one who needs to be honest around here."

Mason wanted to rail some more, work out his aggression here and now. As if he knew that, Jeremy didn't even give him the chance. He simply left.

Mason glanced back into the darkened room with its pile of sophisticated equipment. He'd kept business and pleasure and emotions completely apart from one another. Like a picky child who thought the piles of food on his plate would contaminate each other if they touched. Obviously Mason had been too good at keeping things separate. And while he could forgive EvaMarie for going to the party without him, he refused to take responsibility for her keeping this a secret. That was all on her.

And Mason wanted an explanation.

EvaMarie slowly relaxed into the rhythm of the evening. Laurence had been just attentive enough when she had arrived to soothe her secret ego, but seemed to lose interest quickly. Which wasn't unusual for him. Her parents had been welcoming, without finding any little faults to disapprove of... All in all, she was having a much better time than she'd expected.

Except for the urge to look toward the entryway every ten minutes to see if Mason was going to show up.

She'd already checked her phone once to see if he'd texted or tried to call, but had put it away again when her mother frowned in her direction. Her parents weren't fans of the current trend to have cellular phones constantly in hand. To them, parties were for socializing with the people actually at the party.

Normally, EvaMarie didn't have a problem with that. Tonight was a whole other matter, in more ways than one.

Suddenly her father announced, "I need to sit down."

Her mother assisted him with a concerned look that encouraged EvaMarie to stay close. If her father started having difficulty or limb pain while in the midst of all these watching eyes, her mother wouldn't cope well.

"I'm fine, Bev," he barked as her mother hovered over his left shoulder. "Just tired, all of a sudden. EvaMarie, get me some champagne."

Laurence half rose from his chair. "Would you like me to—"

"Nonsense," her father said in a gruff voice. "She's perfectly capable of fetching me a drink."

Concerned, EvaMarie hesitated, but her mother gave a quick nod in the direction of the bar. It wasn't until she was in line that the first inklings of unease appeared. Several feet away, Liza stood, holding the attention of a court of young ladies. EvaMarie knew them all. They'd grown up together.

What bothered her were the frequent glances in her direction, accompanied by giggles and whispering.

Despite the ache in the bottom of her stomach, EvaMarie took a deep breath and turned slightly away to ignore them. Whatever was happening, she refused to feed the fire by granting it her attention. That was often the thing Liza was looking for—a way to be the center of attention in any given situation. She didn't need EvaMarie to accomplish that.

But the longer she stood there, the louder the giggling grew. EvaMarie didn't think the women were getting louder...they were simply getting closer. She ordered her father's drink and turned to go back to the table with relief.

But Liza had no intention of letting her escape. She'd barely taken half a dozen steps before the woman moved into her path. "EvaMarie, it's so nice to see you here," she cooed, the sugar-sweet tone grating on EvaMarie's nerves. Liza leaned forward as if to impart a secret, only she didn't really lower her voice. "Although I don't remember seeing your name on the guest list, if I recall correctly."

The women behind her giggled, reminding EvaMarie of a gaggle of geese playing follow the leader.

She wasn't going to give Liza the satisfaction of justifying her presence. It was a pointless exercise when Liza knew that EvaMarie could have arrived with any number of people here.

"I was just telling the girls about your new job," she said, her overly mascaraed eyelashes wide enough to show the whites of her eyes. Not the most flattering look, in EvaMarie's opinion.

"Yes?" she said. She was a working woman now. No point in hiding it, which she didn't want to do.

Earning her own living, learning exactly what she was capable of, left EvaMarie feeling pride—not shame. And looking at the women before her, the very epitome of unoccupied children without purpose in their lives, made her glad. This was what her parents had wanted for her when she was young. But it wasn't what she wanted. Her work at the library had given her a taste of creating meaning in her life by helping others. And as hard as the work with Mason had been, EvaMarie ended her days satisfied instead of empty.

"So you're living up there all alone?" one of the women asked over Liza's shoulder.

EvaMarie squinted. "I'm not sure what you mean."

"You know," the woman elaborated, "just the two of you in that big ol' house."

EvaMarie almost expected a *wink, wink* to be added. Was this really what they'd spent their time discussing? "There are a lot of workmen up there. I'm simply directing the renovations for the Harringtons."

"The Harringtons, huh?" Liza giggled. "But you and *Mason* are up there alone at night, right? At least, from what I saw." She glanced over her shoulder at the lemmings behind her. "Gives a whole new meaning to live-in help, if you know what I mean."

"No, I—"

Laurence appeared at her elbow. "Your father wants to know what's taking so long." He lifted the champagne flute from her hand.

"What do you think, Laurence?" Liza interjected. "I'd bet the odds that EvaMarie is securing her job with *the Harringtons* in more ways than one."

EvaMarie felt her cheeks flush as Laurence didn't jump in to immediately defend her. Instead, he cast an inquiring look in her direction.

And even though EvaMarie knew her time with Mason wasn't like that, she couldn't stop the red hot glow from spreading down her throat and chest. "That's not what's happening at all," she choked out, even though her brain told her this wasn't junior high and she didn't need to justify herself to anyone.

"If it was me," Liza said, though her tone made it clear she'd never have to stoop that low, "well, let's just say I wouldn't blame you for milking that relationship for all it's worth. You get to hold on to your home and garner the attentions of one sexy man…although I notice he wasn't the one who brought you tonight. Now was he?"

Just like that, EvaMarie felt her innermost fears laid bare for this uncaring group to dissect and make fun of at her expense. Even Laurence, who'd always stood by her despite her decidedly outcast role in recent years, continued to eye her as if he could see all her secrets behind her fancy retro gown. Finally he asked, "Well, he certainly does have himself a sweet deal, doesn't he?"

"Laurence." Anger started to replace the nerves she felt in the pit of her stomach. "That's completely uncalled for." Regardless of whether or not it might be true. "I keep my job the same way any employee does. I work hard, and go above and beyond for the Harringtons."

"Do you now?"

Mason's voice from right behind her should have been a relief. But the hard tone didn't reassure her at all. Before she could turn, he stepped in close to her back and spoke to the others. "If you all would excuse us, please?"

Then his hand encircled her wrist, a perfect pivot for him to turn her to face him. She had a brief glimpse of Laurence's angry expression before Mason whisked her out onto the dance floor.

His sure touch guided her into a loosely modified version of a modern waltz that allowed them to slowly traverse the lightly populated space. Most people were still enjoying the hors d'oeuvres and drinks and hadn't taken advantage of the live music yet.

The glitter in Mason's blue eyes as he stared down at her didn't calm her unsettled nerves. She'd wondered how he would react to seeing her here. She was about to find out.

"So, was Laurence right? Seems to me you've gotten quite a few perks out of this deal. Though it hadn't occurred to me that you might be milking every opportunity to get exactly what you wanted...until tonight."

"I don't understand..."

"I went into your closet tonight."

Her stumble could have been disastrous, but Mason's smooth save kept them upright and floating across the floor. The whirl of the crowd on the periphery of her vision made EvaMarie a little nauseous.

As if he could read her understanding in her expression, Mason gave a nod, then went on. "So you do understand? How many other secrets have you been keeping from me?"

"What? None." This new assault from a completely unexpected direction left EvaMarie grasping for a response. "Look, I wasn't ready to talk about what I was trying to do..."

"Right." His expression turned into a glare. "It would be a shame for me to encourage you."

"Would you have?"

Mason didn't answer, just continued with his unrelenting glare. EvaMarie wasn't sure exactly what was happening here. She'd made a mistake not telling Mason about her narration job, but they really hadn't had a lot of time to build that kind of trust. Especially in a situation that had an end date in sight...

When he still didn't speak, EvaMarie gave in to her own internal pressure to explain. "I'm just trying to build some sort of career."

"A career based in my house."

His resentment was becoming clearer. "Actually, I can do it anywhere. You know as well as I do that I needed a place to stay—"

"—and work."

"And it helped to be able to continue to work, but that's not why—"

"Why you slept with me?"

The emotions that stopped EvaMarie in her tracks were too complicated to untangle. She found herself searching Mason's face, desperate for any sign of the lover and, yes, friend she'd spent the last few weeks with. The man who had let go of the need for revenge that he'd shown up with on her doorstep. "Is that really how you see me? As a woman who would sleep with you for the chance to stay in my childhood home and—" nausea tightened her throat "—get paid for it?"

In the back of her mind, she realized people were starting to watch them, listen to their conversation. And all of Liza's suspicions were being confirmed. But what mattered right now was Mason and the realization that he hadn't changed as much from that vengeful man as she'd thought.

"Well, you haven't really let me get to know you, the real you, have you? So I can't really say."

"Are you kidding me?" she asked, incredulous. "I keep one thing a secret and now I'm hiding from you? Is that how you really view me? Or is this just an excuse to push me away now that other people are starting to talk?"

"I'm not the one who's always cared what other people think. Am I?"

No, he wasn't. But that didn't really answer her question.

EvaMarie was immediately struck by the sudden awareness of how quiet the other conversations in the large room had gotten. And as much as she'd like to say she didn't care, that didn't mean she longed to air her dirty laundry in front of all of these people.

Without answering, she turned on her heel, stalking back to her parents' table. "EvaMarie," her mother said fretfully as she approached.

She ignored her, ignored her father's hard stare, ignored Laurence's arrival right after her. Instead, she reached for her clutch and shawl. She'd had enough partying for one night.

But Mason wasn't done. "So let's just get one thing straight," he said, the sound of his angry voice scraping across her nerves. "Did you or did you not work with me, sleep with me, so you

328 REINING IN THE BILLIONAIRE

could stay close to your very nice, very free studio in order to build your new career?"

"No," she snapped.

"Then why the secrecy?"

Before she could tell him to go to hell, her father bellowed, "What's he talking about?"

"Nothing."

Still he struggled to his feet, always willing to use his large stature to intimidate an answer out of her. "Why would you need a career?" he demanded. "We agreed you're taking the job with Mrs. Robinson."

"A job?" Mason's voice had gone deadly deep, shaking Eva-Marie far more than her father's at his worst. Mason moved in closer, right over her shoulder. He left no space for her to turn and face him. "What? No two weeks' notice? Or do you only grant others that kind of courtesy when it suits you to do so?"

Sixteen

Mason should have been satisfied as he replayed the memory of EvaMarie running from the Young house, the fragile vintage gown pulled up away from her heels. Instead, he clenched his fists around the steering wheel and hit the gas with considerably more force.

He'd walked away from a blustering Daulton as he demanded EvaMarie tell him what was going on. Their little family drama didn't interest him. She'd run past him across the large main foyer as he'd made his apologies to Liza's parents for disrupting their party. But he had the uncomfortable feeling that the argument hadn't bothered them the way it had Mason.

After all, he'd just made them the talk of the town without any effort. Though Lord only knew what this would do to the Harrington reputation. Probably enhance it, considering how backward things like this worked in the world.

Now he let himself into the house and paused a moment to listen to the stillness. EvaMarie's car was in the drive, not in the garage where she normally parked it.

Was she in her room? The kitchen? Was she planning to continue their discussion? Maybe offer him something special to tease him out of his bad mood?

Mason shook his head. As angry as he was, he recognized that wasn't the EvaMarie he knew. Yes, he'd lashed out and accused her of sleeping with him to get what she wanted. But deep down he didn't want to believe that could be true.

But he wasn't sure the woman he'd come to know as an adult was real. Had she been hiding behind what he wanted to see in order to hold on to the life she hadn't been ready to give up? Even worse, he wasn't sure what to do about that.

Right now, he just needed some freakin' sleep.

Only it didn't look like he was going to get it. As he approached the darkened back staircase, Mason looked up to see EvaMarie seated on one of the upper steps, a pool of frothy material puddled around her. She stared out the arched window opposite, giving him a decent view of streaked mascara and the luxurious wash of hair she'd let down to cover her bare back.

Did she have to be so lovely?

He clenched his fists, wishing he could eradicate all sympathy, all regret from his emotions right now. If only she didn't look like a Cinderella after the ball, after her world had gone to hell in a handbasket. If only she didn't make his heart ache to hold her just once more—even when he knew he shouldn't.

The silence lasted for long minutes more as he stared at her from the bottom of the stairs. Maybe he'd been wrong. Maybe she was justified in keeping her secrets. But what about the job? Or rather, the new job. That familiar anger and hurt flooded his chest once more.

Just when he'd thought she wouldn't, EvaMarie spoke. "I'll be out by Monday."

He drew in a deep breath, but she didn't give him an inch of ground.

"I'd be out sooner, but everything was going so well, I sort of forgot I was supposed to be packing."

"So did I."

And he had, because deep inside, he hadn't wanted to think about EvaMarie leaving. Because her leaving would have made him wonder why being without her left him lonely, why laughing with her made him happy and why knowing she'd kept even a small part of herself from him made him angry.

Because he'd fallen in love, all over again.

She stood, the fall of the gown reflecting the scant moonlight from the window opposite. A few steps was all she gained before she turned back. "I'm sorry, Mason. I know you probably won't believe that. Probably don't even care. But I need to say it for myself. I'm sorry that I kept things from you."

Her huff of a laugh resonated with a sort of despair that startled him. "I thought everything I'd done for you, with you, would have told you what you needed to truly know about me. But I forget that's not the way life works. It never has been. At least, not for me. I've spent a lifetime protecting myself, and old habits die hard, regardless of whether they are serving you well or not. And that's my fault."

"No, EvaMarie." Without thought he moved to the bottom of the stairs, gripping the newel post in his hand. "No, I just didn't expect—"

"That the young, innocent girl you knew would grow up into such a complicated woman. So needy. So scared." Her hand was a pale blur as she waved it to indicate the house at her feet. "After all, I had the perfect life. The least I could do was meet your expectations."

She moved down a step, then stopped to hold herself in frozen stillness as if realizing she'd made a mistake. "That's what everyone else wants. So you should too. Only I thought you wanted me to grow, wanted me to break out from my past—" her voice rose to echo around the black space "—wanted me to take what I wanted." A small sob escaped her throat. "But no one really means that. They just say it to be nice and take it back when it doesn't go the way they expected."

She turned away once more, not speaking again until she reached the top step. Mason's gaze traced the fragile line of her spine where the dress dipped to midback below the fall of her hair, remembering the feel of it against his fingertips.

Her words floated down without her turning her head toward him. "Jeremy was right. No one will ever respect me, because I don't respect myself. So from here on out, I'll accept nothing less...only I figure that means I'll spend a lifetime alone. Funny how that works, huh?"

In that moment, Mason realized he'd let EvaMarie down far worse than anything she'd ever done to him when they were kids. Then, she hadn't stood up for him because she didn't know how. Now, he'd taken advantage of the fact that she wouldn't stand up for herself to exorcise his own anger and conflicting emotions.

Guilt gripped his throat, refusing to let him call out to her as she walked away. He heard the door to her room close, then the distinct click of the lock.

She was done talking, leaving Mason to spend the night contemplating just how big of a jackass he truly was.

She's really done it.

Mason came around the corner of the house to find a long horse trailer parked before the stables. Jim came out the arched entryway leading Lucy, her foal not far behind. Somehow, seeing the horses loaded up with their new owners—without EvaMarie anywhere in sight—told Mason's brain more than anything else that she was gone.

When she'd left him a note telling him she wouldn't be back, she'd meant it.

He hadn't seen her after that night. Her room had been empty the next day, save for a stack of moving boxes in one corner and the furniture. If she had been at the house since that night, it hadn't been while Mason was present. He suspected Jeremy was helping her coordinate her movements, though the other man hadn't said a word.

All of her belongings, including her sound equipment, had been loaded into moving trucks the third day by a group of burly men in uniforms. But it still hadn't seemed real. Until the horses...

EvaMarie had loved those horses. He'd just assumed she would be here to say goodbye to them.

Kane appeared beside him. "What's going on?"

Mason bumped his chin in the direction of the stables. "New owner is here for the Hyatts' horses. Got the stables all to ourselves now."

Kane grunted. "We're gonna need to hire on some help for Jim." He was quiet again for a moment, then said the very thing Mason didn't want to hear. "You okay with this?"

"Hell, yes." But he wasn't. And that was eating away his insides.

"No," he finally conceded. "Hell, no."

Kane slapped Mason's shoulder. "About time you admitted that."

"Why? So you can gloat?"

"Would I do that?"

"Yes." And that was an understatement.

"Nah! But I might have to indulge in at least one *I told you so.*"

As much as he'd like to, Mason couldn't begrudge him that. "You were right."

Kane clutched his heart in a mock death grip. "And you admitted it? Is the world ending?"

"It will for you if you don't drop the theatrics."

Kane chuckled, a sound so rare it startled Mason. "I can't resist."

"Try."

Mason frowned as Jim and the new owner checked over the

inside and outside of the trailer to make sure the horses were safe and secure. "This didn't go how I thought it would."

"Life is full of surprises, Dad used to say."

"And not all of them good, if I remember correctly."

"He did mention that a time or two. And as much as you showing up here was a nasty surprise for the Hyatts, I think it was a good thing for EvaMarie."

"I doubt she'd agree with you now."

"You sure about that?"

Mason studied him.

"Do you remember the year I was in sixth grade?"

"Yeah. That was a pretty miserable year for you." It was before Kane had gotten any height on him. He'd spent the year being picked on by a particularly burly boy at school. "Why?"

"I learned something that year. Oh, I didn't learn it right then. But many years later, looking back, I was taught a massive life lesson."

"That bullies need their asses kicked?"

Kane smirked. "Besides that. I learned that the job of a bully is to make you cower. Not just outside, but inside. To make everything you are shrink until it disappears, including the very essence of who you are."

Mason could see where this was going, and it wasn't helping him feel any better.

"EvaMarie lived with a bully her entire life," Kane went on. "The thing that amazes me to this day is the amount of strength it took for her not to give up, not to lose who she really was. She buried it, and protected it, until the time when it was safe for her to bring it back out."

"So I could stomp all over it." Mason watched the truck and trailer disappear down the drive. Jim raised a hand in acknowledgment before heading back into the stables. They really had to get that man some help. "I completely screwed up. How do I change that?"

"It's easy…"

"For you to say."

Kane squinted as he gazed across the rolling hills behind the stable yard. "Nope. You've just got to help her be who she should have been all along."

Seventeen

"Jeremy, come on," EvaMarie hollered. She couldn't help it. Wondering if Mason was gonna walk in at any minute had her stomach cramping.

Jeremy finally came around the corner from the basement with a grin that made her want to smack him. "Seriously, you could at least be curious as to how the game room turned out."

Oh, she was. More than anything she wanted to take a leisurely stroll downstairs to see all the cool goodness Jeremy had been able to put in place. She wanted to see how the plans they had all discussed and dreamed about had come to life... She wanted to see how the furniture she and Mason had picked out looked in the game room. She wanted to talk party plans and food and music...but that wasn't her place anymore.

"I just want to get my stuff from the safe and go," she insisted, ignoring what she wanted but could no longer have.

"Well, why didn't you go on up and get it?"

Because it was weird.

She knew Mason had now moved the focus of the renovations to the second floor. Honestly, she'd be surprised if he hadn't gutted her room. He probably wanted absolutely nothing to re-mind him of her. Probably the entire floor was unrecognizable now. What had they done with Chris's bedroom? The thought left her cold. She wasn't sure she wanted to see.

Jeremy watched her closely, seeming almost amused. "I told you Mason left the safe on purpose once I explained you'd for-gotten some things in it."

"I'm amazed he didn't blow it out of the wall," she mumbled.

"Oh, stop fussing and get a move on."

She totally wasn't in the mood for his attitude. "Now who's in a hurry?" she challenged.

But she did want to get done before Mason arrived. In the three weeks since she'd left her childhood home, she hadn't seen Mason once. Not driving around town, not out shopping and certainly not here at the estate.

The few times she'd returned for her things, Jeremy had ar-ranged for her to show up when Mason wasn't home. Whether her former lover approved of this strategy or not, she wasn't sure. When she realized that she'd forgotten to get the few real pieces of jewelry she still owned from the wall safe in her closet, it had taken a whole week for Jeremy to find a window for her to come by.

But standing around here in the hall that had seen all the ups and downs in her life made her sink even further into the mo-rass of sadness that darkened her life at the moment. She needed out. As a matter of fact, she almost gave Jeremy the code and asked him to get her stuff from the safe, but she'd done enough wimping out for the day. This she needed to do for herself.

Hard as it might be.

So she forced herself to climb each step, focusing on Jeremy's leather shoes at her eye level in front of her. They shouldn't be so fancy for all the work he did in construction zones, but some-how he managed to pull it off without a single scuff. Amazing.

With a grimace, she acknowledged that she was in deep avoidance mode, but she still refused to look right or left as she crossed the landing to her old room. Her brother's room pulled at her senses, but what good would looking do? He was gone. So was her childhood. Wandering these halls to reminisce about either would probably throw her into a depression she could never crawl out of.

"How are the parents?" Jeremy asked, as he paused outside the door to her old bedroom.

"Currently refusing to speak to me," she confirmed. "Once I told them they could agree to my terms or not see me, they immediately set about breaking every rule I put in place. We're in what I call the tantrum stage."

"Ah, the terrible twos."

"And threes and fours and fives... I feel like it's never going to end."

"It will."

"I hate to say it, but I agree. The minute my dad has his first big health scare and they need me, they'll come calling. I'll just have to remind them that I mean business on a regular basis." Just the thought exhausted her sometimes, but this was life with her parents, since she wasn't willing to cut them out altogether.

Jeremy echoed her thoughts. "I know it's hard, but stick to your guns."

She hated to admit it, but being away from her parents right now was easier than going along with all their demands had ever been. But remembering that would help her keep her backbone strong. It would have been nice to have someone by her side, giving her encouragement and support while she dealt with all of this, but she'd lost that chance the night of the ball.

Without voicing her complicated thoughts, she nodded. "All right. Let's see it."

Jeremy opened the door and stood aside, telling her something had definitely changed beyond the threshold. As much as she dreaded it, this was another good thing. A hard thing, but she needed to remember that this was no longer her home. The past was gone. She couldn't go back.

Especially now that her room had been turned into an office. Her first thought was that it had been turned into Mason's office, but the pale purple of the walls didn't really scream "masculine." With a quick glance, she scanned what appeared to be an antique rolltop desk, a modern ergonomic desk chair covered in a leather that matched the desk's finish and some bookshelves. She didn't look closer. She didn't want to.

Definitely not.

The pale purple had been carried over into the dressing room, but unlike the other space, this one remained unfurnished. Then she opened the door to the walk-in closet and gasped.

Instead of the stripped walls she'd expected, all the surfaces had been reinforced with cushioning covered in some kind of leather. Decorative tufting had been created with upholstery buttons. At the far end, a custom-built shelving unit and desk took up the entire wall. An L-shaped addition on one side was filled with equipment that made the woman who had poured over sound equipment sites to find the best of the cheapest drool.

"Oh my God, Jeremy," she breathed.

"Do you like it?"

That deep voice wasn't Jeremy's. Barely able to breathe, Eva-Marie turned in a slow circle until she faced Mason in the doorway. A remote part of her brain recognized that she'd started to shake, but the rest of her was simply working to keep herself upright.

"Um…" *Oh, real intelligent, EvaMarie.* "It's wonderful."

He stepped farther inside, sending a jolt through EvaMarie's core that she struggled to hide. When his gaze narrowed, she wasn't sure she'd succeeded.

"I'm glad you like it," he said, that deep, soothing tone gliding over her like a calming wave. "I did it with you in mind."

Um, thanks? She could have happily gone years without knowing that she'd inspired a room in his house. Was he crazy? "I don't know what to say," she murmured.

"Say you'll use it to record that sexy voice for me and the world to listen to."

She must not have heard him right. "What?" she gasped.

"I built it for you, EvaMarie."

She could swear she'd heard him wrong, but the acoustics in here were excellent. Perfect for her business. "I lined up two new authors this week," she said, the inane trivia the only thing her brain could cough up. Then she winced. Her "career" was probably the last thing he wanted to hear about.

"That's because you're excellent at everything you put your mind to," Mason said, surprising her.

A deep breath helped her gather the unraveling threads of her cognitive abilities. "That's what you said the last time I saw you. That I'm as good at secrets and lies as I am at cleaning up after the construction crew."

"And this is my way of saying I'm sorry."

She glanced around the impressive space, awed for a moment. "Pretty expensive apology."

"It's worth every penny if it means you'll at least talk to me again."

"Again...it seems like a lot for talking." She just couldn't let it go.

"You're gonna have to grovel, my man!"

"Go away, Jeremy!" Mason yelled back toward the bedroom. "I don't need an audience."

EvaMarie struggled not to smile. What had happened between them wasn't funny, but her emotions were never straightforward with this man. But confusion quickly overtook all her other thoughts.

She shook her head. "I don't understand."

"Understand what?" Mason took a step closer, which didn't clear her thoughts at all.

"I mean, I really don't understand. You hate my family. You hate what I let them do to me. You think I was using you for a place to live and work." She stepped back, struggling to breathe. "After all that, why would you do this?"

Tears threatened to surface. What she'd wanted all along seemed right within her reach, but she couldn't take it, because she couldn't live with him thinking of her that way.

"Remember, we said no other rules. Right?"

Not trusting herself to speak, she nodded.

"Well, I was wrong. There is a third rule."

"What's that?"

"We have to respect each other."

And just like that, her heart shattered. Mason would never respect the woman he thought she was.

"Do you respect me, EvaMarie?"

That was easy. She'd seen the man he'd become—a fierce opponent when fighting what he believed was wrong, utterly loyal and still as hardworking as he had been when he was young. "Of course."

"Even with my faults?"

She'd had enough time to get some perspective on that. "We all make mistakes." Hadn't she?

"And I more than most." This time he moved in close, not giving her a chance to back down. "I built this room to show you that I respect and support the woman you are now." His hands gripped her upper arms, anchoring her to the reality of what he was saying. "The woman who takes the time to read to children, who isn't afraid of hard work or to challenge me when I'm being a total ass."

She tried to smother her grin, but he caught it anyway, shared it with her despite the seriousness of what he said.

"The woman who pays attention to details, and sings to calm the horses. The woman who, even now, is struggling to teach her parents better manners while refusing to abandon them in their time of need."

"Jeremy told you?"

Mason nodded. "He told me. And I'm proud of you."

With that, she could no longer hold back the tears.

Ever so gently, Mason tilted her chin up so her watery gaze could meet his. "Let me be the first to say, EvaMarie, that I'm very proud of you. I know it's not easy. You could have continued to keep the status quo, but you saw that it wasn't the best thing for any of you, and you did something about it."

EvaMarie couldn't explain how his words made her feel. It wasn't just love. It wasn't just about soaking in the rare bit of praise. It was her heart blossoming as she realized someone could get her for the first time—warts and all.

"So you want to, what? Go back to how we were before?" She wasn't sure that's what she wanted anymore.

He buried his hand in her hair, bringing that sculpted mouth so close to hers. "Oh, I want what we had before...but I want much, much more."

His kiss left her reeling, so it was hard to coordinate her feet when he pulled her back toward the door. When they reached the office, she saw a dress hanging from one of the bookshelves. "That wasn't there before."

"Nope."

It was a vintage style with a close-fitting bodice and a full, frilly skirt. The crisp teal cotton was complemented by the lace-edged crinoline beneath the skirt. On the shelf above was a stylish hat with a matching teal ribbon woven through the brim.

EvaMarie pressed her palm hard against her stomach to quiet the butterflies that had taken up residence there. "What's that for?"

"Well, I was hoping you'd still help us with our open house when we put it on."

Her heart sank, and it was a literal, physical feeling. She eyed the dress with longing, wishing it represented so much more than it appeared to.

"As my fiancée."

Turning to look at Mason, EvaMarie found him on one knee right there in her old bedroom. His hand was lifted up to reveal a gorgeous white gold and amethyst ring with a circlet of tiny diamonds supporting it. "Mason?"

"I don't want there to be any more misunderstanding between us, EvaMarie. We're both products of our upbringing, but we're our own people too. And personally, I think you've turned into something incredible. Can you forgive me for letting the past get in the way of the present?"

Heart aching, she stepped in close, pulling his head to her chest. "Only if you can help me be the person I should be."

Mason looked up to meet her gaze. "No, but I can help you be the person *you want* to be."

Standing, he kissed her again with a soft reverence that made her heart ache. Then he pulled her close against his body. As she looked over his shoulder, the pictures on the bookshelves became clear for the first time. Framed pictures of her and her brother. "Mason, how?"

"Jeremy got them out of storage for me. I never want you to feel like you can't talk about your life. All the parts of it."

"I promise this time I will."

Mason scanned the busy rooms on each side of the hall, looking for his fiancée in the midst of the open house chaos. People stopped him frequently. He had to consciously tamp down his impatience with the interruptions. They'd staged this party to make themselves known and extend memorable hospitality.

Mason would just enjoy it more with EvaMarie by his side.

His hunting skills proved apt when he tracked her to the kitchen. There she was in her gorgeous dress, busily helping the caterer fill trays. He watched her for several long moments.

She wasn't anything like he'd expected when he'd shown up at the estate that first day. Instead, she was more.

"Woman, what are you doing?" he finally asked.

She glanced up, giving him a glimpse of her round blue eyes beneath the rim of her hat before dusting off her fingers. "I'm sorry, Mason. I just worry about everything getting done."

Secretly he was amused, but he couldn't resist the blush stain-ing her cheeks. He stepped closer, running his knuckles lightly down the flushed skin. "I understand. But you're the lady of the house. And this dress is not meant for the kitchen."

They left the room to the chorus of giggles from the cater-ing crew. "When you said you weren't big on parties, I thought you were just saying that because of the last time you went to one," Mason said as he led her through the people meander-ing between the front rooms and the hopping activities in the basement.

"Honestly, I've never been big on them. Not nearly as much as my parents," she murmured, sticking close to his side. Mason was amazed at how good that felt. "I'd much rather be upstairs with a book."

The turret library had been bumped to the front of the res-toration checklist. They'd returned a large number of EvaMa-rie's books there, along with Mason's own smaller collection. They spent a lot of quiet evenings in that room, before Mason coaxed her down to the master suite.

He snuggled her closer to his side, bending to her ear to say, "As much as I was looking forward to this event, I'd rather be upstairs too…for a completely different reason."

She gasped as he whisked her partway up the stairs. "Mason, we can't."

A quick maneuver and she was in his arms as they looked out across their guests. Sunlight from the arched window opposite highlighted her cheekbones, reminding Mason of the angel he'd allowed into his life. "I'm teasing you, Evie," he said, grinning at her knowing look.

She knew him all too well.

A particularly loud guffaw had Mason glancing toward the ballroom, which they could see a sliver of from their elevated position. EvaMarie's parents held court in one corner of the room. "Your father is in his element."

"Amazingly." EvaMarie shook her head. "I can't believe they're actually here."

Mason had done his best to support her as she struggled to establish her relationship with her parents on a new footing. There'd been many a time he'd wanted to step in, but he rarely had to do that. EvaMarie, perfectionist that she was, knew exactly what she wanted and stuck to her guns in order to get it.

"You did it, love," he said, kissing her temple. "The house is gorgeous, the party is a hit and your career is gaining momentum. I'm damn proud."

"Thank you."

The tight squeeze of her arms conveyed her heightened emotions. Mason continued to be amazed when she admitted she needed help from him. The admissions were few and far between, but each one made him feel like a superhero as he attempted to give back even a fraction of the support she granted him every day.

"Where's your brother?" she asked.

Mason swept his gaze over the floor once more. "He must still be at the stables. There was a problem getting the stud settled in."

She nodded. "Soon the stables will be set—"

"And we will be the newest stables to win a Kentucky Derby. Just you see."

Her smile gave him the biggest boost. "I'm sure I will."

"It's gonna be beautiful. Just like you."

"No," she said, leaning her head against his chest. "Like us together."

* * * * *

Heartbreaker

Joanne Rock

Joanne Rock credits her decision to write romance after a book she picked up during a flight delay engrossed her so thoroughly that she didn't mind at all when her flight was delayed two more times. Giving her readers the chance to escape into another world has motivated her to write over eighty books for a variety of Harlequin series.

Books by Joanne Rock

The McNeill Magnates

The Magnate's Mail-Order Bride
The Magnate's Marriage Merger
His Accidental Heir
Little Secrets: His Pregnant Secretary
Claiming His Secret Heir
For the Sake of His Heir
The Forbidden Brother
Wild Wyoming Nights
One Night Scandal

Dynasties: Mesa Falls

The Rebel
The Rival
Rule Breaker
Heartbreaker

Visit her Author Profile page at millsandboon.com.au, or joannerock.com, for more titles.

You can also find Joanne Rock on Facebook, along with other Harlequin Desire authors, at Facebook.com/harlequindesireauthors!

Dear Reader,

Sparks flew when Gage and Elena stepped on the scene in my last book, *Rule Breaker*. I couldn't wait to find out what had happened between them in the past to account for all that sizzle!

As it turns out, quite a lot. Elena and Gage have a history, and I enjoyed every moment of their dance around one another to try to avoid repeating past mistakes. Of course, I couldn't resist throwing them together more often than not to see how they would react. I hope you'll have fun joining me for their romance.

And, of course, this wouldn't be a Dynasties story without a big cast of characters in the wings. You can learn more about Jonah and Astrid's romance in a free online read available only on the Harlequin website!

Happy reading!

Joanne Rock

For all my readers going through a hard time,
here's hoping this story lifts your spirit.

One

Gage Striker hadn't been in the same room as Elena Rollins in six years. They'd never spoken after their breakup. Never texted. Never called.

And yet, the exact moment his former lover crossed the threshold of his remote Montana home, crashing his private party, he knew. He sensed her nearness like a breath on the back of his neck—a prickling awareness that set every nerve ending on alert.

How had she gained admittance? He'd hired a security team to prevent just such intrusions. Heads would roll for the oversight, given how many celebrity guests were under his roof at his Mesa Falls Ranch home tonight—guests who rightly expected their privacy to be protected. In the meantime, he needed to contain the problem. Just as soon as he located her.

Gage stood in the massive foyer with his friend and Mesa Falls co-owner Weston Rivera. The DJ was playing a pop song in the great room behind them and a handful of people were dancing. Just then, a commotion erupted near the front door as one of the evening's more prominent celebrities strolled in with her entourage. Social media star Chiara Campagna caused quite a stir with her sleek dark hair and wide dark eyes, but Gage's attention passed over her quickly.

Elena was his real concern.

Guests poured from the great room into the foyer, phones recording Chiara's entrance as she accepted a magnolia flower from a greeter. It amazed him how much attention she attracted, especially among the handful of Hollywood elite who'd been invited to this evening's party, a PR effort to raise awareness about the ranch's environmental initiatives.

And to provide cover for the fact that all six of the owners of Mesa Falls Ranch were scheduled to fly in for a meeting this weekend. They were in crisis mode. The tabloids had been far too interested in the ranch ever since the actress Tabitha Barnes used their holiday gala as a platform to make explosive allegations about one of Mesa Falls' former guests. Gage kept waiting for the spotlight to fade and the public to move on to the next scandal, but tabloid reporters had started showing up to chase the story once they discovered how much time Alonzo Salazar had spent at the ranch before his death.

Much to Gage's personal frustration, Elena had recently embarked on a new career in entertainment journalism. He had a strong suspicion she'd taken the job only when she'd seen a chance for payback given the way they'd parted. With all the gossip Elena Rollins could have covered closer to her Southern California home, of course she'd post a photo of her plane ticket to Missoula, Montana, on her social media account with a provocative caption about hunting down answers.

He'd known all week she was coming for him.

With an effort, Gage returned his attention to his business partner, and the coolly poised blonde at his side. The woman didn't look familiar, but it was clear by the way Weston curled a possessive arm around her waist that she was someone special to him.

"This is more than we planned for, mate," Gage observed

as he took a rough head count of the crowd in the foyer. "We need better security." Then, forcing a more pleasant note into his voice, he peered down at Weston's guest. "I'm Gage, by the way."

"April Stephens," the woman replied, her blue eyes darting around the room and up to the cathedral ceiling where hidden lights cast a warm glow on the partygoers. "And thank you for inviting me. Your home is beautiful."

"Thank you." He had helped design the modern take on a lodge-style home, but he hadn't spent much time on-site since his business interests kept him on the move. At fourteen thousand square feet, the property was made for entertaining more than anything. "I know this isn't everyone's idea of a party, though, love. Come back in the summer when we can kick our shoes off, barbecue some ribs and throw horseshoes by the pool. That's more my speed."

He'd never bought into his parents' belief that appearances were everything. He might have been born with the proverbial silver spoon, but he'd chucked it aside as soon as he realized how much baggage came with it. Now, he had his own wealth. Made his own rules. Funny how he still ended up throwing parties for the overprivileged. At least he called the shots these days.

Weston leaned forward to address Gage. "I need all the help I can get convincing April to spend more time here."

Intriguing that Weston would make his interest in the woman so clear. Gage had known Weston since boarding school days and he couldn't recall a single female in all that time whom his footloose, mountaineering friend had gone out of his way to impress.

Gage nodded, respecting Weston's wishes even though he couldn't imagine diving into relationship waters again. He returned his attention to his friend's date.

"Definitely come back and spend some time with us when there's not so much hype." He snapped his fingers suddenly, remembering why he should know the woman. "April. You're the financial forensics investigator. How's your case going?"

So this was the woman who'd been hired by Alonzo Salazar's son to trace his mysterious finances. Gage's former mentor had recently been unmasked as the man behind a Hollywood tell-all book that had caused Tabitha Barnes and her family a world of trouble.

"It's closed," she assured him. "I've tracked enough of Alonzo's earnings to satisfy my client, so I'm officially finished with my work at Mesa Falls. I'll be flying back to Denver tomorrow."

Gage nodded, realizing she wasn't going to offer any specifics. He would ask Devon Salazar for an update on the case in the morning since her findings could very well turn media scrutiny in another direction. Away from the ranch.

The encouraging thought immediately faded, however, as he felt the hairs at his shirt collar stand on end. The hum of awareness grew to a buzzing sensation until he had no choice but to turn around.

And came face-to-face with his former lover.

Elena Rollins stepped toward him, swathed in strapless crimson silk and velvet. Her dark hair was half pinned up and half trailing down her back, a few glossy curls spilling over one bare shoulder. Even now, six years later, she took his breath away as fast as a punch to his chest. For a single devastating instant, he thought the smile curving her red lips was for him.

Then, she opened her arms wide.

"April!" Elena greeted Weston Rivera's date warmly, wrapping her in a one-armed embrace like they were old friends.

Only then did Gage notice how Elena gripped her phone in her other hand, holding it out at arm's length to record everything. Was it a live video? Anger surged through him at the same time he wondered how in the hell she knew April Stephens.

"Smile for my followers," Elena instructed her friend as the two women eased apart. She lifted her cell to get both of them in the shot.

April hesitated, clearly confused about being in the spotlight.

"Were you unaware of Elena's day job?" Gage asked April as he plucked the device from Elena's red talons and dropped it in the pocket of his tuxedo jacket. "She's now a professional menace."

Elena rounded on him, pinning him with her dark eyes. They stood deadlocked in fuming silence. Weston might have said something to him—Gage couldn't be sure—before Weston and April headed off. Now it was Gage and his ex, surrounded by at least twenty-five other guests still filming Chiara Campagna's every movement on their phones.

"That belongs to me," Elena sniped, tipping her chin at him. "You have no right to take it."

"You have no right to be here, but I see you didn't let that stop you from finagling your way onto the property."

She glared at him, dark eyes narrowing. "My video is probably still recording. Maybe you should return my phone before you cause a scene that will bring you bad press."

Extending a palm, she waited for him to hand it over.

"If you have a problem with me, why don't you tell it to the security team you tricked into admitting you tonight?" He pointed toward the door where two bodyguards in gray suits were stationed on either side of the entrance. "You're trespassing."

The crush of people in the foyer began to ease as Chiara Campagna's entourage made their way into the great room, pausing just inside the open double doors to take a few photos with her friends. At least there would be less of an audience for whatever antics Elena had in mind.

"Is that a dare, Gage?" Her voice hit a husky note, no doubt carefully calibrated to distract a man.

It damn well wasn't going to work on him.

"I'm giving you a choice," he clarified, unwilling to give her the public showdown she so clearly wanted to record and share with her followers. "You can speak with me privately about whatever it is you're doing in my house, or you can let my team escort you off the premises right now. Either way, I can promise you there won't be any cameras involved."

"How positively boring." She gave him a tight smile and a theatrical sigh before folding her arms across her chest. "Maybe using cameras could spice things up a bit."

She gave him a once-over with her dark gaze.

He reminded himself that if she got under his skin, she won. But he couldn't deny a momentary impulse to kiss her senseless for trying to play him.

"What will it be, Elena?" he pressed, keeping his voice even. "Talk or walk?"

"Very well." She gestured with her hands, holding them up in a sign of surrender. "Spirit me away to your lair, Gage, and do with me what you will." She tipped her head to one side, a thoughtful expression stealing across her face. "Oh, wait a minute." She bit her lip and shook her head. "You don't indulge your bad-boy side anymore, do you? Your father saw to that a long time ago, paying off all the questionable influences to leave his precious heir alone."

The seductive, playful note in her voice was gone, a cold chill stealing into her gaze.

He'd known she had an ax to grind with him after the way his father had bribed her to get out of his life.

He hadn't realized how hard she'd come out swinging.

Elena followed Gage through his massive home on unsteady legs.

At well over six feet tall, he cut an imposing figure. His build was as formidable as ever, broad chest and muscular arms filling out his tuxedo. As she walked behind him, she could appreciate the way those broad shoulders narrowed to his waist, how his dark hair brushed the collar of his jacket. She caught a glimpse of the tattoos on his forearms just beneath his shirt cuffs. She used to love tracing the intricate colorful patterns there, asking him the stories behind each. And he would tell her, spinning tales of his past in the New Zealand accent that was an aphrodisiac to her. Or maybe it was just Gage—pure and simple. He could have spoken with a Southern drawl or a Boston accent, and she probably would have thought it the sexiest thing she'd ever heard.

He had affected her that way at one time.

She hadn't been prepared for how seeing him would affect her now. Six years had passed since their relationship ended in an icy goodbye, with Gage believing his father's story that she'd allowed herself to be paid off in order to leave Gage alone. She'd been so angry at his automatic condemnation that she hadn't bothered to correct him. If he thought that poorly of her character, then he'd never really known her at all, and couldn't have possibly loved her.

So she'd told herself that their split was a good thing. An eye-opening moment about someone she'd cared for deeply. She'd even been married since then, a colossal flop of an endeavor that had left her broke and humiliated. Her cooking-show-host husband had taken up with his assistant while Elena was out of town at a conference. She'd become a divorce cliché before she'd turned thirty.

Sadly, even her husband's infidelity hadn't left her as unsettled as seeing Gage tonight. Which spoke volumes about her poor decision in marrying Tomas in the first place.

She thrust those thoughts from her mind as Gage led her from the party to a quiet corner at the opposite end of the house. The sound of music faded as they entered a gray stone corridor illuminated by recessed lights in the pale wood ceiling. The building materials were sleek and expensive looking, the walls mostly unadorned. Even the floors were free of rugs; her high heels echoed in the wide hallway.

They soon arrived in a sitting room with a gray stone fireplace. Or maybe it was an office. She realized the mammoth glass-topped table with steel legs was actually a desk. There was a deep leather couch tucked against one wall and a television screen mounted on the one opposite.

The surroundings were as cold and unwelcoming as her host.

Gage closed the double doors behind them and then turned to face her. The room was soundproof; you'd never know a noisy party was taking place in another section of the house.

"Do you care to tell me what you're doing here?" he asked her now, his brown eyes unreadable as he studied her by the light of two ultramodern chandeliers with sleek white glass spokes. "Or would you like me to get you a drink first?"

The angles of his face were more prominent than she remembered, from the square jaw and high cheekbones to the slash of his widow's peak. His face was shadowed with a few days' growth of neatly groomed beard. He went to a built-in gray cabinet beneath the television screen, raising the wooden lid to reveal a wet bar. There was a small selection of the best whiskeys the world had to offer, cut crystal glasses stacked to one side.

"I've had a challenging year, but I haven't resorted to bourbon yet." She didn't tend to drink hard liquor after seeing what alcohol had done to her mother. "But please, help yourself if you like."

While he poured from the only decanted bottle, Elena had a vivid memory of what Gage's preferred bourbon tasted like on his tongue when he kissed her. The memory—so sudden and visceral it shocked her—sent an unwelcome flash of heat through her. Her skin tightened uncomfortably, and she fought the urge to pace away from him.

To find some breathing room on the other side of this hard-surfaced echo chamber that passed as living space in Gage's world.

But she couldn't afford to give away how much his nearness rattled her.

"On second thought," she mused aloud, thinking this man

and the memories he evoked posed a more immediate threat to her mental well-being than any spirit, "maybe a small taste couldn't hurt."

He glanced her way, but she didn't allow herself to meet his eyes. She pretended a sudden interest in the flames of the fireplace while she tried to pull herself together.

She heard an ice cube clink in a glass. The splash of liquid as he poured her drink. The soft thud of the cabinet lid being shut.

"Here you go." Gage's voice sounded over her left shoulder. "I added ice to yours to mellow it a bit. Would you like a seat?"

"No, thank you." She accepted the glass he handed her, careful to avoid brushing his fingers with hers. She remembered all too well how his touch had affected her. "There's no need to pretend this is a social visit."

She crossed one arm over her midsection and lifted the glass to her nose, swirling the drink as she inhaled the fragrance of toasted vanilla and charred oak.

Neither of which quite captured her memory of the taste on Gage's tongue when they kissed.

"I won't lose sight of that anytime soon," he assured her, gesturing toward the couch. "Sit."

Unwilling to argue, she moved to the far end of the sofa and settled herself on a cushion. He joined her there, leaving a few feet between them. Settling his drink on the window ledge that butted up against the sofa back, he shifted sideways to face her. She did the same.

"Care to tell me why you're here?" he asked, easing a finger beneath his bow tie to loosen it a fraction.

She remembered how much he disliked formal attire, even though his family's living in the public eye had called for it. Then, when they'd been dating, he'd been building his portfolio as a venture capitalist, a role that often put him in business attire. And while these days his tremendous success and wealth surely allowed him to wear whatever he felt like, he was still frequently photographed in bespoke suits.

Not that she went out of her way to find out what he was doing. Given his success in Silicon Valley, his name periodically cropped up at the Hollywood parties she used to attend with Tomas.

And damn, but her memories had sent her thoughts on a wild ride. She refocused on his question.

"Based on the way you labeled me a professional menace, I'm fairly certain you already know why I'm here." She'd been sure to fill her social media with posts about her trip to Montana so that Gage would hear of her impending arrival one way or another. "As an entertainment reporter, I saw an opportunity to unearth a story that readers want right now."

"Since when do you work for the tabloids?"

She shrugged away the pain that came with thinking about that. "Since my faithless ex-husband tied up our assets with frivolous litigation in an effort to make my life miserable. I took a job that would net me enough quick cash to live on until things are settled."

That narrative didn't begin to cover the financial and emotional hardship of her contentious divorce. She'd made the mistake of thinking Tomas would behave like a grown-up and had moved out of the house immediately. Afterward, she'd discovered what a disadvantage it put her at to vacate their shared residence. She'd just wanted him to sign the paperwork and sever their ties. Only later did she realize how shortsighted she'd been to trust that Tomas would be fair.

"I'm sorry to hear about the divorce." The empathy in Gage's voice was real enough. His gaze flicked over her as he took a sip of his drink and returned the glass to the window ledge. Then his tone changed. "But there are only a million ways for one of the sharpest women I know to make a living. Why choose to upend other people's lives to make a buck?"

"I won't thank you for a backhanded compliment intended to make me feel guilty about my job." Why she took it was none of his business. Although if ever there was a time in her life for work that allowed her an outlet for her disillusionment and bitterness, this was it. "For what it's worth, I like to seek out targets for my work that deserve public censure."

"You can't possibly be suggesting that I fall into that category," he replied, displeasure in his voice.

Gage Striker was a man who'd never known a moment's doubt. A man who wouldn't know how it felt to have the world think the worst of him. To have to fight for respectability.

She skirted around his comment, not ready to cross swords with him directly.

Yet.

"I was thinking more of Alonzo Salazar, whose tell-all book ruined lives. The man profited from real people's heartbreak." She shifted on the leather sofa to face Gage more directly and to retrieve her drink. The silk of her dress's skirt swished against her calves, the velvet ruffle at the hem trailing over her foot as she crossed her legs.

Gage followed her movements with his gaze, making her far too aware of herself.

Of him.

"And yet it just so happens that pursuing the Alonzo Salazar story brought you to my doorstep." He lowered his voice as he leaned closer. "That feels a little too convenient to be coincidence, doesn't it?"

To put off answering, she sipped the bourbon, letting the flavors play over her tongue. A hint of caramel. A touch of smoke as she swallowed.

And then, there it was. The afterburn in her throat with a hint of cherry. The scent of leather. The flavor of the last kiss she remembered sharing with Gage.

"It's decidedly inconvenient for me." She resisted the urge to plant the cool glass against her forehead, as her skin warmed at his nearness and the memories of his mouth on hers. "My work here would be much easier if we didn't have such an... acrimonious history."

"Acrimonious," he repeated. "Is that what we're calling it?"

"I wouldn't say we're friends. Would you?" She set the drink aside, knowing better than to play with fire.

"Far from it," he agreed easily. "Which is the real reason you're here, Elena, no matter what you say."

Her heart sped faster at the confrontational note in his tone. A part of her had always regretted not telling him exactly what she thought of him before she left.

"And what reason is that, Gage, since you apparently know me so well?"

She could swear she saw the flames from the fireplace reflected in his dark gaze. It must be that, and not a wicked light in his eyes.

"We both know you're here for revenge."

Two

Gage wondered how she could possibly look him in the eye and claim otherwise.

She sat beside him in his study in her bloodred dress, glossy tendrils of hair winding around her shoulders like Medusa's serpents. It was all an enticing distraction from the threat she posed. To his name, his reputation and everything he'd worked hard to build at Mesa Falls Ranch.

"Revenge for what, exactly?" she asked finally, recrossing her legs in the opposite direction, causing the long slit in her dress to part and expose her lean calves. Velvet ribbons from her high-heeled shoes wound around her lower legs, their soft bows drawing his gaze to her feet, where red-painted toenails peeped from supple leather.

She was a breathtaking woman, even when she didn't dress to turn heads. Tonight, he couldn't look away from her if he tried. And damn it, he needed to try harder.

"For your wounded pride. For the slight from my family when my father bribed you to leave me. You were livid with him." And she hadn't even blinked when he'd asked her if she'd accepted the payment. Her affirmation—the defiant lift of her chin—had iced all the feelings he'd had for her. "With me."

He'd never understood how she could have transferred so much anger to him when she was the one who'd sold out what they had. Later, it occurred to him that his father might have filled her head with lies about Gage not wanting her in his life. But by then, she was long gone and none of it mattered.

She'd moved half a world away, returning to Southern California, where they'd first met, while he remained in New Zealand to help his father campaign for a parliament seat and a more prominent position in his party. For Gage's father, politics had been a paramount concern his whole life, an important way to maintain Striker family interests. Sadly, now that Gage's fortune outstripped his father's several times over, his relationship with his dad seemed even more tenuous.

"It's been six years since we ended things," she reminded him, glancing down at her fingernails as if the discussion bored her. "I moved on. Married someone else."

"And look how well that worked out for you."

The beat of silence afterward told him the barb had hit the mark. It also made him realize how damned petty that had been. Her gaze flicked up to his, her expression tinged with a hint of pain before the walls went back up again.

"I agree that was a foolish move." Her easy response surprised him as she leaned back deeper into the couch cushions, relaxing her rigid posture a fraction. "But my point is that I certainly wouldn't hatch a revenge scheme after all this time."

"I have no business commenting on your marriage." He squeezed the bridge of his nose, the tension in his head a sign that she was getting under his skin. "My apologies."

She inclined her head, gracious as a queen. "And I'm sorry for sneaking into the party under another woman's name. But given our history, I didn't feel comfortable requesting an invitation."

He couldn't help a wry laugh as he forced himself to gaze

into the fireplace flames instead of at the woman on the couch beside him. "Probably because I would have never granted you one. You have to know that it's my job to protect the privacy of my guests. Which means no tabloid reporters."

"Nevertheless, I need to have my phone back." She shifted beside him, running her palm over the expanse between them and drawing his focus to her left hand that bore no ring. Not even a lingering tan line. "My followers will think something happened to me after my video cut off in the middle."

"Then they seriously underestimate your resourcefulness." They'd met the year before he'd taken his first company public. Back then, the tech start-up offering network privacy tools had been the sole focus of his life. Elena had been working for a rival firm, and she'd quit her job because she believed in his product more.

She'd shown up in his office to tell him so, offering her services as an influencer to a younger demographic. At the time, she'd had a homegrown following for her beauty and fashion tips, and he hadn't understood how that could help him. She'd single-handedly taught him the value of never underestimating a target market, making a clever video that brought him fifty thousand converts to his network security product overnight. He'd given her a percentage and a job. In the end, he'd lost more than a woman he loved when they parted. He'd lost a hell of a team member since she'd handed in her resignation the same day they broke up.

"Then what will it take to recover my device?" she pressed, a hint of agitation creeping into her tone. "Let's open the negotiations so we don't take up any more of each other's time."

She reached for the bourbon on the rocks he'd poured her, and then, as if thinking the better of it, she returned her hand to her lap.

"For starters, be honest with me about what you're doing in Montana." He rose from the couch and returned to the wet bar, pouring her a glass of ice water. Delivering it to her, he noticed how carefully she took it from him. Somehow, the absence of contact only ratcheted up the awareness between them as he reclaimed his seat.

"Thank you." She took a long sip before setting the glass beside the first one. A hint of lipstick on the crystal distracted him for a moment. "And I was honest with you. I'm going to get answers about Alonzo Salazar's ill-gotten gains and where the proceeds from his book went. I'm not leaving the ranch until I either find out or have a solid lead that points somewhere else."

Gage already knew from his exchange with the investigator April Stephens that she'd found answers to that same question. But he wasn't going to point Elena in her direction since he didn't want to aid her in her quest.

Alonzo's secrets were tied up with his own. His former mentor had been privy to the nuances of a boarding school tragedy that involved all six of the ranch's owners, something they'd taken pains to put behind them for good. So his primary objective was to keep Alonzo's past on lockdown. For starters, he sure as hell wasn't letting the woman seated beside him anywhere near April Stephens tonight. Thankfully, the investigator would be leaving Mesa Falls Ranch in the morning.

"So you're just here for a story," he concluded, willing to capitalize on their past affair to maneuver her if it came down to that. He happened to know her very, very well. "Not out of any desire to see me again."

He could tell he caught her off guard by the slightest hint of her shoulders straightening. Was it in awareness of him? Or was she just squaring up for the next round of battle?

"You're safe with me, Gage. I promised your father you would be, after all."

They settled back into sparring roles, and if he were being honest, he was more comfortable seeing her as the enemy than a woman out of options after a well-publicized divorce. It spoke volumes about her financial position—and, perhaps, her personal confidence—that she was selling stories to the tabloids. The Elena he'd known had been a fierce businesswoman.

"And you're not seeking some sort of misguided revenge." He stated it as fact, wanting clarification on that point.

Or perhaps he just needed to rile her.

A light trill of laughter bubbled up from her throat. Rising from the couch, she paced closer to the fireplace, peering back over one shoulder at him. "I'd have to feel something for you if I wanted revenge, Gage."

She said it so coolly, he almost believed her. But at the last moment, a hint of something else flitted through her gaze. The look was fleeting, but it had been there before she quickly turned away. In that moment, he'd glimpsed something more than cool detachment.

Getting to his feet, he closed the distance between them to join her beside the sleek stone hearth. Eyes locked on her subtle curves as she stared down into the flames, he remembered a thousand other times he'd touched her. Tasted her. Made her moan with pleasure.

The past simmered around him, hotter than any blaze.

"I don't believe you."

Gage's words, spoken while he stood far too close to her, stopped her short.

Her breath caught. Her pulse stuttered for a protracted moment.

Thankfully, her back was to him. So she closed her eyes and steeled herself against the tingling in her nerve endings that reminded her of how hot they'd burned together, once upon a time. That hint of bourbon she'd sipped danced in her veins, seeming to warm her everywhere.

But she wasn't here to play games with him. And she couldn't afford to let her guard down for a single second. She needed this story to shore up her finances. If she happened to inconvenience Gage Striker in the process, all the better. Revenge? She preferred to view it as a reminder to him that a Striker couldn't pay his way out of all life's inconveniences.

"It hardly matters whether you believe me or not." She shrugged and traced a pattern in the dark gray stone of the fireplace surround with her finger—anything to delay facing him.

"You feel something for me." That voice, pitched so low for her ears alone, was like a fingernail stroke down her spine. "It's probably nothing good, but I am one hundred percent confident you aren't indifferent."

He'd dropped the gauntlet, and they both knew it.

The silence between them stretched. She'd tried acting once, when she'd first fled her father's run-down desert shack for Los Angeles at seventeen. She hadn't been any good at it then, either, but she'd never had as much motivation as she did right now. Taking a deep breath, she spun on her heel to look Gage in the eye.

"Sorry to disappoint you." She flipped a few curls over her shoulder. "But I'm in Montana for work, not to rehash a long-dead past. So if we're done here, I'll see myself out."

She sidled past him, but at the last moment, his palm landed lightly on her elbow.

"Wait." His touch fell away, quickly breaking their connection.

Because he didn't care to make contact with the woman who'd betrayed him? Or because he felt the same jolt of attraction she felt?

She stopped and turned back around to face him.

"You really plan to stay in town to chase this story?" His voice had lost some of its antagonistic edge.

"I'm not going anywhere until I have answers." She would be in Mesa Falls for as long as she could afford it, anyway. Rooms at the main lodge weren't cheap, but she didn't think Gage would ban her from the ranch property altogether given how hard his PR team had worked to bring the place into the public eye. She didn't think he'd risk the potential bad press.

He gave a decisive nod. "Then stay with me."

She blinked, certain she'd misheard. "Excuse me?"

"If you are that indifferent to me, it should hardly be a problem to stay under the same roof while you research your piece," he told her mildly, heading back to the couch to retrieve their drinks. He drained the rest of his bourbon and then returned with her water.

"So you can keep an eye on me while I'm here? Make sure I don't find the answers I seek?" She clutched the glass, savoring its coolness against her palm while she struggled to keep her edge. She had no illusions he was opening his home to her out of the goodness of his heart. "I don't think so."

"Why waste your mental energy figuring out how to sneak into my home when you could have full access?" he asked, his tone deceptively reasonable.

"Why not just kick me out, the way you threatened to upstairs?" She didn't trust the offer. Couldn't trust him.

"While I don't mind negative publicity for myself, I'd rather not stir it up for Mesa Falls." He paced past her toward the huge table that seemed to function as a desk. Withdrawing her phone from the pocket of his tuxedo jacket, he laid it on the glass-topped surface. "So I'd rather not resort to removing you from the property altogether. But to answer your earlier question, I would find it convenient to have some awareness of your movements while you're in town."

Her gaze had dropped to her phone, but his words made her attention snap back to him. "So you admit you want to keep tabs on me?"

"You're hardly making your movements secret when you're posting them online," he scoffed. "But yes. Having you under my roof will help me stay informed so I don't have to check my social media accounts."

He had a point. She'd be deceiving herself if she thought he was going to ignore her presence in town altogether now that she'd made it clear she wanted answers about Alonzo Salazar.

"For that matter," he continued, perhaps sensing her indecision, "you'd have access to me twenty-four/seven."

"For what purpose?" she asked coolly, not appreciating the implication that she might desire such access.

Gage shrugged. "You tell me. I assumed you might have questions about the ranch. Moving forward, I've committed to spending more time on-site to ensure the ranch's mission is fulfilled."

"Are you saying you'd be willing to answer my questions?" she pressed, draining her drink and trying not to think about what it would be like to move into Gage's home for days.

Or weeks.

Her stomach knotted. His easy dismissal of what they'd shared six years ago had hurt her deeply. For the first time, she debated the wisdom of coming to Montana and reopening that old wound.

"I can't promise that. I'm simply offering you the opportunity to ask." He moved toward her again, plucking her empty glass from her fingers and setting it aside on the fireplace mantel. "Put your money where your mouth is, Elena. If you're not out for revenge, and you don't feel a damned thing about me, then work on your story from my home, where you won't have to sneak around my security. And yes, I get to pretend I at least have a chance to influence your work."

She longed to refuse. To walk away from him and the deal with the devil he was offering.

But he'd effectively called her bluff. And bottom line, she couldn't afford to turn him down. Smoothing a nonexistent wrinkle from her velvet-and-satin gown, she told herself it was a welcome opportunity. A chance to learn insider details about Alonzo Salazar's life and legacy.

"I've heard more gracious invitations," she said finally. "But I'm hardly in a position to be choosy."

He gave a satisfied nod.

"Excellent. Are you staying in the lodge? I'll send someone

over to retrieve your things." Gage pulled his own phone from his pocket and began tapping out a message.

"Right now?" She thought about what her hotel room looked like, her meager possessions offering a far more realistic portrait of her desperate finances than the beautiful gown she'd finagled from a local vendor for the event at almost no cost to her.

"I'm sure you're in a hurry to begin pursuing your story." He pocketed the device again. "Didn't you tell me your followers deserve answers?"

She began to see how neatly he'd maneuvered her into doing what he wanted. But what were his real motives? "I hope that doesn't mean I've effectively become your prisoner in this remote home."

"An intriguing idea, but no." The curve of his lips didn't seem quite like a smile. Wolfish anticipation, maybe. "You can, of course, come and go as you please. Although running from me at first opportunity hardly seems like the action of a woman who's indifferent." A note of challenge hung in his voice.

"I only meant that I'd like to retrieve my own things from the lodge." She wasn't sure how much of her life she could hide from Gage if he decided he wanted answers of his own. But she definitely didn't want him to know the extent of her financial hardship.

"And miss the rest of the party you took pains to crash?" He shook his head and moved closer to her. "The evening has only just begun. Enjoy yourself here, and your bags will be in your suite by the time you're ready to retire for the night."

He extended his arm to her, as if he were courting her and not taunting her. Tempting her. Teasing her.

He'd said he didn't believe that she was indifferent to him, and clearly, he still didn't.

She suspected Gage would do everything in his power to prove her a liar on that count. But then, given how quickly he'd believed the worst of her, what was one more black mark against her name?

She'd wheedled her way into his home. Now it was up to her to make the most of the opportunity. So she slid her hand around his forearm, wordlessly accepting his invitation.

His dark eyes met hers and she felt that crackle of electricity between them again. She flicked her gaze away, her darting glance landing on her smartphone.

"My camera—" she began.

"—is off-limits for the rest of the party." He laid a hand over hers where it rested on his arm. "It will be safe here when you return to your suite tonight."

Confused, she peered around the office.

"My suite?"

"This will be your sitting area while you're staying with me. Your bedroom is through there." He pointed to double doors behind the massive desk.

"I see you have plenty of room for me," she noted drily. She'd understood that Gage had achieved new heights of wealth in recent years, but seeing the way he lived firsthand was still eye-opening.

"I do, indeed." He squeezed her hand lightly before letting go and leading her out of the suite and back toward the party. "You'll hardly know we're sharing the same roof again."

Based on the way her pulse quickened when he was near, she seriously doubted it.

Three

Later that evening, Elena went into the kitchen and helped herself to a plate of fruit before declaring the night a total bust. Becoming an invited guest at Gage's soiree tonight had done little to help Elena's story.

Of course, the fact that Gage had attached himself to her for most of the party surely had something to do with it. Sighing with frustration, she drizzled a yogurt dip over her pile of strawberries and pineapple slices. No matter what he said to the contrary, he planned to be her watchdog more than her host.

Which would be easier to deal with, frankly, if his nearness didn't affect her so much. As it stood, her thoughts scattered like dandelion fluff on a spring breeze whenever he was close.

She scooped up some raspberries from a chilled dish on one of the kitchen islands and dumped them on her china plate next to a few wedges of cheese and some baguette slices. She'd given up searching the party for April Stephens, the woman she'd met at their shared dress fitting earlier in the day. April had seemed like a promising lead for more information about the Mesa Falls

Ranch owners since she, too, was in Montana to investigate the finances of Alonzo Salazar.

But by all accounts, the woman had left the party alone shortly after Gage had pulled Elena aside to speak to her. As for the other ranch owners, she'd spotted Weston Rivera drinking by himself in a back den, and his brother, Miles, in a heated conversation with Desmond Pierce out by the pool in the backyard. But they'd both stopped talking as soon as she'd stepped outside, making it impossible for her to overhear anything.

And Gage, the only other owner on-site tonight, was never far from Elena's side. Even now, he entered the kitchen moments behind her, balancing a trio of half-empty champagne flutes in one hand.

With his bow tie long gone, he looked deliciously disheveled. The top button of his tuxedo shirt was undone, and his five o'clock shadow had been darkening steadily as the evening wore on. She noticed that other women's eyes followed him when he walked past. It provided some small comfort that she wasn't the only person captivated by his dark good looks and athletic physique.

But she knew better than to get involved. Again.

"The catering staff not only serves the food, they provide cleanup afterward," she noted, nodding to his handful of crystal stemware. "That's what you pay them for."

"Thank you, Elena, for the entertaining tips. But when one is trapped in a room where the conversation has turned to which lipstick is the longest-wearing, the urge to escape by any means becomes overwhelming." Setting the glasses in the sink, he joined her at the kitchen island. "May I join you?"

He was already helping himself to half a baguette, not bothering with a plate. She hid a smile. His father might have poured a lot of time and money into cultivating an heir with posh manners and social savvy, but Gage had resisted at least some of the efforts to tame him.

"Only if we can talk about something besides makeup." She

found a napkin and retrieved her glass of water to bring with her. "I've had all the party small talk I can bear, too."

It frustrated her that she'd learned so little about the Mesa Falls Ranch owners or Alonzo Salazar this evening. But maybe she could still learn something from her host.

The crowd had thinned out considerably. The only guests still dancing in the great room were younger members of the celebrity entourages. It looked like one of the pop singers was deep in conversation with a European model Elena had spoken to only briefly. The party guests weren't the kinds of people Gage had normally chosen to surround himself with, but then, the evening had been carefully planned by the ranch's public relations staff to showcase Mesa Falls for young influencers who might bring more attention to the ranch's environmental initiatives.

She admired the intent, even if the crowd was far different from what she was used to. They all seemed so damned young.

"Let's sit at the breakfast bar." He nodded toward the coffee station near the back windows overlooking the darkened pool area outside. "That way I can keep an eye on things until these people run out of gas."

Elena slid into the cushioned wraparound bench that surrounded the table on three sides. Even though it was close to the kitchen, the spot was quiet since the catering staff was based in a mobile food preparation truck outside.

Gage slid in to sit near her, closer than she'd expected him to. To converse? Or to prove his point about her not being indifferent? Glancing over at him, she had to concede that she couldn't read the nuances of his expression anymore. Or perhaps he'd cultivated a greater skill in keeping his thoughts to himself since she'd known him. No doubt that was a formidable asset in his business dealings.

"So how long are you in town for?" she asked as she unfolded a linen napkin and laid it over her lap. She might as well dig for answers from the only Mesa Falls Ranch owner she knew personally. "You mentioned staying in Montana beyond tonight, but the last I knew your full-time residence was in Palo Alto."

He'd only just purchased that property when she'd met him. They'd talked about moving in together before things fell apart on the ill-fated trip to New Zealand to meet his family.

"It has been my home base ever since I purchased it." He tore the baguette in half and offered her a piece, but she shook her head. "But Weston is looking for someone else to oversee the ranch full-time."

Sitting so close to him called forth old memories. His aftershave was the same; since they'd broken up, the scent had sometimes tempted her in her dreams.

Dropping a few raspberries into her chilled water, she tried to refocus on their conversation, needing to learn what she could from him.

"Is Weston leaving the group?" she asked, mentally reviewing what she knew about the six partners. Weston Rivera was the younger of the Rivera brothers, both of whom owned a stake in the ranch. Weston had diverse investments around the country—mostly in fast-growth start-ups that had made him a very rich man. Miles Rivera ran their family's ranch in the foothills of the Sierra Nevada Mountains in central California.

"No. But now that we're beginning to attract tabloid attention—" he paused to give her a meaningful look "—Weston doesn't want to be solely responsible for overseeing the security and privacy of the guests."

Either that, or he wanted help ensuring the ranch owners' secrets were kept on lockdown. She was willing to bet the latter.

"So you're moving here more permanently?" She couldn't envision Gage retreating from the world in this remote corner of western Montana.

He might not have gone into politics like his father wanted, and he definitely didn't fit the same spit-shined image his father projected, but he had inherited his family's comfort in social situations. More than that, he was good with people, and seemed to enjoy working in team settings, not on isolated ranches.

"For now, yes." He stabbed a fat strawberry with his dessert fork. "We'll see how the year unfolds with all the media interest in Alonzo."

She sipped her water and watched the antics in the great room as two young men held a dance-off for the enjoyment of the six or seven ladies draped on Gage's leather sofas. Suit jackets discarded, the men spun on the toes of their slick dress shoes and performed hip swivels that had the women cheering and whistling.

The DJ seemed oblivious, spinning records and nodding to herself as she cued one song after another. One of her headphones had slipped off her ear.

"If you keep hosting house parties like this one, your time in town won't be boring," Elena observed lightly, amazed at the agility of the dancers.

Gage looked into the great room and shook his head. "I'm not sure living room dance battles are going to provide much entertainment. Besides, I like ranch life. Don't forget, I grew up on a cattle station before my father turned his attention to politics."

In fact, that detail of his past had slipped her mind. But now it all came back to her. They'd made plans to see the cattle station on her trip to New Zealand with him. But before they could, his father had intervened to confront Elena about her relationship with Gage. She'd flown home early. Alone.

She was still lost in thought when the DJ finished her set. A woman Elena guessed was part of the ranch's PR staff arrived in the great room to urge the last of the guests into the swag room, enticing them with the promise of luxe goods and a fitting for a custom Stetson. The great room suddenly went quiet, as the group shuffled out, drinks in hand.

"What about you?" Gage asked, as she realized they were now alone. "How will you fare in the remote mountains, far from LA life?"

Awareness drifted around her like smoke, clinging to her skin. And yet, remembering how things had ended between them, she forced herself back down to earth. The pain of losing him had led her to a rebound marriage that nearly destroyed her life. She couldn't give Gage any sway over her again.

"In light of my legal battles with my ex, taking some time to clear my head and commune with nature will be a good thing."

Gage made himself a stack of cheese slices and crackers, building his next bite with architectural care that relayed how hard he was working not to show his feelings, too. "I'm having a tough time envisioning you communing with nature."

"I may not have grown up on a cattle station, but I spent my youth in the California desert, sleeping under the stars as often as I slept under a roof. It was remote in its own way." She let herself smile at the good memories. It had taken years of therapy for her to tease out the happy times among the sad and scary ones with her alcoholic mother, but Elena made an effort now. "I hope to explore all that the ranch has to offer."

She'd tried on a lot of hats since running away from home at seventeen. She'd been a beauty influencer with her online makeup tutorials and endorsements that had helped finance college courses. A businesswoman in the years Gage had known her. Then, after that, a supportive wife to her husband's career. None of those things had worked out for her.

She wasn't sure where to turn next, but she knew for sure running hadn't done her one bit of good. She was done being reactive. Over the years, she'd let her family dictate her choices. Then Gage's overbearing father. Then her husband. Now, she was taking her life into her own hands.

For good.

Gage led Elena through his now quiet house half an hour later, not sure what to make of the changes he saw in her.

She wasn't the same woman he'd dated six years ago. But just because he could no longer see her fiercely competitive side didn't mean it wasn't there. No matter how she downplayed her presence in Montana, he couldn't shake the sense that she was here to right an old wrong. To make him pay for not standing up to his father on her behalf.

And yet, what had she expected when she'd completely hidden her past from him? He'd been blindsided by the revelation that her father was a wanted man. That she'd spent much of her teens on the run from the law with him. That her mother was an alcoholic with a violent streak that had landed both parents in jail more than once. Not that any of that reflected on Elena in the least. But it had hurt that she hadn't confided any of it, leaving him to find out from his father's private investigator. Her lack of trust showed how little she thought of him.

Now, she was back. And he didn't know what to think about it other than her presence was still more intoxicating than any bourbon. Even walking four feet behind him, Elena's draw was magnetic, pulling him inexorably backward.

"Thanks for showing me the way," she said as they returned to the living area outside her bedroom, the same spot where they'd spoken earlier in the evening. She retrieved her smartphone that he'd left there.

The velvet flounce hem of her dress swished softly as she moved. He hadn't realized how his ears had been attuned to that sound all evening until it stopped in the quiet stillness of the room.

Grinding his teeth as he tried not to think of her legs beneath the fabric, Gage reached for the double doors into the bedroom and swung them wide. "Your things from the guest lodge are already here, and there are towels in the bathroom."

He nodded with satisfaction to see the bouquet of bear grass on the bedside table. The pretty native wildflowers were protected in many areas, but the Mesa Falls ranching practices had brought the flowers back in abundance on the ranch. His staff had done well prepping her room on such short notice.

And he wasn't going to think too hard about why he wanted

to please a woman who'd tricked his security to get through his front door. He hoped he was only giving her a peace offering so she'd be less likely to backstab him with a tabloid hit piece.

"How beautiful," she murmured, brushing past him and bending over to sniff the white-and-yellow bouquet on her way to the bed. "Thank you, Gage."

If the warmth in her voice hadn't undone him, the sight of her beside the king-size bed would have. She was already reaching for the jeweled clip that held half of her hair up, taking the curls down for the night.

He watched, speechless, as the silky mass tumbled free. Curls danced and sprang around her shoulders as she moved. He knew he should say good-night and retreat. Leave her to get ready for bed.

But his mind had already supplied an alternate ending to the evening. One that included him stepping behind her to lower the zipper on her long, strapless gown. Letting the fabric fall away from her curves so he could touch her everywhere. And finding out if sex between them was still every bit as explosive as it had been six years ago. The connection between them had been so strong; the feelings held him hostage, preventing him from finding a long-term relationship after Elena. Everyone else came up short.

"You're welcome." He edged the words over a throat gone dry, still willing his feet to move. "If there's anything else you need…"

Help with a zipper. A neck massage. Multiple orgasms. He could think of so many things.

"I'm all set." She set her phone and the hair clip on the nightstand beside the flowers. "I appreciate you letting me stay."

He questioned the wisdom of that decision now, realizing how thoroughly she could distract him. How easy it would be for her to slide past his defenses and learn everything about the Mesa Falls Ranch owners that he needed to keep private.

With an effort, he reminded himself where his loyalties lay.

"It's no trouble." He saw it as his duty, actually. He was moving to Montana to keep the past on lockdown. To do that, he'd need to keep an eye on Elena Rollins. "And I'll ask one of the ranch hands to bring over an extra utility vehicle for you tomorrow so you can start exploring the place."

"Thank you." A warm light touched her gaze for a moment—a hint of genuine pleasure.

"I'll clear my schedule for the afternoon to accompany you." Somehow, some way, he needed to rein in his attraction to her before then.

He hoped like hell that it was tough tonight only because he was tired. But he suspected that was a whole lot of wishful thinking.

Her smile faded and he could see her defenses falling into place as he tried to shore up his own.

"In that case, I'll see you then." She gave a regal nod, all but dismissing him. "Sleep well, Gage."

Wheeling around to leave, to put as much space between them as possible before he did something he would regret, he already knew he wouldn't have a moment of sleep that wasn't filled with red-hot dreams of her.

Four

Shortly before noon the next day, Elena caught herself checking her watch again and cursed.

Curled up in the window seat of the spacious bedroom, she adjusted a gray cashmere throw over her legs and told herself to stop thinking about her upcoming appointment to explore the ranch with Gage. The man had dominated her thoughts this morning when she was supposed to be compiling notes for her lawyer to answer her ex-husband's latest bogus claim about their supposed "shared debt." But time and time again, while she was compiling digital copies of her old credit card statements from the months before she and Tomas split, her thoughts veered to the powerful man determined to play host to her this week.

Fluffing a silk pillow behind her back, Elena forced herself to relax. She glanced out the window with its glorious view of the Bitterroot Mountains, still capped with snow even though signs of spring were everywhere else. She had to admit she felt insanely comfortable in Gage's home—on a surface level at least. It wasn't surprising, considering the Egyptian cotton sheets, thick Turkish bath towels and fresh flowers on her nightstand. She hadn't been surrounded by this much luxury since the time she'd visited Gage's family in New Zealand. And despite some vivid dreams of Gage the night before, she'd had the best night's sleep she could remember in ages.

Even in the brief, happy first year of her marriage to Tomas when they'd both been doing well in their careers, her focus had been saving money for the bigger home he hoped to purchase for the family he supposedly wanted. So she'd never indulged in the kinds of high-end touches that graced every corner of Gage's place.

She clicked the Send button, emailing her attorney proof that she hadn't been the one to run up the debt Tomas now wanted her to share responsibility for. It didn't matter that they'd been divorced for months now, he still found ways to violate the terms of the arrangement, or to claim she had, all of which cost them both a fortune in legal fees. Between that nonsense and his live-in lover stationing herself in Elena's former home day and night to make sure Elena never removed so much as a dish towel, her frustration level with the whole process was through the roof.

No sooner had the email sent than her phone lit up with a text from Gage.

The fields are still muddy. I have outerwear for you so you don't ruin your clothes. I'm at your door.

She lightly swiped her thumb over the words while they sank in. Holding on to her enmity wasn't as easy when he did thoughtful things. It made her remember the past she'd shared with him before things fell apart. Before he'd revealed his judgmental side.

Casting aside the cashmere throw, Elena padded in stocking feet across the dense Persian rug and through the sitting room to the outer double doors. She opened them to find her host dressed in a taupe riding jacket trimmed with dark brown leather at the collar. From his jeans and boots to the wide, camel-colored

Stetson on his head, Gage Striker fit the role of an American cowboy with enticing ease.

All the more reason she needed to remember they weren't friends and she wasn't here as his pampered guest, no matter how much she enjoyed the beautiful accommodations. She needed to keep some barriers firmly in place.

"Good morning. I come bearing gifts." He held out a heavy denim jacket with a shearling collar for her. A box with the name of a saddlery shop sat at his feet. "Are you still game for seeing the ranch?" His gaze roamed over her yoga pants and slouchy sweater.

"I'll be honest. I spent half the morning thinking about how to give you the slip." She took the coat, not surprised to see the designer label, and the tag that indicated the garment was the perfect size for her. She didn't waste any time before she reset her defenses. "I'm not sure I should let you buy me off, Gage. Don't journalists frown on bribes?"

He stiffened a moment before recovering himself, no doubt remembering a bribe of another sort—the one his father had offered for her to leave the Striker family in peace. Regret mingled with old anger.

"Real journalists, yes." Retrieving the boot box, he stepped inside the sitting room. "Scandalmongers, however, accept them gladly. Especially the ones who didn't think to pack the right shoes for a Montana spring."

Still clutching the coat, she followed him to the couch, curious in spite of herself. "Is your staff already spying on me? My shoe collection isn't really anyone else's business."

"No one is spying," he assured her, removing his hat before dropping onto the leather seat beside her. "But I did make an educated guess that you left most of your boots at home based on the size of your suitcase when I happened to see it last night." He toed the box closer to her. "Come on and open this. Tell me how I did choosing something for a renowned style influencer.

Will the boots work? Or will you hashtag them 'never in a million years'?"

Her defenses were harder to maintain when he was being charming. Her influencer status had dropped off significantly in the last years she'd been focused on her marriage, but she was trying to be a social media presence again. Picking up the box, she set it on her lap and pulled the top off. The scent of leather wafted up as she peeled aside the sheet of crisp tissue paper to reveal a pair of high-cut black riding boots with a distinctive blue cuff.

"They're gorgeous," she breathed reverently, running a hand over the sumptuous leather. "Now I can go riding, too."

"That was my thinking." He nodded, seeming satisfied as she unzipped the first boot. "You said you were interested in communing with nature while you're in Montana. The boots will help."

She was surprised he'd keyed in on that comment from the night before. She'd forgotten that he was a keen listener and observer.

While she slid her foot into the first boot, Gage was already prepping the second for her. "You're being suspiciously accommodating today," she observed as she slipped on the next one and zipped it up. Standing, she reached for the coat he'd given her, only to have him beat her to it. "It makes me wonder about your motives."

Rising, he held out an arm of the coat for her. Chivalrous. Thoughtful.

Sexy.

"The sooner I show you around the ranch, and give you opportunities to find your story," he said as he helped her into the other sleeve, "the faster you'll learn there's nothing here that will help you in your quest for answers about Alonzo."

He skillfully shifted her hair to one side before he slid the coat into place. For the space of a moment, his hands rested on her shoulders before sliding away again, the touch awakening an awareness of him she didn't want to feel today. Even now, after he retrieved his hat and was escorting her toward the door, her body hummed from that brief contact.

"So all this thoughtfulness is self-serving?" she retorted, desperate to rally her absent defenses as she charged ahead of him. But she still felt hurt all the same.

"Elena." Her name, softly spoken, stopped her. Or maybe it was the unexpected tenderness in his tone when he said it.

Whatever it was, she turned around and locked eyes with him.

"We broke each other's hearts once, but it was a long time ago." His dark eyes seemed to see right through her, past any lame attempt to keep him at arm's length, right down to where she kept all her real feelings. "I don't think we need to keep operating like we're mortal enemies because of a long-ago breakup, do you?"

It was a skillful maneuver, putting her in a position where she would only seem childish and petulant if she kept needling him.

"Maybe I can rein it in," she offered, her gaze sliding away from his. "At least long enough for the tour. Why don't we talk about your former mentor instead? You can tell me all about Alonzo Salazar, a man who truly took scandalmongering to a whole new height."

Gage managed to put off the conversation long enough to get the ranch tour under way. They were in a high-performance utility vehicle that seated two. He'd taken his time snapping the windscreen into place and helping her buckle into the open-air seat, all the while planning his strategy for addressing her question about Alonzo.

Once they were cruising along the dirt path that ran along the Kootenai Creek that fed into the Bitterroot River, Elena gripped the roll bar and pinned him with a frank gaze.

"For a man who offered me full-time access to ask questions, you're noticeably silent on the subject of Alonzo," she observed lightly. She reached to tighten the pink scarf she'd wrapped around her hair, trying to stop the dark strands from whipping in the breeze.

The windscreen helped, but it wasn't the same as riding in a car. They bounced over a rocky hill and he turned sharply to follow the creek bed.

"I said you could ask questions. I didn't guarantee I'd answer." He slowed down to point out an osprey that had been startled from its perch. The huge bird emitted a series of high-pitched whistles as it circled. "It's been my instinct to keep my personal affairs private for as long as I've been in the public eye, so I have to make a concerted effort to be more forthcoming with you."

"You're weighing how much you can share with me." She distilled his answer to the basic point even as her eyes followed the osprey until it settled in a nearby ponderosa pine. "Why don't I help you out by telling you what I already know?"

She turned expectant eyes his way, and he had the impression—not for the first time—that Elena was in a constant state of wariness with him. He understood it, given how they'd broken up. But it meant he had to be far more watchful of her, unsure when her sharp tongue would strike next.

"Fair enough," he agreed, giving the vehicle more gas to take them up a ridge.

"No one knew Alonzo Salazar—a retired English teacher from the prestigious Dowdon School—was the man behind the tell-all book *Hollywood Newlyweds*, which he wrote as A. J. Sorenson, until he was publicly unmasked at the publicity event held here last Christmas." Elena pulled her phone from her jacket and snapped a selfie, no doubt collecting images for the day's social media feed. "The disclosure was all the more shocking because it was made by Tabitha Barnes, the actress whose real-life affair was exposed in the book. After it came out, her powerful director husband divorced her. He also severed his relationship with the girl he'd believed to be his daughter because as the book revealed, she was fathered by another man."

Considering what that girl must have gone through as a teenager—being abandoned and locked out of her childhood home by the man she'd thought was her father—was enough to make anyone think Alonzo was a dirtball. But Gage had known Alonzo well enough to believe the guy had some kind of compelling reason for what he'd done.

"Right. But just to be clear, I didn't know anything about Alonzo's secret pen name until that night." He still didn't know how Alonzo had managed to keep the secret his whole life, especially when Tabitha Barnes had threatened to sue the publisher. But the truth hadn't come out until months after his death. "Neither did any of the other ranch owners. Neither did his own sons."

As they reached the top of the ridge that offered a spectacular view of the river valley below, Gage parked the vehicle at the edge of a clearing and switched off the engine.

Elena unfastened her seat belt and turned more fully toward him. They sat in the open air, birds calling and the creek babbling below them.

"Supposing that's true—and I'm not convinced it is—why haven't you or any of the other ranch owners released a statement condemning his actions?" She tilted her head and gave him a questioning look. Her long dark hair spilled over her shoulder with the movement, reminding him how much he'd dreamed about running his fingers through all those silky waves. "You all were Alonzo's students at the Dowdon School. I know from our past conversations that he was a mentor to you and your friends, so I'm aware that you respect him. But it can't be good for the ranch to be associated with that kind of scandal. Why protect him?"

His publicity coordinator had posed the same question. But when Gage had met with Weston, Miles and Desmond before the party last night, they'd agreed the less said the better. Yet, he needed a different strategy with Elena. He had to keep her close, to buy himself time to figure out why Alonzo had written a book that had torn apart lives. Devon Salazar hadn't returned his calls yet today, but maybe Alonzo's son would share April Stephens's findings.

"Keep in mind that he wrote the book as fiction, and changed all the names, so I don't believe it was his intention to hurt anyone with it." Gage tipped back the brim of his hat to feel the sun on his face, breathing in the spring air to help cool the desire for Elena that was never far from the surface. "Remember the book was out for over a year before some Hollywood gossip columnist got a hold of it and decided to make a game out of matching up the characters to real people. That's when the fascination with the story began on a large scale, not because Alonzo billed it as anything true-to-life."

"I'll definitely revisit that." She nodded thoughtfully, her gaze flicking back to his. "I'd forgotten about that. I think the media frenzy took hold around the time we were dating."

The months they'd been so wrapped up in each other that they hadn't done much of anything else but talk, touch and make love.

"No wonder it didn't make an impression with us back then." He couldn't imagine how she'd left a relationship as intense as theirs only to turn right around and marry someone else. He'd been hurt by that all over again, thinking right up until he'd seen the engagement announcement that she would change her mind.

"No wonder." A ghost of a smile, fleeting and faint, chased over her features. "So you and your partners have decided to withhold judgment until you know more. But what happens when Devon Salazar's financial forensics investigator reveals where Alonzo was funneling profits from the story? No matter what his original intentions, you have to admit it doesn't look good for him to pocket the royalties and essentially profit off someone else's heartache."

Gage hadn't realized how thoroughly Elena had done her

homework, but clearly she knew about April Stephens and her visit to Mesa Falls Ranch.

"My guess is that he didn't personally profit, which is why I'm not jumping on the bandwagon to condemn the guy." He shrugged his shoulders, ready to move on. "And you shouldn't either until you know more."

"You're really going to try to pretend you're as in the dark as I am about this?" she pushed.

"I know more than you only because I considered Alonzo a friend, and I know his character. He wasn't a good dad to his sons, but I like to think he tried to make up for that by being a father figure to my friends and me." Rolling his shoulders, Gage reached for the key in the ignition to start the vehicle. "And on that note, let's move on."

"Wait." She laid her hand on his, halting him before he could turn the engine over. "Why not tell me the good things about him, then? How did you and the other owners end up as lifelong friends with a teacher from your boarding school?"

Her touch short-circuited his brain, preventing him from answering even if he'd wanted to. Which he most definitely did not. Instead, he captured her hand in his, holding it.

"Can we have a conversation, not an interrogation?" he asked, running his thumb over the backs of her knuckles for a moment, savoring the feel of her skin. "Maybe save some of your questions for dinner tonight?"

She shook her head as she withdrew her fingers. "I don't have the luxury of pursuing answers at my leisure, Gage. This is my job, and I don't get paid until I have a story."

He noticed she didn't address the dinner invitation. Because she didn't want to spend more time with him? Or because she suspected it would lead them to act on the heat sparking between them?

"That seems like a mercenary approach." He would be meeting with the other ranch owners later. Even if he couldn't reach Devon Salazar before then, he'd at least be able to talk to Wes to see if he'd gleaned anything from April about her investigation. The two of them had obviously hit it off. "You'll notice I'm not talking to anyone else from the tabloids, so it's not like anyone will beat you to the story."

"What if you don't have the answers I need?" she asked, her words trailing off as a herd of bighorn sheep stepped into view just below the ridge. "Oh wow," she breathed reverently, all her focus on three ewes at the head of the group. "What are they?"

"Bighorn sheep." He glanced sideways at her. "You've never seen one before?"

"Never. Although I might have seen little ones without the heavy horns and thought they were goats." She started recording a video on her phone. The screen showed the animals up close.

He pointed to the ewes at the head of the group. "They'd be some big goats," he teased, liking the smile that curved her lips in response.

She'd been stunning the night before in her vibrant crimson dress, but he was even more captivated by her now, her skin free of any makeup, her mouth a soft shade of rosy pink. One dark curl teased across her cheek in the breeze while the tail of her scarf flapped close to his cheek as he leaned closer to watch with her.

He breathed in her clean scent, remembering the way she used to dot lavender essential oil behind each ear instead of perfume. And, as if that one small reminiscence had been the dam holding back all the rest, memories rushed at him like a rogue wave. Sitting behind her in a tub full of rose petals and washing her hair. Driving up the Pacific Coast Highway with her in the passenger seat of his BMW Z8 roadster, the sounds of Big Sur mingling with her laughter. Undressing her in the private elevator on the way up to their penthouse suite in Seattle on a business trip.

"But I'm no wildlife expert," she exclaimed, snapping him out of his reverie. "How would I know?"

She tapped the screen to stop recording, then turned to catch him staring.

For a moment, the past and present blurred. Maybe it was because he wished he still had the right to wrap her in his arms and taste her. Tempt her into forgetting everything else but how good he could make her feel.

Her breath caught before she spoke.

"Whatever you're thinking," she said with a husky note in her voice until she cleared her throat and started again, "is a mistake."

The determination in her tone helped redirect his brain. Straightening in his seat, he nodded.

"Should we get out and walk around? Stretch our legs?" he offered, not sure there was enough fresh air in the Bitterroot Range to help him keep his thoughts off Elena's lips.

But he'd damned well try.

He'd shouldered the burden of being the point man at Mesa Falls to give Weston a break from a job he'd done so well for years. He couldn't spill all of the owners' secrets to the first reporter who showed up. Even if this particular reporter was causing heat to creep up his spine and flare along his shoulders.

"Sure." She unlatched the simple door that was more like a roll bar, and stepped outside before he could offer her his hand. "It will help me break in the new boots."

Fixing his attention on her legs was almost as dangerous as thinking about the past they'd shared. Both fueled flames he wasn't sure how to tamp down. Cursing himself for the lack of focus, he emerged from the vehicle and met her behind it, pointing to a trail that led down to the creek.

"Let's go this way." He wrenched off his jacket and tossed it in the cargo bed along with his Stetson. "It's warming up," he noted, tugging his long sleeves higher.

Elena's gaze dropped to his forearms, and he remembered her fascination with his tattoos. Seeing the way her dark eyes wandered over him, he vowed to send a generous bonus to the guy back home in New Zealand who'd done the distinctive work.

Because yeah, it was a blissful relief to know he wasn't the only one battling an attraction.

"Can I ask you something?" When she looked into his eyes, her expression was thoughtful. Curious.

"As long as it's not about Alonzo—"

She was already shaking her head. "We never spoke after the day I flew home alone from New Zealand. But I've always wondered about something."

He tensed, guessing he wouldn't like whatever came next. So much for thinking she might be feeling the old attraction, too. "That was the second-worst day of my life," he admitted, already raw from battling the draw of this woman. "I don't remember it that well."

But she kept going, her chin tilting up as she met his gaze. "When your father told you to break things off with me because my family would be an embarrassment to the Strikers, did you even consider asking me about it first?"

Five

Elena's defensiveness was ratcheting up in equal measure to her attraction.

The sight of those tattoos crawling up Gage's forearms had given her vivid memories of times his arms had been pinned to the bed on either side of her, muscles flexing while he moved over her. She'd been moments away from swooning on the spot. So she'd reached for the verbal sword and shield to hang on to the old sense of betrayal. She wasn't proud of herself for the predictable antics, but she was too susceptible to Gage's brand of sex appeal.

"My father confronted you before he shared his findings with me," Gage reminded her quietly, peering out over the herd of sheep still emerging from the pine grove before he brushed past her to keep walking. "I had zero time to process anything he said about you before he finished with his coup de grâce—that you'd already accepted his bribe to remove yourself from my life."

She wanted to believe that she heard a hint of regret in his voice. Over losing her? Or over the fact that she'd hidden her past for the entire duration of their relationship?

Probably the latter, she thought as she hurried to keep up with him. She might not have accepted the payoff, but she was hardly blameless in the breakup. She'd started packing her things before she'd even talked to Gage. It was interesting to realize she'd been that defensive even then—already protecting herself from getting dumped by being the one to walk away first.

"I was furious with him," she admitted, pulling out her phone to snap some more photos of the sharp cliffs jutting up from the creek bed. She appreciated having something to do with her nervous energy during an awkward conversation. "I felt embarrassed, too, that I'd been waiting for the perfect moment to tell you about my family and in doing that, I'd lost the chance to share that story in a less damning light."

She switched over to video mode and filmed another minute of the sheep making their way down to the creek bed, hoping she could find a way to make the nature footage fun for her followers. She was losing her edge in a competitive digital marketplace. One more thing her divorce had cost her since she could no longer afford to attend the kinds of parties and events that people loved to see in her feed.

"Your father was on the run from the law. Is there a way to put a good face on that?" Gage moved farther down the hill leading to the creek, his long strides making it easy for him to cover a lot of ground.

At least the cheerful chirp of birds all around them helped her to detach from the frustration that normally came from discussing her father.

"Of course not. He's a thief, and he should have turned himself in long ago." She hadn't seen her dad since she'd left home at seventeen bound for LA, but she'd always imagined him living in Mexico now, freed from the burden of raising a daughter. "At the time, he convinced me that he couldn't possibly do that—turn himself in—because my mother had left us, and there would be no one to look after me if he went to prison."

"Or so he said." Gage kept trekking down the slope, winding around boulders and trees. As Elena followed, the sound of rushing water grew louder. "But was your welfare really his top priority if he's still running from justice over a decade later?"

"Of course not. But when I was fifteen and still living at home, I will confess I was rooting for him to elude the cops every time we had a close call. If he'd gone to jail, I would have been in the foster system."

"But instead of telling me that, you decided to take the cash my father offered you." He shook his head, obviously still thinking the worst of her.

And didn't that remind her exactly why she'd chosen to leave him in the first place?

"You made it clear what you thought about me," she retorted, anger coursing through her. "There was no way we could have stayed together after that."

Her boot heel skidded on dead leaves, and she stuck a hand out to grab Gage's shoulder.

With lightning-fast reflexes, he reached back to steady her, his hands bracketing her waist. Her heart pounded from his touch. His sudden nearness. All that delectable maleness reminding her that she'd deliberately married someone who didn't make her insides melt, hoping she'd be safe from the rush of strong emotions that made her feel unstable. Unpredictable.

"Are you okay?" He stood too close, fixing her with his gaze, his strong hands lingering on her.

She remained very still, not sure if she was more worried that he wouldn't let go of her—or that he would. Because he was in front of her on the downward incline, his eyes were almost level with hers. He was close enough she could see the fine scar above one eyebrow that she knew was from a hiking accident long ago. She'd kissed that place before, and demanded to know the story.

Too many memories.

"Fine." She forced the words past her lips, her throat dry as she tried to hold on to the anger she'd been feeling just a moment before. "I just wasn't looking where I was going."

His fingers fell away from her, but he didn't step back. For a moment, he seemed to take her measure.

"We're almost there, anyway. I thought you might like to see this." He nodded to his left, where a deer path seemed to lead down a steeper ledge. "Will you take my hand for about ten more steps?"

She wondered why he bothered when he thought so little of her.

He held out an upturned palm, letting her choose. It made her think of how prickly she'd become since their breakup. Not just with him, but probably even with Tomas. She hadn't always been that way—ready to lash out at any moment.

As much as she wanted to protect herself from hurt, she refused to be the kind of person who assumed the worst about everyone. Wordlessly, she laid her palm on his and wrapped her fingers around the back of his hand.

He tightened his grip, leading her down the short embankment to a place where the copse of pine trees opened up, revealing a new view of the creek. Water sluiced down a rocky incline so fast a mist rose above the falls. Glossy dark boulders jutted from either side. The sound of the surge filled the clearing.

"It's so pretty." She still held his hand, remembering the last time they'd stood on an embankment overlooking crashing water. "Montana's answer to Big Sur."

His gaze flicked away from the view and over to her, the shared memory hanging between them. They'd been so incandescently happy that trip up the Pacific Coast Highway, drunk on new love and letting it carry them away. How naive she'd been to think that could last.

She would bet his thoughts were veering down that same dark

path, because his expression clouded. He gave a clipped nod of acknowledgment before he turned around to retrace their steps.

"I have a meeting with the other owners this afternoon," he said as he started up the steep path, tugging her with him. "We should get back."

Retracing her steps up the cliff path beside him, Elena told herself to count it as a victory that she'd weathered the afternoon without letting the old heat between them burn her. But seeing how much the memories affected him, too, didn't feel like a win. Hollowness yawned inside her. She wanted answers to the Alonzo mystery soon so she could leave Montana—and Gage—behind her for good.

Gage half expected Elena to follow him into the private library outside his home office, where he was holding the owners' meeting. She'd made no secret of being in town only for her story.

But she was nowhere in sight as he keyed in the code for the door, a security necessity given his work in investment banking and his access to extremely sensitive financial information. Could Elena be rethinking her decision to stay here with him? Their walk back from the waterfall had been silent and awkward, as though their shared past was riding shotgun in the utility vehicle with them on the way home.

She'd made it clear she wouldn't revisit that time any more than he wanted to. Yet no matter how much they pummeled back the past, it seemed determined to weigh into every conversation. Her casual mention of that day at Big Sur shouldn't have the power to set fire to his nerve endings, but he'd still ended up standing under a freezing-cold shower stream as soon as they'd returned from the tour.

"Wait up, Gage. Right behind you," a familiar male voice called to him before he could pull the door shut.

Peering back, he saw Desmond Pierce charging down the hall toward him, his tie a little askew, but other than that still looking like Mr. Hollywood with his crisp white dress shirt and no hair out of place. His aviator shades glinted under the hallway lights.

"Hiding a hangover under the shades?" Gage asked as he held the door.

"Hardly," Desmond answered drily, pulling off the sunglasses and tucking them into his breast pocket. "Night in and night out, I get to see the way my guests let alcohol make their decisions on the casino floor. I'm probably the soberest guy you know." He paused in the threshold to keep the door open. "Miles is right behind me. He's talking to your security guard in the foyer. Smart move keeping the bodyguards here through the weekend with all the celebrity guests coming and going."

Desmond owned and operated a handful of casino resorts, spending most of his time at his first operation on Lake Tahoe, close to where two other Mesa Falls Ranch owners lived—Jonah Norlander and Alec Jacobsen—both of whom were MIA this weekend.

"What about Weston?" Gage pressed the button to partially open the blinds.

"He texted Miles on our way over here." Desmond took care of switching on the gas fireplace. "Wes climbed Trapper Peak this morning to follow April Stephens, and things must have gone well because now they're in a cabin together somewhere on the mountain."

Gage swore at the same time Miles, Weston's older brother, came into view at the end of the corridor. Phone in hand, Miles jabbed at the screen while he walked.

"Wes can't make it," Miles announced, a hint of disdain in his voice. "He's in love."

"You make it sound like a communicable disease." Gage waved him into the room and allowed the door to shut behind them before he rearmed the lock.

"The end result is the same," Miles muttered, jamming his

phone back into his jacket pocket. "Wes is quarantined for the day and can't be with us."

Miles ran the Rivera Ranch on the California side of the Sierra Nevada Mountains, a huge spread that had once been a point of contention between the brothers. Because Weston and his father had been at loggerheads since Wes was a kid, Miles had been given responsibility for the whole thing. While that sucked for Wes, Gage always figured it hurt Miles more to bear that family responsibility alone when he could have had help. Gage knew how it felt to carry the weight of expectation that came with being an heir. He'd never wanted it.

"That's not a bad thing," Desmond pointed out, already seated in one of four leather barrel chairs positioned around a cushioned ottoman. "We could use an in with April Stephens considering she was hired to track Alonzo's money."

Miles stopped by the wet bar and helped himself to a glass of Gage's bourbon before taking the chair across from Desmond. "If Weston has learned her secrets, though, he hasn't shared them with me."

"She reports to Devon Salazar," Gage reminded them, retrieving the bourbon decanter along with a couple of glasses and a tray. He set all of it down on the ottoman in the middle of the chairs. "We don't have to ask Weston to betray her confidence when we can go straight to Alonzo's son. We might not trust Devon, but he owes us the truth since he kicked off this whole investigation by turning to us for answers."

"So we wait?" Desmond asked, not hiding his discontent with the plan. "That doesn't seem like a wise course of action when we have a tabloid reporter on-site actively trying to shake loose whatever she can about Alonzo."

The other men both looked expectantly at Gage.

He took his time pouring his drink before settling into his chair, the scents of leather, oak and old books providing none of the usual comfort.

"I'm taking care of that," he assured them before he took a sip. "I spent all afternoon with her, keeping her distracted."

He'd distracted himself quite a bit along the way, too, his thoughts alternating between highlights from their past and how much he still wanted her. Recalling the bribe she'd accepted from his father had reminded him he couldn't act on it.

"Why not entice her to write something else?" Miles suggested, scowling into the flames of the gas fireplace. "A tabloid reporter must have more lucrative options for stories than Alonzo. There are enough celebrities still on-site—"

Desmond snapped his fingers.

"Introduce her to Chiara Campagna," he suggested, sitting up straighter in his chair. "Give the tabloid reporter a behind-the-scenes opportunity with one of the world's most sought-after personalities."

Miles scoffed. "Chiara Campagna is famous for nothing."

"There's just one problem. I don't know Chiara," Gage reminded them, wondering if there was a chance Elena would consider it if he offered her access.

"She was here last night for a reason." Desmond pulled out his phone. "She's good friends with Jonah's wife, Astrid."

Jonah had married his college sweetheart, a Finnish supermodel, and the couple had bought a place on Lake Tahoe near Desmond's casino resort. Jonah was the only one of the ranch's owners to tie the knot so far, maintaining a reasonably normal life in spite of the tragedy that had marked their boarding school days. When their mutual friend Zach Eldridge had cliff-jumped to his death during a horseback riding trip, their lives had changed forever. Thanks to Gage's powerful father, the story had been kept out of the papers so it wouldn't reflect negatively on Zach's surviving classmates, but it haunted them anyway. Gage had been particularly troubled; thanks to his father's interference, Zach had never been properly mourned by the school. Gage's father didn't want the good Striker name associated with a death some viewed as a suicide.

Alonzo Salazar had been their class adviser at the time and had helped them weather the aftermath. For Gage, that had meant Alonzo convincing him to stay in school when he'd been determined to quit to spite his dad.

"How does that help us?" Miles asked while Desmond kept typing away.

"Jonah told me Chiara plans to spend a few days with Astrid after leaving Mesa Falls. Gage can take the reporter to Jonah's place in Tahoe for a couple of days so Astrid can introduce her to Chiara. It's win-win. This will get the reporter off ranch property and hand her a story that will net her a bigger payout. With any luck, she'll go back to LA afterward and forget all about us." Desmond spelled out his plan without ever glancing up from his phone. He obviously wasn't concerned that the last thing Gage needed was to spend more time in close proximity to his ex.

"I need to be here," he insisted, figuring that was an argument his friends could appreciate. "We decided I'm the new point man on-site now that Weston's distracted. I can't just take off the day after I dig into the new role."

"Managing a persistent reporter is more important than being at Mesa Falls," Miles countered, draining his drink and setting the glass on the tray. "I can stay until you get back."

Desmond swung to look at Miles at the same time Gage did, mirroring his surprise.

"What about Rivera Ranch?" Gage asked, knowing he wasn't getting out of this assignment if Miles was ready to abandon his own spread for the sake of managing Mesa Falls for a few days.

"I hire good people so I don't have to be there every second." He shot to his feet, looking uncomfortable with the topic and ready to change it. "Are we sure Astrid will share her pseudo-celebrity friend long enough to give Elena an interview?"

Gage hid an amused smile at Miles's obvious distaste for the new breed of fame. He hadn't been a believer either, until Elena had personally demonstrated the power of social media influence. He understood the sway people like her—and, on a bigger scale, Chiara Campagna—could have in the court of public opinion.

Desmond held up his phone. "Astrid already said it's no problem. Chiara is going to visit their new baby, so Gage, you can meet her, too."

"There's a baby." Gage hadn't meant to say it out loud, but he'd forgotten all about the fact that Jonah was a new father. "Has anyone else seen it?"

"*It* is a her," Desmond clarified. "Her name is Katja, and Jonah is over the moon about her. You should have gone to see them already."

"What have you got against babies?" Miles asked, looking slightly more cheerful now that Gage was in the hot seat.

"Nothing." He rose to his feet and finished his bourbon. "It's just one more thing Zach will never have. And I know we try not to talk about him or about how much what happened sucks, but there's something about these life milestones that brings it back, you know?"

Neither of them answered because of course they knew. The ticking of the grandfather clock seemed to increase in volume, filling the room.

When the silence stretched out, Gage set his glass on the fireplace mantel. "It's a good plan to distract Elena," he said finally, hoping he could convince her. "I'll touch base with Astrid before we go, but as soon as she confirms Chiara will grant an interview, I'll call for a pilot."

Desmond nodded. "You're welcome to stay at the casino if you'd rather not stay at Jonah's. I'll make sure there's a suite available."

"Thank you." Gage suspected he'd need that kind of distance. For him, Jonah's happiness as a father would be a vivid reminder of the life and opportunities Zach would never have. "I appreciate that."

Of course, staying in a suite with Elena would present problems of another kind. But he'd gladly face the fireworks he felt whenever she was around rather than think about all the ways he'd failed his old friend.

Chiara Campagna sat in her makeup chair, getting ready for tonight's appearance at a Hollywood premiere and reflecting on her upcoming trip. She'd just returned from Montana and now looked forward to the time in Lake Tahoe to see her friend Astrid. Chiara could count on one hand the people who had elevated her social media status to the precarious heights it had reached two years ago, and former supermodel Astrid Norlander was one of them.

Chiara scrolled through her social media feeds while her makeup artist added jewels along her temple to match her sequined dress. She was looking for mentions of Elena Rollins, the woman Astrid had texted her about, asking Chiara if she'd meet her. Chiara recognized the woman's face; if she remembered correctly, she was a beauty influencer who'd let her profile go quiet during a brief marriage to a well-known cooking show host. A mistake Chiara didn't plan to make; she would never give up her job for the sake of supporting someone else's. She'd come a long way from her hopes of a career as a mixed-media artist, leaving behind her dream of large-scale collage installations and working with found objects to create beauty. But at least she had discovered another way to use her creative skills, honing an online presence.

"Can you tilt your chin up?" the makeup artist asked, changing his brush for a wedge-shaped sponge. "I'm going to highlight the cheekbones a little more."

Chiara tapped off her phone screen and obediently moved her head right and left. She was already planning her time in Tahoe. She would bill it as a girls' retreat weekend and maybe invite a couple of others to fill out the photos she would post. She'd bring lots of outdoor gear and do some things outside. Work-wise, she'd be fine.

But Astrid had mentioned that Gage Striker would be there with Elena, putting two of the Mesa Falls Ranch owners in her path again. And while Chiara adored Astrid, she had a long-standing grievance with the men of Mesa Falls. They'd all been friends with Zach Eldridge, a boy she'd loved and lost when she was fifteen and he was sixteen. She thought she might be one of the few people in the world who knew that Zach had been on a horseback riding trip with those friends when he died. Gage Striker's powerful father had taken pains to cover up his son's connection to the death but Chiara had still managed to find out the truth.

Chiara would never forget how she'd snuck onto the Dowdon campus to find out what had really happened to Zach, a friend who'd loved art as passionately as she did. She'd confronted Gage and Miles separately, asking them for the truth, and they'd both given her canned responses that sounded rehearsed. She'd cried. Begged. Completely embarrassed herself for love of Zach, desperate to understand what had really gone wrong that terrible week.

She knew Zach had been upset about something. He hadn't been himself at the last school art show, a coed event between her all-girls institution and Dowdon.

Yet when she'd seen Zach's friends at Gage's house, neither of them appeared to recognize her as Kara Marsh, the girl she'd been before she adopted her social media persona. Perhaps that was just as well, as it meant they wouldn't be on their guard around her. Because with Alonzo Salazar in the news since Christmastime, and his connection to his former students becoming a point of public interest, Chiara sensed that answers about what really happened to Zach were finally simmering close to the surface. She owed it to her friend to make sure his story was told at last, no matter whom it might hurt.

Six

Elena needed a reprieve from all the feelings stirred up by being with Gage. But when she sat down to her laptop to work the evening after they'd toured the ranch together, her inbox exploded with bad news.

Emails from the bank, emails from creditors, emails from her work popped up one after another. As she scrolled through them all at the massive desk in her sitting room, she realized that her financial situation had turned dire. The woman who was subletting her apartment had given Elena a bad check, and that had made one of Elena's checks for her utilities bounce, too. The news seemed no better on the work front with two tabloid outlets both asking her when she'd have a story on Alonzo. She felt confident that her angle could warrant a bidding war for the piece, but since she had zero to offer them yet, she had no hope for seeing her next paycheck anytime soon.

Worse, her subscriber and follower numbers had taken another downturn, meaning her social media channels were going to be less attractive outlets for advertisers. And while she didn't object to returning to the business world and the kind of job she used to have with one of Gage's companies, she also knew that her value as an employee had gone down, too. What good was a social media expert without the following to back her up?

Staring into the flames blazing inside the sleek stone fireplace, Elena's head throbbed with the new layers of stress. It all served to remind her she should have been more aggressive in her divorce. Taking the high road had not only left her with less access to the marital assets, but being parted from her physical things also robbed her of a surface level of comfort.

A soft rap on the door startled her from the regrets that tormented her and served no purpose.

"Yes?" She swiped a hand across her eyes and blinked. She needed to pull herself together. She couldn't change the past... with her ex or with Gage.

"It's Gage." His deep voice slid straight past her defenses, conjuring up old confidences and quiet conversations. "Can I talk to you for a minute?"

Closing her laptop, she exhaled hard before shoving to her feet.

"Sure," she called, hoping to keep her tone light. Breezy. Like her world wasn't collapsing in on itself. "Come on in."

The door opened and Gage stepped inside, pulling all her focus to his broad shoulders in a steel-gray dress shirt. The fabric skimmed taut muscles, tapering down to the hem, which was untucked from his black trousers. With the sleeves rolled to the middle of his forearms, dark webs of tattoos were left exposed. It took her a moment to drag her gaze from them up to his face. His brown eyes roamed over her; he was studying her as thoroughly as she'd studied him.

Awareness flared to life again, the response more immediate each time she saw him. She stood in front of the big desk, keeping several feet between her and Gage. She wore a long cashmere cardigan over a pink silk T-shirt and matching lounge pants, but she wouldn't have minded a few more layers when her body responded so thoroughly to this man.

"I'm sorry to disturb you." His attention lingered on her face as he moved deeper into the room. "Is everything all right?"

"Absolutely," she lied, unwilling to show vulnerability, especially to this man. "Just going over some of my research on Alonzo."

She played the card most certain to get him to back off.

"In that case, I won't keep you for long." He paused near the fireplace, folded his arms and tilted a shoulder against the dark stone wall. "But I thought I'd mention a potential professional opportunity for you."

Frowning, she couldn't guess what that meant.

"I'm sure you're not here to offer me a job." She pivoted to face him, but stayed by the desk, knowing it was wisest not to stand too close to him when he looked good enough to taste and she was feeling adrift.

"No." His smile seemed more wary than amused. "But I have business to take care of with Jonah Norlander, one of the other ranch owners who is married to—"

"The whole planet knows he married Astrid Koskinen, the former supermodel." Elena's curiosity spiked, and she was grateful for the distraction from the sex appeal of the hot investment banker standing in front of her. "They just had their first child together."

"Correct." Gage nodded. "And apparently Astrid has a close friendship with Chiara Campagna."

"She does." Elena had been studying the new landscape of beauty and fashion influencers in her quest to recharge her social media presence, and was fully aware of the currency Chiara commanded right now. "I would have tried to speak to her last night, but she had left the party by the time you and I finished our talk. She's already back in LA, and I saw on her feed she's attending a Hollywood premiere tonight."

Gage's dark eyebrows lifted, and he straightened from where he'd been leaning against the fireplace. "In that case, maybe you'll be interested in what I have to offer. Chiara is going to be in Tahoe visiting with Astrid this week at the same time I'll be working with Jonah. If you go as my guest, you'd have an opportunity to interview Chiara."

His offer stunned her, and quite frankly, couldn't have come at a better time. But the thrill of what that could mean for her was quickly tempered by suspicion.

"How do you know she'd let me interview her?"

Gage shrugged, the gray cotton of his shirt hugging tighter along one shoulder. "You're a convincing woman, and you'll be meeting Chiara in the home of a friend she trusts. Why wouldn't she give you an interview?"

"Her time is worth a fortune, that's why. She won't just give it away to someone like me, unless…" Her suspicion grew stronger as she recalled how little Gage followed fashion and beauty. It didn't add up that he would tout this meeting as a professional opportunity for her unless he had a very specific reason. "She's doing a personal favor for the Mesa Falls Ranch owners."

He wandered closer to the desk, one hand shoved in his pocket. "Far more likely she'll be there to see Astrid's new baby, but make of it what you will." He skimmed a palm along the glass-topped desk before lifting his gaze to hers. "You told me you're following the Alonzo Salazar story for the paycheck, so I thought maybe the chance to speak with Chiara in that kind of setting would be enticing."

Chiara Campagna was social media gold right now. If Elena could capitalize on that, she would still have a piece that tabloids would vie for, and the payout would probably be even higher than the story she'd wanted about Alonzo.

"What's the catch?" she pressed, certain this opportunity hadn't landed in her lap by coincidence.

A scowl furrowed his brow. "I guess the catch is that you'd have to report on someone who is in the public eye by choice, unlike Alonzo, who never pursued fame and avoided it by writing a work of fiction under an assumed name." He gestured toward her closed laptop on the desk. "But if you'd rather keep searching for dirt about my former mentor, be my guest."

He shifted on his feet as if he was going to leave.

"Wait." Her hand darted out to rest on his forearm before she'd had a chance to think about the wisdom of touching him.

He stilled under her touch, and her heartbeat quickened at his sudden nearness.

For one breathless moment, their eyes met, and there was a world of possibility between them. She resisted an insane urge to stroke her fingers along his skin, forcing herself to let go.

"It's an offer I can't refuse," she admitted, needing this chance he'd given her not only to pay her rent, but to end the hardscrabble months she'd struggled through ever since her divorce. "If you're willing to take me to Tahoe with you, I'd be grateful for the introduction to Chiara."

She hadn't realized until that moment how tense he'd been, but now she could see the lines of his shoulders relax as he nodded.

"Good." He checked his watch, his forearm flexing under the charcoal-colored leather strap. "You'll have time to pack in the morning. I hope to leave by noon tomorrow."

"I'll be ready," she assured him, relaxing a fraction now that they were in agreement about something. "How long will we be in Tahoe?"

"Three days should be sufficient for me." He was close now, near enough for her to catch the scent of his aftershave. "Will that give you enough time?"

She breathed deeply, letting the hint of cedarwood tantalize her senses. She wanted to tell herself that she felt drawn to him only because they'd shared a sensual connection and a romantic history, but she knew there was more at work between them than that. It didn't help that she'd been feeling vulnerable tonight, and Gage had appeared at her door with a chance for her to reclaim some financial independence.

The gift may have been dropped into her lap in an effort to

distract her from pursuing the mystery of Alonzo Salazar, but it was still a gift. And she was grateful.

"Three days is fine," she answered, suspecting the hardest part about the trip would be avoiding the draw of the man beside her.

"Excellent." He gave a clipped nod. "I'll let the pilot know there will be two of us for the flight. We'll head over to the airstrip at noon."

"Thank you." She hugged her arms around herself, mostly to ensure she didn't do something unwise like reach out and touch him again. The memory of his skin under her fingertips burned in her brain. "I appreciate the invitation, Gage."

His name sounded intimate on her lips. Maybe because it was late, and they were alone. Maybe because a bed waited in the next room.

His attention dipped to her lips for an instant and her mouth went dry. It seemed like forever since they'd kissed, and yet she remembered with perfect clarity how he'd savored her lips with infinite tenderness. Devoured her with all the hunger and urgency of taut, fiery need.

But before the moment could spin out of control, he took a step back.

"It's no problem." He shoved his hands in his pants pockets. "I'd better let you get some sleep."

"Good night." She pushed the words past her chalk-dry throat, her body mourning the loss of his nearness even as her brain applauded the boundaries.

He was already stalking toward the door, his footsteps sure and quick. Running from the same seductive thoughts plaguing her? She couldn't be sure, but she knew that three days in Tahoe together were certain to push the issue.

But perhaps between his business, her interview with Chiara and visiting his friends with a new baby, they would be too busy to indulge in the desire that smoldered between them. She'd just have to make sure they were alone together as little as possible. Because she already knew that underneath all that red-hot attraction, there wasn't enough trust to hold them together.

Gage had done his level best to distract himself with business obligations during the two-hour flight to Tahoe. After how close he'd come to kissing Elena the night before—an impulse he felt every time he was around her—he'd been determined to lose himself in work for the course of the trip.

Things had started off well enough, with each of them taking seats on opposite sides of the aircraft. Wearing a tailored jacket and matching skirt in deep emerald, with her mass of dark hair piled on her head, she looked every inch the businesswoman he remembered. He'd assumed she'd been working for the past hour.

But something in her tone distracted him as she spoke to a friend on a video call. She sounded upset.

Glancing up from his tablet, he saw her seated at the built-in workstation in the front of the plane, her laptop open while she engaged in an animated dialogue with a woman he didn't recognize. Up until now, Elena had kept her head down and her eyes on her work, seemingly as committed to ignoring the sparks jumping between them as he was.

Yet how could he pretend not to hear her when her stream of agitated whispers indicated she was obviously distressed?

She peered back over her shoulder, catching him staring. Any guilt he might have experienced at not giving her more privacy was immediately negated by the sight of her red-rimmed eyes.

He unfastened his seat belt but by the time he made it to her, she was already stabbing the button to disconnect the call, her screen going black.

"Is everything all right?" He wanted to touch her, to offer what comfort he could, but he also didn't want to overstep those prickly defenses of hers. "Can I get you anything?"

"No. Thank you." She blinked fast, tugging tissues from a slim, sapphire-colored bag. "I'm fine."

"Elena." He lowered himself to kneel in front of her, need-ing to see her face. "You're obviously not fine. What's wrong?"

She squeezed the bridge of her nose for a moment, then pat-ted her eyes with the tissue, seeming to pull her emotions back under control. "That was a friend of mine from LA." She stuffed the tissue back in her bag. "She'd offered to help me retrieve a few things from the home I once shared with Tomas, but ap-parently his new fiancée refused to allow her inside to collect them." Elena looked like she'd been about to say more on the subject, but stopped herself. "It's nothing that plenty of other people haven't been through when they split up. I don't know why I let it get to me."

"These items are legally yours?" he asked, recalling she'd been separated for a year. At her nod, he asked, "Wasn't that all spelled out in the paperwork?"

Sighing, she seemed to surrender to the topic she clearly hadn't wished to discuss.

"Yes, but I kept waiting for a good time to return to the house, trying to avoid his fiancée."

"I remember hearing he proposed to his assistant on his cook-ing show," Gage said drily, hating the guy on Elena's behalf. "Sounded like a ratings ploy to me. But you have a legal right to your possessions, Elena. There's no need to be diplomatic with people who are denying your rights."

The aircraft hit a pocket of turbulence, forcing Gage to grip the arms of her chair to steady himself.

"I realize that. I just really didn't want to play out that whole drama of confronting the woman who wormed her way into my life, pretending to be my friend right up until the weekend she slept with my husband." She gasped as they bounced through another air pocket, her fingers covering his briefly where they rested on the arms of her chair. Her gaze flicked to his before she took hold of her seat cushion instead. "It's so trite. So not what I imagined for myself. And I kept thinking Tomas would man up and send me my things, but now I think he's just dragging his feet in the hope I'll forget about it. His new fiancée is spiteful and—sadly—my size."

She shook her head, obviously frustrated, a dark curl sliding loose from her topknot. The strand caught her eyelashes, and Gage couldn't suppress the urge to peel it gently away from her eyes. Her glossy hair gleamed under the soft cabin lights, the strands smooth against his finger as he let them coil back into place alongside her ear.

"So your friend was denied entrance to your former marital home to retrieve your possessions?" He wanted to be sure he had his facts straight, already seeing a way to be of assistance.

Because it bugged the hell out of him to think Elena had been going without personal effects for months in an effort to be reasonable. He'd understood her financial position had taken a hit in the split from her ex, but given her drive and resourcefulness, he'd assumed she would bounce back. It hadn't made sense to him that she'd arrived in Montana with little luggage and few clothes when she had once been a successful lifestyle blogger. When they'd been together, her closets were full; she'd never lacked for fashion samples from all the big designers.

Now? She hadn't even brought boots to the mountains for the weekend. Whether she admitted it or not, Gage suspected she was struggling.

"Yes." Elena confirmed his understanding of what had happened, sounding more resolved and less upset now that she'd had a few minutes to settle down. "Which only confirms for me that it's long past time to go over to the house and deal with the situation personally. No more deceiving myself things will work out for the best."

Gage studied her, curious about this side of Elena that he hadn't seen when they'd been dating. She'd always been so sure of herself. So fiercely committed to whatever path she chose.

He realized he'd probably been watching her for too long, his body too close to hers. His hands were still braced on the armrests of her seat. The scent of the perfume she favored—

something tinged with lavender—teased his nose. And damn, but this was not the time to touch her.

"Do you need anything in the meantime?" he asked, wanting to help ease the burden of her months of frustration. To say nothing of the heartache that must have come before it. "Is there anything I can do to make things easier for you until you return to Los Angeles?"

"No. Thank you." She made a point of peering out the window off to one side, as if she wasn't ready to accept any favors from him. "I really appreciate you bringing me with you today. That's plenty."

She might not be looking at him, but he could sense her awareness of him in the way she gripped the seat cushion more tightly.

He would let it go for now.

Easing away from her, he took the seat closest to Elena as the pilot descended toward the northwestern edge of Lake Tahoe. Gage would contact a friend in security to ensure Elena's things were retrieved at a time when her ex-husband was present. For that matter, Gage had seen the name of the friend who'd attempted to help her today on Elena's tablet before she ended the call. He could solicit input from her to be certain they collected what belonged to Elena—quickly, legally and without having Elena inconvenienced another minute.

He liked the idea of doing this small thing for her, even if he hadn't forgiven the way she'd allowed his father to buy her off. There was blame to go around for their unhappy split, and Gage had never felt right about bringing Elena to New Zealand in the first place when he'd known the way his father liked meddling in his life. How might things have been different between Elena and Gage if she'd come around to telling him about her past on her own, instead of having the details thrust into the spotlight by his father?

There was no way to know, of course. Elena had to live with the consequences of her actions in their breakup. But with this one simple act, helping Elena out, Gage could rest easier knowing he'd tried to atone for his role in the split.

Too bad it wouldn't come close to fulfilling his need to kiss her. Touch her. Make her forget that bastard of an ex-husband of hers had ever existed.

Seven

Three hours later, Elena sat ensconced in comfort inside Jonah and Astrid Norlander's mountainside mansion overlooking Lake Tahoe, the hospitality of her hosts almost making her forget what a frustrating day it had been up until then.

"Would you like to sit outside while we wait for Chiara?" Astrid asked her, pointing through the wall of windows toward the huge deck with deep couches built around a fireplace table that was already lit. A long, lithe Finnish beauty, the former supermodel had ethereal blue eyes and platinum shoulder-length hair. She wore not one smidge of makeup that Elena could see, and she was still so striking that it was difficult not to stare. "There are patio heaters and blankets, but with the sun on us, I think we'll be warm enough without them."

Even the woman's accent was gorgeous. She went to the kitchen and added a couple of orange slices to her seltzer water, then padded to the back door and slid into a pair of fur-lined clogs.

"Sure, I'd love to join you outside." Elena rose and picked up her white wine spritzer from the table. It was a light drink, the type she didn't mind sipping to be social. "The guys look fairly absorbed in their game."

Jonah and Gage sat at the bar between the kitchen and great room, their eyes on a flat-screen above the fireplace, where coverage of college basketball was in full swing.

"They both went to UCLA as undergrads," Astrid reminded her, pushing the sliding glass door open. "I think Gage timed his flight to make sure he was here for the game."

Elena smiled, recalling sitting courtside a few times with Gage while they'd dated. Back then, when he was working almost all the time, she had enjoyed seeing him relax for a couple of hours. "That wouldn't surprise me in the least," she said, stepping through the oversize glass door before Astrid slid it back into place.

"Your suit is gorgeous, by the way," Astrid observed, stroking her fingers over the fabric of the sleeve in a friendly way. "Is the designer anyone I know?"

"It's one I made, actually." Flattered, Elena took a moment to enjoy the compliment, glancing down at the angled cuffs and buttons she'd found in salvage shops three years ago.

"Wow." Astrid's gaze zeroed in on the boning around the corset-style waist. "There are so many unique details. You're incredibly talented."

Elena searched the woman's face, wondering at first if she was just making polite conversation, but seeing genuine interest in her eyes, she explained, "When I blogged more regularly, I made some pieces that I wanted to wear and couldn't find. I did a few social media stories about the process of picking fabrics and finding a tailor for sewing samples."

The reminder of the hard work she'd done to build her blog and connect with followers made her regret slowing down when she'd married. Why had she turned her full attention to supporting Tomas in his work instead of being loyal to the people who had been loyal to her? Why hadn't she found a healthy balance between Tomas's career and her own?

"You are very talented," Astrid repeated, underscoring the words by pointing with her index finger. "Wait." She froze, turning her head toward the house. "Did you hear the baby cry?"

Astrid pulled her phone from her pocket and checked the nursery monitor feed that she'd already viewed a handful of times since Elena and Gage arrived. Katja had been sleeping the entire time.

"Is she okay?" Elena asked as she moved to the sleek steel-and-wood railing surrounding the deck. The springtime air was cool, and there was still snow on the mountaintops, but the sun felt warm on her face and the breeze was scented with green and growing things.

"She's fine." Astrid laid the phone on the marble tabletop surrounding the row of flames that shot up in the center. "But I just buzzed Chiara in at the front gate. Do you mind if I go greet her and then I'll come right back? I can't wait to introduce the two of you."

"Of course." Elena walked the dark wood planks of the raised deck as Astrid disappeared inside the house.

Elena's gaze lingered on the wall of windows, and she caught sight of Gage for a moment. He met her gaze, and perhaps because he noticed she was alone, he stepped outside a second later. He'd worn a black suit over a gray-and-white-striped T-shirt for their visit. The cotton shirt stretched smoothly across his chest in a way that called to her fingers to touch. Beyond the obvious attraction, there was also a new level of appreciation for how he'd treated her today. She'd felt so defeated when she struck out with her latest attempt to retrieve her possessions from her former home. Her friend Zoe had been upset by the hostility she'd experienced from the moment Tomas's new fiancée opened the front door. And worst of all, Elena had been so frustrated herself that she'd nearly broken down in tears in front of Gage.

Thankfully, he'd been extremely kind about it, listening to

her concerns, not judging, and allowing her to move past the anger to focus on their trip.

"How are you doing?" he asked, concern in his dark eyes as he closed the distance between them. "Can I get you something else to drink besides the wine?"

She appreciated his thoughtfulness since he knew she imbibed very little—the bourbon that first night at his house being a notable exception. But there had been extenuating circumstances.

"It's mostly club soda. But thank you." She felt at a loss for how to navigate her new relationship with him. Between his kindness on the flight to Tahoe and the way he'd set up an interview with a woman who could single-handedly reignite Elena's lapsed social media presence, she could no longer pretend that Gage was her enemy. "Astrid went to greet Chiara, by the way. Thank you again for setting up the meeting."

Turning to look out over the mountains, she sipped her drink, grateful for the cooling effect of the chilled wine and soda. With Gage standing so close to her, she definitely wouldn't be needing the patio heater to keep warm. His shoulder brushed hers and a thrill chased up her spine.

"Good. We'll stay long enough for you to obtain what you need, see the baby and then return to the casino residence." They'd dropped their bags at the posh four-bedroom house earlier before continuing to Jonah's in a rented Land Rover. Desmond Pierce owned the casino and was letting them stay there for free.

Gage leaned closer to speak in a tone meant just for her, even though they were alone on the patio. "You can give me the high sign when you're ready to leave."

"What's the high sign?" she pressed, hearing Astrid's voice inside the great room, and guessing her hostess was returning.

"Whatever you want." He kept his dark eyes fixed on her in a way that made her heart beat faster. "A wink, maybe." He lifted his attention to her updo. "Or you could let your hair down." His focus shifted back to her eyes. "I'd definitely notice that."

With an effort, she restrained a shiver at the thoughts those words ignited. "That would be a bad idea, as I'm sure you already know."

Behind them, she heard the sliding door open. The noise of the game on the TV and the voices from the house grew louder.

"Then I'll have to settle for a long, smoldering look," he told her softly, still speaking for her ears alone. "Once I see that, I'll have you out the door in no time."

She wanted to tell herself he was just teasing. Just trying to rile her. But his lingering attention suggested otherwise in the moment before he pivoted to greet Chiara Campagna.

Elena did the same, forcing herself to flip the switch into professional mode. Still, the breathless anticipation of their flirtation didn't fade.

Not when Gage excused himself to return to the house and give Elena space for her interview. And not when she delved into a conversation with one of her generation's most sought-after beauty and fashion icons. But no matter how often she found her thoughts straying to Gage Striker, Elena refused to consider the scenarios he'd painted in her mind as anything more than outrageous fantasies that had no place in her real life.

Seated in one of the paired leather recliners in Jonah's great room, Gage peered out the wall of windows. Chiara Campagna was lifting her phone to take a photo of herself with Elena.

He could only see Elena's face in profile, so it was difficult to read her mood. He knew he'd caught her off guard when he'd voiced his desire for her, but it wasn't as if she'd been unaware of it. They'd been sidestepping it since their first meeting at Mesa Falls, circling and taking each other's measure after all this time. By now, he'd seen enough to know he wanted her as much as ever, no matter how things had ended between them before.

He refused to pretend otherwise.

"She's still there," Jonah observed drily from his seat beside Gage, his voice even louder than the TV's impressive surround-sound audio. "You've checked out your date at least five times since we sat down."

Caught.

"She's been an unexpected complication at Mesa Falls," Gage explained, forcing his attention back to the game even as Jonah stabbed the remote to lower the television volume. "I didn't anticipate having to take a role on-site in Montana, and I sure as hell didn't expect to have to confront my ex in the process."

He'd known Jonah since they were thirteen, meeting him the same way he'd met the other owners of Mesa Falls Ranch: as suite mates at Dowdon. There'd been four of them in a room at the end of the hall, and three in the room across from them. Seven friends. Six who graduated. The six who remained now owned and operated the ranch together as a way to honor the life of the one they'd lost.

Jonah made a dismissive sound. Dressed in a weathered college T-shirt in honor of the game they watched, he didn't look much different from how he had in their school days, except his dark blond hair was cut shorter and he had some kind of verse in Finnish tattooed around both biceps. "With the way you two look at each other, she won't be an ex for long."

"Old flames die hard. Or so the saying goes." Gage retrieved his craft beer from the table between their chairs and tipped the bottle to his lips, wishing he could quench his thirst for Elena as simply.

Jonah sat forward in his recliner so his leather loafers were back on the floor. "You're not concerned about starting a relationship with someone who's actively trying to put Alonzo's name back in the public eye?"

"Who said anything about a relationship?" Gage resented the question. It was as if he was betraying the memory of a guy who'd helped them through the aftermath of a hellish trauma. "I've got no choice but to keep an eye on the situation. I need to stick close to her, and I can't pretend the attraction doesn't exist."

"Call it what you will," Jonah conceded. "But Elena Rollins means trouble for the ranch. You know that as well as I do."

"That's why we're redirecting her with the Chiara interview today," Gage reminded him, refusing to feel guilty about distracting her with this trip since the resulting story would further her prospects far more than anything she might learn about Alonzo Salazar. It benefited them both. "I'm taking what precautions I can, but I can't prevent her from finding out the truth about Alonzo if she's determined to dig."

"If only we knew the truth as well, maybe we could prepare for the consequences." Jonah's final words were drowned out by the sudden wail of an infant from somewhere deeper in the house. Unbelievably, the guy broke into a broad grin. "Duty calls. Excuse me."

Gage watched as he wound through the house to the main staircase and took the polished steps two at a time, his hand running along the mahogany banister. A moment later, Astrid appeared in the doorway from the outdoor patio, hurrying through the great room with a quick wave to Gage before she followed her husband up the stairs.

The sight of their commitment to their new child reminded Gage of the hopes he'd once harbored for his future with Elena. There'd been a time they'd discussed their dream home, designing and decorating it over shared meals or in stolen conversations between business meetings. They'd even talked about having a family together.

They'd spoken about most everything, it seemed, except her past. Instead, she'd allowed it to blindside him, unwilling to give him any time to process it before she boarded a jet and took it right out of his life. Now, he knew better than to expect more from her. They could have a physical relationship instead. Straightforward. No strings.

His thoughts were interrupted by the sound of the patio doors opening again. Chiara and Elena entered the great room. Chiara was showing Elena a photo on her phone. He caught the end of a conversation about dyeing techniques for silk kimonos.

Elena's gaze flicked to his, the eye contact as tantalizing as any touch after their exchange on the deck earlier. He liked thinking he'd invaded her thoughts as surely as she dominated his.

"Gage, will you take a photo of us by the fireplace?" Chiara asked suddenly, passing him her phone. "I took some of us outside, but I need to be sure I have some images of Elena's suit."

"Of course." He was surprised the woman remembered him by name from the party the other night since they hadn't been formally introduced. But he was glad to see Chiara seemed as enthused about the meeting with Elena as Elena had been about interviewing her. "It's a beautiful jacket," he remarked as he adjusted the focus.

Of course he'd noticed Elena's stunning emerald-colored skirt and jacket, even though he'd been determined to focus on his work and not her during their trip here. But that plan had fallen by the wayside, and now that he'd allowed himself to consider the possibility of being with her again, he couldn't peel his eyes off her.

The double-breasted blazer was sewn with corset details, making the fabric hug her narrow waist. Even viewing her through the phone's camera, Elena set him on fire. He clicked a few shots and then passed the device back to its owner.

Chiara reached for it, then pocketed it in the long white cardigan she wore with brown suede pants and silver pumps. "But did you know that Elena designed it herself? I'm so impressed with everything from the fabric choice to the clever boning sewn into the seams."

Gage hadn't known that. New facets of this woman kept cropping up, making him wonder how well he'd ever known her.

Something he was determined to change, if only to anticipate her next move.

Before he could respond, their hosts called them from the stairs.

"Friends, we'd like to introduce you to someone." Jonah stood beside his wife, who cradled a pink blanket in her arms. The smallest hint of an infant's face was visible from Gage's vantage point.

What struck him most was how damned happy Jonah appeared. His eyes filled with paternal pride as he gazed down at his daughter in his wife's arms. Though Gage hadn't thought about marriage in six years, he could still understand the appeal as long as you were with someone you trusted implicitly. And how often did that happen in life?

The women rushed to surround Astrid, cooing over the baby and admiring everything about her. Gage moved more slowly, clapping Jonah on the back when he got to him.

"Congratulations, man. I'm so happy for you."

"Thank you." He lowered his voice for Gage's ears only. "I'm still scared out of my mind I'll screw up something. But apparently, from what I hear from other parents, that feeling doesn't go away for at least eighteen more years."

Gage's father hadn't invested that much concern in Gage's upbringing, shipping him off to the United States for school to ensure his antics—youthful attempts to capture his dad's attention—didn't taint the family reputation. Alonzo Salazar had been more like a father to Gage than the man who'd sired him.

"The fact that you worry about being a good parent says a whole hell of a lot about the job you're already doing," Gage assured him as he watched Astrid pass the pink bundle to Elena.

Something about seeing her hold the little girl, an expression of tender fascination on her face, felt like a sucker punch to Gage. A reminder of the chance for the family they'd never gotten.

Still, he couldn't have looked away if he tried. Transfixed, he was still watching her fifteen minutes later when Astrid and Jonah disappeared into the kitchen to oversee preparations for the evening meal. Chiara followed them, leaving Gage alone with Elena in the front room near the foyer.

"Would you like to hold her?" Elena asked, approaching him with Katja in her arms. "You have a lot more experience with children than I do given all those cousins who have kids."

And in a flash he was transported to that time he'd taken her to New Zealand to meet most of his relatives at a family party. It had been a huge deal for him, introducing her to everyone. His mother had insisted on holding a big reception on his father's estate, inviting half the country.

He reached to take the baby from Elena, his arm brushing her breast in a purely accidental way. Awareness of her exploded. Bending closer to speak into her ear, he said, "I hope you're contemplating giving me that high sign sooner rather than later."

Elena quickly stepped back once she'd safely passed him the infant. "You speak as if I would be green-lighting a whole lot more than an exit strategy, but I haven't given you any cause to think I'm foolish enough to get close to you again, Gage."

"Foolish or not, you can't deny there's a strong sense of unfinished business between us." He tucked the pink blanket around the little girl's foot, keeping her wrapped up tight. Her blue eyes were open, her focus vague. She smelled like baby shampoo.

And she seemed a whole lot happier for his attention than Elena, who paced in front of the windows overlooking the horseshoe-shaped driveway.

"Perhaps. But I promised your father I'd leave you alone," she reminded him, falling back on that old rift between them and using it to keep a wedge there. "I can't go back on my word."

"That didn't concern you when you snuck past my security to get into my house, so I can't imagine you're all that worried about what Nigel Striker thinks about you now." He found himself parrying her maneuvers, and forced himself to stop. "But if going back on your agreement concerns you, I'll repay the old man as a way to buy you out of the deal."

That stopped her pacing.

She stared at him from across the living room, her jaw dropping in disbelief.

"You can't be serious." She shook her head, as if trying to convince herself she'd heard correctly.

"On the contrary, I couldn't be more sincere, Elena. I've already wasted too much time trying to ignore an attraction that refuses to die. I'm done deceiving myself that this thing between us will end up any way but in flames." He moved toward her, his boots echoing on the polished marble. "I think, in your heart of hearts, you know that, too."

"Leave my heart out of it," she warned him, dark eyes narrowing.

He didn't stop until he was standing much too close to her, the only barrier between them a contented baby.

"As you wish." He nodded, agreeing to her terms. "But I'll take all the rest of you just as soon as you're ready to give it."

She was still staring at him in a wordless standoff when Astrid called them into the dining room for the meal. Gage already knew the food wasn't going to do anything to take the edge off the real hunger.

Eight

Back in the Land Rover after dinner, Elena buckled her seat belt for the short drive to where they were staying. The day had been more fun than work, even though she'd signed on for an interview with Chiara Campagna. As it turned out, Astrid and Chiara were not only smart, creative women with tons of knowledge about fashion, they were also a blast to be around. The evening had gone better than Elena could have hoped.

The only moments that had given her pause involved Gage making his renewed interest in her known. Because although she'd felt the sparks fly between them from the moment he'd filched her phone at the party the other night, she had thought he was firmly opposed to reigniting the flame. Now, she knew otherwise, and she wasn't sure what to do about that.

She'd been floored when he'd offered to repay his father for the bribe he'd offered her. It made her regret that she'd never come clean about that. In the past, she'd told herself that it wouldn't matter to Gage that she hadn't accepted the money because Gage had been so quick to believe the worst of her anyway. But this week had forced her to rethink that perspective—a viewpoint she'd formed in the heat of anger and hurt. In truth, she'd been quick to believe the worst of him, too, and the realization was more than a little uncomfortable.

"Did you get everything you needed from Chiara tonight?" Gage asked as he pulled the SUV out onto the main road. Keeping one hand on the wheel, he changed the screen on his dashboard map for directions to the casino. "Or will the two of you be getting together again?"

Elena peered across the dark interior of the vehicle. With shadows playing across his face, his bone structure was all the more defined, the shadow of bristle along his jaw sending her into a tantalizing daydream about kissing him there.

Clearly, her body was rebelling against her for all the times she'd put up barriers between them. She tried to remember his question.

"While I definitely have enough to run a series of spotlights on her and her work, *she* asked *me* if we could get together again this week," she answered finally. After two years of focusing on the social media for her ex-husband's cooking show, Elena had been floundering to get her own voice back for her own brand. But tonight had reminded her how much she had enjoyed what she did. How much she had to offer her followers.

"It seemed like you two hit it off." Gage nodded, sounding satisfied. "Good for you."

His obvious pleasure in her success confused her, after they'd been at odds so often this week. That dynamic anchored her, helping her to stay strong against his undeniable appeal. But he'd shifted the playing field on her tonight and she didn't know what that meant for where things would go next. She wasn't ready to jump back into a relationship. Even a hot, passionate fling.

No matter how fun that might be.

To distract herself, she turned on her phone and idly opened her most active social media platform.

And nearly had a heart attack. Gasping, she fumbled her phone.

"What's wrong?" Gage asked. "Should I pull over?"

"No. Sorry. Nothing's wrong." She stared in disbelief at her number of followers, refreshing the page to see if there'd been a mistake. "My following has more than quadrupled in size tonight."

"What did you post?" he asked, brows furrowing.

"Absolutely nothing." She clicked open her mentions and found the posts from Chiara and Astrid. "But your friends posted about my suit. I can't believe this."

There were more comments than she could ever hope to reply to personally. In the course of one evening, her social capital had grown to more impressive proportions than ever, even bigger than when her blog had been at its most successful.

"I'm glad to hear it." He steered the SUV away from the lake, into the hills overlooking the water. "With the boost in followers, will your piece on Chiara fetch a higher price?"

The evening had quickly grown cold after the sunset, and now she was grateful for the vehicle's heated seats keeping her warm. Her gaze roamed over Gage, his nearness sending another jolt of heat through her.

"Definitely. It also takes the pressure off to lock in a quick sale for the interview since the increased reach expands my options for revenue streams." She couldn't begin to quantify what a gift this meeting had been for her, but her brain worked overtime strategizing her next move to solidify the growth.

Besides, thinking about business helped keep her thoughts off the upcoming night with Gage as he turned into the driveway of the four-bedroom vacation home perched above the lake. She should address his proposition. Make it clear that indulging in the attraction wasn't a good idea, even if thoughts of him dominated far too much of her brain space lately.

The dense stand of pine trees all around the house kept it hidden from view of the main casino building nearby, giving them the illusion of total privacy. Gage had told her Desmond managed nine other residences in addition to the main resort.

While the high-roller suites were glitzy and modern, the villas were positioned as elegant mountain retreats.

Gage thumbed the remote door opener for the two-bay garage tucked under one side of the house. Light flooded from the space, spilling out onto the stone driveway. The garage was vacant except for a couple of kayaks stowed on one wall rack, and two bikes on another.

Elena was about to tuck her phone back into her purse when a new message caught her eye, this one from Zoe, her friend in California who'd attempted to collect her things from Tomas's house that morning. Unable to ignore Zoe, who'd been even more distressed than her about not making it past Tomas's fiancée, Elena clicked open the message while Gage shut off the vehicle and came around to her side of the Land Rover.

He opened her door and offered his hand, the simple courtesy reminding her she was being rude to keep checking her phone.

"My apologies." Bracing herself for the thrill of his touch before taking his hand, she gripped her phone in the other. "I just saw a text from my friend in Los Angeles and I wanted to thank her for her efforts to obtain my things from my old house, even though her mission wasn't a success this morning."

"Of course." Gage's touch didn't linger once she was on her feet, and Elena couldn't deny that she missed it. "It's been a long day, and I'm sure you've got a lot on your mind."

Perhaps she should be relieved that Gage wasn't pressing the issue of taking their relationship further this evening. Especially when he'd already done her a tremendous kindness in that valuable introduction. No doubt, her feelings were a confusing knot. His willingness to give her space was welcome, and yet she thought about his touch whenever she wasn't actively experiencing it.

That didn't bode well for maintaining her boundaries.

He held the door to the house for her and they went inside, passing through a mudroom before entering the kitchen. They'd been in the house only briefly earlier, mostly focused on stowing their bags. Now, Elena took in the gourmet kitchen with top-of-the-line appliances and custom maple cabinetry. Industrial-looking pendant lamps went well with the French country decor, the contrast of antique and modern style giving the room character. Red accents in the leather bar stools and the knobs on the Wolf range broke up the natural tones of the tan granite and ivory-colored travertine floor.

"Your friend Desmond maintains a beautiful property," she observed, stepping out of her shoes to pad barefoot toward the countertop. The granite was spotless, and there was a hint of lemon cleaner in the air. It was so different from the crappy temporary apartments she'd bounced around in as a kid.

"He does. And his advice was instrumental as we began accepting guests at Mesa Falls Ranch when we expanded it from a working ranch to a luxury retreat." Gage eased out of his jacket and tossed it over a bar stool before turning back to the cabinets, opening and closing a couple. "Can I get you something warm to drink to take the chill off before bed? There are a few flavors of tea."

While it might be tempting to escape to her bedroom and avoid the inevitable draw of being around him, Elena knew hiding from the attraction wasn't going to make it disappear.

"Tea would be nice. Thank you." She dragged one of the leather bar stools away from the counter and slid onto the seat. She placed her phone facedown on the granite, waiting to read Zoe's note until she retired. Right now, she owed Gage her full attention.

Somehow, she needed to address the proposition he'd made earlier in the evening. She wouldn't sleep with his suggestive proposal left open-ended, clinging to the corners of her mind. Tempting her.

She stared at him as he pulled mugs and a basket of teas from a cupboard, mesmerized by the tattoos visible on his forearm. Or maybe it was the whole man who mesmerized her.

Just watching him walk toward her sent a shiver down her spine.

"So what did your friend in LA have to say?" he asked, setting the basket of teas near her before he tapped the back of her phone with his finger. "Feel free to reply to her if you want. It will take the water a few minutes to boil anyway, and I should shoot Desmond a note to thank him for the accommodations."

"I haven't read her text yet," she replied automatically, even though she reeled from the ping-pong of her thoughts as they veered from steamy to practical and back again. She flipped over her phone to read Zoe's text, trying not to think about Gage's nearness.

Or those long, smoldering looks he'd shared with her.

Still, it took several moments for her mind to refocus on Zoe's message, the words swimming in front of her eyes. Finally, they came into focus, even though they made no sense.

I have your things! All your things, Elena! The pictures and mementos, the kitchenware, the clothes and the shoes.

"I don't understand," she murmured, clicking on the image attached to the note that showed Zoe's smiling face as she hugged a box containing one of Elena's vintage designer handbags. Only then did the reality of Zoe's words start to sink home. Behind Zoe, Elena could see rolling racks full of clothes. "How did she retrieve my things?"

"Is everything all right?" Gage asked, setting his own phone back on the counter before returning to the kettle and filling two mugs with hot water.

"I'm not sure," she explained distractedly, returning to her friend's original message to try to focus on the rest.

The security team your friend sent worked like magic. I didn't have to say a word! Tomas's fiancée ended up leaving the house. Tomas spent whole time apologizing while I went through your list. Security guys had your moped and bike delivered, too. Your doorman put in your storage unit.

This message required reading twice, but she had an excellent idea of the identity of the mystery "friend" who'd sent a security team with Zoe. The only friend who had witnessed her near meltdown when Zoe failed the first time.

"Gage." She realized her fingers were trembling when she set down the phone, her emotions all over the place. "Did you help orchestrate the retrieval of my things from my old home?"

"Absolutely." He carried over the steaming ceramic mugs, setting them on either side of the basket of teas. "I have zero remorse for interfering, and I'd do it all over again."

He met her gaze steadily before he chose a tea and added it to his cup.

He must have contacted Zoe without her knowing. Hired the security people and put her in touch with them, coordinating all of it while he was on the road. With the resources at his disposal, it wouldn't have been *difficult*, but it had surely inconvenienced him. And it must have cost far more than she could ever afford to repay.

Gratitude filled her along with tenderness for this man who'd done so much to help her today. She'd been determined to keep her boundaries in place with him, to deny herself the hot attraction that pulled her toward him whenever he was near. But with this one act of kindness, he'd stripped away her last defense.

She was more than grateful. She was touched.

"Thank you." She wasn't sure she had appreciated how fully the burden of Tomas's games had weighed her down until this moment, when she felt lighter, freer than she had in years. "Truly, I can't thank you enough for making that happen."

Gage slid the basket closer to her, as if to redirect the conversation toward something more concrete. "It was really no trouble, and I'm happy to help."

The part about it being no trouble had to be a massive understatement. She wasn't sure exactly what drove him to orchestrate the task, but she knew for certain that she wouldn't have all her worldly possessions back under her own control if it hadn't been for Gage.

The many feelings she'd been suppressing for him these last few days returned in full force, and then multiplied. The attraction flared hotter until it was impossible to ignore.

Impossible to deny.

So this time, when she met his eyes over the steaming cups, she didn't bother giving him any long, smoldering looks. Instead, she rose from the leather bar stool and rounded the island to stand on the same side of the counter as him. She was done denying that she wanted him.

Later, she'd figure out how to handle the aftermath of giving in to this attraction. For now, she planned to give herself to the moment. Without hesitation, she levered up on her toes and kissed him.

Gage tried like hell to remind himself that gratitude wasn't the same thing as passion.

But having Elena's slender arms twine around his neck, her sweet curves pressed against him and her lips teasing over his, made it damned near impossible to distinguish the difference. For a moment, he allowed himself to breathe in the hint of lavender fragrance on her skin; he wanted to lick every inch of her to find the source. He savored the silken brush of her mouth despite the need to deepen the kiss and tangle his tongue with hers.

All of which meant he was breathing like he'd run a marathon by the time she eased back to study him with her dark eyes.

"You're holding back on me?" she asked, pursing her lips as she tipped her head sideways to look at him. "After all those seductive words in stolen moments at Jonah's house?"

This. Woman.

She seemed to have an IV right into his bloodstream and could heat it up at will.

"After the way things ended last time, I think we need to be very, very clear about what we're getting into before we let passion burn away all of our best intentions." He ached to touch her. To peel away every last stitch of clothing and run his fingertips over her bare skin.

He wanted to see her shiver with pleasure. Give her goose bumps. Watch her come undone from nothing more than his touch, his breath on her most sensitive places.

"Then I will make what I want very, very clear." She mimicked his cadence, reaching up to unfasten the clasp that held her long dark hair in an updo. She opened it, the waves tumbling down her back. "I don't want this night to end any other way but with us in bed, and I trust you, Gage Striker, to make sure that happens."

Wordless, he could only stare for a moment while she held the jeweled combs between her fingers, then let them fall to the countertop. He hadn't thought this would happen tonight. But he'd be damned if he would argue when Elena looked at him with fire in her eyes and in her words.

He'd fallen hard for that strength and passion. Seeing it resurrected now shredded any last restraint.

"Count on me," he vowed to himself more than her.

Spearing his fingers into that long, lush mane, he cupped her head and drew her close for the kiss he wanted. Slow, deep, thorough.

He licked his way inside her mouth, tilting her head for full access. The soft, needy sounds she made kept him there for a long time, until her knees seemed to give way and she sank more heavily against him. Still, he didn't break the kiss he'd waited forever to taste. He stroked an experimental touch down her throat, pausing to circle the hollow at its base.

She reared back to look at him, her pupils dilated, her eyes passion-dazed. "I will combust out of these clothes if we wait any longer to get naked."

"We can't have that." He kissed his way along her collarbone while his fingers worked the buttons on her suit, unfastening each one until the jacket opened to her narrow waist. Her camisole was next.

The sight of her pale breasts straining the navy blue lace of her bra cups made his mouth water. He spanned her waist with his hands, skimming up her ribs to mold his palms against the swell of her enticing curves. When he tipped a bra strap off her shoulder with one finger, he watched the lace cup roll down to free an enticing taut nipple. He bent to capture it between his lips, drawing on her while she arched toward him, her hands roaming over his chest, down to his waist and underneath his T-shirt.

She wriggled closer, her nails lightly scoring his abs as he turned his attention to the other breast.

Her efforts to undress him slowed as her breath came faster. He helped her by dragging his shirt up and off, leaving it on a bar stool before he turned her in the direction of his bedroom.

"Come with me, sweetheart." He hadn't meant to take things so far in the kitchen. By now, his whole body was on fire.

"That's the plan." She stripped off the lace bra as she walked, letting it fall on a hall table outside his suite. "Now that I've committed to this conflagration, I'm requesting as many orgasms as you deem manageable."

Stepping deeper into his bedroom, she sent him a saucy look over her shoulder, that dark tangle of hair nearly brushing her waist.

"You'll have to beg me for mercy." He toed the door shut behind them, his eyes on Elena as she eased down the zipper on the back of her pencil skirt.

He couldn't lose his pants fast enough—but left on his boxers—before he reached for her skirt. He wanted to feel the way the fabric slid down those memorable hips.

Wrapping an arm around her waist, he drew her back against him, watching her in the silver-framed mirror above the mahogany chest. Her head lolled back against his shoulder while he touched her, tracing the scalloped edge of her blue lace panties. He kissed her hair, his eyes never leaving her reflection, visible thanks to the light of a desk lamp in the sitting area behind them. She trembled against him.

"I've missed you." He spoke into her ear, knowing from her flushed cheeks she was already close to the first orgasm. He remembered she was exquisitely sensitive. "I've missed this."

He meant the passion between them, but he cupped her sex as he said it. She shivered hard, and her nipples beaded.

"Please, Gage," she murmured softly, her hips swaying in a way that threatened his restraint.

He obliged her by skimming aside the panties. Finding the tight bud between her legs. Circling the slick heat.

She went still, her lips parting. She reached back to grip his thigh, her fingers clenching tight until the sweet, convulsive shudders began. Seeing her come apart filled him with hunger, even as a new, fierce protectiveness surged.

When the shudders subsided, she turned into him and he lifted her in his arms, carrying her to the king-size bed. Raking back the white duvet, he settled her in the middle of the mattress before he went to get condoms from his toiletry bag.

He returned to the bed to find her propped against the gray leather headboard, hugging a white pillow to her chest as she watched him come toward her. As he set the condoms on the nightstand, she tossed aside the pillow and dragged him down beside her, her arms locked around his neck.

She was so damned sexy.

With an effort, he managed to strip off his boxers. She arched up off the bed to kiss her way around his chest, interspersing gentle bites while he rolled a condom into place.

Levered above her, he positioned himself between her thighs, and their gazes locked. He caressed her cheek before running his thumb along her lower lip. Then, finally, he eased inside her. Inch by incredible inch, he lost himself in Elena.

Wrapping her legs around him, she anchored her ankles behind his hips. They moved together with the rhythm of two people who've memorized one another's bodies. They started slowly at first, and then picked up the pace, revisiting all the touches that drove one another wild.

For a while, she wanted to be on top, teasing him with her long hair by dragging it across his sensitized skin. Later, she rolled underneath him so she could trace the patterns of his tattoos with her fingers. The movements were intensely seductive and familiar at the same time, calling down memories he wasn't ready for.

In the end, he held her questing fingers captive, pinning them to the pillow on either side of her head to focus solely on the moment. She gave herself to that plan, rolling her hips in time with his thrusts, intensifying every movement. Once he was close to completion, he bent to lave one nipple, tugging it in his mouth until he felt her tense. Letting go, he thrust deep. Hard.

They came together in a rush of sensation. He lost track of everything but how she made him feel. Mindless with pleasure. Whole.

Once he recovered himself enough to move off her, Gage knew that last feeling was a problem. He couldn't rely on Elena to make him feel fulfilled. This relationship wasn't about that, and he'd be wise not to mix up the past and the present.

Still, it was impossible not to hold her tight for long afterward. He told himself it was because he wanted to be ready for the next round of orgasms he had every intention of giving her.

But he feared he knew better.

Nine

Elena awoke to warm sunlight on her face, her body pleasantly aching and thoroughly sated. Memories of the evening before swirled through her mind, from the first kiss in the kitchen to a late-night refrigerator raid and lovemaking in front of the fireplace.

Now, reaching for Gage, she felt empty air on his side of the bed. And flowers? Wrenching her eyes open, Elena discovered a pool of pink rose petals on Gage's pillow, trailing to the floor of the suite. There was also a note on the resort's stationery propped against the fluffy down, two words written in a sure, masculine hand.

Join me.

The rose petals led out the door.

Anticipation hummed warm in her veins even though they'd rolled in these very sheets together just a couple of hours ago. What was it about this man that captivated her so thoroughly? Sliding from the covers, she set her feet on the floor and padded to the bathroom to brush her teeth. Afterward, she found one of Gage's clean T-shirts folded neatly in the top drawer of a bureau, and slipped it on.

She hoped things wouldn't turn awkward between them now that the sun had risen. But she knew inevitably they would because she hadn't told him the truth about what had happened between them six years ago when they broke up. Trust hadn't come easily for either of them then, and it wouldn't return now in light of the way they'd treated each other—red-hot encounters notwithstanding.

For just a little while longer, though, she would live in the moment. Take all the joy she could from this time together.

Grabbing one of the resort robes from a hook in the bathroom, Elena slid it over Gage's shirt and followed the trail of pink petals out of the master suite. She wound an elastic around her hair and scooped up a handful of the rose remnants from the hardwood, bringing them to her nose for a sniff. Her mother had taught her that—take time to smell the roses. She didn't have many good memories of her mom, but it helped to hug close the ones that weren't tainted by her parents' drinking. Fighting. When her mom abandoned the family, it had eliminated the arguments that too often turned to violence, but the hole she left behind had been too big to fill no matter what Elena tried to put there. Work. Ambition. Relationships.

It was simpler to just smell the roses and savor the present, especially since Elena couldn't change the past. Hiding it hadn't worked with Gage's family. And altering herself to fit into Tomas's life had been foolish.

From now on, she was embracing the journey that had made her the woman she was today. As she made her way through the family room, she saw that the petal path led through the double doors leading out to a patio overlooking the lake. She stepped outside to find a bubbling hot tub steaming white puffs into the cool mountain air.

Gage sprawled in the far corner, his arms spread wide along

the edges of the tub, ropes of muscle drawing her eye, the black ink of his tattoos shiny and wet. Her personal Poseidon.

"Good morning, lovely." His New Zealand accent wrapped around her ears, the words as unhurried as his gaze. "I thought you might like a soak to start the day. The view isn't bad, either."

He nodded toward the lake visible through the trees, the mountains in the distance still capped with snow even though spring buds were visible on nearby branches. But she preferred the view of Gage's naked chest rising from the water.

"As it happens, I might have a few muscles that would benefit from the pulsating jets." She slid off the robe, setting it on the wooden bench that wrapped two sides of the tub. She reached for the hem of the T-shirt, then hesitated. "What would you rate the level of privacy out here?" She peered around.

Gage's pupils darkened with satisfying speed. "Maybe for my sanity you should keep the T-shirt on."

"As you wish." Elena stepped over the edge of the partially sunken tub, then tucked the end of her ponytail through the elastic to keep her hair out of the water before she sank into one of the seats. "How did you sleep?"

"Did we sleep?" He reached for a towel at the edge of the tub and dried his hands before grabbing his phone. "Let me just send a text for room service to set up breakfast while we're out here."

Elena waited, appreciating Gage's thoughtful efficiency. But as she took in the luxury of their surroundings, she realized the sharp contrast in their lifestyles. She knew that Gage's level of wealth was even more staggering than when they'd dated before. More daunting. A private jet brought him where he wanted to go. Catered meals appeared with a text. Expensive vehicles and exotic vacation destinations were the norm while Elena had worked her way up from virtually nothing. People like Gage's parents would always view her past as a liability, an unfair burden for their son. And although she liked her life just fine, she would always be an outsider in Gage's privileged world.

Tipping her head back to breathe in the mountain air, she

closed her eyes and soaked up the sensations of the jets against her shoulders. Bubbles burst at the surface, spraying her face with a light mist. Birds called to one another in the nearby trees, a boat motor sounding in the lake below. The hot tub water sloshed side to side as she heard Gage settle deeper into the spa a moment before his palms landed on her waist through the wet shirt, his fingers wrapping around her hip.

She didn't open her eyes, simply feeling him come closer as he repositioned himself next to her. His thigh brushed hers and her body stirred, still hungry for him.

"How do you want to spend your day?" He spoke into her ear, the sound giving her shivers before he kissed her neck. "Keeping in mind I want to spoil you."

The temptation to lose herself in his touch nearly overwhelmed her. But how long could they indulge this attraction before they addressed the inevitable problems that came with it?

Starting with the fact that she'd let him believe she'd accepted his father's bribe all those years ago. The thought felt like a bucket of cold water despite the heat of the spa tub.

"We should probably talk first." Sitting up straighter, Elena opened her eyes. "Last night happened so fast."

Easing back, Gage looked wary. Water droplets clung to the bristles along his jaw. "What's there to discuss? Last night was a gift. Today can be, too, if we let it."

The temptation to defer an unhappy conversation was strong, but she'd gone that route before and lived to regret it.

She swiped away a damp strand of hair that came loose from her elastic.

"Six years ago, I let myself get caught up in the idea of living in the moment so much that I never acknowledged my past." She hadn't wanted to taint Gage's opinion of her, so she'd kept it to herself that her father was a wanted man. "And when you finally learned the truth about my family, you didn't learn it from me. I'm not making that mistake again."

The warmth in Gage's dark eyes cooled, his expression growing distant as he leaned back against the hot tub wall. His gaze turned assessing.

"Meaning you're keeping more secrets from me?" he asked.

Guilt stung. She didn't know how else to broach the subject, so without preamble, she admitted, "I never took the bribe your father offered me."

His dark eyebrows lifted in surprise for a moment, then swooped low in a scowl. "What are you talking about?"

"That day in New Zealand with your family," she began slowly, remembering the waves of pain she'd felt from Nigel Striker's cruel words, followed by Gage's automatic assumptions regarding her character. "I was devastated by your father's dismissal of me from your life when I believed…" She'd thought Gage had brought her home to propose. The turn things had taken had been so far off course from what she'd envisioned she hadn't weathered the storm well at all. "When I'd thought things were going so well between us."

"You weren't the only one devastated, Elena." The flash of pain she saw in his eyes was all too real, and it hurt to know that she could have lessened that ache if she'd reacted differently. "My father was merciless in characterizing you as secretive and deceptive about your past. But none of it would have mattered if you hadn't jumped at the chance to take a lucrative detour out of my life."

Had she always known that? Had she subconsciously sabotaged things between them even more than Nigel Striker tried to do? The humming of the hot tub motor seemed to grow louder in her ears, or maybe it was the buzzing of a guilty conscience.

"I didn't take the bribe, Gage. I ripped up the check and threw it at his retreating back." She sat forward on the hot tub bench seat, not feeling at all relaxed despite the rush of the jets on her shoulders.

Gage shook his head in disbelief. "You led me to think you took it."

She bit her lip. "You immediately assumed I had."

"So you lied to me?"

She closed her eyes for a moment, regretting her temper as the buzzing in her ears grew louder. *Yes.*

"I was hurt and angry," she explained. "And I figured you'd learn the truth eventually—"

"Six years later?" There was no way to miss the growing anger—and yes, disillusionment—in his voice. "When it doesn't matter anymore? After you *married* someone else?"

The buzzing sound almost drowned out Gage's words, and Elena turned to see a four-wheeler bump over a ridge and onto the lawn from the tree line.

With a curse of frustration, Gage was on his feet instantly, grabbing a towel and wrapping it around himself as the rider came into view. Desmond Pierce had sharp, aristocratic features like she envisioned on a Mediterranean prince. As he rolled to a stop near the edge of the deck, Elena could see his cool gray eyes as he met Gage's stare.

"What's wrong?" Gage asked, still dripping wet as he tied the towel around his waist and stepped up onto the deck.

Desmond's eyes shifted to her briefly before they moved back to Gage.

"News from Weston. We need to meet this afternoon if you can be at the casino by midday. I've been trying to reach you all morning." Then the man turned to her once more, his posture relaxing somewhat now that his important news was, apparently, delivered. "Sorry to interrupt your morning. I don't think we've been formally introduced. I'm Desmond Pierce."

"Elena Rollins," she said, frustrated and relieved all at once to have her conversation with Gage end abruptly. She knew his ranch partners would take precedence over her, especially in light of what she'd just confessed to him. "And I'll go get dressed so the two of you can speak privately."

She was about to stand up, awkwardly reaching for the robe since she wore nothing beneath Gage's T-shirt, but Gage already had a towel outstretched for her.

"We'll continue our conversation later," Gage spoke to her in low tones, his voice warm against her neck as he draped the towel around her.

"I'm not sure there's much more to say." They'd both made mistakes that had led them to this point. There was no going back to change them now. "I'd be more interested to hear what Desmond has to share with you. I'll bet anything it has to do with Alonzo Salazar."

Gage didn't bother to deny it. He retrieved her robe before setting it on her shoulders.

"Lucky for you," he said as his hands lingered on her upper arms, bringing memories of their night together flaming from her mind through her body, "you have a whole new story to cover that will be far more lucrative than whatever you might dig up on my former mentor." He gave her a meaningful squeeze, eyes flaming with heat, then opened the French doors leading back into the house for her. "I'll finish up as soon as I can here."

Closing the door behind her, Elena didn't linger in the great room. She darted past the breakfast area where the catering staff were arranging the table for their meal, then took refuge in a hot shower to try to figure out what to do next.

She wanted to accept Gage's olive branch—the Chiara Campagna introduction—and forget about Alonzo Salazar. Except what if Gage's former mentor was the same caliber of father figure as Gage's actual dad? What if Alonzo had been a man without scruples, driven to achieve his own ends no matter the cost?

It bugged her to think of letting a man like that get away with bending the world to his will. But for today—for Gage—she'd call Chiara and see about setting up another meeting instead. Maybe focusing on her career and her future would help her to forget about the knot of emotions she felt for Gage.

Ruminating over the view of Lake Tahoe out the window of her luxury hotel suite, Chiara Campagna hurried to pick up the call when she spotted Elena Rollins's number on her caller ID.

"Hello, Elena," she answered, needing to make the woman feel at ease with her. "I hope we're going to hang out today while we're both still in Tahoe."

She regretted manipulating someone as genuinely nice as Elena seemed, but she couldn't afford to lose this chance to find out what information Elena had gathered for her story on Alonzo Salazar and how the Mesa Falls Ranch owners were involved. Those six men knew more about Zach's death than they admitted, and Chiara would never get to the bottom of it without stirring the pot.

Starting with Elena.

"As a matter of fact, I'm free for a few hours. Gage is meeting with Jonah and Desmond Pierce at the casino this afternoon, so I thought I'd see if you and Astrid wanted to see the sights."

"Astrid sounded wiped out when I talked to her this morning." She stretched the truth a bit, but she didn't want to share Elena with Astrid, especially when she needed to pump Elena for information about the Mesa Falls owners. Even though Astrid's husband was one of the owners, too, Chiara had never gotten the impression Jonah had been as close with Zach as Gage Striker. They'd been roommates at school.

"Why don't you and I meet at the casino for drinks?" That would put them in close proximity to where the secretive ranch owners would be getting together.

"You don't get swarmed by fans at places like that?" Elena asked curiously.

"I'll have my secretary call ahead to make sure we have some space to ourselves." Ideally, somewhere close to the meeting among Gage, Jonah and Desmond. She didn't have a plan for crashing it, but being nearby like that might yield an opportunity to find out more.

"Sounds good," Elena said warmly. "I'm so grateful for the help you've already given me, Chiara. I don't know how I can repay you."

Chiara had seen the way Elena's followers jumped after her

posts the day before. Ideally, Elena's gratitude would make it tough for her to turn Chiara down when she asked for some favors in return.

"It's my pleasure to tout talented friends," she told her honestly, typing a list of questions she wanted answered about Gage's partners. "Although I assure you, the big following comes with as many heartaches as joys."

Not that anyone ever believed her about that. But as far as she was concerned, the view from the top of the social media world was a study in terror. The only direction to go was down. For Chiara, the question every day became, would she fall fast in a stomach-churning nosedive? Or would her decline be a slow and steady destruction of everything she'd earned these last few years?

If her time as reigning social media queen was coming to an end, it was all the more reason to hasten her search for answers about Zach. Whatever power she possessed, she was going to leverage it for the sake of the truth.

"That's the story of my life, Chiara," Elena admitted drily. "Just when the joys become their most wonderful, heartache kicks in. I'm still glad for the boost."

"It's no trouble at all." Chiara was already calculating how fast she could get out the door so she'd be there during the owners' meeting. "I can meet you at the casino anytime after noon. We can hit the shops and talk over lunch."

"I'll message you when I'm there," Elena promised before disconnecting the call.

Rushing to dress, Chiara dictated a few more questions into her phone, including what role Gage Striker's father might have played in making sure Zach's death wasn't reported in school for months afterward.

She chose a couture pantsuit for spring that a designer had sent her the week before, slipping into the champagne-colored fabric while she texted her hairdresser to fix her blowout. Another perk in her life she didn't feel worthy of.

It was probably an unhealthy sign that she couldn't simply enjoy life as a macro-influencer, raking in big checks for sponsored content and personal appearances. Instead, she lived with constant imposter syndrome, and a nearly crippling fear that she'd make the wrong choice about what to allow on her feed, wondering if the next sponsored post she agreed to share would label her as a sellout to the world.

Her therapist told her survivor guilt was common in people who'd lost a loved one. Especially when the loved one was someone like Zachary Eldridge, a boy who'd been on track to be a phenomenal artist. His work and friendship had given her all her best ideas for what would one day become her celebrated social media feed—touted as creative and artistic, appealing to multiple sensibilities. Without him, she felt like a fraud.

Sometimes she hoped for her downfall to come sooner rather than later. Because maybe then, when she wasn't on top of the world, she wouldn't battle the sensation that she didn't belong there every single day.

Gage paced the high-roller suite in Desmond's casino. He knew whatever Weston Rivera had reported to Desmond, the news was important if it warranted a meeting. He'd been the first to arrive, and one of the resort's support staff was still in the suite to ensure the hookups were live for a video conference with Miles, Weston and Alec, the partners who couldn't attend in person.

Pausing by the billiard table in the middle of the suite, Gage rolled the cue ball back and forth between his palms. The lake glittered bright blue outside the floor-to-ceiling windows, while indoors the fire in a smooth stone hearth warmed the room. A wooden bar cart had been rolled in from the wine cellar containing a few select bottles and—thankfully—Gage's preferred bourbon.

He poured himself a glass, trying not to think about Elena's news this morning.

She hadn't taken the bribe.

He knew in his gut as soon as she'd said it that it was the truth. He should have known it—if not at the time, when he'd assumed the worst of her, then shortly afterward when she'd left in a fury. It turned out she hadn't been furious with his father for offering to pay her off to make her leave Gage's life. She'd been livid with Gage for believing she could be bought.

Tipping back the measure of aged Kentucky bourbon, he set the stopper back in the decanter and turned away from the bar in time to see Jonah and Desmond enter together. Desmond thanked the AV staff member before dismissing her.

"What gives?" Gage barked more sharply than he'd intended.

Jonah shook his head. "Dude, I've got the newborn. If anyone should be tired and out of sorts about the snap meeting, it ought to be me."

"Right. Sorry, mate." Gage had been in the middle of the most significant conversation of his life when he'd been interrupted, but he didn't mention that now. He'd have to figure out how to proceed with Elena later, once he knew what was so all-fired important to get everyone together now.

Desmond switched on his laptop and brought online a specially made ninety-inch television screen over the fireplace. The screen divided into three windows, one for each of the other owners. Miles arrived first, with Alec and Weston flickering into view shortly afterward.

"Looks like we're all here," Weston observed, kicking things off while Gage and Jonah took seats on a leather sofa by the fireplace. "I've gotten Devon Salazar's permission to share this information, which came from April's investigation of the money trail for Alonzo's book. She discovered the majority of the income has gone toward the support and education of a thirteen-year-old named Matthew Cruz."

Jonah coughed on the sip of coffee he'd just taken. Gage felt his jaw drop. Alonzo was supporting a kid?

"Is there any reason to believe it's Alonzo's son?" Desmond asked. "Did Devon run DNA?"

"Matthew Cruz looks nothing like any of the Salazars." Weston glanced down at his own laptop as he spoke, and with a keystroke, he shared a photo of a lean, gap-toothed preteen. With dark blond hair and gray eyes, he bore no resemblance to Alonzo, or his sons Marcus and Devon, who owned Salazar Media and had worked with the ranch on branding and promotion.

"If the kid is thirteen years old, it means he was conceived during the worst year of our lives," Alec observed, leaning closer to his computer screen, maybe scrutinizing the photo. It made his face loom large on the television screen. "The boy looks most like Jonah."

Jonah shook his head, his expression thunderous. "Don't even go there. I'm still reeling that Alonzo did all this without breathing a word to any of us. Besides, you know damned well if the kid was any of ours, Alonzo would have kicked our asses if we weren't accountable."

"Why would Alonzo take financial responsibility for anyone that wasn't a blood relative?" Gage asked, trying to make sense of a day that had taken a fast downward spiral after beginning with a trail of rose petals.

"First, we make sure it's not a blood relative," Weston chimed in again, apparently knowing more about the case because things had worked out well between him and the financial forensics investigator. "Devon is going to reach out to Matthew's guardian and see if she'll agree to paternity testing."

"Who's the guardian?" Desmond asked, one shoulder tipped against the stone wall near the fireplace. It was barely past noon and the casino owner was already dressed in an impeccable custom suit.

Weston clicked another button and a new face appeared on the screen where Weston had been a moment ago. "This is Nicole Cruz. She worked briefly at the ranch under the alias

Nicole Smith, but she was fired suddenly by a supervisor who said it was performance-related. When I tried to follow up on that incident, I discovered the supervisor quit the next day and didn't leave a forwarding address."

"Which means the supervisor could have been lying. Or someone at the ranch applied pressure for Nicole to leave," Miles pointed out. The two brothers frequently didn't see eye to eye. "Is Nicole the mother?"

"According to her, no," Weston replied. "When she introduced herself to April several weeks ago, she claimed Matthew is her sister's son, and that her sister died suddenly without naming the father. So far, we don't have a photo of the mother since Nicole and Matthew disappeared after Nicole was fired from her job at Mesa Falls."

"So we hire someone to track the kid and his guardian using a last known address," Gage suggested, already itching to start piecing the puzzle together before someone else did. Someone like Elena. Could he trust her to be honest with him about her next move? Despite their night together, he couldn't be sure. "Or are the Salazar heirs already doing that?"

"At the very least," Miles added, "we need to ask around Mesa Falls to figure out who knew her. I'm ready to take some time away from Rivera Ranch, Gage, if you want me to come help out at Mesa Falls."

Gage wondered who was the most surprised by that comment. Weston reared back from his screen like someone had just shoved him. Jonah coughed through another sip of coffee. Desmond made a long, low whistle.

Miles swore and shifted in his seat, the Sierra Nevada Mountains visible out the window of his ranch office behind him. "Every one of you takes time off. I've earned it. Besides, I'm going to ask the Mesa Falls foreman for some recommendations to bring sustainable ranching practices to Rivera Ranch."

One of the reasons they'd founded Mesa Falls was to highlight more green practices in raising cattle, and the experiment had turned Mesa Falls into a successful showplace.

Gage was the first to recover from his surprise since Miles had already indicated to him that he'd be willing to cover for Gage this week. "I'd appreciate the help for as long as you care to stay. Elena Rollins should be leaving Montana soon and won't be doing a story about Alonzo."

Even as he said it, he realized how much he didn't want her to leave, no matter how upset he'd been by her revelation in the hot tub this morning. Something incredible had happened between them last night, and he wasn't ready to turn his back on it just because she'd shaken his whole view of their past together. They'd been too quick to call it quits the first time. What if they kept things simple this time? Instead of worrying about how they would fit—or not fit—into one another's lives, they could simply spend night after scorching night in one another's arms and not worry about the future.

He hadn't realized how fully he'd lost the thread of the meeting conversation until Desmond said his name.

"Gage? You still with us?"

Damn it.

"Sorry." He wasn't used to being distracted. Especially not by a woman. In his work, he normally juggled ten different tasks at a time. But the lack of trust and honesty between him and Elena burned raw. "Just thinking about how quickly I can tie up loose ends here and be back at Mesa Falls."

Jonah gave him a sympathetic glance as he leaned deeper into the sofa. "We're on to party planning. Miles suggested we host another celebrity shindig on-site and release a statement offering our own narrative about Alonzo. Maybe if we share a story of our own for where the money went, the public interest will die down."

"You mean we lie?" Gage couldn't imagine his friends would sink so low.

"Of course not," Miles was quick to clarify. "Alonzo funneled some of the profits from his book to building infrastructure in poor neighborhoods in cities around the world. We have photos and concrete evidence of those travels, right, Wes?"

"We do," Weston confirmed, clicking more keys before a picture of an old-fashioned bulletin board covered with photographs held up with thumbtacks appeared on his screen. The shots showed Alonzo in foreign countries around the world, posed with volunteer groups in front of a variety of building projects.

"So we have a party," Gage agreed, wondering if he had ever felt in less of a party mode in his life, "and reveal Alonzo's secret life as a philanthropist."

Desmond straightened from his spot near the fireplace. "Do you think Elena will take up the cause? Be the vehicle for the story we want to circulate about Alonzo?"

Gage's gut knotted at the thought of asking her to use her newfound social media cache to share a story that he knew wasn't the full truth. He refused to lie to her after the way he and his father had treated her six years ago.

"I'll see what I can do," he said, unwilling to promise anything.

Especially when feeding Elena a story like that meant she'd be all the more likely to leave Montana—and Gage—for good.

Ten

While she waited for a boutique owner to finish her conversation with Chiara in the casino resort shops, Elena glanced up at the door of the high-roller suite in the second-floor gallery, where Gage was in a meeting.

What had been so important to tear him away from their conversation this morning? He'd closed himself in the den of their suite after Desmond's arrival, not reappearing until it was time to leave for his meeting. She wasn't necessarily hurt by his lack of communication. She understood business didn't stop just because she'd revealed a long-held secret to Gage. But she couldn't deny she was curious to pick up where they left off, to see if her revelation changed anything in their relationship.

Chiara's voice interrupted her thoughts. "Elena, will you hop in a photo with Mimi so I can tag you both and help her find you in case she wants to place a future order for your designs?"

Shaking off the romantic preoccupation with Gage, Elena hurried over, amazed at how Chiara's hustle never took a day off. While Elena had been daydreaming about Gage, Chiara had been talking up Elena's potential future business. Both Astrid and Chiara had insisted she had a real talent for fashion.

"Of course." Elena posed with the woman, one of the boutique's mannequins between them, while Chiara took several photos. "You have a beautiful store. Thank you so much the tour."

After shaking hands with the owner, Chiara and Elena left the store and returned to the shops that fanned out around a courtyard fountain. The water bubbled and splashed from the mouth of a sea dragon before falling into a marble pool at its base.

Again, Elena glanced up at the second-floor gallery toward the high-roller suite, but the door remained closed. She noticed Chiara followed her gaze.

"Astrid made it sound like the Mesa Falls owners were meeting for supersecret reasons." Chiara's green eyes sparkled with mischief, like they shared a secret of their own. "Have you made any progress cracking the code of silence from them about Alonzo Salazar?"

Caught off guard by the question since Chiara was close with Astrid, Elena took a moment to consider her response while a group of young tourists photographed the sea dragon.

"Honestly, I'm backing off the story." She hadn't consciously made the decision until that moment, thinking she'd wait to see how things played out with Chiara. "I was convinced that Salazar had greedy ulterior motives for writing his book when I first started digging, but now I'm not so sure that was the case."

"Really?" Chiara turned her face away from the tourists' cameras, then leaned closer to Elena, green eyes wide. "Do tell."

Her obvious interest gave Elena pause. She wasn't entirely sure why, but she hadn't survived her teens with a drunken nomad for a father by ignoring her instincts. So she spoke more cautiously than she might have otherwise.

"The Mesa Falls owners all trust Salazar. And that says a lot to me." She peered up toward the meeting place again and spied Jonah emerging with Desmond Pierce. "They must be finished now."

"You know they all attended a boarding school where Alonzo was a teacher, right?" Chiara asked, her gaze narrowing as a tall man dressed like a casino employee approached Desmond Pierce and seemed to receive instructions. "I attended a girls' school nearby, but none of them remember me."

Elena did a double take as the words sank in. "You knew them from their school days? Does Astrid know?"

"I mentioned it to her once, but I'm not sure if she remembers. But it's not as surprising as it sounds that none of the owners remember me. I was just plain old Kara Marsh back then—tall and gawky and a long way from being comfortable in my own skin."

As much as Elena longed to find Gage upstairs and pull him into a quiet corner to finish their earlier conversation, she couldn't deny a strong curiosity about Chiara's tie to Gage and his friends. A tie he apparently didn't know about.

"You changed your name?" Elena wondered how many of her followers knew about this.

"No. I simply use Chiara like a stage name. When I started out, it made it easier to have some separation between my professional world and my personal life." Chiara pointed toward the stairs. "Shall we go up? I'm sure you're eager to see Gage."

Was she that obvious? But as much as she'd thought about him all day, she also feared she was getting in over her head with him. His reaction to her news this morning had been difficult to read. Instead, she delayed a bit longer, asking Chiara another question.

"Doesn't it bother you that they don't remember you?" she pressed, not moving toward the steps.

The sound of the fountain splashing filled the air. A group of young women wearing T-shirts printed with "Bridesmaid" in frilly font giggled as they passed Elena, fruity drinks in hand.

"Not really. I don't want to be Chiara Campagna forever,"

she mused wistfully, gazing down at a wristwatch with a huge yellow diamond in its face. "But if you change your mind about looking into Alonzo Salazar's connection to the ranch owners, I'd be game to develop an angle with you."

Stunned by the turn the conversation had taken, Elena followed her new friend up the steps to the gallery, where Chiara greeted Jonah. Why would Chiara take an interest in dredging up a past the Mesa Falls Ranch owners clearly wanted to keep quiet? The woman's words stirred Elena's curiosity, making her wonder if she'd allowed Gage to lure her away from the Alonzo Salazar scoop too easily. She needed to see him. Speak to him.

Elena lingered a moment with Chiara to say hello to Jonah, then excused herself to peer into the suite where the owner meeting had taken place.

Gage sat with his back to her on a huge, curved leather sofa, a fitted black jacket drawing attention to his broad shoulders. He was tapping away on his phone. There was an artful arrangement of birds of paradise on the glass-topped table in front of him, and a fire burned in the sleek, modern hearth. A massive flat-screen television was mounted over the fireplace, but the display was dark. On either side of the fireplace, windows overlooked Lake Tahoe, the clear sky making the water look impossibly blue.

A moment of nervous anticipation threaded through her at the sight of Gage. Attraction, uncertainty and a whole lot of other emotions she didn't bother to unpack all clamored for her attention.

"Gage?" she called to him and he spun around immediately.

"Elena." His shoulders relaxed a fraction. He remained unsmiling, yet somehow seemed relieved to see her.

Or maybe that was wishful thinking.

"Am I interrupting you?" She hugged her handmade hobo bag more tightly to her side, the fake jewels from repurposed old necklaces digging into her forearm where she pinned the purse to her body. "I met Chiara downstairs a couple of hours ago to share ideas about a potential new business venture."

She was still in a daze that one of the world's most famous faces was interested in helping her move into the fashion world, potentially developing an experimental line of her own as a guest appearance for another brand.

Elena had never visualized something like that for herself, but she would be crazy not to pursue the opportunity while she had it. Although something made her uneasy about the woman's second proposition, suggesting she would support Elena if she wanted to write a piece on Alonzo Salazar despite her growing feelings for Gage.

"I'm glad you're here." Standing, Gage tucked his phone in his jacket pocket and strode toward her, his dark eyes making her melt inside even though she couldn't quite read his expression. "I owed you my undivided attention this morning. My apologies for the interruption."

Her body hummed everywhere as he approached, something that always happened around this man, but the effects were more pronounced after the vivid reminder of what it was like to be with him the night before.

"You're a busy man." Her thoughts traveled back in time to their first encounter. "I understood that from the moment we met, considering how long it took to get a meeting with you."

"These days, I clear my schedule for you." His gaze tracked over her. "How about we have dinner at the resort tonight and we'll pick up where we left off in the hot tub?"

Her pulse thrummed faster, awareness surging through her bloodstream.

"I look forward to it," she confessed, needing to clear the air about their past once and for all.

And once that was done—like it or not—she needed to confront Gage about the mysterious Alonzo Salazar. Because whether or not she shared her findings about the author with the public, she was beginning to suspect the man was the key to a larger story that Gage was keeping hidden from her.

Gage couldn't take his eyes off Elena.

He watched her swirl her dessert fork through the meringue on her fruit-covered *boccone dolce*, her one-shoulder evening dress shimmering in the candlelight. The champagne-colored tulle hugged her curves and turned other men's heads.

The casino's Italian-inspired restaurant was decorated like a Florentine palazzo, with white moldings around the ceilings, neoclassical paintings and elaborate chandeliers. The walls were covered in frescoes between the windows overlooking Lake Tahoe. They sat at a pedestal table on a raised dais encircled by pillars. White curtains were strategically draped through-out, giving them a modicum of privacy within the small dining room.

Throughout the meal, he'd bided his time, not wanting to ambush her with questions about her revelation this morning. So he'd asked her about plans for merging her growing social media platform with her new interest in pursuing fashion more seriously. He'd offered to invest in her next venture, but she'd declined before steering the subject back to him and his movement away from investment banking to pursue his personal investments. Now, he guided things back to her.

"We never spoke about your family when we dated," he reminded her as he dug into his hazelnut torte. In retrospect, while he'd been content to accept her at face value, he'd done them both a disservice by not being more curious about what made her tick. "But I wondered—after learning about your unconventional upbringing—how you managed to catapult yourself to the level of business savvy you possessed when I met you."

A waiter refilled their water glasses, and Elena sampled a raspberry before answering. "I was very honest with you about how I started my social media platform. I chronicled my drive to surround myself with beautiful things, from flea market finds to freecycling. Those posts were very popular because there are a lot of struggling people who appreciate the need to create a physically appealing space with truly limited resources."

"And sponsorships for the blog paid for college?" He remembered her telling him that she'd built the platform out of nothing, but at the time, he'd assumed that was euphemistic. Now, knowing she'd run away from home before she was eighteen, patching together waitressing jobs to pay her rent, he had a far greater appreciation for how hard she must have worked.

"Yes. I took online courses at night and worked during the day, massaging the blog on my breaks." She met his gaze over her water glass before taking a sip. "I was driven, yes. But that time in my life didn't feel nearly as difficult as managing my father had been. Once my life was under my own control, a lot of stress went away."

"How so?" He couldn't imagine navigating adult life as a seventeen-year-old being anything but stressful.

His own father might be a manipulative, controlling bastard. Nigel Striker hadn't approved of his friends, and he'd hurt Elena badly. But at least Gage had never had to worry about where his next meal was coming from, whereas Elena had to deal with that kind of poverty.

She stabbed a strawberry with her fork. The pair of violinists who'd been playing throughout the meal shifted from a complicated allegro to a lilting waltz.

"I didn't have to worry about getting kicked out of a house because the rent didn't get paid," Elena explained, dabbing her lips with her napkin. "Or the police carting off my dad and putting me into a foster home. I trusted myself far more than I trusted my father, and that made my life easier."

Gage finished the late-harvest zinfandel the sommelier had recommended with his dessert, realizing that this woman didn't put her faith in anyone lightly after the way she'd been raised. "On that note, Elena, I have to wonder what it will take for you to trust me again after the way I assumed the worst of you six years ago."

"You believe me now?" she asked, lifting an eyebrow. "Because I have a photograph of the destroyed check somewhere. I thought your father would come clean and tell you the truth one day, but apparently that never happened."

"I don't need photo evidence," he said firmly. "I shouldn't have jumped to that conclusion then, either. And there will come a time of reckoning between my father and me, but right now, I'm going to deal with the PR crisis the ranch is facing first."

"Fair enough," she agreed, pushing aside her half-eaten dessert plate as she studied him across the table. "But if you're asking about how I might trust you again, I think a place to start might be with some honest answers about Alonzo Salazar."

Wariness surged at the reminder of her reason for coming to Montana in the first place.

"Because your followers deserve the truth?" he asked, unable to suppress the trace of bitterness in his voice.

"No." Her dark eyes never wavered from his. "Because I do."

Gage recognized the line she'd drawn in the sand. If he wanted to move forward with their relationship, he needed to share something of himself. They'd dodged the difficult parts when they'd dated six years ago, and that had resulted in a bond that broke when they encountered the first major obstacle.

Now? He wasn't sure he was ready for the kind of relationship they'd been building toward back then. The aftermath when it ended had been painful for them both, and being with Elena would mean a permanent rift between him and his family. He'd dodged that kind of break his whole life, hoping that it wouldn't come to that since it would make things painful for his mother and his sisters.

But he didn't have to decide the future right now. He only had to decide that he wanted Elena for one more night.

And from that perspective, his choice was simple. Gritting

his teeth, he told the most painful truth of his life in the sparest of words.

"Alonzo Salazar was a mentor to me and all the Mesa Falls partners. And he was there for us after one of our friends jumped to his death in an accident that every damned one of us feels responsible for."

Elena felt Gage's hurt in those terse words.

Shock delayed her response, and in that stunned silence, their waiter had returned, effectively shutting down the talk. Gage signed his name on the check and helped her from her chair, no doubt wanting more privacy for a conversation that had moved in a completely unexpected direction. She waited while he settled a long satin trench coat on her shoulders—a gift from Mimi, the boutique owner Elena met today, after Elena had posted a photo of the garment.

Wordlessly, Gage escorted her through the casino to the valet stand out front, where the Land Rover quickly appeared. They made the short drive to the private residence Desmond had offered them for their stay, and once the vehicle was parked inside the garage bay, Gage opened the passenger side door for her.

"I'm so sorry for your loss," she told him quietly, not sure if he'd heard the words back at the restaurant when she'd said the same thing.

He seemed to have retreated from her somehow, but perhaps that was only because they'd been in a public space. Now, she kept hold of his hand, wrapping it between both of her own.

"Thank you. It's nothing I've shared with anyone else in my life." His jaw muscle flexed. "But you wanted to know why I remain loyal to Alonzo, and that time at school with my friends is at the heart of it."

She realized then how little she'd known him six years ago. They'd both coasted along on attraction without digging deeper to see the real people underneath. Was he finally ready to share something about himself?

"I'm surprised a tragedy like that could remain a secret for so long." Especially given the public interest in Alonzo Salazar over the past few months since his authorship of the bestselling novel had been revealed.

"It shouldn't have been such a secret." He gave her fingers a light squeeze before leading her into the house and closing the door behind them. "It's been one of my deepest regrets in life that my father threw his political clout and money around to ensure that the story of Zachary Eldridge's death didn't cast a shadow on us or the Dowdon School, even though all six of the Mesa Falls partners were with him when he died."

The bitterness in his voice was unmistakable.

"What happened?" she asked, letting Gage remove her coat, even as she realized he'd used the task to tuck behind her so his face was hidden from view. And she couldn't blame him. Even hearing about it—about a person she didn't know—chilled her to the core. At least his fingers provided a welcome warmth as they brushed her shoulders.

Gage led her into the sunken great room, switching on the fireplace before pulling her onto the twill sofa cushions with him. He sat forward on the seat, elbows on his knees as he looked into the flames.

"The seven of us were on a horseback riding trip. Our school had stables. We'd taken the horses out longer than we were supposed to—overnight—being rebels and not caring what kind of trouble we got into. Zach had been mysterious all week about some drama in his life, saying he needed us to 'man up' and be there for him."

Elena edged closer, laying her hand on his upper arm. Stroking lightly. "What was the drama?"

"Who knows? We didn't really ask straight-out at first. We just drank stolen hooch and forgot our collective worries, riding deeper and deeper into the mountains until we were mostly lost, but in a good way."

She tried to imagine Gage as a rebellious teenager, before

he'd diverted all of that energy into finance. After seeing the posh, fussy home of the Striker family in New Zealand, it was easy to see that his big, expansive personality would have been stifled there. She remembered him saying that his father had sent him to school in the States specifically so Gage wouldn't embarrass their family.

"Did you ever ask? Even when you stopped for the night?"

He shook his head. "I fell asleep because I had too much to drink. I thought most of the other guys did as well, but later I learned Alec, Miles and Zach stayed awake late, talking. Maybe Zach told them more." Gage repositioned the wooden stag statue on the coffee table, tracing the antlers absently. "But the accident didn't happen until the next day."

"Accident?" She zeroed in on the word. When Gage had said before that a friend jumped to his death, she had thought the boy committed suicide. Had she misunderstood?

"Some of the guys wanted to go cliff jumping, but it had rained the night before and the conditions were all wrong for their plans." Gage shook his head, his eyes seemingly fixed on some distant point in the past. "I didn't think they were serious. I thought it was just posturing that would end with all of us getting on the horses and going back to school."

Her stomach knotted; she knew that must not have happened. She tipped her temple to his shoulder for a moment, offering what comfort she could.

"What came next was hotly disputed afterward." Gage moved the stag farther away from him, sliding the wooden creature along the table on its weighted, felt feet. "We all saw counselors in the weeks that followed, thanks to Alonzo's intervention. And the professionals helped us understand that our brains can rewrite traumatic events to make them…bearable."

Elena lifted her head, peering over at him. "What do *you* think happened?" She wound her hand around his upper arm. Squeezed gently.

"I believe Zach jumped. I never viewed it as a suicide because that was just the way the guy was wired—especially that weekend. He pushed boundaries because he said that a good thrill 'fed his art.'" Gage shrugged and drummed his fingers once on the coffee table. "He liked to live on the edge. But after one jump, he never resurfaced."

A pit opened in her stomach.

"Did anyone go in after him?" She hugged closer to Gage, rubbing her cheek against his shoulder. Comforting and taking comfort at the same time.

"Every damned one of us." His dark eyes flared with something like defensiveness. "Weston was the only one to jump, which could have killed him, too. The rest of us went down to the rocks below and slid in the water that way. We searched until we could barely breathe, knowing all the while we were too late."

"I'm so, so sorry." She couldn't imagine the trauma of an experience like that for sixteen-year-old kids.

"My father showed his true colors in the aftermath, threatening to pull his support of a new library if the school didn't handle the press releases about the death the way he wanted." Gage closed his eyes for a moment. When he reopened them, there was a flinty determination in his gaze. "Our names were never mentioned in connection to the accident, nor was the school's. But while Nigel Striker was being a first-class selfish bastard, Alonzo Salazar did everything humanly possible to help us weather the loss of a friend."

The fierce loyalty of the Mesa Falls Ranch owners toward the *Hollywood Newlyweds* author began to make sense. No matter what Alonzo might have done after the boys went on to graduate, he'd been a friend and mentor to them through unimaginable pain after the death of their friend.

"No wonder you're protective of his legacy," she observed softly, shifting positions to stroke a hand along Gage's back. She felt the ripples of tension relax under her fingertips.

"He might not have been much of a parent to his own sons, but he was the best teacher imaginable to a bunch of kids hanging on to their sanity by the skin of their teeth. He found local jobs for the ones who needed physical activity, and he found causes for the ones who needed something to shout about. Wes ended up as a lifeguard, where he found his passion for saving people." Gage turned toward her, cupping her cheek in his palm. "For me, Alonzo knew that I'd been interested in investing after I did well on a project where we invested in an imaginary company. So Alonzo signed me up for an electronic trading account and put a few hundred bucks in it. Said I could lose it if I wanted, but if I made money, he wanted ten percent of everything."

"Really?" She hadn't expected that. She plugged in what she'd learned about Alonzo with this new glimpse of Gage's past. "Didn't he teach English classes?"

She tipped her cheek more firmly into Gage's hand, drinking in the feel of his caress. Craving more. Sensing that he needed the physical connection, too.

"Yes, but our school had a lot of curriculum overlap. He was friends with the business teacher and knew about the project." Gage lifted a dark eyebrow. "Good thing for me, I guess. I made both of us a tidy sum that year, and I became obsessed with investing."

"What about your friends—" she started to ask, but Gage laid a finger over her lips.

"I think I've had all the sharing I can handle for one night." The serious look in his eyes told her how much the conversation had cost him. But he didn't remove his finger from her lips, and his focus slowly lowered there. "I need to think about something else...or better yet, not think at all."

Elena's breathing quickened. Heat flared along with keen awareness of that sensual touch. His finger shifted slowly, back and forth, along her mouth. Her eyelids fluttered closed as she relished the feel of him there. Anticipating what was to come.

"In that case, let me share something with you," she whispered against the blunt fingertip before nipping it between her teeth.

She opened her eyes to see his pupils widening.

That was all the response she needed. Standing, she reached for the side zipper under one arm of her dress. Lowering it, she let the heavy sequined tulle fall away from her body. The gown pooled at her feet and she stepped out of it along with her metallic leather sandals.

Desire flared in his eyes, the heat of one look burning its way up her legs and over her belly and breasts.

Clad only in her panties and a strapless silk bra the same tan shade as her skin, Elena stepped between his knees.

"I don't know about you..." She skimmed her hands along his broad shoulders, wanting to make him forget everything else but this. Her. "But I've been dreaming about this moment all day."

Eleven

Stepping into his arms felt like coming home.

For a woman who'd never lived in the same place for more than eleven months until after she'd turned eighteen, that sense of homecoming was all the more potent to Elena. She tried not to think about that, not trusting the emotions as Gage's hands wrapped around her hips.

Instead, she lost herself in the warmth of his lips as he brushed a kiss along her ribs. In the huff of his breath along the scalloped lace of her bra. She began unbuttoning his white dress shirt, slipping open one fastening after the next while he skimmed touches up her sides. In the end, he had to help her with his cuff links, but she wrestled the shirt free, baring all that golden muscle to her hungry gaze. Standing, he spun her in his arms so her back was to him before he pulled the pins from her hair, letting the waves fall down her back briefly before he swept it to one side and kissed her neck.

For a moment, their reflection in a wall mirror captivated her. The sight of Gage wrapped around her, his muscles shifting as he caressed her, seemed pulled straight from her fantasies.

She traced a finger through the maze of tattoos on his arms where they banded around her waist, desire heating her from the inside out. His tongue darted beneath her ear, igniting a fresh wave of tingling sensations down her spine.

"Take me," she demanded, reaching up to comb her fingers through his hair. "Please."

She twisted around to face him again, cradling his face and drawing him close to kiss her. He tasted her lips with the skillful finesse of someone who knew his way around her body better than anyone. Better than she did. He wrapped one hand around the length of her hair, tilting her this way and that to give him the best access to her mouth. Her body quivered with pleasure and they weren't even naked.

He lifted her against him with one arm, hauling her close. She helped him by wrapping her legs around his waist and locking her ankles there. With his hands anchored under her thighs, he carried her easily to the bedroom, each stride a delectable torment that brought the hard length of him more fully against her sensitized flesh.

When he set her in the center of the puffy duvet, she unclasped her bra and tossed it aside while he unfastened his belt. His pants. Anticipation coiled inside her until one long, hot look from Gage threatened to send pleasure boiling over.

He hooked a finger in the silk of her thong and drew the fabric slowly down her legs. When they were naked at last, he was about to roll a condom into place when she nudged his hand aside to take over the task. He shuddered with her touch before he stretched out above her.

Breathless, needy, she skated caresses along his arms and chest until he anchored her thigh against his hip and entered her. The shock of sensation buried deep inside her was both sharp and sweet. She held herself still, waiting, adjusting, her fingers twisted in the duvet cover.

When he began to move again, she knew she wouldn't last long. Her gaze shifted to his and she found him looking at her intensely, with a tangle of emotions that confused her as much as her own. Closing her eyes again, she refocused on the physical sensations, feelings that made sense to her.

Gage leaned over her, whispering sweet words in her ear before he fastened a kiss on one taut nipple, drawing on the peak. Elena gasped, her hips bucking.

He drove deeper. Faster. And she was lost.

Her release rolled through her, burning away everything but the sweet fulfillment that came with it. She clung to Gage, hands on his shoulders, moving with him until he couldn't hold back any longer. He came with her, his back arching and his legs tensing. She held him tighter, savoring every moment that was too perfect for words.

When the sensations eased, Gage lay down beside her, wrapping an arm around her and tucking her under the covers. She waited to catch her breath before she moved closer to kiss his shoulder. His chest.

He stroked her hair and she wondered if he was as reluctant as she was to speak. To shatter the bubble of time where they seemed to understand one another. It was an illusion, she knew, a false sensation perpetuated by all the amazing things they could make one another feel.

Wasn't it?

Not sure she was ready to find out, she tipped her forehead to his chest and felt the beating of his heart instead. Steady. Comforting.

For tonight, she was going to savor that much. The morning was soon enough to wade through the complicated ties that still bound them. She owed him something for turning her life around. It hadn't happened yet, but she could sense her world shifting, surging with new opportunities that hadn't been there before, thanks to him introducing her to Chiara.

Tomorrow would be soon enough to come up with a plan. To thank him and leave him to find someone suitable who would make the Striker family proud.

She just wished the thought of walking away didn't make her chest feel so incredibly hollow inside.

Leaning back into the buttery leather seat of the Learjet, Gage told himself it was a good thing that Elena had agreed to return to Mesa Falls Ranch so readily.

He'd been concerned that she would prefer to stay in Lake Tahoe for the rest of the week, given her new relationship with Chiara Campagna. No doubt Elena would want to explore the business opportunities that the friendship offered, and he certainly couldn't blame her for investigating those possibilities. Yet she'd complied with his wish to fly to Montana today.

He turned to watch her use the photo editing software at the workstation near the front of the aircraft. She'd been manipulating images for the last hour, testing fonts with the graphics and different filters. He recognized some of the garments in the shots—clothes she'd discovered in the casino's boutique or that she'd made herself. There were close-ups of hems and stitches, shoulders and necklines.

To a certain extent, filling her time with work was the norm for Elena Rollins. But Gage couldn't help but wonder if she was busying herself purposely to avoid talking to him. To avoid whatever was happening between them.

He'd sensed her pulling away somehow last night after an incredible sexual encounter. Or had it been the story about his past he'd shared that had left things feeling uneasy between them?

"How's it going?" he asked, unfastening his seat belt to join her at the workstation as the plane began its descent.

Glancing up at his approach, she combed her hair from her face as her brown eyes flicked over him. Memories of her dark hair sliding along his bare skin threatened to derail all his good intentions.

"I'm putting together an inspiration board that can double as creative content on my blog." She leaned back in her chair, her red-tipped fingernail tapping against the mouse, as he took the seat closest to her. "Now that I won't be selling scandalous news bits to the tabloids, the pressure is on to ensure I can leverage a new revenue stream."

"If you need financial backing, Elena, I can give you extremely favorable terms." He'd barely gotten all the words out when she was already shaking her head.

"Thank you, but no." Shifting in her seat, her calf brushed his for a moment. Quickly, she repositioned herself to avoid further contact. "Too much potential for conflict of interest."

He bit back a retort, knowing the defensiveness he felt had more to do with this damnable sensation he had that she was pulling away from him.

Already.

She'd been back in his life for a handful of days, hardly enough time for them to iron out anything from the past, let alone think about what came next. And there hadn't been nearly enough time for him to enjoy having her back in his bed again.

"You might change your mind about the loan when I tell you I have a big favor to ask of you." He should have brought it up the night before when he'd told her about Zach. But when she'd given him the chance to leave the conversation behind and lose himself in her beautiful body, he'd been powerless to refuse.

"Gage Striker needs a favor from *me*?" She gave a self-deprecating smile. "Do tell."

Frustration knotted in his shoulders.

"I'm not sure why that would surprise you." He didn't understand how or why she'd lost herself in her unsuccessful marriage, but he wouldn't listen to her sell herself short. "You're a smart, enterprising woman on the verge of an exciting new chapter in your life."

For a moment, the only sound was the hum of the engine as the pilot throttled back the speed of the aircraft.

"Thank you." Elena nodded, a single wavy lock slipping in front of her shoulder. Vibrant red cashmere hugged her curves, the V-neck drawing his attention to a silver necklace consisting of her initial beside a diamond-encrusted star. "How can I help?"

"When Desmond called the meeting yesterday, he revealed some startling news about Alonzo's profits from the tell-all book." Since he was done doubting her, he shared the truth without hesitation. "The funds have been supporting a thirteen-year-old boy."

She frowned, sitting up straighter in her seat. "Didn't you say the accident was fourteen years ago?"

"Yes." He suspected his friends had all been awake late into the night trying to piece together that particular puzzle, but Gage felt confident the child didn't belong to Alonzo. DNA testing would prove it soon enough. "And we will continue to investigate that. But since the funds were also financing Alonzo's humanitarian efforts, we wanted to announce that. We hoped a concrete response to the public interest in the story would put an end to the speculation."

"And you're comfortable with only providing half a story?" she asked, crossing her legs in a way that drew his eye to the hem of her black pencil skirt where it grazed her knee.

"I don't think any of us feel compelled to account for every nickel of the guy's money." Gage lifted his attention from her legs, wishing they could have spent this flight in the sleeping suite through the door in the back of the plane. "But I thought I'd give you the right of first refusal for the piece to see if you want to pedal it to whatever outlet you planned to approach when you first came to Montana to explore the issue."

How damned ironic that he'd brought her to Tahoe in the hope of making her lose interest in the Salazar story. Now, he needed a way to entice her to stay in Montana long enough to figure out how to keep her in his life.

She nibbled her lip, a hint of pink gloss disappearing as she did so. "It's not like I'm writing for a venue winning journalism awards," she admitted drily. "I'll do it, but with the understanding that I'll donate my payment to one of Alonzo's humanitarian organizations."

"You would do that?" He hadn't anticipated her generosity, especially when she would need financing to start her next business.

He knew she'd arrived in Mesa Falls with precious little to her name, although perhaps his retrieval of her personal effects from her former home would make things easier for her.

"I won't allow any of your friends to think I was trying to make a buck off a—" her eyes lowered for a moment "—from the hard times you've all been through."

The reminder of Zach always nudged a dark, painful place inside him. Yet somehow, sharing the story with Elena and having her understanding eased a layer of the pain this time.

"Very well. You have my thanks. Our thinking was to offer you the scoop a few hours before we share the details publicly at a party similar to the one that brought you into my home in the first place." He had already sent a memo to the ranch's public relations director. Plans were in place to drop hints that an announcement was forthcoming, ensuring the event was well covered in the media. "We're coordinating a party for next Saturday."

That was over a week away. If he could convince her to stay on at the ranch for that long, Gage hoped it would be enough time to move past whatever barriers Elena was putting up between them.

The aircraft shifted slightly as the landing gear came out with a soft thud that vibrated through his feet. The movement sent her hand darting out to steady herself, her fingers landing on his forearm. The crackle of awareness was there for her, too. He saw it in her eyes before she pulled away.

"Okay." Elena shut her laptop and unplugged the cord, packing up her things for their arrival. "I can use the next week to brainstorm my business plan with Chiara, but I'll remain in

Mesa Falls through the party as a way to thank you for the help you've given me this week."

A kind offer, but not at all what he wanted from her.

Gage considered his next move, not wanting to scare her off if she was already planning her life after their affair. He would simply use their remaining time together to remind her how good life could be at his side. For today, he would be grateful for the gift of one more week.

"Thank you." Picking up her hand where it rested on the workstation, he brushed a kiss across the knuckles, inhaling the orange blossom scent of her skin. "I can't deny that I'm looking forward to having you under my roof until then, Elena. I plan to make the most of every day."

A week later, Elena walked through a fashion studio in New York's Garment District, perusing a breakout Italian designer's new collection for a venerable French fashion house with Astrid and Chiara at her side.

Sample sizes of all the clothes shown in Paris last week hung neatly on rolling racks outlining the big, open space where natural light slanted through huge windows. It was a dream girls' trip, helpfully orchestrated by Gage in his quest to remind her of the perks of continuing their affair. Her stomach knotted at the thought of how much his thoughtfulness swayed her.

But for all the things he'd offered her, never once had he suggested he loved her. Better to enjoy this last hurrah with her friends before she returned to a more down-to-earth life on the West Coast. Alone.

"I can't believe you got us in here, Chiara." Elena sighed wistfully, sliding one hanger farther down the rack to take a better look at a pair of crepe de chine pants with a sexy silhouette that hugged the hips and billowed into a tulle puff midway down the calf. "Let alone that we have a private showing."

Nearby, Astrid squealed over a cashmere sweater dress with cutouts around the waist.

Chiara stood at one of the long windows, gazing down at West Thirty-Eighth Street. "Frankly, it was tougher getting you two to join me than it was to convince Noemi's assistant to let us in here for the day." Chiara fixed Elena with a sidelong stare, her perfectly drawn cat-eye makeup enhancing the sage green of her eyes. "Astrid gets a pass as a new mom, but I'm surprised I had to twist your arm, Elena, when Noemi is actively interested in seeing your drawings."

The invitation from the fashion luminary was both exciting and a little scary, but Elena couldn't pretend fear had anything to do with her reservations about making the trip to New York for the afternoon. She shifted the crepe pants to her left, fingers walking down the remaining hangers on the rolling rack.

"It isn't that I didn't want to be here," she admitted. "But I sense my time is drawing to a close in Mesa Falls and I hesitated to miss a single day with Gage."

The days were fun. The nights were hot enough to fuel a lifetime of sensual fantasies. But she'd indulged that kind of surface relationship with Gage before and knew it wouldn't be enough to keep them together long-term. It had been a careful balance this week to protect her heart and still savor the fun of being with him. She knew even before they'd returned to Mesa Falls that she wanted more from him.

And she felt deserving of more after selling herself short for too long—both with Gage and in the ill-fated marriage that came afterward.

Astrid tugged a silk skirt from the rack, the handkerchief hem floating gracefully around her ankles as she held the garment to her waist. "Gage loves you," she informed Elena matter-of-factly. "I'm not sure if he realizes it or not. But I've never seen him look at anyone else the way he looks at you."

The comment felt like a hit to her solar plexus, robbing her of breath for a moment and making her see stars behind her eyes as if she was oxygen deprived. Of course, Astrid was only guessing. She couldn't know Gage's feelings any better than

Elena did. Blinking rapidly, she moved to the next rolling rack with new determination to find an outfit for the party the ranch's publicity department had put together for the following evening. It wasn't a gala or a fund-raiser, just a private house party with a DJ and a select guest list including a handful of Hollywood celebrities, world-class athletes, a Formula One race car driver and a couple of heavyweights from the music industry.

All of whom sounded like safer candidates for her affection than the man who'd already broken her heart once, no matter what Astrid believed about the way Gage looked at her.

"Gage and I have had a long and complicated relationship," Elena explained, unwilling to get drawn into those old feelings for him even though they'd resurfaced at an alarming speed during her time with Gage. "But whatever he might feel for me comes second to his loyalty to his family."

Astrid peered up at her curiously, settling an embroidered denim romper back on the rack. "Jonah once called Nigel Striker a judgmental asshat. I remember because Jonah gets along with almost everyone."

A sad smile pulled at Elena's lips. Chiara returned to the rolling rack, her hand moving unerringly to a turquoise-and-green sari-inspired dress. She held it up for their inspection, a light-as-air coordinating scarf fluttering where it wrapped around the hanger.

"This is you," Chiara announced. "It's a gown to slay in, and exactly what you need to wear to the house party."

Elena moved closer, drawn by the featherweight of the layers printed with swirls of blue and deep purple. The sheer fabric around the shoulders and the effect of the scarf made her think of a butterfly.

"It's beautiful," she murmured, running her hand down the fabric. "The question is, will it be a gown to usher in a new chapter or end one?"

Saying goodbye to Gage wouldn't be easy, but she would fulfill her promise to share the story the ranch owners wanted to spread about Alonzo. After that, she had nothing tying her to Montana. Gage might romance her, but that didn't mean he loved her enough to break with his family to be with her. Nigel Striker had already proved he'd stop at nothing to ensure she stayed far from his son.

"Maybe the party will be a little of both," Chiara informed her, giving her a level look. "But that's okay. There's nothing wrong with walking away from what isn't working so you can move on to new opportunities."

Of course, she was correct. But crazy as it might be, Elena held out a sliver of hope that maybe things would be different this time. Gage had shared a deeply held secret with her. He'd given her a level of trust he'd never bestowed on anyone else. It had to count for something.

Because whether or not Astrid was correct about Gage's feelings for Elena, Elena knew without a doubt about her own emotions where he was concerned. Based on the deep fear in her gut about leaving him after the party, she understood that she'd passed the point of no return.

Somehow, she'd fallen for Gage for a second time.

Twelve

Finishing his meeting with the interior decorator he'd hired as a surprise for Elena, Gage checked in with the contractors who were already tearing out a media room in his home to remake the space into a work studio for her. The construction was moving quickly, and he appreciated the accelerated timetable since he wanted to unveil the new suite to her tonight after the party. She'd known the contractors were on-site at his house all week, but he'd told her they were installing a tasting room in another wing, forestalling more questions about his secret project.

He'd wined and dined Elena all week, hoping to convince her to continue their affair even after she left Montana. When he'd encouraged her to visit New York City with her friends, he'd used the time to take estimates from a handful of highly recommended decorators, finally choosing the guy who'd flown in for today's meeting.

The dude was someone familiar with Elena's blog, and he'd insisted she should be brought in on the decor before they went any further in planning. Gage had appreciated the decorator pushing back on his plans since he had raised a valid point.

Elena's future as a designer seemed more and more probable. She'd surely want to weigh in on fabrics and colors for the "home within a home" Gage hoped to create for her. Surely if she had her own retreat space at his house on the ranch in Mesa Falls, and at his place in Silicon Valley, she would be enticed to visit both spots with him as often as possible. She would see that she was the only woman he wanted in his life.

Now that he'd seen how rootless she'd been as a kid, how much her father had dragged her from town to town hiding from the cops and battling his own demons, Gage hoped she'd understand the significance of what he was trying to offer her. A place she could always call home.

Stepping out of the studio, where new windows were being installed to increase the natural light, Gage thanked the head contractor and walked around the exterior of the house to make sure the work crew were being respectful of the grass and gardens. He needed to dress for the evening's event, the party where the owners would share the news about Alonzo Salazar's humanitarian efforts as a way to end the public interest in his story. The PR staff had chosen Miles Rivera's residence as the site for the get-together, hoping to maintain the security of the celebrity guests more easily in a private venue.

Satisfied with the work crew's use of a side lawn to park their trucks, Gage rounded the front of the house and pulled out his phone to let Elena know he would be ready in half an hour for the party.

Only to have a woman's familiar voice stop him cold.

"Gage?"

He stopped. Confounded.

Because there, in his front entryway, stood his smiling mother and expressionless father. A designer suitcase rested between them. A liveried chauffeur wheeled a second piece of matching luggage from the back of a luxury SUV idling quietly in the driveway.

His parents looked older than when he'd seen them last. Not

just because they were a little grayer. A network of worry lines crawled across each of their faces. The reality of the changes in them brought home to Gage how many years it had been since he'd seen them in person. Guilt pinched at his chest.

"Mom?" Gage stared at her in shock, wondering what on earth they were doing in the States and on his doorstep, tonight of all nights. "What's going on?"

"We're here for the party, Gage," she announced, her pink traveling suit and lightweight trench coat neatly pressed as if she'd journeyed from across town rather than across the globe. She appeared tentative for a moment, perhaps unsure of her welcome. Then she stepped forward to hold out her arms to him.

Regret burned that he'd made his mother doubt his affection for her. No matter what had transpired between him and his father, he didn't blame her for it. Gage embraced her, pressing a kiss to her cheek as the scent of lemon verbena drifted from her, punching him in the gut with nostalgia despite his strained relationship with his parents.

"I don't understand why you'd come all this way to attend tonight's event." He addressed his father as he stepped back, knowing his parents' presence could send Elena running if he didn't handle the situation carefully. "The event is a publicity function for Mesa Falls Ranch."

A venture they'd never supported since it involved his friends from school, friends who'd been a source of aggravation for Nigel Striker more than once.

His father inclined his head a fraction. His gray suit lapel was decorated with a pin of the New Zealand flag. "Yes. A publicity function carefully calibrated to suggest a revelation about the ranch's tie to Alonzo Salazar." He spoke the name with obvious distaste. "A man I would have hoped you'd have erased all connection to long before now."

Frustration simmered, and Gage felt the painful tension in his temples. Behind them, his housekeeper was already opening the door to usher in Gage's mother. The driver brought the bags inside.

Foreboding loomed like a thundercloud, smothering him with the sense of inevitability. Tonight was going to be a disaster if he didn't get a handle on this unexpected visit fast. The last thing he needed was his father upsetting Elena after how hard Gage had worked this week to make tonight special.

"That's my business, not yours," Gage reminded his father, knowing he'd need to hang on to his patience with both hands if he wanted the evening with Elena to unfold the way he'd hoped. He'd invested too much time in his plans to have his father spoil them now. "And tonight's party is a private affair, but I'd be happy to meet with you tomorrow morning once you've both had a chance to recover from your trip."

New Zealand was nineteen hours ahead of mountain time in the United States. They had to be exhausted. He gestured to his housekeeper to prepare a guest room for them.

"We spent last night in Los Angeles," his mother assured him, sliding a coaxing hand around Gage's arm as she lowered her head to speak softly to him. "We've had plenty of time to acclimate. We're only in town for a couple of days, Gage. Attending the party will give us an opportunity to catch up."

Had his father urged her to guilt Gage into letting them attend? Suspicion mounted along with his irritation. He didn't have time for a big confrontation right now when the driver was due to deliver him and Elena to Miles's house in—he checked his watch—fifteen minutes.

What if Elena was ready early? She could make an appearance in the foyer at any moment. He needed to get his parents out of there.

"Nevertheless—" Gage freed himself from his mother's coercive hold "—we'll have to speak tomorrow. My housekeeper, Mrs. Merchant, will show you to your rooms."

Gage was unconcerned about how his father interpreted his limited hospitality, but his conscience niggled at leaving his mom standing in the hallway with her bags for the staff to oversee. In the end, he had no choice. He headed down the hall toward the back of the house, where he still had just enough time to change.

He'd almost reached the door to his suite when his father's cold voice echoed along the corridor, raking along Gage's last nerve.

"Elena Rollins. What in bloody hell are you doing here?"

The moment seemed surreal enough that Elena briefly hoped she was just having a nightmare.

When she'd arrived in the foyer to ask Gage's housekeeper to snap a few photos for her blog before the party, Elena came face-to-face with the harsh, disapproving man who still occasionally haunted her dreams. Nigel Striker, the man who'd attempted to buy her off and then failed to tell his son for years that she hadn't taken the bribe, was now blocking her path to the living room. He loomed almost as large as Gage, although his shoulders were more stooped now and his gray hair had thinned.

Nigel glared at Elena, while his wife—almost a decade younger than him, but looking equally world-weary at the moment—hurried closer to them.

"Nigel, please. We're Gage's guests," Rosalie Striker murmured, her eyes lingering on Elena briefly before returning to her intractable mate. "Let them get to their party and you can speak to Gage tomorrow."

Something about the woman's intervention freed Elena from the paralysis that seeing Nigel had induced. She wouldn't be intimidated by this man, even if he'd been needlessly cruel to her six years ago. Nigel Striker had simply exploited the weakness that had always existed in her relationship with Gage—the lack of deeper understanding and core trust.

"What am *I* doing here?" she parroted, minus the expletive. "I'm doing a favor for your son, who asked me to attend an event with him this evening."

Anger and an old resentment balled in her stomach. And as Gage entered the foyer from the opposite corridor, seeing him did little to ease those feelings, even if his expression registered concern for her.

Pivoting on her heel, she retreated down the hallway, charging back the way she'd come. She heard quiet, furious voices behind her, but she wasn't even mildly compelled to glance backward.

Gage had asked her to share a story about Alonzo that would feed some of the public fascination with him, and she had. More media outlets would pick it up tonight after the announcement at Miles Rivera's party. Gage had wanted her to attend the event with him, but as far as she was concerned, that part of the deal was off the table now that his parents were under his roof.

"Elena. Wait," Gage called to her as she reached the door to her suite.

The door to the same room where they'd hashed through the logistics of her visit just two weeks ago.

She paused with one hand on the knob, wishing she could scavenge a fraction of all that defensiveness she'd felt around him then. She'd come to this house ready to do battle with him, to take the story she wanted and—yes—maybe have a little revenge for how he'd treated her six years ago.

Now that she'd seen another side of him, a facet of his kindness and a hint of the difficult journey he'd taken to be a different man from his father, Elena didn't have the heart to do battle with him the same way.

"I'm leaving," she told him quietly, forcing herself to meet his dark eyes. "I've filed the story you asked me to with *The Hollywood Metro*. I'll forward the check to your publicity director so she can give the proceeds to one of Alonzo's preferred charities. But I'm done here."

"No." He opened the door for her, apparently waiting for her to step inside. "Please, Elena. You can't go without giving me a chance to explain."

His gaze roamed over her, and she felt self-conscious in the turquoise-and-green gown that had made her feel so beautiful just half an hour earlier when she'd dressed for the evening with care. The fluttery fabric had matched her light, airy hopefulness. Now, the frothy material reminded her how foolish she'd been to hope for more from a man who still wanted—deserved—closeness with his family.

"You don't need to explain anything, Gage." She cut him short, fearing if they talked much longer she would humiliate herself by bursting into tears. She didn't move to enter the room. She felt so fragile at the moment she feared she might break if she took a single misstep. "Your parents are in town to see you, not me. And I'm not going to add fuel to the fire by remaining here when you and your dad already have a strained relationship."

"I'm not interested in repairing a relationship with my father after the way he's treated you." His words were softly spoken, but the fury behind them was still apparent. He stood just inches from her, still waiting for her to enter the office outside the bedroom he'd given her for her stay.

A visit that had come to an end, as much as she wished otherwise. She couldn't afford to ignore how this would inevitably turn out. Heartbreak delayed would only be heartbreak doubled.

"And what about your mother? Your sisters?" she prodded, trying to help him see the facts he'd been ignoring. "How happy are you going to be alienating your whole family for my sake? They're your flesh and blood, Gage. I'm just the woman sharing your bed temporarily."

"I want you in my life for more than that," he shot back, emotion flaring in his eyes.

Anger? Passion? She couldn't be sure. Her own emotions were so mixed up where he was concerned, she didn't have the clear-eyed judgment necessary to try to interpret his. She felt weary.

"For how long?" she asked, making one last effort to help

him see that they were wrong for each other. To think otherwise had been delusional. "Right now, we have great chemistry. But will that still be there three years from now after you've cut yourself off from your family in order to be with me? Or will you wish you'd found someone that your family could embrace instead of someone they're determined to hate?"

"I don't need their approval, Elena." His tone was resolute. Final. "What my father wants doesn't mean a damned thing to me."

She'd like to think things could be simpler, but she couldn't help but remember her own father. No matter his shortcomings, she still wished she could have found a way to have him in her life. To fix the rifts between them so she still had someone she could call family.

"I understand that, Gage," she said sadly. "And what you want doesn't mean a damned thing to him, either. Which makes you far more alike than you realize."

That, at least, seemed to sink home. Some of the determined fire faded from his eyes.

"You really mean that?" he asked, his jaw jutting forward. "You can just walk away thinking I'm as unbending as my old man and I'll only get tired of you anyway?"

It would be different if he loved her. But he'd never said anything to give her that impression, and she refused to put her heart on the line for him a second time. Whatever feelings she'd developed for him again would remain her secret.

Her private heartbreak.

Gage reached for her, but she backed up a step, afraid that the attraction would make her lose sight of reason. Again.

"Why would I believe otherwise?" She stepped into the office outside her bedroom, ready to change out of her party clothes and forget this night ever happened. "I'm going to pack now, Gage. I'll get a flight back home as soon as I can."

His nod was jerky. Abrupt. And it was the only hint that he might be hurting, too.

"I need to put in an appearance at the party," he said finally. "If you leave before I return, would you consider taking a look at the room renovation before you go?"

She couldn't imagine why he would ask her such a thing. Why he would care about her opinion?

"I'd prefer not to run the risk of stumbling into your father." She had no desire to cross swords with Nigel Striker. Especially when Gage could obtain design advice from dozens of other people. "Good night, Gage."

Closing the door between them, Elena told herself it would be the last time she'd ever have to face that level of pain. And she prayed that was true, because one drop more and she would be destroyed. This was almost too much to bear. She'd encouraged him to maintain his ties with his family, but in doing so, she'd cost herself the closest relationship she'd ever had with someone. Because no matter that she'd married Tomas at a sad point in her life, Gage Striker had always held her heart.

Thirteen

Where the hell are you?

Gage read one text while five more rolled in, his phone blowing up with notifications from his friends as the evening wore on. He'd changed into his tux for Miles's party, but hadn't called for his car in case there was a chance he could figure out a way to keep Elena from leaving.

Anger at his father still clouded his head. How could he show up here—tonight—and ruin any chance he might have had with Elena? Again.

Now, Gage sat outside in the dark by the pool, staring up at his own house. The lights were still on in Elena's rooms. They were still on in his parents' suite on the other side of the house, too. The studio his contractors were working on remained dark. It had been foolish of him to ask her to look at it since the space hadn't fully taken shape yet. Without him there to explain what he was doing, she would just think he was putting in a tasting room, like he'd told her several days ago.

Defeat weighed heavy in his chest as he settled deeper into the cushion of the wooden pool lounger.

She was right here in his house, a sexy, beautiful and giving woman he wanted to be with, but he couldn't think of a damned thing to do to make her stay.

When his phone chimed again, he had the urge to chuck it into the pool to stop the buzzing. But seeing the notification from Miles—the host of tonight's shindig and the most level-headed of the bunch—made him read the message.

How well do you know Chiara Campagna? Found her in my study, and I would swear she was rifling through my notes. Looking for something.

Seriously?

Gage wondered if Miles had been drinking, because it made zero sense that one of the most famous women in the world would want to find out secrets Miles Rivera was keeping. Of all the Mesa Falls partners, Miles would win the award for most apt to do the right thing.

Astrid and Jonah have known her forever. She's cool.

Unconcerned, Gage shot back the text and pocketed his phone. By the time he looked up again, he saw his mother heading his way. No longer wearing her travel suit, she was dressed in a long knit skirt and sweater with a cardigan over the top. He stood out of habit, even though he wasn't sure he wanted to talk to her. His frustration might be with his father, but then again, she hadn't done anything to help defuse the tension earlier.

"Mom, I'm not in the best frame of mind for a conversation. I'm going to have to confront Dad tomorrow, and I want to warn you, I feel certain it won't go well." He figured he might as well give her fair warning.

She settled onto the chaise beside him, her skirt billowing

around her, the watery reflection of landscape lights illuminating her face. There was concern in her expression as she looped her arm through his.

"You mean about Elena Rollins refusing his bribe all those years ago?" she asked, picking lint from the arm of her sweater.

"He told you?" It shouldn't surprise him that his mother was party to his dad's deception. And yet it still stung.

"We were never sure what to make of it that you believed she'd taken the money when she hadn't." Rosalie Striker fluffed her dyed brown curls, her hairstyle still exactly the same as the one she'd worn in his youth. "We assumed she wanted you to think she took it. That she used the misunderstanding as a way out of the relationship."

"Only because I was quick to believe the worst of her. Since Dad lied to me." He had to take some ownership for his own actions back then, as did Elena.

Yet he placed the biggest blame firmly in his father's court.

"He did a foolish thing, Gage," his mom admitted, crossing her ankles. "I hope you won't hold it against him forever. In his own way, he does love you."

And this was how he showed it? Defensiveness ate away at him, especially considering that Elena had just told Gage he wasn't all that different from his old man. Was he that unbending?

"Elena traveled halfway around the world as my guest only to be treated like a viper and asked to leave. Is it any wonder I'm not inclined to roll out the red carpet for Dad when he shows up here?" Gage's attention flicked back to the house, where a light snapped on in the media room he had been remodeling into a studio for Elena.

With no blinds on the new windows the work crew had installed, he could see her inside the house, dressed in jeans and a simple white blouse, pulling a suitcase behind her.

His heart stopped in his chest for a long moment before kicking to life faster.

"I've got to go." Standing, he didn't know what he was going to say to her, but he knew he had to try to find the right words.

Fear of her leaving ate away at his insides.

"Do you love her, son?" His mother's hand circled his as he stood, but her words were what glued his feet in place.

"Love?" Not that it was a foreign concept, per se. But he hadn't thought about it. Or maybe, more truthfully, he'd tried not to think about love and Elena in the same sentence.

Maybe because love hadn't worked out well for him in the past. His relationships with his parents—his father especially—had always been difficult. His closest friendships as a kid had resulted in a loss that left a lifelong wound.

"She's gotten closer to you than any other woman, Gage. Twice." His mother's eyes were wise, her tone gentle as she probed at the edges of his hurt. "Elena Rollins seems too important for you to let her get away."

"I'm going to do my best to make her stay," he assured her, needing to talk to Elena now. Before she got on a plane and never came back.

"You might have to tell her you love her, son." She tipped her cheek to the back of his hand. "Don't keep denying yourself happiness just because Zachary Eldridge didn't have the chance for a long, full life."

When she let go of his hand, it took him a minute to process that he was free to walk away now. Her words looped in his head, making no sense because he'd never thought that way. Never consciously made that sacrifice for the sake of a friend who'd been dead for almost half of Gage's life.

Had he?

Worry fueled his steps as he kept an eye on Elena turning in a slow circle inside the studio space he'd built for her. He feared her leaving, yes. He could admit that. And was it because he loved her?

Gage tried the idea on for size. Found it fit everything he was feeling. Explained everything that had perplexed and infuriated him about his relationship with her over the last couple of weeks.

He loved Elena Rollins. He'd been blind and unbending, but he could fix that. The one constant—the one thing that was never going to change—was how much he loved her.

Elena might not have realized what she was looking at in the room under construction in the back corner of Gage's mammoth house. Except that the work crew had left a big inspiration board propped up in a corner of the room, with drawings of every architectural element to be incorporated in a design project called "Elena's Studio."

Just seeing the title had made her knees feel a little weak. But then, peering back and forth between the half-finished space and the poster, Elena could see where the ideas on the outline were coming to life in the physical setting. Releasing the handle of her suitcase, she walked across the dark hardwood floor to read the notes under the heading "Window Nook" with a series of photos pinned beside it. The board showed ideas from a built-in chaise surrounded by bookshelves to a candlelit, faux-fur-covered bench with retractable blinds on three sides for privacy. The actual window seat in progress was a bump-out of floor-to-ceiling windows.

In another corner of the room, a raised platform was taking shape and the inspiration board suggested it could have mirrors on three sides for designing clothing on mannequins or doing fittings on real-life models.

Stunned to see the space that propelled her dreams that much closer to reality, Elena was speechless when she heard the door creak open behind her. She knew who would be there: the man who'd created this haven for her by listening to all of her half-formed dreams over the years, then translated them into workable goals for a crew that he'd said was building a wine cellar for him.

"I can't believe you did this." Her hand trembled a little as she reached out to touch a new window with deep moldings above and below. "It's so much different in here than in the rest of the house."

Gage's home was a modern take on Western design, with natural stone and timber elements in a relentlessly masculine style. Here, the aesthetic was more formal and traditional, with architectural salvage pieces to give the place an older feel.

She glanced back at him, taking in his tuxedo shirt. His jacket was missing, and his bow tie remained undone, as if he'd dressed partway for the event and then reconsidered. He moved deeper into the room, his dress shoes lightly tapping the hardwood.

"I wanted it to look like a New York fashion house. Or a Paris artist's garret. Something that would transport and inspire you to create." He jammed his hands in his pockets, looking thoughtful. "I hired an interior decorator who's a real fan of your blog. But he said we needed to consult you on the design before I did anything else since the style should reflect you."

"You know me well, though. I couldn't have described what I wanted any more perfectly than what you've done here." She pointed to the inspiration board, where all the ideas were laid out with a range of design options for each.

"These are all your ideas, Elena," he said cryptically, his dark eyes moving over the poster. "Six years ago, on that trip up the Pacific Coast Highway, I asked you to tell me what your dream office looked like." He withdrew a hand from his pocket to gesture toward the style specs. "This is what you described."

He couldn't have surprised her more. Turning to face him, she tried to remember that talk. They'd shared so much about their dreams. The future they both wanted. They just hadn't revealed much about their pasts.

"You kept all of those notes from that conversation?" she marveled.

"I made some notes that night in the hotel and tucked them in a file for one day down the road." His lips curved at one corner. "Believe me, at the time, I didn't think there'd be a six-year delay before I consulted them again."

And yet, he'd kept them.

Her heart melted into a puddle of love for him, and she wondered how she'd ever recover from loving him so much.

Then again, what did it matter if he didn't say the words that she wanted to hear when she had the proof of his feelings in front of her? All around her?

"I can't believe you did all of this in such a short amount of time." She blinked rapidly, daring to look at Gage with new eyes.

With hope.

Wasn't her time with Gage better than any other period in her life?

"It was my pleasure, Elena." He took a step closer to fold her hand in his, his warmth wrapping around her fingers. "I wanted to put everything I had into convincing you to stay with me. To be a part of my life."

She wanted to question him about that, but she sensed he wasn't finished yet, and she didn't want to forestall any insights on this man who confused her even when he made her deliriously happy.

Their conversation echoing slightly in the mostly empty room, she realized it had been perfectly quiet for a long moment while they collected their thoughts.

"But I've been so busy trying to find tangible ways to make you stay that I may have missed something more obvious." He stared down at their clasped hands, and she could see his jaw flexing as he chewed on a thought she couldn't see.

Hopeful that he was trying to find an answer, pleased to know that making her happy was important to him, Elena lifted his hand and rubbed it against her cheek. The scent of his soap stirred sensual memories, reminding her how much pleasure they could find together. How in sync they were in so many ways outside the bedroom, too.

"It's not as though I haven't been tempted, Gage," she reminded him. "But I think I've wanted something more long-term than you. Knowing that your family doesn't want me in your life is a serious deterrent when my dreams of us have been more…" she pointed to the room around them where pillars and walls had been built to last "…permanent."

"Mine, too," he agreed quickly, unthreading their fingers so he could stroke a hand under her jaw. "I wanted to build this for you. Not just here, but at the Silicon Valley house, too. I've already lined up contractors to remodel a space for you there, as well."

His touch bolstered her as much as his words, the connection between them both physical and something more… But she needed to be sure, for him to be sure.

"Really? What about your family?" she asked, lifting her head up to remind him of that sticky dilemma. "I can't change my past."

"And I'd never want you to," Gage assured her. "My mother already understands that, but I'll have a conversation with my father in the morning. I'm letting him know that while I want them in my life, you come first. And if he wants to be welcome here, he'll find a way to embrace the unique person you are."

She didn't think it would be that simple, but she could live with that if Gage could. "You sound certain."

"I am. Elena, I love you." He caressed her cheek with his fingertips, then combed over the spot with the backs of his knuckles.

She was sure she'd misheard. His touch had distracted her. She went very still. "Excuse me?"

He leaned closer, tipping his forehead to hers. "I love you. I didn't know how much I was denying letting myself feel that way until—" He shook his head. "I'm sorry that I didn't see it before. That I didn't know it six years ago, because it was a mistake to let you go then, too."

She couldn't quite follow all the nuances of what he was

saying, but the "I love you" had been as clear and plain as she could ever ask for. It cut through everything else to soothe her heart and assure her this could all work out.

"I love you, too, Gage." She lifted up on her toes to kiss the corner of his lips where he'd been frowning. "It's okay that you didn't know then. As long as you feel sure now."

"Sweetheart, I'm so sure." His New Zealand accent was thick as butter, making her smile even as it tantalized her. "I let my past do a number on me and I knew that was true on a lot of levels, but I didn't realize until just now that I let it rob me of the future I want with you, too."

"How so?" Now that he seemed as relieved as she felt to recognize that what they had was too special to let go, she couldn't help but wonder why he hadn't seen that sooner.

"The role modeling for love in my family—" He shook his head. "Well, you've seen what that looks like. But it didn't matter as a kid once I found friends. Solid, meaningful friendships that were better than any family as far as I was concerned."

Shadows moved through his eyes.

"And then Zach died." She was so grateful he'd shared his past with her, offering her a window of insight she'd been missing six years ago.

"Losing him made it tough for me to let good things into my life. But I know that was wrong of me." He skimmed a touch along her shoulders before tracing the path of her hair down her back. "I should be honoring his memory by living life to the fullest—the way he always did."

"I know what's between us is right." She'd tried loving someone else and the results had been painful for them both.

"I do, too. And I know we'd be damned fools to let go of it again."

"I don't want to be a fool." A laugh bubbled up in her throat, a new happiness crowding her chest. "I feel so lucky to have a second chance."

Hope filled her heart.

"So you will consider a future with me, Elena Rollins?" he asked, wrapping both arms around her and pulling her flush against him. "Will you unpack your suitcase and stay right here? Let me build you a space that's just for you here and in Silicon Valley?" He tilted her face to look deep into her eyes. "Because I want you to always know that whenever you're with me there's a permanent home for you that's just the way you want it."

His words—the sentiment behind them—showed her how thoroughly he understood her. Emotions clogged her throat. "That's a really nice thing to offer a woman who never stayed in one place for more than eleven months until after I turned eighteen."

"You'll always have a home with me." He brushed a kiss over her lips. Soft. Tender.

With the promise of so much more.

* * * * *

Keep reading for an excerpt of
Hot Zone
by Elle James.
Find it in the
Ballistic Cowboys: Trace & Rex anthology,
out now!

Chapter One

Trace "Hawkeye" Walsh checked the coordinates he'd been given by Transcontinental Pipeline Inspection, Inc., and glanced down at the display on the four-wheeler's built-in GPS guidance device. He'd arrived at checkpoint number four. He switched off the engine, climbed off the ATV and unfolded the contour map across the seat.

As with the first three checkpoints, he wasn't exactly sure what he was looking for at the location. He wasn't a pipeline inspector, and he didn't have the tools and devices used by one, but he scanned the area anyway.

Tracing his finger along the line drawn in pencil across the page, he paused. He should be getting close to the point at which RJ Khalig had been murdered. Based on the tight contour lines on the map, he would find the spot over the top of the next ridge-line and down in the valley.

Hawkeye glanced upward. Treacherous terrain had slowed him down. In order to reach some of the points on the map, he'd had to follow old mining trails and bypass canyons. He shrugged. It wasn't a war zone, he wasn't fighting the Taliban or ISIS, and it beat the hell out of being in an office job any day of the week.

That morning, his temporary boss, Kevin Garner, had given him the assignment of following the pipeline through some of the most rugged terrain he'd ever been in, even considering the foothills of Afghanistan. He was game. If he had to be working with the Department of Homeland Security in the Beartooth Mountains of Wyoming, he was happy to be out in the backwoods, rather than chasing wild geese, empty leads and the unhappy residents of the tiny town of Grizzly Pass.

In the two weeks he'd been in the small town of Grizzly Pass, they'd had two murders, a busload of kids taken hostage and two people hunted down like wild game. When he'd agreed to the assignment, he'd been looking forward to some fresh mountain air and a slowdown to his normal combat-heavy assignments. He needed the time to determine whether or not he would stay the full twenty years to retirement in the US Army Rangers or get out and dare to try something different.

Two gunshot and multiple shrapnel wounds, one broken arm, a couple of concussions and six near-fatal misses started to wear on a body and soul. In the last battle he'd been a part of, his best friend hadn't been as lucky. The gunshot wound had been nothing compared to the violent explosion Mac had been smack-dab in the middle of. Yeah, Hawkeye had lost his best friend and battle buddy, a man who'd had his back since they'd been rangers in training.

Without Mac, he wasn't sure he wanted to continue to deploy to the most godforsaken, war-torn countries in the world. He wasn't sure he'd survive. And maybe that wasn't a bad thing. At least he'd die like Mac, defending his country.

He'd hoped this temporary assignment would give him the opportunity to think about his next steps in life. Should he continue his military career? His enlistment was up in a month. He had to decide whether to reenlist or get out.

So far, since he'd been in Grizzly Pass, he hadn't had the

time to ponder his future. Hell, he'd already been in a shoot-out and had to rescue one of his new team members. For a place with such a small population, it was a hot zone of trouble. No wonder Garner had requested combat veterans to assist him in figuring out what the hell was going on.

Thankfully, today was just a fact-finding mission. He was to traverse the line Khalig had been inspecting when he'd met with his untimely demise. He was to look for any clues as to why someone would have paid Wayne Batson to assassinate him. Since Batson was dead, they couldn't ask him. And he hadn't been forthcoming with a name before he took his final breath.

Which meant whoever had hired him was still out there, having gotten away with murder.

Hawkeye double-checked the map, oriented with the antique compass his grandfather had given him when he'd joined the army and cross-checked with the GPS. Sure of his directions, he folded the map, pocketed his compass, climbed onto the ATV and took off.

At the top of the ridge, he paused and glanced around, looking for other vehicles or people on the opposite ridge. He didn't want to get caught like Khalig at the bottom of the valley with a sniper itching to pick him off. Out of the corner of his eye, he detected movement in the valley below.

A man squatted beside another four-wheeler. He had something in his hands and seemed to be burying it in the dirt.

Hawkeye goosed the throttle, sending his four-wheeler over the edge, descending the winding trail.

The man at the bottom glanced up. When he spotted Hawkeye descending the trail on the side of the hill, he dropped what he'd been holding, leaped onto his ATV and raced up an old mining road on the other side of the ridge.

Hopping off the trail, Hawkeye took the more direct route to the bottom, bouncing over large rock stumps and fallen branches of weathered trees. By the time Hawkeye arrived at the base, the man who'd sped away was already halfway up the hill in front of him.

Hawkeye paused long enough to look at what the man had dropped, and his blood ran cold. A stick of dynamite jutted out of the ground with a long fuse coiled in the dirt beside it.

Thumbing the throttle lever, Hawkeye zoomed after the disappearing rider, who had apparently been about to sabotage the oil pipeline. Had he succeeded, he would have had the entire state in an uproar over the spillage and damage to the environment.

Not to mention, he might be the key to who had contracted Batson to kill Khalig.

At the top of the hill where the mining road wrapped around the side of a bluff, Hawkeye slowed in case the pursued had stopped to attack his pursuer.

Easing around the corner, he noted the path was clear and spied the rider heading down a trail Hawkeye could see from his vantage point would lead back to a dirt road and ultimately to the highway. With as much of a lead as he had, Dynamite Man could conceivably reach the highway and get away before Hawkeye caught up.

Hawkeye refused to let the guy off the hook. Goosing the accelerator, he shot forward and hurtled down the narrow mining road to the base of the mountain. At several points along the path, he skidded sideways, the rear wheels of the four-wheeler sliding dangerously close to the edge of deadly drop-offs. But he didn't slow his descent, pushing his speed faster than was prudent on the rugged terrain.

By the time he reached the bottom of the mountain, Hawkeye was within fifty yards of the man on the other ATV. His quarry wouldn't have enough time to ditch his four-wheeler for another vehicle.

Hawkeye followed the dirt road, occasionally losing sight of the rider in front of him. Eventually, between the trees and bushes, he caught glimpses of the highway ahead. When he broke free into a rare patch of open terrain, he spied the man on the track ahead, about to hit the highway's pavement.

"I'LL BE DAMNED if I sell Stone Oak Ranch to Bryson Rausch. My father would roll over in his grave." At the thought of her father lying in his grave next to her mother, Olivia Dawson's heart clenched in her chest. Her eyes stung, but anger kept her from shedding another tear.

"You said you couldn't live at the ranch. Not since your father died." Abe Masterson, the Stone Oak Ranch foreman for the past twenty years, turned onto the highway headed toward home.

Liv's throat tightened. Home. She'd wanted to come home since she graduated from college three years ago. But her father had insisted she try city living before she decided whether or not she wanted to come back to the hard work and solitary life of a rancher.

For the three years since she'd left college with a shiny new degree, she'd worked her way up the corporate ladder to a management position. Eight people reported directly to her. She was responsible for their output and their well-being. She'd promised her father she'd give it five years. But that had all changed in the space of one second.

The second her father died in a freak horseback-riding accident six days earlier.

Liv had gotten the word in the middle of the night in Seattle, had hopped into her car and had driven all the way to Grizzly Pass, Wyoming. No amount of hurrying back to her home would have been fast enough to have allowed her to say goodbye to her father.

By the time Abe had found him, he'd been dead for a couple of hours. The coroner estimated the fall had killed him instantly, when he'd struck his head on a rock.

Liv would have given anything to have talked to him one last time. She hadn't spoken to him for over a week before his death. The last time had been on the telephone and had ended in anger. She had wanted to end her time in Seattle and come home. Her father had insisted she finish out her five years.

I'm not going to get married to a city boy. What use would he be on a ranch, anyway? she'd argued.

You don't know where love will take you. Give it a chance, he'd argued right back. *Have you been dating?*

No, Dad. I intimidate most men. They like their women soft and wimpy. I can't do that. It's not me.

Sweetheart, her father had said. *You have to open your heart. Love hits you when you least expect it. Besides, I want to live to see my grandchildren.*

Her throat tightening, Liv shook her head. Her father would never know his grandchildren, and they'd never know the great man he was. The tears welled and threatened to slip out the corners of her eyes.

"If you sell to Rausch, you can be done with ranching and get on with your life. You won't have to stay around, being constantly reminded of your father."

"Maybe I want to be reminded. Maybe I was being too rash when I said I couldn't be around the ranch because it brought back too many painfully happy memories of me and Dad." She sniffed, angry that she wasn't doing a very good job of holding herself together.

"What did Rausch offer you?"

Liv wiped her eyes with her sleeve and swallowed the lump in her throat before she could force words out. "A quarter of what the ranch is worth. A quarter!" She laughed, the sound ending in a sob. "I'll die herding cattle before I sell to that man."

"Yeah, well, you could die a lot sooner if you go like your father."

Liv clenched her fist in her lap. "It's physically demanding, ranching in the foothills of the Beartooth Mountains. Falling off your horse and hitting your head on a rock could happen to anyone around here." She shot a glance at Abe. "Right?"

He nodded, his voice dropping to little more than a whisper.

"Yeah, but I would bet my best rodeo buckle your father had some help falling off that horse."

"What do you mean?"

"Just that we'd had some trouble on the ranch, leading up to that day."

"Trouble?"

Abe shrugged. "There've been a whole lot of strange things going on in Grizzly Pass in the past couple months."

"Dad never said a word."

"He didn't want to worry you."

Liv snorted and then sniffed. He was a little late on that account. She swiveled in her seat, directing her attention to the older man. "Tell me."

"You know about the kids on the hijacked bus, right?"

She nodded. "I heard about it on the national news. I couldn't believe the Vanderses went off the deep end. But what does that have to do with my father and the ranch?"

Abe lifted a hand and scratched his wiry brown hair with streaks of silver dominating his temples. "That's only part of the problem. I hear there's a group called Free America stirring up trouble."

"What kind of trouble?"

"Nothing anyone can put a finger on, but rumor has it they're meeting regularly, training in combat tactics."

"Doesn't the local law enforcement have a handle on them?"

Abe shook his head. "No one on the inside is owning up to being a part of it, and folks on the outside are only guessing. It's breeding a whole lot of distrust among the locals."

"So they're training for combat. People have a right to protect themselves." She didn't like that it was splitting a once close-knit community.

"Yeah, but what if they put that combat training to use and try to take over the government?"

Liv smiled and leaned back in her seat. "They'd have to have a lot more people than the population of Grizzly Pass to take over the government."

"Maybe so, but they could do a lot of damage and terrorize a community if they tried anything locally. Just look at the trouble Vanders and his boys stirred up when they killed a bus driver and threatened to bury a bunch of little kids in one of the old mines."

"You have a point." Liv chewed on her lower lip, her brows drawing together. She could only imagine the horror those children had to face and the families standing by, praying for their release. "We used to be a caring, cohesive community. We had semiannual picnics where everyone came out and visited with each other. What's happening?"

"With the shutdown of the pipeline, a lot of folks are out of work. The government upped the fees for grazing cattle on federal land and there isn't much more than ranching in this area. People are moving to the cities, looking for work. Others are holding on by their fingernails."

Her heart ached for her hometown. "I didn't realize it was that bad."

"Yeah, I almost think you need to take Rausch's offer and get out of here while you can."

Her lips firmed into a thin line. "He was insulting, acting like I didn't know the business end of a horse. Hell, he doesn't know the first thing about ranching."

"Which leads me to wonder—"

Something flashed in front of the speeding truck. A rider on a four-wheeler.

Abe jerked the steering wheel to avoid hitting him and sent the truck careening over the shoulder of the road, down a steep slope, crashing into bushes and bumping over huge rocks.

Despite the safety belt across her chest, Liv was tossed about like a shaken rag doll.

"Hold on!" Abe cried out.

With a death grip on the armrest, Liv braced herself.

The truck slammed into a tree.

Liv was thrown forward, hitting her head on the dash. For a moment gray haze and sparkling stars swam in her vision.

A groan from the man next to her brought her out of the fog and back to the front seat of the pickup. She blinked several times and turned her head.

A sharp stab of pain slashed through her forehead and warm thick liquid dripped from her forehead into her eyes. She wiped the fluid away only to discover it was blood. Her blood.

Another moan took her mind off her own injuries.

She blinked to clear her vision and noticed Abe hunched over the steering wheel, the front of the truck pushed into the cab pressing in around his legs.

The pungent scent of gasoline stung her nostrils, sending warning signals through her stunned brain. "Abe?" She touched his shoulder.

His head lolled back, his eyes closed.

"Abe!" Liv struggled with her seat belt, the buckle refusing to release when she pressed the button. "Abe!" She gave up for a moment and shook her foreman. "We have to get out of the truck. I smell gas."

He moaned again, but his eyes fluttered open. "I can't move," he said, his voice weak. "I think my leg is broken."

"I don't care if both of your legs are broken—we have to get you out of the truck. Now!" She punched at her own safety belt, this time managing to disengage the locking mechanism. Flinging it aside, she reached for Abe's and released it. Then she pushed open her door and slid out of the front seat.

When her feet touched the ground, her knees buckled. She grabbed hold of the door and held on to steady herself. The scent of gasoline was so strong now it was overpowering, and smoke rose from beneath the crumpled hood.

Straightening, Liv willed herself to be strong and get her foreman out of the truck before the vehicle burst into flames.

She'd already lost her father. Abe was the only family she had left. She'd be damned if she lost him, too.

With tears threatening, she staggered around the rear of the truck, her feet slipping on loose gravel and stones. When she tried to open the driver's door, it wouldn't budge.

She pounded on it, getting more desperate by the minute. "Abe, you have to help me. Unlock the door. I have to get you out."

Rather than dissipating, the cloud of smoke grew. The wind shifted, sending the smoke into Liv's face. "Damn it, Abe. Unlock the door!"

A loud click sounded and Liv pulled the door handle, willing it to open. It didn't.

Her eyes stinging and the smoke scratching at her throat with every breath she took, Liv realized she didn't have much time.

She braced her foot on the side panel of the truck and pulled hard on the door handle. Metal scraped on metal and the door budged, but hung, having been damaged when the truck wrapped around the tree.

Hands curled around her shoulders, lifted her off her feet and set her to the side.

Then a hulk of a man with broad shoulders, big hands and a strong back ripped the door open, grabbed Abe beneath the arms, hauled him out of the smoldering cab and carried him all of the way up the hill to the paved road.

Her tears falling in earnest now, Liv followed, stumbling over the uneven ground, dropping to her knees every other step. When she reached the top, she sagged to the ground beside Abe on the shoulder of the road. "Abe? Please tell me you're okay. Please."

With his eyes still closed, he moaned. Then he lifted his eyelids and opened his mouth. "I'm okay," he muttered. "But I think my leg's broken."

"Oh, jeez, Abe." She laughed, albeit shakily. "A leg we can get fixed. I'm just glad you're alive."

"Take a lot more than a tree to do me in." Abe grabbed her arm. "I'm sorry, Liv. If it's messed up, I won't be able to take care of the place until it's healed."

"Oh, for Pete's sake, Abe. Working for me is the last thing you should be worrying about. I'll manage fine on my own." She rested her hand on her foreman's shoulder, amazed that the man could worry about her when his face was gray with pain. "What's more important is getting you to a hospital." She glanced around, looking for the man who'd pulled Abe from the wreckage.

He stood on the pavement, waving at a passing truck.

The truck slowed to a stop, and her rescuer rounded to the driver's door and spoke with the man behind the wheel. The driver pulled to the side of the road, got out and hurried down to where Liv waited with Abe.

"Jonah? That you?" Abe glanced up, shading his eyes from the sun.

"Yup." Jonah dropped to his haunches beside Abe. "How'd you end up in a ditch?"

Abe shook his head and winced. "A man on a four-wheeler darted out in front of me. I swerved to miss him." He nodded toward Liv. "You remember Olivia Dawson?"

Jonah squinted, staring across Abe to Liv. "I remember a much smaller version of the Dawson girl." He held out his hand. "Sorry to hear about your father's accident."

Liv took the man's hand, stunned that they were making introductions when Abe was in pain. "Thank you. Seems accidents are going around." Liv stared from Abe to Jonah's vehicle above. "Think between the three of us we could get Abe up to your truck? He won't admit it, but I'll bet he's hurting pretty badly."

"It's just a little sore," Abe countered and then grimaced.

Liv snorted. "Liar."

"We can get him up there," the stranger said.

"Yes, we can," Jonah agreed. "But should we? I could drive

back to town and notify the fire department. They could have an ambulance out here in no time."

"I don't need an ambulance to get me to town." Abe tried to get up. The movement made him cry out and his face turn white. He sagged back against the ground.

"If you don't want an ambulance, then you'll have to put up with us jostling you around getting you up the hill," the stranger said.

"Better than being paraded through Grizzly Pass in the back of an ambulance." Abe gritted his teeth. "Everyone knows ambulances are for sick folk."

"Or injured people," Liv said. "And you have a major injury."

"Probably just a bruise. Give me a minute and I'll be up and running circles around all of you." Abe caught Liv's stare and sighed. "Okay, okay. I could use a hand getting up the hill."

The stranger shot a glance at Jonah. "Let's do this."

Jonah looped one of Abe's arms around his neck, bent and slid an arm beneath one of Abe's legs.

The stranger stepped between Liv and Abe, draped one of Abe's arms over his shoulder and glanced across at Jonah. "On three." He slipped his hand beneath Abe.

Jonah nodded. "One. Two. Three."

They straightened as one.

Abe squeezed his eyes shut and groaned, all of the color draining from his face.

Liv wanted to help, but knew she'd only get in the way. The best thing she could do at that point was to open the truck door before they got there with Abe. She raced up the steep hill, her feet sliding in the gravel. When she reached the top, she flung open the door to the backseat of the truck cab and turned back to watch Abe's progression.

The two men struggled up the hill, being as careful as they could while slipping on loose pebbles.

Liv's glance took in her father's old farm truck, the front wrapped around the tree. Smoke filled the cab and flames shot up from the engine compartment. She was surprised either one of them had lived. If Abe hadn't slammed on his brakes as quickly as he had, the outcome would have been much worse.

Her gaze caught a glimpse of another vehicle on the other side of the truck. A four-wheeler was parked a few feet away.

Anger surged inside Liv. She almost said something to the stranger about how he'd nearly killed two people because of his carelessness. One look at Abe's face made Liv bite down hard on her tongue to keep from yelling at the man who'd nearly caused a fatal accident. Once Abe was taken care of, she'd have words with the man.

Jonah and the stranger made it to the top of the ravine.

The four-wheeler driver nodded to the other man. "I'll take it from here."

"Are you sure?" Jonah asked, frowning. "He's pretty much a deadweight."

Jonah was right. With all the jostling, Abe had completely passed out. Liv studied the stranger. As muscular as he was, he couldn't possibly lift Abe by himself.

"I've got him." The stranger lifted Abe into his arms and slid him onto the backseat of the truck.

Despite her anger at the man's driving skills, Liv recognized sheer, brute strength in the man's arms and broad shoulders. That he could lift a full-size man by himself said a lot about his physical abilities.

But it didn't excuse him from making them crash. She quelled her admiration and focused on getting Abe to a medical facility. If the stranger stuck around after they got Abe situated, Liv would tell him exactly what she thought of him.